The
Gypsy
Bride

Katie Hutton is Irish but now lives in northern Tuscany, with her Italian husband and two teenage sons. She writes mainly historical fiction on the themes of love and culture clash. *The Gypsy Bride* is her debut novel in this genre, with a sequel to follow in 2021. Katie is a member of the Historical Novel Society, the Irish Writers Centre, the Society of Authors and the Romantic Novelists' Association, and reviews for Historical Novel Review. In her spare time she volunteers with a second-hand book charity of which she is a founder member.

The Gypsy Bride

Katie Hutton

ZAFFRE

First published in Great Britain in 2020 by
ZAFFRE
80–81 Wimpole St, London W1G 9RE
www.zaffrebooks.co.uk

A CIP catalogue record for this book is
available from the British Library.

ISBN: 978–1–83877–025–9

Also available in ebook and audio

1 3 5 7 9 10 8 6 4 2

Typeset by IDSUK (Data Connection) Ltd
Printed and bound in Great Britain by Clays Ltd, Elcograf S.p.A.

Zaffre is an imprint of Bonnier Books UK
www.bonnierbooks.co.uk

For Anne Booth – who insisted

PART ONE

CHAPTER 1

Short days ago
We lived, felt dawn, saw sunset glow,
Loved and were loved . . .

John McCrae, *In Flanders Fields*

Last Leave

Chingestone, Oxfordshire, 29th April 1917

'I can't stay out long, Charlie. I musn't go annoying Grandfer.'

'Oh, Ellen. He'll cut you some slack, surely! He knows I'm due back tomorrow.' Charlie leaned against the flint wall of the cottage and pulled her closer, but Ellen held back, her palms flat on his chest.

'Can't you pretend the old wound is troubling you?' she said.

'You know I can't. "Lying lips are abomination to the Lord, but they that deal truly are his delight".'

The girl made an impatient movement, glad that in the dusk he couldn't see her expression.

'They've lied to *you*, Charlie,' she said. 'They said it would be over long before now.'

'They haven't said that in a long time,' he said gently. 'Please, Ellen, it'll be a while before I can kiss you again. I want to remember your kisses. I need them in that place. You know I've given my word; I have to go back.'

'At least tell me where you're going.'

'You've to tell no one, mind.'

'Who would I tell, Charlie?'

'Arras. Now please hold me and stop talking.'

He folded her in his arms and kissed the top of her head, the way he always began. Then he lifted her chin and quietly fed on her mouth, easing her lips open.

Oh, Charlie! Yet she knew even kissing like this was something he'd learned in France. A conversation in a dug-out, he'd said, with those boys from Poplar, who had laughed at him when he'd told them of their chaste embraces, the dry pressure of his lips on hers. Well, three of them had their mouths full of earth now.

'*Please . . .*' he murmured.

*

Three weeks later Ellen hid behind the curtains, as she always did when the motorcycle came puttering up the lane, as if not seeing its rider meant not getting the news he carried. But that day, swathed in her mother's faded chintz, she

4

could not help but hear, in a heart-stopping moment, the click of the latch of Grace's cottage gate further up the lane; the sound she'd always heard just before Charlie came to call for her. She stumbled out of the cottage without shutting the door, and ran to where Grace Lambourne, white-faced, sagged against her doorframe. The man looked round, unable to disguise the relief on his weary face that he could leave this woman with someone else. He had other telegrams to deliver.

Wordlessly, Grace held out the piece of paper. 'Died of his wounds', the telegram said. The two women clung to each other, but Ellen could not cry. She heard her own thoughts as though she had spoken them aloud. *You must be strong, for Grace!* Eventually, hearing a shuffling, she looked round, into the faces of ten or eleven villagers, her mother amongst them. Someone said, 'I'll make tea,' and Grace stood aside to let the woman past.

Ellen broke free of the little crowd, and ran unseeing down the lane, onto the path leading to Surman's Wood.

How long did he take to die? Was he left hanging on wire, or did one of his pals put him out of his misery? Was there a stretcher, with the Quaker men sliding about in the mud?

She tried to picture instead Charlie's face, pale against a hospital pillow, a kind nurse holding his hand, hearing his last words. Her own name, or 'Mother' – poor Grace, who had no other child. Alone, Ellen howled against a tree, pounding the trunk with her fists until they bruised.

That evening the doctor called, and administered a bromide. A week later, he came again, and after he'd gone her mother came up and sat by her bed.

'He wants you to go to Littlemore Asylum,' said Flora Quainton. 'For a rest. Only your grandfer won't hear of it. Says you mightn't get out of there.'

'I wouldn't care if I didn't.'

Yet the following morning, Ellen dressed, crept downstairs and twisted the prospectus for the teacher training college into kindling.

'Ellen!' exclaimed her mother, coming in with eggs fresh from the hens.

'I'm just going for a walk.'

'Just give me a minute . . .'

'No, it's all right. I want to go alone.'

By the time Ellen returned, the card advertising for an assistant in the window of Colton's Drapers had been taken down.

*

Many times after the telegram came, Ellen went to lean in darkness against that cottage wall, unbuttoning her blouse to the cool autumn air.

'Charlie, oh, Charlie,' she wept, trying to remember the touch of his lips on the secret skin of her breast. 'Don't leave me!' But with each day another detail of face or gesture was lost.

CHAPTER 2

One day I saw a few blades of grass growing between two slabs of stone in the exercise yards. Young and green, they excited me like wine. I feasted my eyes on them each day.

Fenner Brockway

Lincoln Prison

20th August 1917

'C3.46! On your feet, slacker! Fight me, if you dare!'

The voice crashed round the cell. The prisoner unfurled, stiff and confused, from the bare board on which he had been fitfully sleeping. The warder looked down into a pinched, swarthy face, a young man's, whose cropped hair and obligatory beard made him look tougher and older than he really was. The warder knew little more than the prisoner's number, but enough to hate him.

'Sir?' said C3.46, bleary with fatigue. He glanced up at the high barred window – pale dawn.

'Talking not allowed!' screamed the warder, and punched him in the mouth where he sat. The taste of blood woke the prisoner completely. C3.46 swayed to his feet and put up his fists. He'd been taught to box as a boy without ever taking to it, other than as a means to defend himself. He had the advantage of the warder in height and youth, but was faint from lack of nourishment. His opponent laughed, though his face was wet with tears.

'No Queensberry rules in here!' he shouted, and brought up his knee. The prisoner doubled up, his hands clutching at the agony between his legs. As his head went down, the guard grabbed the little stool that was one of the few furnishings of the cell, and smashed it over the prisoner's cropped skull. That stool was the reason the prisoner had only a plank bed to sleep on. A warder padding silently in felt overshoes had seen him, through the spyhole in the cell door, standing on it as he tried to look through the window bars; the offence had been listed on a notice he could not read. The blow brought him to his knees. He tried to rise, but a kick knocked him sideways.

'Bloody funk! Gippo! Englishmen are dying for cowards like you!'

The prisoner put up his hands in surrender, but got more blows to his head. Blood ran into his eyes. He had no thought of hitting the guard back; he only wanted him to stop. As he lost consciousness, he thought, *I could not hit a man who is weeping.*

The tapping on the bars that had begun in the adjacent cells grew to a crescendo until the entire wing rang with it, but it was the guard's screamed oaths that brought his colleagues running from their command post at the centre of the spider. He continued to kick the prisoner's inert form, his rage concentrated on C3.46's face. He still held the slop bucket he had emptied over his victim; his trouser-ends and boots were soaked and stinking.

*

C3.46 came round to an exquisite stinging above his left eye. He confusedly made out a white-clad figure bending over him, touching his forehead with gentle fingers yet nevertheless intently inflicting pain. The room beyond his tormentor gleamed white and indistinct. Heaven? But heaven surely would not smell so strongly of disinfectant.

'Can you see me?' whispered the figure.

The prisoner murmured his assent – it came out painfully, 'yesh'. He brought his fingers gingerly to his mouth, and winced. His lips were twice or more their normal size. He held his fingers near to his right eye; the other remained obstinately sealed. Blood.

'Better if you don't move. I'll be finished with you soon,' muttered the orderly. 'If you'd stayed out a bit longer you'd have spared yourself.' He was tugging at the skin of the prisoner's browbone.

9

'It's all right, Rawlins, you can speak normally – and see if he can,' said a voice nearby. 'Helps us see what damage has been done.'

'Thank you, Doctor. Can you tell me your name, prisoner?'

'Shampshon,' he replied. 'Shampshon Luff-widge.'

'Shampshon? Samson? Can you spell it for me?' He was now dabbing at the patient's face with antiseptic. It burned. Tears seeped through the closed lid.

'Shpell? Can't hread an hvrite.' Despite the pain, the chance to talk was as welcome as running water. 'Hvwhat happen'?'

'Whitelam? He got a telegram last night. His second. He shouldn't have been at work today; the chaplain's taken him back to his quarters. You'd find it hard to believe, I'm sure, but he's not a bad chap, mostly. I don't know why he chose you; it could have been any of us.'

'Ush?'

'Yes! I'm a conchie too. Thought I was a doctor, did you? I'm a schoolmaster from Barrow-in-Furness. Gosh, you'd never think a face as battered as yours could show that much surprise.'

The patient felt about him. He was wearing something loose, of starched cotton. He smelled clean – of tar soap and something chemical.

'Try not to move too much . . . They trust me to do this patching up because I've loved to go fishing ever since I was a lad, and I'm a dab hand at tying flies. It's made me good with a needle, but I wouldn't recommend you look at my stitching just yet.'

The prisoner passed his hand lightly over his head, his fingertips searching. His already close-cropped hair had been shaved. Tentatively he explored his cheeks and chin, mindful of bruises. His unwanted, eclipsing beard was gone.

'Three lots of stitches in your skull, and another lot on your browbone. That's catgut, that is, pure protein – absorbed into the body when it's done its work.'

'Hat-hut?'

'No, not your dear old tabby. Cow's tripe. Don't know why they don't just call it that. The doctor says your eyes will do. They're colourful, but that's only bruising. Fortunately he missed your nose. He's broken one of your teeth; try not to chew on the right side of your mouth – it'd be painful. Lips are best left to mend themselves – with a bit of ice to help. You'll not be kissing anyone for a while anyway.'

C3.46 smiled for the first time in weeks. It hurt.

'I'm afraid I had to shave your eyebrow. But you've been lucky. No bones broken.'

'Phor Fwhitela'. He pwobly dunt like Shypsies, thass all. Shawl frong he losht hish boysh. Waysht.'

'You're right, prisoner. It is a waste. A bloody, senseless un-Christian waste.'

*

11

Three mornings later, C3.46's left eye opened. His lip was still tender and painful to the touch, but he could talk almost normally, and revelled in the chance of conversation with Rawlins after three months of imposed silence. The whiteness of the long room still hurt his eyes after the gloom of the cell. Two other beds at the far end of the infirmary were occupied by a man coughing up his lungs and another who muttered to himself incessantly. C3.46 was forbidden to call out to either. The pain of his bruises was fading to a dull but constant ache, but whilst he could see clearly enough, sometimes he saw double. Rawlins frowned and talked of concussion. The conchie deftly washed him as he lay on the infirmary sheets, talking incessantly to distract both of them from the most intimate of his ministrations.

'I do what I can for the poor little beggars, though I've been told often enough that as they're destined for the shipyard I shouldn't waste too much effort on them. That's the biggest obstacle I'm up against in teaching a boy to think for himself. Turn over that way, would you? Splendid – no, don't try to get up. I wonder sometimes if the boys miss me.'

'How long did they gev you?'

'Me? Ten years, hard labour. That was after going to France and a court-martial. I'd the death sentence read out to me before the entire regiment – but after a pause that was as long as they could make it, they told me it was commuted. The medical officer got the hard labour scrapped, though – my weak chest. If I'd gone on with the call-up I would likely have been rejected anyway, but me and my principles didn't want to take that risk. I was brought up as a Congregationalist, you see, and though the chapel doesn't see me much these days, some of it has stayed with me. Father comes to see me when he's allowed, poor man, and gives me courage. Cup of tea, Loveridge?'

'Oh please!'

'I'll get you a straw. We'll see if we can't feed you up a bit before you have to go up before the governor. When was it they put you on bread and water?'

'Oh, days ago. Can't tell. I missed the cocoa most of all. That pale meat they gev us, that's horse, ain't it?'

'Yes – not to everyone's taste, of course, but nourishing enough. What's the matter?'

'I was right not to eat it, then.'

'You mean you've not eaten any meat since you came in here?' asked Rawlins.

'Could you eat a dog?'

'Of course not. I have a dog – at home, that is.'

'Well, we can't eat horses,' said the prisoner.

'Good Lord, man, no wonder you're so famished.'

'I dunt know about them boys, bein' boys, but *I'd* miss you, Rawlins.'

*

'Take off your cap, Loveridge, when you're talking to me.'

'Yes, sir, sorry, sir.' C3.46 pulled off the arrowed cap and passed a hand nervously over his sand-grained scalp. The stitches were itching; Rawlins had assured him this was a good sign.

'Do you intend persisting in this business?' asked the governor, frowning at him from behind his desk. C3.46 stood in a raised dock, a warden with a truncheon either side. For a short, bewildered moment he had thought himself back before another tribunal. An assistant sat at the back of the office, recording the meeting in shorthand. The place was spartan: a book-case held a Bible and a few box files. The one barred window was as high up as a cell's. But a fire in the small grate kept the room pleasantly warm, and its austerity contrasted oddly with its club-like smell of hair oil and tobacco. The longing for a cigarette made C3.46 feel even more light-headed.

'Business, sir?' he asked.

'Don't cheek me, Loveridge.' The governor waved a hand over the papers on his desk. 'At none of your hearings has any evidence of conscience been found . . . You don't claim the Almighty and you don't talk about the international brotherhood of the proletariat or other such rot – your justification is, quote, "Don't know as it has anything to do with me". You're hardly an Englishman, are you, Loveridge?'

'I dunt know what else I might be . . . sir.'

'Are you an absolutist?'

'A what . . . beg pardon, sir?'

'Evidently not . . . Loveridge, you cannot get out of your duty by saying it has nothing to do with you – oh, Bateman, walk round and get C3.46 a chair, would you? He's not quite steady yet.'

The warders grasped the prisoner's upper arms firmly enough to bruise, forcing him to attention. Bateman put down his notepad and, wearing an expression of compressed irritation, left the room by a side door and shortly afterwards the door behind the prisoner was unlocked and a chair brought in. There was silence until Bateman reappeared in the office; the governor was writing notes as though he'd forgotten the prisoner was there. Then, without looking up, he said, 'I don't want you in my prison, Loveridge. As soon as the medical officer says you are fit to travel, you'll go to Princetown Work Centre. Anyone you need to inform?'

'No, sir. If I may ask, where is that, sir?'

'You may. Dartmoor.' The governor picked up a hand-bell, and the two warders turned the prisoner round.

*

'Cigarette, Bateman?'

'Thank you, sir.'

The governor leaned over Bateman's match.

'So, what do you think? Trouble?'

'No. He could hardly write to the newspapers, even if he got hold of the means.'

'But the Bolsheviks or the Bible-thumpers could do it for him.'

'I don't think so. It's difficult enough for them to do that for themselves. The socialists, most of 'em, have an expensive education and he's not one of their class, and he's a Godless sort of animal anyway. The cat that walks by himself. If it did get into the papers, not even *The Socialist* could make anything of "nothing to do with me". Whitelam would come off best, I should think: "grief-stricken father of fallen heroes goaded beyond endurance by cowardly Gypsy".'

'The M.O. says he's been refusing meat – won't eat horse, apparently. You can see how starved he is. I don't want to have to explain a death.'

'He'll do better in Princetown, then. They've got vegetarians and all sorts of cranks there.'

'I suppose you're right. He doesn't seem to have been that much trouble anywhere – always the same misdemeanours: trying to look out of the window or raising his head at exercise. And every place he's been sent he starts by curling up in his corner like a hedgehog. It's beyond me why a man who hates to be penned up doesn't just get outside with the others and do his duty.'

'He has no sense of duty, sir. Gypsies don't. Parasitical, I call it – always a foot in the door to get something from those who do an honest day's work. They're like the Jews, sir, their loyalty is only to themselves.'

'Except that Jews stick together – always helping their own. No one has ever come to see Loveridge. And he's never given us a next of kin.'

CHAPTER 3

But the boys who were killed in the trenches,
Who fought with no rage and no rant,
We left them stretched out on their pallets of mud
Low down with the worm and the ant.

Robert Graves, *Armistice Day, 1918*

Armistice

Chingestone

With the peal of bells, the tension broke. Unbuttoning her overall, Mrs Colton rushed to the door, flinging it open to the cold air and the running feet. She turned back to the counter. 'Ellen!'

'Yes, Mrs Colton?'

'Leave those tablecloths. It's over! I'm shutting up shop. There'll be no more work done in fields or forge today. We'll be expected at the chapel.'

Ellen ran her hand across the crisp linen. She could not look up. 'I'll give thanks here, in my own way.'

'But—'

'Please. I don't feel able to celebrate – and I don't want to spoil anyone else's joy.'

'Come out from behind that counter at least.'

Ellen obeyed, and her employer embraced her. The girl caught a whiff of the rose-scented face powder that was Mrs Colton's only vanity.

'"The Lord is nigh unto them that are of a broken heart", Ellen.'

*

The girl bolted the door after her employer and pulled down the blinds that were used to protect the window display on days when the sun shone brightly – not that day. She sat in the chair reserved for customers and folded her hands in her lap, thinking about the other girls who would come to the shop for their bottom drawer, those whose sweethearts would return. She heard a brass band strike up 'Abide with Me', the sound pinched by the cold air. *I am alone,* she thought, picturing the scene in the tiny Primitive Methodist chapel, crammed to the doors. *I shall always be alone.* In the lengthening shadows she began to whisper a prayer, but the well-known words meant nothing and were soon engulfed in sobs.

*

At No. 2 Army Remount Depot in Abbeville, Picardy, Corporal Loveridge (Farrier) found himself on a charge of insubordination – again. This time he had simply asked when he might go home.

CHAPTER 4

What Hath God Wrought!

Numbers 23:23

Chingestone

4th June 1922

Ellen looked up at the ridge of the Chiltern Hills for reassurance, a habit learned over five lonely years.

'Leave the path men have made and all God's greatness is there,' her grandfather was in the habit of telling her. She thought of those hills as clay in the Creator's hands, long ago when the world was made, and how they would still be there when she herself was clay, having passed through the arc of life with only one memory of a man's lips on her skin. She'd never bear any husband's name, nor suffer the pains of childbed ordained for all mothers ever since Eve ate the apple.

Ellen walked swiftly, crossing the road to avoid passing in front of one of the small Victorian villas lining the high street, then recrossed twenty yards further down.

Feeling eyes on her, she glanced up and saw the wife of
the Wesleyan minister watching her from the baywindow
of the manse, and looked away. *Let them all think I'm
touched!*

Ellen passed the forge, then the general store and the
butcher's, turning right past the Red Lion, the reek of beer
and Woodbines reaching her from the open door of the
public bar. Five taverns in this village, one to every forty
inhabitants, and as a member of the Band of Hope she had
never entered any of them. But it was easier to pass the Red
Lion than that pretty house on the high street with that
imagined fireside, her foot rocking a wooden crib, Charlie reading to a little girl in a starched pinafore. Walking
home on the day their engagement had been announced
in chapel, he'd tucked her arm under his, and said, 'Now
tell me, Ellen, which of them houses would you want for
ours?'

'*Those* houses, Charlie!'

'You're not in the school today, Mistress Quainton!'

'And you know we can't afford it. Besides, I love your
mother. I'd like it, just the three of us in her cottage.'

'Won't be just the three of us for long, God willing!
Anyway, *I'd* like that one there!'

Ellen remembered those words now more accurately than
the face of the man who had spoken them. She turned onto the
green, the old heart of the village with its cluster of thatched
and slated flint cottages. The grass was newly mown, its fresh

scent mingling in the warm, still air with that of the flowers in the gardens. This little quadrangle, along with the Primitive Methodist chapel and Sunday school – two knocked-through cottages just where the village tailed out into the fields – were now the limits of her world.

*

In the Wesleyan manse, Rose Newcomb was laying the table for Sunday dinner. Standing in the doorway, her husband said, 'I think, Rose, I shall need to speak to the rector again. I know it's none of my business but those Wixon children have been making a nuisance of themselves with the Prims again. Their father thinks it's funny. He dared me to go to the squire when I cornered him about it the last time, if you'll remember.'

'You didn't, of course.'

'You know as well as I that I'd have been wasting my time. The corn factor – I never can remember the fellow's name – told me that this morning the brats threw home-made fireworks into Grandfather Quainton's path.'

'Can't Quainton speak for himself? Or that fussy solicitor's clerk who is always with him?'

'Of course,' he said, nettled. 'But Quainton is an awkward old cuss when he's not in his pulpit – up there, apparently, he can chill the blood if he wants to. And anyway, we're more . . . more . . .'

22

'Respectable, Frank?'

'Yes. I believe the rector will listen more readily to me.'

*

C.G. Lambourne – Private – Fifth Dorsetshire.

Ellen reached down and touched her fingers to the name plate on the handsome Portland stone cross. It had been a dignified ceremony in its own way, despite the lady of the manor being all got up like a galleon in full sail, and the mayor squat and sweaty and a little tawdry beside her, longing to be back in his favourite armchair in the masonic lodge, pipe in hand, where such shrill and bossy beings could not reach him. The Rector had spoken in that peculiar sing-song way of his that he employed in the pulpit. Mr Newcomb had read a poem; Ellen thought she might ask him what it was, but not yet. For the Prims, her grandfather Oliver had read from Ecclesiastes, as usual without notes. Ellwood the Quaker, who had been a stretcher-bearer, asked that the fallen be remembered in silence, but no one knew when to end it, until the mayor had cleared his throat impressively and her ladyship had said, 'So be it!' in her brittle voice. Poor Grace Lambourne had drooped and wept throughout the ceremony, batting away those who urged her to 'be strong for your boy's sake!', with only a tearless, pale Ellen at her elbow allowed to comfort her, because Ellen had said nothing, just held her upper arm and stroked it gently with her thumb. Finally the village band played, inevitably, one verse of 'Abide with Me', and it was over.

'Oh, Charlie!' Ellen murmured. 'One day I'll come to France and see where they've put you, and I'll put some earth from your own vegetable plot over you. I don't know when, but even if I'm an old lady you'll wait for me, and I for you.'

First a telegram, and now a monument. She looked at the other names, and saw all those young men as though still alive, walking off the fields at supper time, bringing the cart back on Tuesdays from the market, bending and striking at a horseshoe, standing up in the chapel and crying aloud that God spoke within.

Grace Lambourne now stood at a short distance, head bowed. She and Mrs Munday held each other's elbows and leaned gently into each other. The Munday twins were listed, in strict alphabetical order, beneath Charlie's name.

Couldn't they have put their Christian names? wondered Ellen. Then, as if she read her thoughts, Grace said, 'It's the same as his headstone, Ellen, only there he'll have a little poem I wanted too.'

'Oh Grace,' said Ellen, turning, crying at last.

*

The two women were the last to leave, and Ellen looked back more than once as they walked away. The cross resembled, more and more at a distance, a sword thrust into a rock.

'It don't look right, do it, Ellen? What was wrong with our local stone what those poor boys knew?'

'They say it's the same as the cenotaph that way – and the stones they're putting above them in France.'

Grace's grip on Ellen's arm tightened. 'I hate to think of him lying there amongst strangers.'

'They won't be strangers, Grace. They'll be the boys he wrote to us about. His pals.'

'I shall never get over it, Ellen.'

No more shall I, thought the girl, but had no intention of comparing her grief with that of a mother. 'It's the worst sorrow,' was all she said.

Grace stopped on the path.

'Thank you, Ellen, for not quoting scripture at me today,' she said. 'That's all everyone else has done, but it won't . . . it won't *do*, you know. I am too angry with God,' she added, with the sudden frankness of one at ease with her faith. 'I hope I don't offend you talking like that?'

'No.' Ellen smiled. 'I'm angry too – perhaps not with God but with all those that think they speak for Him. But you've reminded me I needed to speak to Mr Chown about the tea-meeting. I'll see you indoors and then I'll go round to his.'

'Go now, Ellen. I shall be fine. But come and see me soon. If I'm not seeing things, then that's Judith Chown up there on the gate by the stables, looking cross. You could go along with her.'

Ellen laughed. 'Judy always looks cross! All right, I shall call tomorrow after work.'

*

'Blessed waste of time all that was!' spat Judith, scrambling down from the gate and planting her hands on her hips. Where Ellen was reticent and self-effacing to the degree that not everyone noticed immediately the charm of blue eyes in an oval face, framed by a soft cloud of light brown hair, Judith Chown was a force of nature, with her black shingled bob and mobile red mouth.

'Ah, Judy, it gives comfort to some.'

'To you – to *her*?' Judith inclined her head in the direction of Grace's cottage.

'No.'

'And my Reggie's name oughter been on there too.'

'He lives and breathes, Judy.'

'What's left of him. I'm supposed to be grateful for that – I know. Luckier than your poor Charlie, but he don't see it that way. Not the way he is. But we've been through all that and he won't see reason and won't see me. So there it is. You going home now?'

'I was going to see your pa,' said Ellen.

'Old misery guts? I'd've thought you'd heard enough of 'im after this morning's preaching. He oughter been called Job, not Harold, for the way he goes on about 'im all the time.'

26

'He's a good man, your father.'

'So was Job, I expect. Don't suppose he was much fun to live with either!' said Judith.

*

Harold Chown stood at the door of his cottage. A little above middle height, Judith's father, on passing fifty, had begun to put on weight. His hair was still plentiful, though now iron-grey, and his face retained the vestiges of good looks, marred by the muddiness of complexion of a man who has worked most of his life indoors, and by his own reluctance to smile.

'Miss Quainton.'

'Good evening, Brother Chown. I just called for the readings for next Sunday. And Grandfer wants to know if the date of the tea-meeting has been decided.'

'Ah. Um . . . come in,' Chown said, as he ducked his head and backed into the little parlour. Judith followed them in without greeting her father and went to crash amongst the saucepans in the back scullery.

'I don't want to be any trouble,' said Ellen.

'You're none whatsoever. I must say, Miss Quainton, that it is rare to encounter round the circuit such conscientiousness as yours.'

Ellen smiled faintly at this. Judith regularly made a mock of her father's slightly pompous choice of words ('You'd think he was a judge in a wig to hear him, Ellen, not Lightfoot's old clerk!').

'Um . . . I know of no other Sunday school teacher who takes the trouble to plan her lessons on the readings of that day,' he went on.

'Oh . . .' Ellen reddened a little at his compliments, and with her left hand rubbed the back of her neck. 'Well, it makes it easier for me, you see. I don't have to think of something new.'

Harold took a step forward and grasped her right hand in both his own.

'Today cannot have been easy for you, Miss Quainton. But one must not question the will of God.'

Mustn't one?

Ellen gently extricated her hand.

'Indeed, Brother Chown.'

'It's not quite the same thing, of course,' he said with unconscious clumsiness, 'but when I lost Judith's mother—'

'Of course, a terrible loss,' she said, echoing his words and wishing the conversation over. Judith had told her friend that Harold seldom spoke of his dead wife, so why now? 'I expect you never get over it,' she added with finality.

'No . . . yes . . . um . . . I mean, you are right, of course.' He rubbed his palms down the sides of his thighs, as if they were damp, though when he had grasped Ellen's hand they had felt cool and dry, and slightly rough.

'Let me get you those readings,' he said.

CHAPTER 5

Tis thus they live – a picture to the place,
A quiet, pilfering, unprotected race.

John Clare, *Gipsies*

Stopping Place

Surman's Wood, Chingstone, Summer 1922

Unobserved except by the rooks circling above, three brightly painted Gypsy caravans rocked and swayed off the road and into the cool depths of Surman's Wood. Two ragged children ran ahead under the trees. A lanky young man in shirtsleeves and a fedora walked backwards before the first wagon, guiding it.

'Mind that rabbit hole, Mother!'

'Mind it yourself, boy!' laughed the old woman holding the reins of a piebald horse, easing her pipe into the corner of her mouth. Both of the *vardos*[1] that followed were driven

---

[1] Romani: wagons.

by thick-set, frowning men – clearly brothers – each with a silent woman beside him, and smaller faces clustering behind. A woman of about twenty-five came next on foot, leading a roan pony. She wore a loose white blouse, a velvet waistcoat too warm for that evening, but which she wore fastened to emphasise her slender waist, and a skirt that flowed with her undulating walk. Her black curling hair was held back by a red silk scarf tied about a head that she held with the air of a princess. Lucretia Loveridge had learned early to charge a decent fee to amateur photographers; a stinging slap rewarded any man who attempted more than a photograph. A melancholy barefoot teenage boy in a too-large man's jacket leading another horse ended the little procession.

'Pick up your long face, little brother,' the young woman called to him. 'We're on this *atchin' tan*[2] till September.'

There would be work – first the hay harvest, and then the crops. This would bring enough money to pay for the new *vardo* ordered from the carriage-works in Reading. Camped by the stream in the wood, they would need to disturb no one for water, but the villages were near at hand for Lucretia and her two sisters-in-law to hawk clothes pegs and fortunes, and to beg cast-off clothes. And who would miss the occasional rabbit when they were so plentiful?

*

[2] Stopping-place

Judith and her father sat opposite each other, the tea things between them.

'Does your friend have any followers, Judith?'

'Who, Ellen? No, she's too particular – or too wedded to the memory of the dear departed. Why you asking?'

'Well, I don't know ... um ... a pleasant girl like her. And Charlie Lambourne dead five years – a more than decent interval.'

'I think she's given up, Pa, like the rest of us. And who'd brave her grandfer to walk out with her, anyways? Poor Charlie went in fear of him as it was.'

'I am sure Oliver merely wishes to protect her.'

'Why do you ask? Sweet on her yourself, Pa? Doubt she'd look at you twice!'

Harold flushed. 'Really, Judith, you can be quite vulgar sometimes. I don't know where you get it from – not from your poor mother, I'm sure. Can you not eat faster, daughter – we shall be late for the prayer meeting.'

'We?'

'I merely remind you of it, Judith. Whether you attend is a matter for your own conscience.'

'It is, isn't it?'

He rose from the table and went out the back to wash. It would take him little more than five minutes to walk to the chapel, but he liked to be early. He might have a chance to speak to Ellen that way.

*

A mile or so away from where the prayer meeting was getting underway, the tall Gypsy sat on the steps of his *vardo* and demonstrated the making of wooden chrysanthemums to a small shock-headed boy and his elder sister. He rested the blunt side of the knife against his knee and, with determined movements of his right hand, drew the stick of soft wood back and forth, turning it almost imperceptibly as he did so.

''Tis magic, Sam!' exclaimed the girl, watching the spiralling petals of the flower grow beneath her eyes.

''Tain't, though, Sibela. You must work at it, like anything, and have patience. Choose a nice dry one of them sticks Righteous has peeled for us; they're the ones that curl best and come all nice and frilly, see? Now I'm going to trust you with my knife, but you must hold it this way, or you'll hurt yourself or your dress, and your ma'll be angry at me.'

He settled the girl beside him on the step and fastened her fingers carefully round the knife. Frowning with concentration, and wishing her brother Righteous far away, the girl attempted to whittle as she had seen her teacher do it. The first petal appeared, but short to the point of atrophy, the second too long and broad, and too far from the first; Sibela had jerked the stick round in her hand rather than nudged it gently forward. But Sam encouraged her, and eventually the stick was worked round, although the result resembled more a part-peeled leek than anything saleable. Sam took it from her and whittled a little further until the untidy, straggling head separated from the body of the stick.

'Can I keep this, Sibela?' he asked her. 'I'd like to, seeing as it's your first 'un. See if there's a bit of that applewood as'll make for a stalk . . . What colour will we make it?'

'Pink – and green!'

*

'You wasted good colour-papers on that?' exclaimed Lucretia. ''Tis good only for burning.'

'It's the little maidy's first try, Lukey. You'd take the heart out of her if you burned that flower. I'm keeping it – and it dunt look bad in that beer bottle.'

'You're soft, Sam! How is she goin' to learn?'

'She'll never want to learn nothing if you dunt sell her flowers along of yours – and you won't, not yet, so that's why that one and all the other ones she spoils afore she gets good, I'm going to keep.'

CHAPTER 6

When Gorgio mushe's merripen and Romany Chal's
merripen wels kettaney, kek koso merripen see.[3]

'Betie Rokrapenes: Little Sayings', George Borrow,
Romano Lavo-Lil

Cows

Chingestone, Harvest 1922

Ellen hesitated before taking the footpath round the edge of
the pasture, but she had had some particularly irritating customers and was keen to get home. The short cut would gain
her seven or eight minutes, to be prized as time for a cup of
tea and to rest her aching feet. Farmer Horwood's cows were
grouped peaceably at the far side of the field, giving her time
to get to the opening into the wood before they lumbered

---

[3] 'When the Gentile way of living and the Gypsy way of living come
together, it is anything but a good way of living'

across to investigate her. Sure enough, as soon as she ventured onto the path, they caught sight of her and started to move.

'Get away, silly girls!' she called at them. 'I've nothing for you!' But being cows, they kept on coming. Concentrating on being annoyed as a way of not being fearful, Ellen ignored them and marched straight ahead, counting the trees beyond the bramble hedge to her right until she would reach the stile. *They're not dogs – they can't tell you're afraid,* she told herself and then, with a cry, she fell headlong, her foot caught in a rabbit hole. Face to the ground, she could now feel the thud of their advance as well as hear it.

Oh no, she thought, *my only chance is the hedge, and I'll get it for muddying my work clothes!* She got to her knees – she was hemmed in by the cows, heard their low breathing, their restless pacing as they surrounded her – but she dared not look up. Then she heard a low whistle, some murmured, unintelligible words, and the cows shifted and backed away.

'Can you get up?'

A stranger, an odd lilt – not quite that of the Chilterns, but not so distant either – deeper, the vowels stretched out lazily. Two pairs of mud-caked labourer's boots came into her line of vision. She looked up slowly, into the faces of a man and a boy, the man's face shaded by his hat, the boy's expression fearful – Ellen could not imagine why. Then the rest of the man rushed towards her as he squatted down and faced her, probably the dirtiest human being she had ever seen. Even the poorest cottage children that came to the Sunday school had been passed under a pump first. Then she realised that it wasn't dirt; except for a white scar running through his left eyebrow, his skin was simply darker, as dark as the 'old clo'' Jews she had seen in London, darker than the Italian boys who'd hawked the pretty Parian ware heads her mother had admired so much but never dared to buy. *And horrors!* she thought, he was wearing a small gold hoop in one of his ears.

'You didn't ought to have called 'em silly girls, you know. Might be true but they dunt care for it all the same.'

'Who are you?' she blurted, though she guessed. Even without his swarthiness, the broad face and high-bridged nose alone would have proclaimed what he was.

Her rescuer laughed, revealing strong but uneven white teeth, one of them in the top row broken.

'Sam Loveridge at your service – Sam for Sampson. Vanlo here is my wife's brother. Can you stand?' He got to his feet, and reached both hands down to her. The palms were as pale as her own – and they were clean. She hesitated for a moment, then placed her hands in his and allowed him to pull her up. He held them for a moment longer, then let go, and plucked a blade of dried grass from her hair. He wore an aged collarless shirt, open at the throat, and a crumpled red silk neckerchief. His faded moleskin trousers were held up with string. Everything about him was scruffy – the black hair under the battered but jaunty fedora too long and tangled – and he smelled not only of unwashed clothes and sweat, but of tobacco, horse and woodsmoke, yet some-where behind all of that was the unmistakeable presence of carbolic. Sam Loveridge was taller than most men she knew; looking up, she held her head back.

'Aren't you going to tell me your name, then?' he said.

'I am Ellen Quainton. My grandfer's cottage is the other side of that wood.'

'And where is your husband's home?'

'I have no husband.'

'That's hard. A woman should have a husband. If I was your relation I should find you one. I'd be your husband myself if I wasn't already spoken for.'

Ellen opened her mouth to retort that he had no busi-ness to say so, but stopped as she saw the genuine concern on Loveridge's face – and anyway, the little gallantry had pleased her.

'I was to have had a husband . . . He was killed in France.'

'I'm sorry. And I'm sorry to have spoken out of turn.'

He lifted her hand suddenly, and kissed her fingers. She felt his breath warm on her knuckles.

'Are you all right now?' he said, releasing her hand.

'Yes. You have been most kind.'

'Let us see you home, Miss Quainton.'

'Oh, no, no, that won't be necessary, Mr Loveridge,' her unwillingness making her suddenly formal, their little moment of intimacy shattered.

'We shan't let your grandfer see us.'

She looked up quickly, and both smiled. He pulled her arm under his and she heard Vanlo gasp. Ellen was too startled to protest, and anyway, she didn't want to appear churlish. The boy followed them silently.

'We'll be here until harvest end,' the man said as they walked. 'P'haps we'll meet again.'

Reaching the lane, he released her arm, touching a finger to his hat. 'I can see you're troubled you med be seen with me,' he said, smiling. 'Same med be true for me! I'll wish you a good evening.' Then he and Vanlo turned back into the trees before Ellen had time to thank them. Thinking of the encounter later, she realised the boy hadn't spoken a single word.

*

Oliver Quainton was standing in the doorway of his cottage, watching Ellen walk slowly along the lane.

What's Grandfer about? she wondered. She had never known him to be idle and had often heard him raging against others for being so. He disapproved in particular of cottagers lounging in doorways. Whatever he was doing now, it certainly wasn't lounging. Yet he took comfort from his own doorframe, for unlike most of his neighbours, he could truly say that it was his own. Oliver, in all the years he had worked in London, had secretly and implacably saved, so that when he returned to his native village, staggering under the blow of his son's death, he carried in a cloth bag inside his shirt twenty hard-won guineas.

'I seen families turned out at a week's notice for nothing more than the rumour the father had joined Mr Arch's union, and if it hadn't been for the chapel many would have starved,' he'd told his astonished daughter-in-law, brandishing a key in one hand and title-deeds in the other. 'I'll not have you nor the little maidy on the parish.'

Her mother Flora was sitting outside this evening on a stool plucking a fowl. She looked up at her daughter and her face was an unmistakeable warning.

'You're later this evening,' said Oliver. 'Came by the road, did you?'

'Yes, Grandfer.'

Her ear stung with the blow and for a moment Ellen staggered. Tears came to her eyes.

'"Ye shall not steal, neither deal falsely, neither lie one to another." I came that way just now, and I saw no sign of you! You're a poor liar, girl, and perhaps that will save you. There's mud on your skirt and your shoes. You've come through Surman's Wood, though I've told you not to often enough!'

'I did, Grandfer, I was tired. And then I thought I would be trampled by the cows—'

Flora whimpered.

'—so I sat on the stile a while till I got myself together again.'

'"He causes the grass to grow for the cattle, and vegetation for the labour of man, so that he may bring forth food from the earth . . ."'

'Psalm a hundred and four, Grandfer.'

Oliver smiled at last. 'Now what about: "The man gave names to all the cattle, and to the birds of the sky, and to every beast of the field . . . "? I'll not go on, for I'll make it too easy for you.'

She smiled back, the tension broken. ''Tis too easy anyway, Grandfer. Genesis chapter two – but I can't remember the verse.' She could, but allowed him to supply it.

'I don't know that Farmer Horwood gives his cattle names,' she added.

'But they are still His instrument, child, if they teach you obedience.'

She pressed home her advantage. 'They frightened me – the way they all came towards me, as if none of them could think for themselves.'

'I shall preach on that come Sunday,' he said, 'for there are plenty of men made in His image that don't think for themselves either – most of 'em that are drinking their wages away in the Red Lion at this very moment. Come in, child, wash your hands and then go and help your mother. I hadn't the cows in mind, though. Horwood told me there are Gypsies in Surman's Wood. He gives work to some of 'em and doesn't complain; his excuse is that it's easier for him as he don't need to find anywhere for them to sleep, seeing as they have their own wagons and tents and all. But you must keep away from them – they're no company for a young woman and their ways are not our ways, even if they be God's creatures same as us, wandering the world as a lost tribe of Israel.' He paused. 'Some, I will say, have been brought to our Lord and that by the words of preachers of their own. I knew two good men of their tribe in London – the Lord inspired them to bring many home, both Gypsies and Englishmen – but I don't know anything about them as are in Surman's Wood.'

Ellen tried to read her grandfather's expression, but saw nothing other than his usual conviction that he knew what was right. No, her conversation with Sam hadn't been observed. She went in to wash her hands in the basin of clean water her mother had drawn from the pump, but not before she had gently stroked the fingers the Gypsy had brought to his lips, and sniffed them to see if he had left any trace of himself. He hadn't. *Silly girl*, she reproved herself as she took hold of the tar soap, *it's not as if he's a fox.*

*

'Mebbe best if we dunt mention the *rakli*[4], my Vanlo,' said Sam as they approached the clearing, where the dark woman in the headscarf – his wife – was building the fire.

'O' course!' said the boy, glad that they shared a secret.

*

---

[4] Non-Gypsy girl

41

'Where you bin then, Sam Loveridge?'

'And a very good evening to you too, Lukey,' he said. 'You know me, idling about, annoying good honest folk.'

'I expect that's about the size of it! Whilst I've had wood to gather and other people's children to mind. It's what a woman does when her man has no arrows in his quiver.'

'Rest it, Lukey, please,' said Sam quietly, without expecting or getting a response. He and their companions heard regular gibes about their childlessness. He had long ago given up suggesting that his wife might be the cause.

'Have you seed Horwood about work yet?' called one of the men.

'No, my Liberty. I'll go tomorrow.'

'I seen him today. He's taking me an' Caley. I said you'd be along – he'll take Vanlo too if he thinks 'en big enough,' said Liberty.

'He'll want 'en. Fine strong *chavvi*[5] he is now.'

'You coulda gone along of my brothers, Sam,' cut in Lucretia. 'Too afraid of him asking again what you did in the war, I expect.'

He flared. 'Dunt know why you complain. There are thousands of women who wish their men hadn't gone – thousands! And anyway, I did go.'

'Eventually.'

---

[5] Gypsy boy

The other adults gathered round the open fire looked steadily into the flames, avoiding each others' eyes, but at Sam's raised voice a shawled old woman took her pipe out of her mouth and nodded in his direction. "Bout time he stopped her,' she muttered to her nearest neighbour, a younger woman who gave no indication that she'd heard.

'I don't suppose you thought to bring back a rabbit, did you?' asked Lucretia.

'I'll get you your rabbit – as many as you want. No point in looking for them early; it's now they come out.' He climbed up the steps of the *vardo* and opened the half-door. 'Hello, old girl,' he muttered, addressing the wagon his father had had built for him on his marriage. To give her her due, Lucretia kept it spotlessly clean. His father's own wagon had been burned with all the rest of his belongings, as was customary at a death; without it his ghost could not be at peace. But this meant that Harmony Boswell, Sam's mother, had had to join him and Lucretia in their *vardo;* in the cold months she slept in the narrow cot that had been intended for children beneath the big built-in marriage bed. As soon as there was a breath of spring, however, she would ask Sam to plant and curve the willow branches for her bender tent. The green, gold and red paint of the *vardo* was still fresh and vivid, and Sam never got bored of the twined carvings of foliage and horses. The brass lamps and handles shone, polished to perfection with rotten-stone and oil. This left Lucretia's palms as rough as pumice and there were times when he shivered at the touch of her strong hands on his bared skin – but she knew what to do with them all right. It wasn't for want of trying that there was only the two of them. He sighed, seeing the empty beer bottle, and stepped down, carrying his catapult.

'You coming, Vanlo?' he called.

'Why can't you set a trap like any man with a bit of sense would?' said Lucretia.

'You know why. They're slow – cruel.'

'Nets.'

'Dunt have the patience.'

*

Sam and Vanlo walked back along the path that led to the field, an old lurcher trotting companionably alongside them. They leaned against the stile. Sam watched the rabbits innocently feeding; Vanlo watched Sam.

Dignified. A real lady, Sam thought. *But when she smiled – that poor sojer had that to think on out there in that mud, that and them blue eyes. I've never seed a* gauji[6] *rakli smile at me like that – her whole face so lively. And she fitted so nice and neat under my arm. Come on, Sam, you're dreaming, and none of it's right by Lukey.*

He rummaged in his pocket and loaded the catapult.

*

---

[6] Non-Gypsy girl

The following evening a light drizzle was falling as Ellen paused at the entrance to Horwood's field. She glanced at the cows absorbed in their grazing, pulled her hat down a bit further and pressed on to where the chalky path met the high road at the crest of the rise. Reaching the junction, she was rewarded by the sight of bandy-legged old Mott walking back from her village to his own lone cottage.

'Good evening, daughter!'

'Good evening, Brother Mott!' She was fond of old Mott, and grateful to him for being there. He would surely have been to see her grandfather, and now she could say she had met him.

From the cover of the trees Sam and Vanlo had watched Ellen, had seen her pause and her moment of decision before moving on.

'Come on, bruv, let's get back,' said Sam.

Vanlo looked up into Sam's face, and feared what he saw.

*

Sam lay awake. Birds clicked and scuffled across the roof of the wagon. He could hear faintly the tobacco-stained snore of his mother settled in the bender tent close by. Lucretia's breathing was low and regular, but Sam knew that the moment he reached for her she would wake as quickly as a cat. He put a hand on the promontory of his wife's hip. In a rustle of bedding she was up and straddling him, and their battle recommenced.

*

Ellen again dutifully took the long way home the next day, skirting the wood, telling herself it was because of the cows, and that she couldn't count on being rescued a second time. *Silly enough he'd think me then!*

The day after she did the same again, but this time a man detached himself from the trees and stood in front of her, not quite barring the path.

'Miss Quainton!'

'You startled me, Mr Loveridge.' Ellen looked round. 'Where's Vanlo?'

'I sent him to get kindling. We've been to see Horwood about the harvest.'

'Did you get work, then?' Ellen spoke as lightly as she was able.

'Oh yes. I've been there before. He knows me for a good worker, but he made me go through the hoops for him anyway.'

'I've never seen you before.'

'P'raps you wasn't looking!'

Ellen coloured.

'What do you mean, he made you go through the hoops?'

'About the war. I didn't fight, see, not really.'

'Perhaps he'd a right, then. Mr Horwood lost a son, and the other, Reggie, came back not much good for farming!'

'I'm sorry for it. I've to take Reggie out in his chair, he said.'

'Take him out on a horse and cart, Mr Loveridge. Reggie would like that best,' she said, in an inspired moment. 'He loved getting up on the trap . . . before. I remember he used to get into trouble for going out in it on a Sunday. And if you sit him alongside you he'll look the same as any other man – and that will mean a lot to him.' Ellen looked away, close to tears.

'I've known Reggie Horwood all my life,' she added. 'When we were little he got put in the corner time after time at Sunday school. And once he told the teacher I had my eyes open during prayers! He got ribbed about that for ages! But he's precious little chance to be naughty now.'

She faced him.

'So how *was* your war, Mr Loveridge?' she asked.

'Various clinks to start with – then Dartmoor. Hard labour – stone-breaking under the rain, mostly. In with all those varsity men, the conchies. I was like a cat in a cage.'

'Better than being a dead rat in a ditch.'

'I know that. Lost my brother Noah – Verdun. We dunt even know where he lies.'

'Oh – I'm sorry.'

'Ain't your fault. But dunt be angry with me – it dunt suit a face like yours. I didn't wait for you to make you so.

47

Anyways, I didn't stay in Dartmoor long. I'd avoided call-up because I didn't know how I'd manage with someone bawling and shouting at me what I should do, that was all; I can't say as it was my conscience – I just couldn't see the why of it.'

'You couldn't see *why*? How were we to defend ourselves?'

'Defend what, Miss Quainton? I dunt see much thanks for them that came back. I meet plenty of them in my life – *mumpers* – tramping up and down the country begging – all they're fit for now. They tried all ways to trick me into soldiering; the first place I was held with these other fellows, our togs was taken away, every stitch, and we had the choice of wearing a blanket or wearing a uniform. I'm sorry, I can see from your face I shouldn't be saying these things to a lady.'

'No, please – go on. I have never met anyone who did . . . what you did. I heard there were some in the connexion – in the chapel – that wouldn't enlist, though everyone round here did that was called up. There was a lot of division and argument about it, though.'

'And what did *you* think?' he asked.

'I thought . . . oh dear, I thought it wasn't fair that some went to die and some stayed behind in the lap of luxury.'

Sam laughed. 'Tole you that, did they? 'Twas hardly luxury! Well, I didn't put the uniform on and was glad of it, for those that did went to court-martial like they was already soldiers. Then after a bit I'd be brought five minutes before some bristling moustaches at another tribunal and they said a Gippo didn't have no conscience beyond what was comfortable to his own self and gave me prison. Never met anyone that's been inside, have you?'

'No!' said Ellen, thinking herself very daring.

'Well, I was in a cell on my own, no mattress to begin with, and then only let outside for half an hour a day, just to walk round in a line. And you mayn't look at the sky. You chapel children you say are tole to shut your eyes 'gainst God's creation, but just looking at it I think's a prayer itself. I was forever doing that, by getting on a stool and looking through the bars, but they always catched me at it – and then I'd get put on bread and water and no mattress again for a bit. And in the yard, you'd to keep your eyes to the ground. My ears was all cold 'cause my hair was cropped, but my face all bristly because they left us to grow beards whether we wanted 'em or no – and I never did. Made us all look the same. I'll tell you, taking your hair off you is worse than having no clothes, just about. I got a whopping too, off a guard. Don't they do prison visiting, your chapel people?'

'They do, but not round here. I've never been let to go, anyway.'

'Not a place for the likes of you, Miss Quainton.'

She looked at him sharply, but could see no trace of sarcasm in his expression.

'The worst was the silence rule. Couldn't speak to the other men, not even to the wardens, and them not to us 'cept to tell us what to do. Must be why I talk so much now.

Not that anywhere was quiet – iron staircases and wardens' boots. Dartmoor was better that way. We were let to talk and the cell doors wunt locked – must be a bit like what living in a reg'lar house is like.'

'So hard for you! Whilst other men were fighting and the poor women that loved them not knowing if they'd ever see them again, or if they'd come back like Reggie!' Ellen fumbled for a handkerchief but Sam was quicker.

'Here,' he said. She stared at the piece of cloth in his outstretched hand. It was crumpled, but looked clean.

'Thank you, but I have my own!' She wiped her eyes, then blew her nose, turning her head away.

'We never got Noah's telegram for a long time after – he'd given them a pub near Maidstone for his address. Only o' course my old mother said she knew.'

'I am sorry, Mr Loveridge. You must think I've been inexcusably rude to you today – rude and ignorant. But I must go now – they'll be wondering where I've got to.'

'I'm grateful to you for listening to me, Miss Quainton. But would you give me your hand again, like you done last time?'

'Oh – of course.'

*

'Ellen! Where've you been?' Flora came out of the scullery drying her hands on her apron. 'Butter the bread, would you? The table's already laid ... Wait, child!' Flora laid damp, cool fingers on Ellen's forehead.

'Your eyes is all bright – but you've no fever I can see. You've not the curse, have you?'

'I'm fine, Mother. I've never been better.'

'I dunt know how I should bear it if I was to lose you too,' quavered Flora. 'I still ask myself what I done to offend the good Lord, that He saw fit to take my little girl.'

Ellen turned back and put her arms round Flora. Her mother's bones felt as fragile as a sparrow's.

'Hush, Mother, Grandfer'll be in soon.'

'I know what he'd say. That I mun never question the will of God. That He has His reasons. But did He have to take *my* Sally? *And* your poor father so soon after?'

'Let me get the bread buttered, Mother. Then after tea we could walk over to the churchyard, if you'd like that.'

'Bless you, child. And bless your Grandfer for bringing them back home. I couldn't have borne it if they was in one of them grett big burying places in London. There's nowhere so lonely as a city, and that's as true when you're dead as when you're alive, I'm sure.'

'But you've always said the dead went to their reward, Mother.'

'I have, haven't I? Let's just hope it's true.'

'Ssh! That's Grandfer now, scraping his boots.'

*

The following morning Ellen followed her usual routine, of preparing and wrapping her sandwiches in the back pantry whilst her mother laid the breakfast table.

'Morning, Mother! Morning, Grandfer!'

'Morning, Ellen,' said her mother, and paused. 'Why've you your best frock on?'

'Thought I might as well wear it. It's only going to waste in the wardrobe.'

'But nobody'll see it under your overalls.'

'Doesn't mean I won't know it's there.'

'Can I get on and say grace, daughters? Then perhaps our day's work can begin,' growled Oliver.

*

Ellen dawdled on the path home. She had almost reached the ridge, feeling drear with disappointment, when she heard a twig snap, and turned round.

'I'm sorry, Miss Quainton, I'm a bit late. I was kep' back to physic one of Horwood's nags.'

'There is no need to apologise, Mr Loveridge. It is not as if we made an appointment,' she said, trying hard to hold back a smile.

'Mebbe not, but like I said, I like talking to you.'

'The horse?'

'He'll do. Them togs suit you.' He fingered the short sleeve of the cotton dress: sage green sprayed with forget-me-not flowers. 'That blue matches your eyes.'

'Charlie said that too – my fiancé.'

'You ain't worn it since, have you?'

'Not much.' *Not at all.* 'But I'd taken a lot of trouble over it, back then.'

'You made it? Is that your work then, doing the stitching?'

'No, I'm a draper's assistant. I just sew for myself, and for my friend Judy.'

'You dunt talk like a shop girl – not that I talk to a lot of 'em, but they're not usually so fine-natured as you, Miss Quainton.'

'Oh . . . well, I was a teacher.'

'Why ain't you now, if I may ask?'

'It got harder to go on – after Charlie died. I've been urged often enough to go back, and to go away to college to qualify properly. I still teach the Sunday school.'

'Ain't that meant for a day of rest?'

'Our busiest day!' laughed Ellen. 'Sunday school and worship in the morning, then again in the afternoon.'

'So what does a young woman like you do to enjoy herself?'

'Oh, there's plenty. Camp meetings, if there's a visiting preacher. Sewing meetings. Picnics . . .' She faltered, look-ing up at him. 'I expect you think I have a very dull life.'

'No, but I think a girl like you should have more call for pretty dresses.'

'It's not all I hoped for, of course. But there are so many girls in my position. So many babies not born . . . I do like the Sunday school, though, even if they aren't my children. Do you go to church, Mr Loveridge?'

Sam laughed. 'We're Christian children all right but we've our own ways of being so. We dunt hold with much in the formal way. My old mother'll go and sit in a church for an hour at a time, but run off if ever a parson comes near her. It ain't so easy to go to a service when all those good Christians turn and look at you and draw in their skirts. Or when you're handed a prayer book and dunt know which way up to hold it because you can't read what's in it anyway. But I was christened in a church, several times over in fact!'

'*Oh!*'

'I was born to the north of this county, I'm tole. The parsons thereabouts would give money to a poor family for the baby, so my father would hitch up the wagon and take us from parish to parish. I see I shouldn't have told you that, only I had no say in the matter.'

'And have you done the same with your own children, Mr Loveridge?' she asked coldly.

'I wish you'd call me Sam. I have not – I've not been blessed with children.'

'I'm sorry. Perhaps they'll come soon.'

'No. I've been wed as long as I can remember – as soon as they saw I needed to be!'

Ellen flushed and looked away.

'I'm wed regular, Miss Quainton,' he said in a changed voice.

'I don't know why you're telling me this!'

'Because you've the kind of face that says you'd listen! I did think about getting free once or twice, but I was too young to find the courage to say what I thought, and I wasn't sure what that was anyhow. Where would I have gone to? We was rubbing along all right, even without a *tickner* to cry us awake at night. I just wondered in a way if there wasn't greater happiness on offer somewhere than what we seemed to have.'

Ellen could not meet his eyes.

'You understand then why I'm idling about here instead of at the camp,' he said quietly. 'It is a pleasure for me to hear your gentle voice. If you never speak to me again I'll always be grateful that you did at all.'

'I think it's time I went home, Mr Loveridge. I really shouldn't let you talk to me about such things.'

'Let me kiss your hand again and I'll let you go, then.'

'Here.'

He took her hand but this time examined it intently, passing the ball of his thumb across the clean, oval nails with their sickle-moon rims.

'You've pretty hands. Go with your pretty dress.'

'Thank you,' said Ellen, pink with delight. Her hands were one of her few vanities, along with the bright brown hair, which she wore unfashionably long but wound in a bun low on her nape, to allow her hat to fit. But for her twenty-first birthday her mother had given her a manicure set that she treasured. She knew the watered lining of the zipped pigskin wallet could only be artificial silk, and that the implements themselves were of plated base metal that would eventually flake, and their handles resin, not tortoiseshell. But it was a secret pleasure to use each of them in turn, in a weekly ritual. And this Gypsy, with dirt under his own nails, and hands scabbed by work, actually noticed her effort! Finally he kissed her fingers, holding her gaze and smiling.

Walking on afterwards, Ellen looked round to make sure that he was gone, then stopped and hugged herself.

Oh where's the harm? I thought nobody would say such nice things to me ever again. And he'll be gone by September.

*

The following Monday, her mother stopped her just as Ellen was leaving for work. 'I nearly forgot, daughter. Would you go and see Mrs Hempton after work?'

Flora heard the slightest intake of breath and looked into Ellen's face; the disappointment vanished as quickly as it had appeared, and the veil of obedient resignation that was the girl's usual expression slipped back into place.

'I thought you liked going to Mrs Hempton's, Ellen? She's always pleased to see *you*. Her poor little Joan has the whooping cough, and I said you'd go as you're safe, seeing as you had it yourself years ago. The tea-meeting voted that we'd pay the doctor for her. You could pop by his house on your way and settle what's outstanding.'

For the next three days Ellen called at Mrs Hempton's cottage after the shop closed and tried to find hope of recovery in Joan's damp, exhausted face. She was convinced she could hear the child's gasping cough wherever she was: walking home later along the now deserted path, in the kitchen garden pulling carrots, unpegging the washing. Then the doctor was due again, so she told the child's mother she would call instead on Saturday, and set off home, telling herself Sam would have already given up on her, that it was better that way.

But just ahead of his usual place, with a rustle quiet as a squirrel's, he stepped out onto the path.

'Oh . . . you look very smart today, Mr Loveridge. Sunday best but not on Sunday?' *Where did I learn to be so pert?*

'I've took Reggie out on the cart. Thought I'd go to a bit of trouble for 'en – a clean shirt and trousers 'stead of my working togs.'

'That was a kind thought.'

''Twas a pleasure to do it. Where you bin, though?'

'There's a widow in a cottage in Chinnor whose little girl has the whooping cough. I've been keeping her company.'

'How does the little maidy?'

'She's bad – worn out. She's never been a strong child. Her mother is beside herself – she comes out to the door with me when I leave and holds my arm and asks me again and again, "Will Joan live? She's all I have!" Joan's father died in Flanders without ever seeing her. If it weren't for the kindness of neighbours they'd both be in the Union.'

'I s'll ask my old mother,' said Sam. 'What to do for the cough, I mean.'

Ellen hesitated.

'I dunt mean she'll call there. She med be the mother of a fallen hero, but it dunt mean she gets treated any better. I'll tell you what she says, so you'll know what to do. Tomorrow I'll be off the harvest at six. Shall I see you here?'

'Yes – and thank you.'

'I'll go, then, but it's done me good to have seen you again. I thought you was avoiding me, maybe.'

'Oh no, not that!'

He touched a finger to his hat. 'I mun see where my Vanlo has got to. Goodbye, Miss Quainton.'

*

The following evening Ellen walked as slowly as she could. She wanted to be late, just a little late. *This is foolishness*, she thought to herself. *I don't suppose he can even tell the time. And I'm only coming for Joan's sake.* She scented a faint drift of tobacco on the cooling air, and looked up, aware that she was being watched. Sam was leaning against a tree, smoking. He threw down the stub and carefully stamped it out.

'Coltsfoot and thyme, Miss Quainton. Brew it as tea, like it was nettles or sage – the leaves, not the flower. You know the difference, don't you, 'tween coltsfoot and a dandelion?'

'What country child doesn't?'

'Begging your pardon. But that should ease the little maidy's cough. My mother physicked all of us. She lost two babies, mind, but not to the cough. I'm all she's got left, after my sister went too, and I'm healthy enough.'

'You had a sister?'

'Have, I suppose, for strictly speaking she ain't dead. Just dead to us.'

Ellen's hand went to her face.

'Married a *gaujo* – a ploughboy. Not seen 'er since.'

'Your poor mother, Mr Loveridge.'

'Yes, I reckon she'd agree with you there.'

'I was wondering, Mr Loveridge . . . on Sunday we have a circuit preacher coming from Banbury. He has brought many to God. It'll be a camp meeting, outside, I mean. You and your mother – and any of your family – would be welcome. You wouldn't have to come into the chapel – if you didn't like it, you could slip away and no one would be the wiser.' She stopped abruptly, embarrassed at her babbling.

'Them mission vans come round on the hopping,' he said. 'Tea and tracts – they always want you to take 'em even if you can't read 'em. Kind enough people – I can see that. But they always want you to give up the road.'

'Give up the road?'

'Settle down, live in a house. Have the same master year-round. I'd feel like a tombstone, I would, buried up to the ankles so's I couldn't move. I worship God's work every day, in every little animal I hear scuttling at night. When I've the sun in my face and the horse trotting the road before me, when I've to clear snow from the wagon steps, or when I see the new leaves putting out. Every road I go, and every new place I see. Every new face – your face.'

'We've been here, in this place – Quaintons, I mean – for hundreds of years. There was a vicar when Grandfer was a child, told *his* father – they were church people then – that our name comes from somewhere in France, men that came over with the Conqueror and ruled here. Of course, none of us rule anything now.'

'Not even yourselves! But all this,' he waved an arm at the trees behind him, 'in a few years if they go on as they do, it'll all be gone. My people'll be huddled in there waiting for the end, for by then there'll be no place for us to go – like the poor rabbits and mice hiding in the last patch of a field before the crop's all cut. Then if they dunt set about us with sticks like they do with them, they'll put us in them boxes they call houses, with a poor naked patch of grass front and back to plant flowers in and pretend it ain't a prison, and a ball and chain round our ankles, one you can't see but you know is there. And rules, dockiments, and flags and duty! Look what duty did for my poor Noah! When I was inside, them scholars and holy boys tole me how it was wrong to kill a fellow man, same as the good Lord said, a man you dunt know, who in the ordinary way of things would do me no harm – but in France they was all the Boche, even the padres said so.'

'So you *did* go to France?'

'O' course I did. Anything to get out of prison; some of what you might call the finer-natured men were driven mad by it. I went to France in their uniform in the end. I saw men die. I'd help the stretcher-bearers when I could, and sometimes it was only a case of gathering up the pieces after, but I killed no one.'

'Kept your head down, did you, and fired in the air?' said Ellen.

'I'm more than a middling shot, as it happens. Even in poor light – and especially by moonlight. But I never let 'em know that. There's not a thing I dun't know about horses, so I went for Remount Services down in Romsey. Sorry, do I talk too much?'

'No, no – but that sounds a good number, a long way behind the lines.'

'Actually, it was.' He was unabashed. 'One and six a day and all found. Only problem was being roused at half past five every day, whether it was light or not. I didn't see the sense in it.'

'No different from anyone working on a farm.'

'I know that well enough – I've worked on farms since I was a little lad. I only meant that for that work you might as well have stayed snug another half hour in winter.' He rummaged in a trouser pocket. 'Here – look. My badge. Pretty, ain't it?'

It lay in her palm, warm from his body, a little leaping horse with the letters *GR* above and the words *Army Remount Services* on an heraldic belt.

'I s'pose you can read it, too?'

'Can't you?' she said.

'I *know* what's writ there but no, I never had no learning. I got on all right without it, even there. Started as a rough rider, breaking the horses in, I mean, then worked up to being farriery corporal.' He clicked his heels and saluted. Ellen laughed.

''Tis good I've made you laugh. You look like you haven't done that for a good bit.'

'What makes you say that?'

'Because the way you laugh looks very close to crying, I'd say.'

She averted her face and said in a queerly suffocated voice, contemptuous, 'An easy war, then.'

'It was. In Romsey. But they tempted me with twice the money and something for Lukey – that's my wife – if I'd go to France. I was fed up with the quartermaster too. In Romsey the officers was all *gentlemen* –' the word sounded like an insult – 'the kind that rode with the hunt and had their own stables. Most of the time he left me alone to look after the draught horses, them being of no interest to a man like that, but he hated it when the other men would ask advice of me rather'n him. And I wanted anyway to know where all them horses I'd trained up and led down to Southampton had ended up. They'd sent them to hell, Ellen. Can I call you Ellen? I can't talk of them things and say "Miss Quainton".'

She nodded.

'I swear to you those poor beasts can get shell-shocked as readily as any man – and gassed, and bombed . . . I'm sorry. I've upset you.'

'No, please go on. I wish people would talk more about what happened – the war, I mean. You'd think sometimes they were trying not to remember it.'

'Some wunt want to, after what they've seen, Ellen.'

She flinched. 'You said – about the horses.'

'I love horses, see. There they came in all sorts – like men do. There was poor nags as had only ever known the shafts of a butcher's cart and a country lane, driven mad by the noise. And there was gentlemen's chargers what had only ever ate grass, kicking up to find themselves in a strange stable with stranger company and throwing off their nose-bags. I killed no men but I had to shoot horses when there was no more could be done for 'em, they being poor flesh and blood just as ourselves. It doesn't much matter to a horse if he's German or English – he's a horse and does like one.'

'My grandfather says your kind cheat with horses.'

'He isn't the first to say it,' Sam said without rancour. 'And I wunt say there aren't Gypsies as would, same as other men. We might know well enough how to whistle a horse out of a field – or get cows to stand out of the way for that matter – but it's hard on a man to be told he is cheating when all he does is know more than another. The man who befriends us always gets good advice.'

'I'm sorry, I spoke too hastily.'

'Forgiven! Especially if you smile at me again,' he said.

'I don't know how I smiled, I'm sure. Like this?'

'No, that's too polite. It has to come nat'rel. That's better ... An' you'll let me know how the little maidy does, will you?'

CHAPTER 7

*At all times it is of use to have a Friend to whom you
can pour out your heart without any disguise or reserve.*

John Wesley, 1776

Lace

'Come outside a minute, Ellen, I'm gasping for a smoke!'

'Oh Judy, what about your pledge?'

'Pledge my pretty arse!'

Ellen looked round the school-room, now with the
forms pushed back and thronged with tea-drinkers and
cake-eaters, the reward of the righteous for having sat
through a sermon and prayers on a Wednesday evening.

'I think I can be spared now,' Ellen said.

*

'Oh, that's better.' Judith leaned against a fence, drawing
the smoke deep into her lungs. 'I don't get better at this,

do I?' she said, holding out the crooked little cigarette she had been at such pains to roll.

'How do you keep it from your father, Judy? He must smell it on you.'

'If he does, he never says. Anything for a peaceful life, that's him.'

'I think he must be afraid of you,' said Ellen.

Judith laughed, delighted.

'Oh, then I should make more of it! What life is this, Ellen? Doing Boddington's books for him day after day. Tea-meetings. *Sewing* meetings – even worse, you only get the old cats, not even the old tom-cats. Band of Hope . . . more teas for the missions, so's over in Fernando Po they can have tea-meetings too.'

'That's unkind, Judy. Grace is hardly an old cat. You forget how much good comes out of it – holidays for orphans, the workhouse visits . . .'

'But we make 'em pray morning, noon and night for it. If I was them people, I'd want the help for being me, not because someone was hell-bent on saving my immortal soul. The chapel's like commercial travellers sometimes – how many stockings can I sell on this circuit? How many tracts can I give out? How many souls can I save before they give me a book with an inscription in it that I'll never want to read? You know what I want before I'm too old, Ellen?'

'A man, knowing you!'

'O' course. And I don't believe for a minute you're any different – you just hide it better. I want a man to kiss me and tell me I'm pretty and that he'd die for me. Instead, they're too old, too married, or too common for Pa's liking. And there's poor Reggie stuck at home because he's no use to anyone from the waist down and won't even see me, when we could have had a houseful of brats by now if that Boche bullet had gone into the next man instead. And I daren't find myself another man because I'd be afraid of hurting Reggie.' Judith swore and flung down the cigarette butt.

'He gave you your freedom,' said Ellen.

'I know – but what freedom is it? It just don't feel right all the same. I wish . . . I wish I could go away. You too. We could find a room in a city, have ourselves some fun.'

'You've said this before. But you know I can't leave Mother.'

'And I'm stuck with Pa.'

'Did you really want a houseful of brats anyway, Judy? Look at Sarah Figg – old before her time.'

'Figg beats her, they say,' said Judith.

'You see?'

'Reggie would never have beaten me. He wouldn't have dared! Don't tell me, Ellen, that you wouldn't want a fellow to hold you and tell you you're the best thing that ever happened to him?'

'Judy, you could write his lines for him! You'd do it better than poor Charlie ever did. You know, I can't really remember what he looked like. There's only that horrible photograph of him in uniform. I've stared at it that many times I can only remember a man in black and white who didn't smile. And he did smile. He was always smiling at me.'

Judith watched her carefully. 'You might find someone else, you know.'

Ellen hesitated. 'Round here? I don't think I could do it, Judy. If I stood up in the chapel with another man, he'd be taking *Charlie's* place. It'd be like settling for second best – he'd know it too. I'd have to go away, like you said.'

'You won't, though, will you? If you'd gone on with the teaching, maybe you could have. Not now you're a draper's assistant.'

'Don't, Judy! Do you think, though, that hearts can mend? Even when you'd thought yours was all broken in pieces and buried in France in a place you've never seen?'

'What is it, Ellen . . . ?'

'Oh, nothing, Judy.'

*

The old woman sat on the steps of the *vardo* gazing intently at the small, fat pillow on her knees. The smoke from the incessant pipe in the corner of her mouth obscured the pricked paper pattern that lay pinned to the pillow alongside the strip of lace that grew beneath her flashing fingers, but that didn't matter as by now her hands had memorised the rhythm of the design. The threads twisted as the little bobbins danced and shivered, their glass beads glinting in the light.

Lucretia put her foot on the bottom step.

'Pretty, that. For me, is it?'

The fingers didn't slacken. The old woman tightened the corner of her mouth to hold her pipe firm. She would not look at her daughter-in-law.

'No. I'm making this for a lady.'

Lucretia's face congealed. Then, shrugging, she said, 'But they gets all their trimmings from factories now, Mother Harmony. They'll not be wanting your efforts. All smelling of baccy, that's going to be.'

The old woman said nothing, but the tinkling glass beads flew back and forth a little faster.

*

Ellen had just walked up onto the path across the fields when she heard her name called. She said nothing, but her shoulders stiffened in disappointment.

No Sam this evening then! Nobody to tell me he likes the sound of my voice or wanting to kiss my hand!

She turned round, trying not to look vexed, and waited for Judith's father to catch up with her.

'Good evening, Brother Chown.'

'Good evening, Miss Quainton. May I walk with you? I was going to see your grandfather about Thursday's class meeting.'

'Of course.'

'Um . . . will you be attending yourself, Ellen?'

'Well, yes, I expect so,' she said.

'I wish you could persuade Judith. She might listen to you when she won't listen to her father.'

'I have tried,' said Ellen. 'We can only pray for Judith's conversion, Mr Chown, and trust to a will that is greater than ours.'

'I have much faith in your influence on her, Ellen.'

Only now did Ellen look at him directly.

'She is my dearest friend, Mr Chown. I love her for what she is.'

Chown's greyish face flushed.

'You do right to rebuke me,' he said.

'But I never meant—'

'No, no, your loyalty to Judith does you credit. I only trust that *she* does not have a bad influence on *you*.'

'I sometimes wish I were more like her,' she said, half to herself, 'more high-spirited, saying what I think, instead of worrying about how others judge me.'

'Judith is in want of tact, Ellen. I, like you, am anxious about how I am seen by others.'

'But you're—'

'I'm what? Old? I must look that way to you, of course. But for me worrying about the judgement of others is a matter of pride – a grave sin. For you, I think it is more that you want to avoid hurting people. Whereas Judith, I think, simply doesn't care enough.'

Ellen didn't know what to say to this, and looked away from him up the path. They were approaching the ridge where the track met the road leading to Chingestone. To the left of the junction, Surman's Wood cut a rich green swathe across the vale, up towards the ridge of hills that marked the border with Buckinghamshire. Where the trees edged the path as it rose to the horizon a man and a boy stood watching them. The man's fedora alone gave him an unmistakeably un-English air, though quite why Ellen couldn't say. But she did know that she didn't want Judith's father and Sam Loveridge to meet.

'Um . . . I've noticed that *you* care, Ellen. I have heard reports from Quartermaine at the board-school that the children you teach on Sundays are neater, more attentive, more biddable when they are in his classroom the day after. Even the youngest members of our connexion can spread our Lord's message if they set the right example – apostles not only to their companions but also to their elders. Quartermaine misses your help, you know. Not one of the girls he has engaged since you left has proved acceptable . . . Ellen?'

The figures up ahead had disappeared into the trees.

'Oh . . . I'm sorry, Mr Chown. I was distracted . . . What were you saying?'

'Mr Quartermaine says his best pupils are those who attend your Sunday school.'

'It's their parents who deserve the credit, not me.'

'But we must dare to be a Daniel, Ellen. There are Gypsies camped in that wood. Their women have been seen peddling fortunes to the credulous in the villages, dragging their filthy children with them to elicit sympathy. Just think if those little ones could be brought to the Lord by you as His instrument! If the children can be brought to godliness and cleanliness, then so may their parents follow!'

'You want to make them like us, then?'

Harold stared at her, perplexed.

'Don't you?'

'I think they mayn't be here much longer – not beyond the end of harvest.'

'How would you know that?'

'Farmer Horwood isn't expecting to keep them,' she said evasively.

'Oh, yes, of course. But would you not consider going back to the board-school, or to think about the teacher training again, Ellen? Now that you are . . . recovered? The connexion would look after you in Birmingham if you were willing to go, and Quartermaine would certainly take you on afterwards – that is if you wanted to use your talents other than in the chapel's mission.'

'No, and please don't mention it again. If Charlie and I had married, it would have been different.'

'But a married woman should not work anyway, Ellen! Her task is to please her husband and make a home for him, not belittle him by pretending to a wage the same as he has. It's not the natural way of things – no more than a woman voting when she can have such little idea of what government means. One must be grateful for the small mercy that at least she may not vote until she is thirty – that she may devote the best years of her youth to her children and her lord, without troubling herself with matters that should be of no concern to her!'

'But I have no children, no lord, Mr Chown! So why does it matter what I do? If I spent any more time with other people's children I'm sure I would come to hate them because I'd none of my own. I think you must see me, Mr Chown, as a better person than I really am.'

'We all try to show ourselves as better than we really are, Ellen. That's the weakness of our pride. But your honesty does you credit.'

'You see? First my loyalty and now my honesty. You will persist in thinking well of me. But I must work, whether it's ladylike or godfearing or not. When Grandfer is called to his rest who will support Mother and I? Or do we return to London to be a burden on my brother John, who struggles enough just to keep himself?'

'I have annoyed you, I see. I am sorry. I didn't mean to offend – I think I don't know how to speak to young women. I believe I didn't even when I was a young man. That is why I need your help.'

'My help?' Ellen scanned the path in both directions, but no one was coming.

'Yes. I don't believe we are reaching those who need to be saved. Look round you next Sunday afternoon. Apart from your scholars – and you, of course – when I preach I look down mostly on grey heads. Other chapels have a young ladies parlour, cricket teams; they dress up and put on plays – operettas even.'

Ah! Safe ground after all.

'Grandfer doesn't hold with play-acting and singing, except for hymns.'

'I know. But there have to be stronger attractions than Mrs Stopps on the harmonium.'

Ellen looked at him in surprise. But there was no leavening humour in Harold's face.

'We have to do something about the Overseas Mission collection. The task there is pressing,' he said.

How dreary this is! Aloud to Harold she said, 'I shall give it some thought, Brother Chown.'

They had drawn level with the wood. Ellen's eyes flickered over the path towards the stile, and over the trees that had absorbed Sam and Vanlo.

'There is something else I wanted to ask you, Ellen, if you do not think I speak out of turn. Um … might I enquire as to whether anyone has entered your heart since Charlie's loss . . . ? Whether you have ever considered marriage?'

'I have not,' she said, her heart pounding. 'I have met no one else I could marry. I must accept this as part of His plan. Just as you have, Mr Chown.'

'You are right, of course. "It is of the Lord's mercies that we are not consumed, because His compassions fail not." Forgive me my presumption. The ways of the Almighty are inscrutable at times. I have sometimes wondered . . . How can I put this? That the loss of Charlie was also part of His plan for you. I cannot see, Miss Quainton, that you live out that plan in that draper's shop, pandering to the whims of those idle women, though Sister Colton is an excellent woman. It pains me, if I may speak honestly, to see one of your talents and personal graces exposed to the eyes of any casual observer. I find it hard, personally, to think of you as a shopgirl. Whatever is the matter?'

'Poor Charlie! Poor, poor Charlie!' she cried.

'My dear Ellen – Miss Quainton – I didn't mean to offend—'

'Leave me alone!'

'Miss Quainton—'

'I don't know who your God is that makes plans like that! A cruel God, Brother Chown! Not any God I want!'

She turned and ran, as Chown observed, like a child, her knees raised as far as her skirts would allow. Then, aware that she was being watched, she slowed to a march, arms swinging, fists clenched, shoulders rigid. She was saying something, but he could not distinguish her words.

Harold Chown put his head in his hands. *You old fool!*

*

'Son?' Harmony leaned over the half-door of the *vardo*. 'Come in here a minute, will yer?'

Sam got up from feeding the fire with sticks, wiping his hands down his trousers.

'What is it, Ma?'

'Up here and I'll tell yer.'

The old woman was rummaging in the drawer under the bed where she slept in wintertime, amongst what she called her 'private treasures'. Sam had been shown these at times over the years: baby teeth, curls of dark childish hair, some little pieces of jewellery.

'Where's that one?' asked his mother.

'Lukey? Washing the pots in the stream with the others.'

'Here, Sam,' she said, turning round and handing him a small brown paper parcel. ''Tis a present. Fit for a lady.'

'Mother?'

'Don't play the innercent, Sam.'

''Bout what? I ain't done nothing.'

'I 'ope not, but you're thinking about it. I seed it in your face. I know my own son.'

'So why this? This present?'

'Cause you're all I got, my Sam! There's not a day goes by I don't think about your sister Miselda, and wish her well, wherever she may be, and 'ope her *gaujo* still loves 'er and she 'im, and that their *tickners* are handsome and strong – them as I should've helped into the world. Only your father wouldn't have it any other way, an' I dunt want you coming to the same end. It's breaking my 'eart, seeing you with that look about you and you wandering all over, young Vanlo along of you. No use you looking away, my Sam. I'm right, aren't I? If I can see it, Lukey'll not be far behind me. Give the *rakli* 'er present and tell 'er she'll not see you again.'

'I done nothing, Ma, we only talked a bit.'

'She know you're *rommered*[7]?'

'I tole 'er. First time I saw 'er.'

Harmony's face cleared a little. 'Well, if she's a good gel she'll not want to get 'erself mixed up with some other woman's man. An' if she ain't, she'll be easier for you to forget, Sam.'

'What's Vanlo said, Ma?'

'Him? Nuffing. Best not go gettin' him into trouble. You're the world to him.'

'I dunt know what to do,' he said in a low voice.

'I've just tole you. You can't live two lives, my Sam. But I know it's not Lukey keeps you here,' she said, with a tilt of her head in the direction of the campfire. ''Tis me.'

---

[7] Married

'I ain't leavin' *you*.'

'Can't say I'm not pleased to hear it.'

'Can I open it, at least?' he said, holding up the package.

'Go on then.'

He unwrapped the brown paper, kneading its contents. 'Oh, who wouldn't love this?'

Sam put his arms round his mother and kissed the top of her head through her scarf. The old woman pushed him away, passing him in the narrow space, stumping down the steps. Sam sank onto a three-legged stool.

Gev the girl her present, then, and stop this. Ma's right; I ain't got two lives.

*

For the next three evenings Sam forced himself to spend the last hours of daylight going round the farms with Vanlo in search of scrap.

On the fourth evening he went back to the path and waited.

'Good evening, Ellen.'

'Mr Loveridge.'

'Sam – please. Only the *gavvers* call me Loveridge – they don't bother with the mister.'

'*Gavvers*?'

'*Gavengros* – the constables. Sometimes I tell 'em my name is Tom Boswell.'

'You use a false name?'

'Not really. My grandfer's. We do that all the time. Anyways, who was that old *mush* you was with the other day, then? Him that went upsetting you?'

'Oh, that was Harold Chown – my best friend's father,' she said as dismissively as she could. *So he was there, all the time.*

Ellen couldn't say what *mush* meant exactly, but 'that old *mush*' hardly sounded complimentary. She felt ashamed of knowing Harold, whereas that evening, in his presence, she had tried to convince herself that it was knowing the Gypsy she was ashamed of. Now, with Sam's dark eyes gazing at her from under the brim of that extraordinary hat, what dull, sanctimonious old Harold might have thought didn't matter at all.

'He's very attentive to *you*,' said Sam.

'What, *Harold*?'

'He couldn't keep his eyes off you, Ellen – not that he's to blame for that, o' course. So what's your friend's mother like, then?'

'She's been dead more than ten years; Mr Chown is a widower.'

'Well, he don't want to stay one, evidently!'

'You talk as if you're jealous, Mr Loveridge.'

'Sam. Well, I am. Or I would be if he wunt such a *dinilo*[8] of a wooer.'

---

[8] Idiot

He has a wife, Ellen! A wife!

He hesitated in the face of her silence. 'Here, I brought you a present.' He pulled out the small brown paper package. 'Sorry, it's got a bit crumpled.'

The strip of bobbin lace had been rolled quite tightly. She unfurled it gently: a pattern of acorns and leaves stood out against her palm. 'Oh Sam, it's beautiful! There must be three yards at least here. I have never had anything so lovely – but I have no idea how I can use it.'

She glanced down at her plain blouse and skirt; the experiment of the pretty dress had not been repeated, Ellen lacking the courage to withstand her mother's questioning looks.

'They will ask me where I got it. They don't like girls to wear finery.'

'So don't. Trim something they can't see,' he said, smiling. Ellen's face flamed.

'Oh, I don't know that I can accept such a thing . . . It wouldn't be right.' She gazed at the lace, feeling its fineness between finger and thumb.

'It's only something to remember me by, Ellen. I can see you like it. I shall tell Mother so.'

'Your *mother* made this?'

'Yes. She made it for you. Don't look so surprised, Ellen. A mother can read her own son.'

'Who else knows about this . . . this present?'

'No one.'

'I am very grateful . . . but . . .'

'Please accept it, Ellen. Mother would take it badly if you didn't. I would too.'

'I will. Please thank her for me. I shall write her a note to say so.'

'You needn't go to that trouble. None of us can read.'

'Oh, of course.' To hide her embarrassment, Ellen concentrated on wrapping the lace again in the brown paper, and then held out her hand, awkwardly. He didn't shake it, but as before lifted it to his lips, then with a swift twist turned it over and kissed her palm.

Now, Sam. Tell 'er she'll not see you again.

'Shall you be here tomorrow, Ellen?'

'I expect so.'

'Till then.' He touched a finger to his hat and turned into the wood. Then, 'Ellen!' he called after her. 'Your Harold is wrong, you know. God don't send men to war. It's other men as do that.

After he'd gone she unwrapped the little parcel again. *It's a keepsake, that's all. As he said, something to remember him by. Once the harvest is over.*

CHAPTER 8

I afterwards found that what is called the long sight of the Gypsies . . . is not long sight at all, but is the result of a peculiar faculty the Gypsies have of observing more closely than Gorgios do everything that meets their eyes in the woods and on the hills and along the roads.

Theodore Watts-Dunton, *Aylwin*

Falling

'*Vanlo!*'

The boy turned round reluctantly. He was afraid of his sister, though he admired her – but he loved Sam more. Lucretia had brought Vanlo up, for he had been six years old when their mother died, and nine years later he struggled to remember her. Lucretia had striven to make him her own when it became apparent that she would bear no child herself. Several days a month she spent sleeping alone in a bender, as custom dictated. No, there was clearly nothing amiss with her! But Vanlo hated it when his sister mocked

Sam for their childlessness. He could see that she used it to get her own way – with this half-man who, for all his effort, could not plant a seed of his own in the world.

'Sam ain't hisself,' said Lucretia. 'He's more of a dreamer than ever. He washes hisself mor'n he ever did and I've seen 'im with a comb. What do you and him get up to on them walks you take of an evening?'

'You know what we do. We always brings back a rabbit – or a pheasant. You've seen. I keep watch for the keeper mostly. But I'm getting better with the catapult too.'

'You was always good with it, little brother.'

The boy flushed.

'I like talking to him. An' it's easier without them children earwigging.'

'You was always more like him than like your brothers, my Vanlo. Go on with you then. But if he gets up to anything, sees anyone, them holy boys included, you mun tell me. All right? 'Cause if I didn't know 'im better I'd think he'd've got God but not wanted to say so.'

Lucretia watched Vanlo walk off towards his eldest brother's wagon. She turned her face away, feeling tears start to her eyes. *Please let it only be the holy boys, my Sam!*

*

'Take the catapult, Vanlo,' said Sam. 'I'll whistle when I want you.'

Vanlo hesitated.

'What is it, bruv?' asked Sam.

'She's been on to me – Lukey. Thinks you've mixed yourself up with the chapel people.'

'I s'pose I have, after a fashion. What've you said to 'er?'

'Nuffing. Just said we went for walks. But I'm mortal scared, Sam.'

'I ain't *done* anything, my Vanlo. And if I had, it'd be me to blame, not you.'

Vanlo looked over Sam's shoulder, seeing a slight female figure coming along the path.

'Nuffing?'

'Go on, Vanlo, get me that rabbit.'

The boy went reluctantly into the trees, and Sam turned round to watch Ellen's approach.

'You're earlier this evening,' he said. 'I med've missed you altogether.'

'I asked to get away smart. There's something I need to do.'

She looked round.

'There ain't no one,' said Sam. 'I make sure of that, every time I sees you. And if there is, I make myself scarce. I dunt want to cause you trouble.'

'You make it sound as though you're spying on me.'

'Not spying, watching out for you. And anyway, I wanted to ask you about the little maidy.'

Ellen's face lit up. 'Oh, I should have said! She is much better – not completely well but getting there. Please thank your mother!'

'Well, I'll not hold you back. You said you was going somewhere.'

'He'll wait for me, Sam. I'm going to the war memorial. It's Charlie's birthday.'

'Oh my poor girl.' Sam took her hands, stroking her fingers. 'You never tole me where you lost 'en.'

'Arras.'

He sighed. 'I know the place. More than once I was there, bringing up the poor beasts I'd cared for from Abbeville to wherever it was they'd decided men and horses had to die next.' He hesitated.

'What is it, Sam?'

'I had to lead a column of horses and mules along this road – a channel of mud was more like it, an endless battle with mud, always. It rots their hooves, you see. It was summer, but the only way you'd know that was the smell; it's in my nose now. It was on my skin then, always, greasy-like. There was some trees left, but like spikes, twisted metal. No leaves, no grass underfoot. Warm rain – dirty rain. And the ditches both sides, full of dead horses, their bodies all puffed up – scores of 'em. And I had to take the new ones to the same end, after talking to them that morning, stroking their noses. And they knew I was betraying them. There was one time I passed a horse up to his hocks in the mud, unable to move. I promised him I'd dig him out when I came back, but when I did, there he was, on his feet still, but stone dead of exhaustion. I've never talked to anyone about that sight, Ellen.'

'But what about the men? If there were dead horses, then surely . . .'

'Don't ask me about the men. Please.'

She started to cry, quietly at first, then with great gulping sobs. Sam put his arm round her and pulled her towards him. She grasped fistfuls of his shirt, pressing her face into his chest. Gradually, against the insistent thud of his heart, with the rhythmic stroke of his hand on her hair, her cries subsided into shuddering. She felt his chin resting gently on the top of her head, and heard him whisper, 'Ellen, oh my Ellen!'

'I had a sort of collapse, you know,' she said, her cheek against his shirt. 'When the telegram came. I couldn't look into a child's face, for I was always looking for the little girl – or boy – who might've been ours. The doctor wanted me taken to Littlemore Asylum.' She felt Sam flinch. 'Grandfer stopped that,' she went on. 'Prayer and fellowship would pull me through, he said.'

'And did they, Ellen?'

'I live, don't I? But my hopes – no, they're as dead as that poor horse.'

*

That night she dreamed of Charlie. He was standing at the pump behind Grace's cottage, stripped to the waist, splashing his face, his chest, his armpits. He turned to Ellen and smiled, talking volubly, but she couldn't hear a word, and when she opened her own mouth, she couldn't make a sound in reply. Ellen woke to find her pillow wet. But she found that she could remember Charlie's smile.

*

'I have never slept outside a house in my life,' Ellen said. She and Sam faced each other on the edge of the path, shaded by a beech tree.

'What, never fallen asleep in a field beneath the wide dark sky? It's the most wonderful thing, Ellen. There's a skylight in our wagon so when we're in the woods, I can see the branches of trees waving in the moonlight. When it rains, it don't wake me, but if I'm awake already the sound of it drumming on the roof is a comfort – because I am inside and warm and dry. The horses I can hear snuffling at night – a horse is as good in his own way, if you'll hear him, as any guard dog, though we've got them too. I can hear the birds – not just their song but the beating of their wings. If a fox steps on a twig I'll hear him, or a badger's grunt.'

'I hear the birds too. My grandmother taught me to tell their names from their warble. Sometimes on a quiet night I can hear the panting of the hedgehogs at the back door but other times there are cats creating unless Grandfer goes out and throws a pail over them. I never know if they are fighting or . . .'

'Or loving. I wonder sometimes how different the two are, Ellen.'

'And there are the bats, of course,' she said, rushing on. 'I've to fasten the casement against them.'

'Do you sleep alone, Ellen?'

'Oh! Well, yes! Since my sister died – she was six.'

'Poor little maidy. Just you two, was there?'

'No, there's my brother John, but he stayed up in London for work. He was a carter, like Grandfer – like Father was – but now he works in Covent Garden. He says it's the closest he can be to the country, to be up in the dark to handle vegetables with the earth still on them. John misses us, and I miss him. But it's God's will, he says, and he finds righteous people in the city as much as in the fields.'

'He your elder brother?'

'Younger by three years or so, though you wouldn't think it to see him, big strapping fellow that he is.'

'Missed the war, then?'

'Thankfully. He was all for joining up to start with but he was too young. Then when so many didn't come home, or came home like poor Reggie, he got fearful. When he couldn't avoid conscription any longer they took him off to Aldershot. But it was all over before they'd finished training him.'

'Do you go and see him in London?'

'No. Grandfer wouldn't like it, so we wait for when he can come home. We all lived in London for a while; Grandfer and Father worked hansom cabs – closest they could get to carting. But then Father died and Grandfer could see that the hansoms and horses were going to be put out by those motors – he said anyway it was better to toil in the vineyard of the Lord at home than in the richest of mines.'

'We'd find something to agree on, at any rate.'

'I think, though, that some in the chapel were relieved when we left. Grandfer is a bit stuck in his ways, and he hates to be crossed. Of course, Mother and I had nowhere to go but back here with him, though I know she was happy to come home.'

'Where was it you lived?'

'Clerkenwell.'

'I never went up there – they tole us Italians live there so maybe they take the work we would do. We go to London, if there isn't enough work in Kent after the hopping, and pass the winter there – on Wandsworth Common if we dunt get moved on. But I dunt care for it. All them people stuffed into lodgings where you mun breathe everyone else's air and hear their clatter at all hours – and share a privy instead of looking for a nice, clean ditch. We don't like houses – people die in 'em. And in a London house you can't go out of a morning and walk barefoot on grass.'

'And what do you do there?'

'Anything. Collecting old iron, rags, some tinkering. The women like London better than I do – it's good for the *dukkerin*.'

'*Dukkerin*?'

'You know, the palms, the fortin-telling.'

'Work of the devil!'

'Not really,' he said mildly. 'Sometimes people need their dreams, and sometimes they just need to be told something about themselves they know already but haven't the confidence to think on.'

'"There shall not be found among you anyone who burns his son or his daughter as an offering, anyone who practises divination or tells fortunes . . . " I can't remember rightly how the next bit goes, but it's something about abominations. Grandfer would know.'

'Oh, Ellen, I wonder what life it is you have! You're wonderful quick with them scriptures. I can tell you I've never set fire to anyone yet. And it's the women who do the palms, mostly. Lukey can be an abomination when she wants but there is no harm in my old mother, I'm sure! All the fortin-telling does is gives a person something to hope for.'

'For money!'

'When you work in that shop you take money for the time you pass there, don't you?'

'But the ladies go out with parcels. They get something for the coins they hand over.'

'And so they do with the *dukkerin*, even if most of the time it's just a way to amuse themselves at a fairground, something for the *raklis* to laugh over afterwards, to see if they can spot the tall strangers they've been promised. I can't believe your ladies buy things they really need half the time, or they wouldn't have 'em to give to us when we come calling.'

'I've never been to a fairground.'

'Never wanted to know your fortin?' He took hold of her hand. 'They say it's all hiding in them creases. Never wanted to know if there was some man who loved you enough to die for you, and you never knew he was there?'

'That's not funny, Sam. Give me back my hand.'

'Why, because you don't want me to tell your fortin or because you don't want me to hold it?'

'Because I don't want to know – 'tis wrong! "But of that day and hour knoweth no man, no, not the angels of heaven, but my Father only."'

'I wunt want to know either, if I'm truthful.'

'Let go of my hand, Sam!'

'Sorry,' he said, relinquishing it. 'I can't tell your fortin anyroad. There's too much in the way now . . . I mean, I know you too well.'

'It would be horrible to see the future. What if Charlie and me had known when it was his last leave? If I'd screamed it to the hills no one would have believed it.'

'My poor girl. I wish I could make you happier. Do they let you laugh much at home, Ellen?'

'"There's a time to cry and a time to laugh", and if I don't get home soon it will be a time to cry and no mistake!'

'I'll hold you back no further, then,' he said, looking rapidly up and down the dirt road. 'Come a bit further into the wood. I've something to ask you.'

'What is it, Sam?' she said, following him. Now they could not see the path nor be seen from it. She looked up at him expectantly. He took her face between his hands.

'I'd like very much to kiss you, Ellen.'

'You may not!' She tried to lift his hands away, but he was immovable.

'I'd thought to ask you to close your eyes, so that I might give you a surprise. But that won't do. I want you to want me to kiss you, you see.'

'You have a wife, Sam,' she said coldly. 'Let go of my face.'

'I do, don't I? I was married to her when I was no more than seventeen years old. I can't even be sure if that's right, for I don't know when my birthday is.'

He let go of her face and grasped her hands.

'A boy of that age don't know what he wants but he knows he must find relief for his urgings and if he's promised that, then he'll accept any price, not being old enough to know better. But you – you're the best thing I ever did see. And if you tell me to take myself off now, and never set eyes on you again, I'd do it and never forget your face my whole life long. But let me kiss you now, dear Ellen, for pity if nothing else, and then go and marry that old man if you must.'

'He hasn't asked me and I wouldn't if he did!'

'Then you hurt no one, Ellen.'

'I hurt your wife!'

Sam sighed. He released her hands. Ellen thought of Harold's pursy mouth. She saw the man before her transformed as Harold would have wanted him: short hair, naked ear-lobes, half-strangled by a collar and tie, stooping in the chapel porch and taking off a respectable homburg hat identical to those of the other Prim men. She thought of Charlie's mouth full of Picardy earth, and of her own loneliness. She lifted her face.

'Ellen!' he whispered. His face, shadowed by his hat, came towards her and she saw his eyes close as though he was giving himself up to sleep, lashes thick and dark against his tawny skin. Her own lids closed as his warm, dry lips met hers, at first tentative, shy. Then his arms closed round her, pulling her to him; she felt her breasts crush against his chest. Then gently, gently, the tip of his tongue probed the corner of her mouth and moved delicately across her lower lip until she opened to him. She felt as much as heard the moan in his throat and tears came unexpectedly to her eyes.

I don't deserve this happiness. It's wrong, all wrong, but I love him – I love him! Her hands went round his neck, exploring the skin beneath his neckerchief, dislodging his hat; it fell to the ground with a tiny thud, no more noise than an acorn would make. *I could live on the smell of him!* Her fingers meshed in the darkness of his hair. *Oh Sam, if I could just hold you like this forever. I daren't think of anything else.*

*

'Cat got your tongue?' asked her grandfather, frowning at Ellen across the tea things.

'I'm sorry. I just had a busy day, that's all.'

'You ain't eating much, either,' put in her mother.

Ellen reached obediently for another slice of bread and butter. 'I think I might go up early, if I may.'

'We'll say prayers then as soon as you've done with the washing-up,' said Oliver.

'Mother, could I take the bicycle tomorrow?'

'Of course, dear. Give yourself a bit of a lie-in,' said Flora, averting her face from Oliver's disapproving expression.

*

Ellen lifted her face to the breeze as she sped hatless along the road, letting the air fill her lungs, her hair lifting. Glancing left through fencing into Horwood's fields, she saw a knot of men working the reaper-binder, but looked away as the man atop the machine turned in her direction. The bicycle wobbled, but then mercifully the road went into a dip, and the fence gave way to hedgerow.

*

Mrs Ansell met Mrs Larden coming out of Colton's Drapers, clutching a small parcel of haberdashery.

'Oh Nellie, lovely to see you, dear! Fancy Rumsey's for a cup o' tea? If I don't sit down for a minute these shoes will be the death of me.'

'Oh, that would be just the thing. Who was it served you in there, if you don't mind me asking?'

'The Quainton girl. Why?'

Her friend took her arm confidentially and bent her head closer.

'She's been seen on the footpath by Surman's Wood, talking to one of 'em Gypsies.'

'No! And her quite the Miss Prim!'

'Then she went with him into the wood, I was told.'

'The little fool!'

'Perhaps someone ought to warn the girl. Her mother is too afraid of her own shadow and of that old curmudgeon Oliver to do anything. That's if she even knows.'

'Oh, I wouldn't tell her – spoil all the fun, that would! And besides, it's not as if it's any of our business, is it?'

*

'Ellen, you are distracted. I've asked you twice now to get me down the blue worsted but you're in another world.'

'I'm sorry, Mrs Colton. I'm a bit tired. I'll fetch the steps.'

'Tired?'

'Cats.'

*

After prayers that evening, Ellen went up to her room and hunted in her New Testament for those ominous words in the Epistle to St James: ' . . . *every man is tempted, when he is drawn away of his own lust, and enticed. Then when lust hath conceived, it bringeth forth sin: and sin, when it is finished, bringeth forth death.*'

'I'm sorry, Sam,' she wept. 'I can't see you again. I'll pray for you, and hope someone will pray for me!'

For the next two days she rode her mother's bicycle with eyes resolutely forward.

*

'Can you walk the path again tomorrow, Ellen?' asked her mother as they prepared the tea. 'I s'll need the bicycle to get to Mrs Lindow's about the Mission returns.'

That night Ellen in her prayers gave thanks for Mrs Lindow and her book-keeping for putting her to the test.

Perhaps he won't be there, and if he is, I'll just be polite and tell him not to speak to me again.

She woke up during the night. *He'll be there, of course he will! He won't see me on the bicycle, so he'll know I'll be walking.*

*

He was there.

'Oh, it's you.'

'You're stiff with me now, Ellen.'

'I should think so. You had no business to take that liberty.'

'Well, I'll say I'm sorry as you'll expect it of me, but I'm not. And the way you kissed me back, nor was you. I'm only sorry you ran off so fast afterwards. Thought better of it, did you, once you'd given me a try?'

'I'd best go.'

'Stop – at least let me explain myself. I've been wanting to kiss you ever since I saw you that first time. I thought you the prettiest thing I had ever seen, a real lady. Not a high and mighty lady, a gentle lady like in the old tales, good and kind – too much so for the likes o' me. I'll have to move off with them when autumn comes and I mightn't ever see you more, and I wanted that to remember you by – and I will, for always.'

'Oh Sam, you mustn't think of me that way!'

'Mustn't? Can't help it, more like! I've fallen for you as deeply as I can, Ellen. I know I'm not allowed to, but it don't alter the case any. And I can't regret it, even if it makes for misery my whole life long. I'll have your words in my head forever. I can't read none, as you know, but that means I dunt forget nothing. I've to think on a thing instead over and over – that's my way of writing things down. Let me just ask you one thing, and if you want, I'll disappear into that wood and you won't see me for dust ever again.'

'Ask me, Sam,' she whispered, her throat tight.

'Do you think anything of me at all – or did you just like my company enough to talk to me?'

'Oh yes . . .' said Ellen.

'I mean more than you just being polite to me?'

'Sam,' she said, trying to steady her voice. 'I think you talk too much sometimes.'

'What?'

She took a step closer to him and held out her hands. He took them. She looked up at him, and all the feverish resolutions of the last three days evaporated. Astonished at her own boldness, she tilted her face towards his. Their kiss was long and deep, and she exulted as he drew her close, feeling his heartbeat, his urgency.

'Are you my girl?' he murmured into her hair.

She stroked his cheek.

'Ellen!' He looked up and down the path – empty. 'Come into the wood with me a little way,' he said. 'I want to walk with you and hold your hand, like we're reg'lar sweethearts, I mean.'

'I can't be late home, Sam.'

'Five minutes. I'll take you another way that'll bring you back to the road so no one will be any the wiser.'

'All right.' Now that they had kissed, she didn't know what to say to him.

'I like your quietness,' he said, as though he had read her thoughts. 'You make a man feel rested, like he doesn't need to prove himself. He can just be who he is, with you.'

*

Vanlo crouched, barely daring to breathe, though he was getting cramp. Through the tangle of branches he looked down on them standing in the glade. They had stopped murmuring and Sam was kissing her again, the *gauji* girl's arms up round his neck and his across her back. Then Vanlo saw his hands move downward and rest on the curve of her bottom, pulling her closer to him. The girl wriggled a little at this, but their faces didn't separate and Sam didn't let go, and Vanlo finally saw her respond by pressing closer to him. Sam's hat came off and rolled on the ground. Vanlo had never held anyone as Sam did now; in the Romani life a kiss was never casual. Looking at them he knew with thrilling intuition that these two longed to be naked.

At last Ellen broke away, though Sam held her hand and tried to retain her. She made one more little rush at him, swiftly kissing his mouth, then hurried away back towards the path, the shortcut forgotten. Sam stood some time looking after her, then picked up his hat and brushed it down before slowly walking away. Vanlo got up, stretched, wincing at the snapping of a twig, and stiffly went to catch up with Sam.

'Vanlo, boy!'

'I thought I'd lost you!'

'That's what I'd meant, truth be known.' Sam looked at the boy intently.

'I'll not say, Sam!'

'I know that.' He passed an affectionate hand over Vanlo's hair. 'It ain't fair on you, though.'

*

Ellen's happiest memory of her dead father was of a day when the spring air was sweet with expectation, and he took her on the cart with him along a road edged with primroses, to make a delivery to a farm near Monks Risborough. It was two years before the family uprooted and went to London. Ellen was five years old, exultantly sitting higher than the cow parsley nodding in the hedgerows, looking over the fields from her vantage point to where newborn lambs staggered bleating behind their mothers.

'I'll show you something partikler after we've got shot of that old plough,' said Luke Quainton.

The little girl stared perplexedly at the white scar cut into the slope of the hill, the turf peeled away to reveal chalk in the shape of a solid triangle, with atop it a cross.

'There's only one. Where's the thiefs, Pa?' she asked eventually.

Luke raised his eyebrows. 'We ain't Catholics, child. We don't need any cross to remind us. But you're a clever girl to ask me that question.'

'They didn't ought to have done it, though,' she went on.

'Done what?'

'Scratched the hill. What if it wakes up and is angry?'

Luke laughed. '"Ye shall say unto this mountain, Remove hence to yonder place; and it shall remove." Oh daughter, 'tis the Almighty as'll shift mountains, not mortals with spades! Anyway, there's prettier cuts than this. Horses and that.' He twitched the reins and the mare moved for home.

But the child Ellen could not shake the idea that the impassive hills looking down on her world could, if provoked, rouse themselves and send all tumbling. Lying in bed later in the twilight, she raised knees and elbows beneath the blanket, making of herself a mountain range. The slightest movement, and the whole terrain shifted.

*

Now the adult Ellen lay in the same bed, no longer believing that mountains could be awakened, not even by the Almighty. Had He not stood by and seen pastures, cornfields, forests and the poor mortals they contained blasted out of existence, and done nothing? She tossed off the blanket, shifting restlessly, unlacing the neck of her nightgown for air. She looked down at the landscape of her body shrouded in white poplin, and trembling at her boldness, raised her knees into two peaks. Then she lifted her arms up to embrace the empty air. 'Sam, Sam!'

*

Sam always enjoyed the opening of a new field at harvest. He took his place in the row of men, each an equal distance apart, scything down the first row of corn so that the horses wouldn't trample it. As the other men tied up the first sheaves with twine, the only ones that would be made up by hand that day, he went to prepare the three horses who would be pulling the reaper-binder. This was the part of the work he liked best, setting the rhythm of the animals to the turn of the machine. The mechanism was simple, but it delighted him: an invention that would cut and also tie, but which depended, as farming always had, on the tractability of the animals that pulled the machine forward. He liked being the man most trusted to operate Horwood's apparatus, chosen for it by his employer as the one with the best touch with horses. Caley, Liberty and Vanlo worked with the other men to build the sheaves into stooks as they fell, fashioned as if by magic from the machine. Sam whistled and sang tunelessly above the thrum of the motor, as if his heart would burst with happiness.

'Yorn Gippo is like a boy in love, to hear 'en,' called one of the older hands to his nearest companion. Liberty swung round to scowl at the speaker, but the man had turned to catch the next sheaf and didn't see him.

CHAPTER 9

Pawnie birks my men-engri shall be;
Yackors my dudes like ruppeney shine;
Atch meery chi! Ma jal away:
Perhaps I may not dick tute kek komi.[9]

George Borrow, *Romano Lavo-Lil*

Virgin Knot

'I brought this . . . it's quite clean.'

Sam spread the blanket on the ground. 'Come, sit here next to me. It's a good place. Nobody can see us here, but if someone comes along the path down there we'll hear them.'

'But won't they hear us?' said Ellen.

---

[9] *I'd choose as pillows for my head, those snow-white breasts of thine;*
I'd use as lamps to light my bed, those eyes of silver shine:
O lovely maid, disdain me not, nor leave me in my pain:
Perhaps 'twill never be my lot, to see thy face again.

'Depends what we do . . . but we'll hear what comes up from the hollow more than what goes down. I can hunt, remember?'

'Poach, you mean.'

'If you must. But no keeper's took me yet.' His fingers drifted over her cheek. 'Don't be afraid, Ellen.'

'Are *you*?'

'How could I not be? I'm wronging my wife—'

'No, *we* are.'

'Me most of all – I made her a promise. If they get wind of it back there I'll cop it from her brothers so's you wunt recognise me again. But I'm more scared of how much I want to be with you. *We'll* move on, as we always do, but then I'd not see you till this time next year – when I dunt know how I'm to stand a world without you.'

'I'm only scared of what my life would've been if I'd never met you, Sam,' she said, nestling against him. 'But harvest always comes round again.'

'It does. But a whole year . . . *Choomande,* Ellen!'

'What?'

'Kiss me, lovely girl.'

When they at last drew apart he said, his breath warm on her face, 'Will you unbutton my shirt? I want you to feel my heart beating.'

She did so, and cautiously slipped her hand inside, mar-velling at the warmth of the taut, tawny skin, stroking the drift of silky dark hairs on his breastbone.

'You're so . . . *alive*, Sam!'

He laughed. 'I've never bin so glad to be so.' He covered her hand with his and guided it to where the hairs grew more densely, round his navel. She heard his breath catch.

'I've never been touched so gently, Ellen . . .' He removed his hand from where it held hers. Her heart tight, she tentatively explored the secret skin of his waist, his ribs.

'May I?' he murmured, fingertips tentatively at the collar of her blouse.

'Yes, Sam,' she whispered, her face burning.

'Them buttons of yours is tiny, though.'

'Let me.'

He pushed the blouse back and kissed her shoulders, then nuzzled into her neck.

'I love the smell of your skin, Ellen.' His hand slid across her chemise, coming to rest beneath her breast. 'Oh my girl!'

I could die of this, she thought, and hardly believing her own daring, guided his hand upwards. He kissed her, kneading her breast gently, groaning softly into her mouth. Ellen opened her eyes to see his closed. He opened them, drew back, smiled. He looked young, ecstatically so, warm and flushed, his chest rising and falling within the opened shirt.

He said, 'Oh Ellen, if you could see your lovely face. What a flower it is! Do you . . . do you love me, Ellen?'

'Oh yes!'

'Will you come here tomorrow? Will you let me love you then?'

'I . . . yes, yes, Sam.'

He walked her to the path, and looking in both directions before he did so, kissed her again.

'Tomorrow, then.'

'Tomorrow, Sam.'

'I love you, Ellen. I daren't, but I do all the same.'

*

Judith called at the Quainton cottage after tea. 'Come out a minute, can you, Ellen?' she said, leaning against the door into the scullery where Ellen was drying crockery.

'Just a minute then,' said Ellen, glad of the distraction. She hung up the tea towel on its rack and untied her apron. They went out onto the lane and walked in the direction of the bench by the parish church.

'What about this one?' said Judy, flopping down and waving a three-month-old copy of the *Illustrated London News* under her friend's nose.

'What? Oh, those pictures . . .'

'You're jumpy, Ellen. What is it?'

'Oh, nothing,' said Ellen. 'Which one is it?' Her head on one side, she concentrated on studying the photograph.

'That one.'

'Yes, I could do that, I think. Maybe box pleats instead of these knife ones – they'll stay in better. Where did you get this?'

'Lightfoot's secretary – her with the bristly chin. Pa's terrified of her. She thinks he needs to be married, see, and is nice to me because of it.'

'Oh dear, poor lady!'

'Poor *us*, Ellen.'

'Judith,' began Ellen, her heart jumping in her throat. 'What would *you* do if you liked a man, but knew you couldn't have him?'

Judith looked intently at Ellen. Eventually she said: 'I'd have him anyway. I'd *let* him, I mean.'

'Oh Judy!'

'Only if I thought he liked me as much as I liked him, I mean. I'd rather have a memory of him than nothing at all – something to think about more'n looking at pictures in magazines, and dreaming.'

'But it's sinful . . . and what if you started a baby?'

'Sinful?' said Judy. 'You don't still believe that, do you?'

'I don't know what I believe now, Judy.'

'That's what they'd say in the chapel, of course. But it's different now, I'm sure of it. Since the war, I mean. Life's too short.'

'I'm sure a girl always has to pay, Judy, same as she's always done.'

'Ellen, what are you up to?'

'Oh, nothing. I just wondered was there more than this – this life we have.'

*

Beneath the canopy of beech trees, he murmured, 'Am I hurting you?'

'No, Sam,' she lied.

Tight, he thought. *It's been a long time for her, poor girl.*

'I *am* hurting you. I can stop,' he said, not sure if he could.

'No, don't!'

'*Dordi!*[10] Oh Ellen! Hold me!'

So this is what it's like, she thought. *What no one talks about but everyone must do when God joins them. I've done wrong but I'd do anything to have Sam's face looking down on me always. I love him. I don't care if it's wrong. I have this, forever, no matter what happens now.*

She moved her hands under his unbuttoned shirt, stroking his back, down to the rise of his buttocks, cool in the evening air, feeling him dwindle and slip out of her.

'Let me look at you, Ellen!' He smiled down at her, then eased away, uncovering her opened blouse, her rucked-up

---

[10] Oh dear!

skirts. His gaze fell on her white splayed legs and he thought with immense tenderness: *Pale and weak as a little frog on its back.* Then she saw with horror his expression change; he looked away from her, tugging frantically at tufts of grass, trying to clean himself.

'*Ratti!*'[11] he shouted, forgetting the need to be quiet. '*Mochadi!*'[12]

'Sam?' She sat up. 'What did you say, Sam? Tell me what I did wrong!' Starting to cry, she pushed down her skirts and fumbled with her blouse buttons. *So all the warnings were true, then. Give him what he wants and he'll not want you more.*

'Couldn't you have said, Ellen? I'd have waited if you'd only said you'd your sickness. Oh *dordi!*'

'What sickness?' she wept.

'It's unclean! This . . . blood. You've made me unclean!'

'Isn't it meant to be like that – the first time?' she sobbed. 'You must know better than I!'

A moment later he was holding her close, crying, 'Ellen, I'm sorry, I'm sorry, I didn't know!' and rocking her from side to side as if she was a child needing to be comforted.

'You never did this before?' he whispered.

'No!' she gulped between sobs.

'What about your Charlie?'

---

[11] Blood

[12] Unclean

'*No!* Poor Charlie . . . We were going to wait, do what was right, obey what we were told was God's law, but God took him just the same!'

'Oh my poor girl . . . But that makes you mine, always and always.'

'What if I got in the family way, Sam?'

'You can't with me.'

'How can you be sure?'

'Lukey's sickness is that reg'lar it comes nearly at the same time of day – that's how I know the fault must be mine. But I don't want to talk about her – not now. If I got a baby with you no man could be more pleased than me.' He kissed her rapidly, all over her face.

'I don't want to go home, Sam.'

'No more do I.' But a note of resignation had crept into his voice. The mention of 'home' for each of them brought into focus a place where they were not together, where other rules applied, where both would have to lie.

'I'm sorry, Ellen, it's not much of a wedding night, this. But lying here like this we can pretend it is.'

They lay facing each other; she turned back his shirt and laid her cheek against his skin, her head beneath his chin. With his arms round her, Ellen felt protected from the entire world.

'I don't think I've ever been so happy, Sam – nor so scared!'

'Me too.'

'Look up at those trees. Look how friendly they are, stretching their branches across to shelter us – better than any bed canopy.'

For a moment Sam was transported back to his *vardo,* the built-in bed behind the sliding engraved glass panels, his mother's cot beneath. He tensed.

'What is it, Sam?'

'I want to be with you like this forever, Ellen. Not just harvest time, I mean. I mun work out how – how I can have you by me.' His arms tightened. 'It won't be easy – not for me, nor for you. Too many rules to break. Laws of the tribe and laws o' God – or what men say the laws o' God are.'

'I wonder, Sam, what God they're talking about when they talk about His laws. Seems to me they make the laws themselves then stick God's name on them, so nobody questions them.'

'That's what I thought in France.'

'When I was a little girl it was all so certain. We were the converted. We lived by the word of the Lord who would not abandon us in our need. But He did, Sam, He did! Even though we were supposed to have all the answers, it was all there for us in the scriptures and every preacher who stood in that pulpit made us even more sure we were right – right when the church people weren't and when even the Wesleyans were on the wrong path. We were promised the joys of heaven but sometimes I wish there was a little room for joys now. We had all those prayers for victory, but there must've been German girls who gave out the same prayers, to the same God. I don't know what I believe now, I'm sure I don't, and that's made me feel more alone than I've ever been. And the Lord knows I've been so lonely, though I've a mother who loves me and Grandfer who protects me. But I've spent my life, Sam, being good, doing what I was told . . . and for what? To lose Charlie. To be on my own, always wondering. Then you came along . . .'

'And you saw your chance?' He was smiling.

'No, not like that! I couldn't stop thinking about you after that first time I saw you. I feel special when I'm with you; I feel *pretty,* which I haven't felt since the telegram came and I thought I'd never smile again, let alone that anyone would kiss me – or that I'd want him to.'

'I'll kiss you for the rest of your life if you'll let me.'

'Oh Sam, how?'

'Come away with me. You'll have to, now you're mine.' He said this as a thing obvious and decided.

'What about your wife?'

'She dunt love me. I dunt know as she ever did, really. But once our names was linked it'd have been shameful for her if I'd walked away. Pa wouldn't have lived that down either – I'd've been sent away, like I'd be sent away now, for you. Come with me, Ellen. Only, I'll have to take my old mother with me . . . I'll need to tell her that's what we mun do. I can't leave her with them Bucklands. I'll tell her tonight, once I've made sure nobody is earwigging . . .'

Ellen lay quiet as the world pressed in on her. She'd go anywhere with Sam, she knew. All he had to do was pull her to her feet and take her hand. If it could only be like that: to walk up onto the road and hail the next farm cart going towards Oxford, or Reading. But this old lady, his mother? She thought of Grace Lambourne alone in her cottage with the photograph of Charlie in his puttees, posed incongruously beside the photographer's flower pot, against a painted backdrop of a countryside that looked nothing like the one he had grown up in. She thought of her own timid mother, fearful of her father-in-law, but more fearful of being alone.

'I'll need to tell mine, too. But she'd never come with us. I don't know how I should get to see her again. Oh Sam, it's too much for me to take in! You do a private thing but then it's suddenly everybody's business.'

'There's time to think what to do – how to do it, I mean,' he said gently. 'The wagons won't pull off now till into September. But when they do, I shan't be with 'em. It'll be you and me as will face the world together.'

'Do you mean that, Sam?' she said wonderingly.

'Do you love me, Ellen?'

'You know I do!'

'Then I mean it all right. Now, seeing as them blouse buttons aren't done up, let me show you how much I mean it.'

*

The shadows were lengthening as Ellen walked slowly home. She looked with wonder at her familiar surroundings. How could they still be the same, when she was so utterly changed? How could the cottage still be there, with Oliver pulling off his boots, her mother spooning the tea leaves into the warmed pot?

How will they not know what's happened? I'm not the person they thought I was – not now.

*

Ellen woke the following morning at cockcrow, but instead of immediately fumbling for her slippers to run out to the privy, she lay in bed, a bar of sunlight slanting the floorboards through the gap in the curtains. There was no urgency to move, but she'd have to empty the chamberpot, for her night had been restless. Under the bedclothes, she stealthily lifted her nightgown and explored. *Ow! He said it only hurt the first time, but when does it stop hurting?*

*

The morning passed in a daze. Voices came at her from far-off, her actions automatic, until one customer jolted her into consciousness. Mrs Larden came in, wanting a spool of ivory twist. Ellen nodded and opened the drawer, and in that action remembered that the woman had come in for precisely that item only days previously. She looked up in surprise, to be met with Mrs Larden's unswerving gaze, and flushed.

'I thought you already had this, Mrs Larden?' she stuttered.

'P'raps I have. No law against coming back for more, is there?'

'Oh . . . no, of course not.'

'That's what you do when you're onto a good thing, don't you? Go back for more, I mean,' said Mrs Larden, smiling unpleasantly.

'Indeed . . . Shall I wrap it for you?'

'No need. Thank *you*.'

*

Ellen ran to their appointment. *What if he's not there? What'll I say to him if he is?*

He was.

'My Ellen!' he exclaimed, bending his face to hers.

'Come to the stream with me,' he said eventually. He took her hand and they walked on the springy earth under the trees towards the babble of water.

'When did you last bathe in running water, my Ellen?'

'Me? Oh, not since I was a little girl – with Judy. It was about here, in fact. I've never told anyone that.'

'Well, I'm going to bathe you now. However does this come undone?'

'We can't, Sam, someone might see us!'

'They've not seed us before now, lovely lady mine.'

'But it's one thing to . . . to have to button things up in a hurry if we hear a twig snap, and quite another to be all wet and to be spied on. And besides, we'll have precious little warning if someone comes this way for we'll not hear him for the sound of the water.'

'I have you thinking like a Gypsy already, Ellen!' he said approvingly, but went on steadily undressing her.

'You're wearing them horrible underthings again,' he said. 'You ain't kind to them pretty *birks* keeping 'em all crushed like that. And as for all them clips . . . they're put there to drive a man mad. Turn round.'

She obeyed, slipping the linen blouse from her shoulders. Behind her, Sam bent forward and kissed her neck. She heard his frustrated intake of breath as he began to work his way down the clips that held the flattening corset in place and shivered in anticipation.

'God gives you this abundance and you strap it all flat and pretend it's not there. 'Tisn't nat'rel, Ellen.'

Eventually the hated garment was peeled away and Ellen's pale breasts breathed in the dappling sunlight.

'Oh you are lovely, lovely,' he murmured, cupping them in his hands and kissing her shoulders. 'Now take off them drawers, pretty *rakli*.'

As she did so, Sam untied the string that held up his trousers, pushed them down and pulled his old collarless shirt over his head. She turned towards him, putting her arms round him and resting her forehead on his chest.

'In the water first,' whispered Sam. 'I want to wash those horrible togs away. I want to see that lovely skin all aglow.'

'That was my best underwear,' she said sadly. 'Worn specially for you.'

She'd put aside something from her wages for some weeks to buy them: 'dainty things for modest means' the accompanying advertising had said, and she'd asked Mrs Colton to keep her size by until she could pay for them in full, without knowing then what occasion she might have to wear them.

'I like them,' said Sam, conciliatory. 'I liked best taking 'em off. It's the dull blouse and skirt I don't like. A pretty girl deserves better.' He stepped back from her, holding her shoulders. She shut her eyes, to not see his arousal.

'Water after,' he said. 'I can't wait longer for you.'

*

'I don't want to, but I have to wash you off, Ellen.'

She murmured in her sleep.

'Ellen,' he said, kissing her awake.

She sat up suddenly.

'Oh Sam, what time is it? I've been asleep forever. I'll get such a hiding!'

'Not for sleeping, you won't. It's all right, *rawnie*[13] mine. It's not been long. I've been watching you. Now come in the water with me.'

Sitting up, her knees folded primly sideways, she watched him go before her. She would have to pay for such beauty, surely!

'If you ain't bathed here for years and years,' he said, 'how *do* you get clean, then? At the pump?'

'I could hardly do that, could I? Saturday night is wash night for me,' Ellen said. 'Heat the water in the copper and then the hip bath in the outhouse. How else?'

'What, sitting in your own dirty water? No one ever got clean that way! Come here, girl, till I bathe you myself.'

Ellen stood up and, sheltering breasts and sex with her hands, hobbled awkwardly with bent shoulders towards the stream, feeling Sam's warm sap damp on her thighs.

''Tis too late for that,' laughed Sam. 'I know all of you, pretty white *birks* and that dear *minge* of yours – see, all wet from me!' He eased her hands away. 'Put your shoulders back, look proud!' And before she could stop him, he had pulled out her hairpins and tousled her soft brown hair about her shoulders.

'Now, into the water – no, t'other side. You mun go downstream of me.'

'Why, Sam?'

---

[13] Lady

'How it should be. You can wash in my water but I mayn't wash in yours.' He thought for a moment. ''Tis all along of the liquids a *chi* makes, I suppose – I never stopped to think on it before now, it's just how it is. Now you stand there and I shall wash you, and you shall wash me.'

'It's so cold!'

'You see when you get out, that you'll be glowing so warm that I could bake bread on you, though I'd rather do something else, but then I'd need to get in here again.'

'Oh Sam, what'll happen to us?'

'Don't fret. Haven't I told you I'll always be yours, no matter what? I know you're mine.'

'And Lucretia?'

His face clouded. 'I've told you before, don't you worry on account of her. Since I bin with you I ain't bin with her, nor will I be. 'Tisn't her should trouble you. My old mother, though . . .'

'Have you spoken to her?'

'Not yet. One or other of them Bucklands are always there, ears pinned back. The only one of 'em I trust is young Vanlo, but he's mortal afraid of the others.'

Then his face brightened as though the sun had come out. 'Nay, Ellen, I'd do anything for you! I'd even wash in a dirty old hip bath if you wanted me to! Come here, girl, and let me stop your shivering! Ah, you're as slippery as an eel . . .'

*

Though the days dragged, after the incident with Mrs Larden, Ellen's instinct for survival began to take over. But subterfuge was hard work. Several times her mother had complained: 'I have to repeat myself every time to get a simple answer from you. Anyone'd think you was in love!'

'Mother!' cried Ellen in distress.

Judy, of course, had to be told something, if only to enlist her help.

'I'm not telling you any more than that I've met someone, Judy, in case . . .'

'In case it comes to nothing? Don't look like nothing, with your face like that. Who *is* he?'

'I daren't say!'

'All right, then, you've said he's handsome – at least tell me has he any brothers? You *know* I won't split – and if you told me just a tiny bit more I'd know how I could cover up for you, you goose!'

'Not yet.'

*

Mrs Larden and her nasty smile seemed to be everywhere. Leaving the shop one afternoon Ellen encountered her standing a few yards further down the pavement with her friend Nellie Ansell. To avoid them, Ellen would have had to cross the road, and that would have looked even worse. Mrs Larden nudged her companion's arm as the bell of the shop jangled on Ellen's exit, and they stopped talking – and stared instead. Her face heating up, Ellen approached, murmuring, 'Good afternoon.' Neither woman acknowledged this. Ellen was forced to step off the pavement, and felt their eyes on her back until, sweating, she turned the corner and let out a tiny animal cry of distress. It was a trembling and tearful Ellen who went to the stream with Sam that evening.

*

'What is it, Ellen?'

'I've told them all lies, Sam, as I never have in my life before! I told them I like to walk and pray, for that is a thing Grandfer often does – he says it's a way for a man to get closer to his creator without any flummery and pride in the way. But I don't pray, Sam, do I? I mean, I know the words but they don't go deep – I don't let them, because any moment I have to myself, and those I don't, I think about you. Then I come here and find you and we do these things and afterwards I fear what will happen to us both!'

'What'll happen is that you'll come away with me, Ellen! I mean that I find a place where they'll give me reg'lar work, and you come along of me as my wife. No one will be any the wiser. I can turn my hand to anything – be it in the cattle line, or smithing, or hedging, or ditching. If there is land to be tilled and animals to be cared for, I can do it – most of all if it's horses. I can't stay on in this life and love you, Ellen, and if you love me you can't stay on in yours.'

'If I love you? Oh Sam!'

'I want you to take this, Ellen,' he said, unknotting the red silk scarf he wore round his neck. 'If you and I were to be wed in the reg'lar way of my people, I'd be giving you this and if you accepted me you'd tie it round your head so everyone would know that you were going to be mine. If you want a ring of me you shall have one, Ellen, even if I don't have no right to give you one.'

'But I can't wear either.'

'No more you could now, but I would know that you were mine. And when you come away with me I'll walk proudly with you on my arm in the busiest streets in the land if you'd let me. Will you tie my *diklo* round your hair for me now?'

'Tie it on for me, Sam.'

His hands were busy round her head.

'Oh, what a picture you are, my Ellen.'

'But won't they notice it's gone?' she said.

'They'll notice all right. But they'll notice when I'm gone too.'

*

Lucretia crouched in the bender like a wounded animal.

'We'll sort 'en, my Lukey,' said Liberty, sitting on a pile of blankets. 'He'll pay. He'll not want to do it again after.'

'P'raps he's been 'dulteratin' me for years and years,' she cried, her face averted.

'No, we'd've known. You'd have known.' He tentatively put a hand on her shoulder, but she twitched it away.

'I'd do anything for you, Lukey.'

'An' I'd thought it was only them holy boys,' she sobbed.

He shifted his position. 'We'll do it quick, then. And move off after. There's other farms.'

'But leave Vanlo out of it.'

'All right. But he'll see it. And that'll learn 'im too.'

'Leave me, brother. I need to think a bit.'

Oh Sam, I thought you was a soft mush sometimes. But I never took you for a cruel one!

*

'Ellen?'

She looked round from where she stood at the sink scraping potatoes.

'Mother?'

'One of 'em Gypsies came asking for you today!'

'What did he want?' she stammered.

'Never said it was no he, did I? A bold-looking young woman, it was, along with another one that never spoke a word.'

Ellen's heart hammered. She held onto the edge of the sink for support.

'I don't know any Gypsy woman, Mother! What did she look like?'

'Pretty enough in a hard, dirty sort of way. Black curly hair tied back and a man's old hat on her head. A man's jacket and boots too, atop an old skirt all long and draggled, the way they wore 'em before the War; I couldn't say what colour it was meant to be anymore. And a yellow scarf knotted round her neck. But as proud and staring a look as though she was the Queen of England.'

'I've never seen such a person. I don't know how she should know me, I'm sure.'

'She don't know you by name. She came here with them pegs they make – and I took some of 'em for I'll always use them and I don't want trouble – and some of them pretty elder-wood flowers. Then she asked could she see the young woman of the house so as to read your palm and say what your fortin was. She said she would do it for free just for the pleasure of your company. But she wasn't kind with it, nor wheedling the way her sort often are. She said it like it was a threat. I told her thank you for the pegs and the flowers but to get packing for we'd have no truck with sorcery and that your fortin was in God's hands alone. Then she laughed, but nasty-like, and the pair of 'em took off. Well, if you say you don't know her then I'm sure you don't. Perhaps she spied the place, or saw your linen out to dry. I oughter go and see is it all still there. I'll be glad, though, when they've upped sticks and gone on their way. I did see one of 'em today out in Farmer Horwood's trap with poor Reggie up alongside him, talking away as if they'd known each other years. Reggie looked happier than he has in a while, I will say that.'

Ellen put down her knife and stared at the wooden flowers that Lukey had brought. Had she made them? Had he? She tapped them gently.

'They're very pretty, aren't they,?' she said, her voice shaking. 'If you didn't touch them you'd think they were the real thing, real chrysanthemums.'

'We had a neighbour in Clerkenwell couldn't abide chrysanths. An Italian lady. Said they were the flower of death. I've always liked 'em, myself.'

CHAPTER 10

Had a Romany chal kair'd tute cambri,
Then I had penn'd ke tute chie,
But tu shan a vassavie lubbeny . . .[14]

'Song of the Broken Chastity', George Borrow,
The Romany Rye

Account Rendered

'This water isn't right, mother!'

'What do you mean, Ellen?'

'Was it in a tin can before you put it in the jug?'

'No, indeed. It's fresh from the bucket, fresh from the well, and that not half an hour since.'

'So why does it taste all metallic, then?'

Her mother's hands stilled at the copper. 'Oh Ellen,' she muttered. 'I wasn't mistaken then.'

'Mother?'

---

[14] 'Had a Romany man got you with child, then would I have said unto you girl, you are a wicked whore . . .'

'You do right to sound fearful.'

'What are you talking about?'

Flora Quainton said nothing, but started to cry into the washing.

'*Mother!*'

'I dunt know what your grandfather is going to say, but it'll be none of it good. My poor little girl!'

Mrs Quainton turned round to face her daughter. Cold fear gripped Ellen's insides. Her mother's face was pouchy, defeated.

'Your undies are tight on you today, ain't they, child?' Mrs Quainton crossed to the table and traced her daughter's jawline with her index finger.

''Tis a first sign, the face going softlike round the edge.' With three fingers she swiftly prodded Ellen's breast.

'Ow!'

'Tender, is it there?'

'How did you know?'

'I'm a mother – your mother. Who was he, child?'

'*He?*'

'Telling *me* is the least of it. 'Tis your grandfather you have to think of!'

Ellen's glance darted round the cramped kitchen, looking for escape. The humble deal furniture she had known all her life seemed to rise up against her, leering, the mocking plates jostling on the dresser, the ladle in the jar poised to strike at her, the fly whisk against the wall readying itself to beat against her calves. She stood up, felt again that dizziness and nausea, and rushed out of the cottage door into the misty rain to throw up.

If Mother knows, it must be so!

Flora followed her, and put her arm across Ellen's back as she retched uselessly on an already emptied stomach.

'It med be all right, Ellen. We dunt need to say anything yet. Sometimes they dunt keep, babies.'

'I *can't* be having a baby, Mother . . . *He* can't . . .'

'That's what he tole you, is it? Offer to marry you too, did he?'

'No . . . no.' The full realisation of her situation hit her at last, but within it quivered a little flame of hope. She remembered his words, that first time: '*If I got a baby with you there'd be no man more pleased than me,*' and saw herself and Sam walking along the road, waiting for the carrier, going into their future.

'Go in and lie down, Ellen. I'll get Doris's boy to run to Mrs Colton's and say you ain't coming in today.'

*

'Ellen sick?' Oliver leaned his stick slowly against the wall. 'Can't be – Ellen's never sick. Has she a fever, Flora?'

'No, just the vomiting – and tired. A face like paper.'

Oliver was silent for a moment. 'The little maid started that way,' he said.

'No,' Flora said quickly. 'It's not that.'

'You're a doctor now, are you?' said Oliver.

'Maybe she ate something not right,' tried Flora.

'What do you mean, woman? She ate same as you and me and we're hale enough. I'll go for the doctor and stop your foolishness.'

'Couldn't we wait a little . . . ? Mayhap it's nothing serious.'

Oliver stared at her. 'My granddaughter – she'll have the doctor, whatever it costs.'

Flora's shoulders sagged. There was no escape, then. The doctor would come, a judge in a black cap, condemning Ellen to a kind of death, the death of respectability, of name, of hopes.

*

Oliver and Flora sat wordlessly either side of the fireplace, listening to the murmurs from above – the doctor's rumble and Ellen's short, muffled replies. At last they heard the man's slow tread down the creaking staircase, and saw him pause as he ducked his head under the doorframe at the foot. He closed the staircase door.

'Bad news, is it, Doctor? Something my girl shouldn't hear?' asked Oliver, getting to his feet. For the first time Flora sensed Oliver's agitation.

The doctor's face was inutterably sad – disappointed, Flora thought.

'There is some good news, Quainton. Ellen is in perfect health. Please, sit down.'

Oliver obeyed. The doctor spoke to him as though Flora wasn't there. *He blames me,* she thought. *It's me 'as let her go astray.*

'Ellen is going to have a child.'

The silence seemed endless. The blood drained from Oliver's face. He stared at the doctor, his mouth moving soundlessly. He shrunk in his chair; those few words had turned him into a frail man of ninety. The doctor leaned towards him, fearing a stroke, but Oliver at last spoke, though in a cracked whisper.

'No – not my poor maidy.'

'I'm sorry.'

Flora started to cry. Ignoring her, Oliver creaked to his feet. 'I'll get you your fee, Doctor,' he said, leaning on the mantelpiece with one hand whilst rustling the notes in a tin tea caddy.

'No, not this time, Quainton. I'll need to come back anyway.'

*

'Who is the man as did this, daughter?' asked Oliver.

Her face in her handkerchief, Flora shook her head.

'You knew about this?'

'No – only hours before you did,' wept Flora. 'I guessed – but I have no idea who the man is. She won't say. She hardly believes it herself. It's my opinion she don't know what she was doing. He mun have taken advantage of her – of her innocence.'

Oliver sat down again and covered his face with his hands.

'She mun go away,' he said. 'She mun go away and come back without 'en – without the baby. I'll enquire – maybe Birmingham, friends in the connexion who can help.'

'Send my child away?'

Oliver glowered at her.

''Tis that or the poor ward, woman! "He that commiteth fornication sinneth against his own body . . . the temple of the Holy Ghost!" I mun think now what best to do – and pray for guidance. Keep her in the house, Flora.'

*

Where is she? What did I say that she won't see me? It was the fourth evening that Sam had waited for Ellen by the chalky path. As usual, Vanlo had accompanied him part of the way before melting into the trees. The shadows were lengthening; there was a hint of autumn in the air's cooler breath. Then at last he heard a woman's hurried step. A dark-haired, scowling girl was approaching.

Judith Chown looked over her shoulder before speaking. 'You Sam Loveridge?'

'That's me.'

'She can't come,' said Judith.

'Why – where is she?'

Judith looked away.

'Ill.'

'*Ill?*'

'Don't ask me what of as I'm not going to tell you. But she'll live.'

'Well, can I see her?' asked Sam.

'I'd advise you not if you want to keep your skin whole. That's all I'm saying. I've done what I told her I'd do – to stop her fretting.' She turned round and began walking briskly back the way she had come.

'Wait!' called Sam, and started to follow her. Judy took no notice, except to walk faster.

*

Sam waited three more evenings, in the hope of seeing Judith, if not Ellen. He found he could not stay in the clearing, but walked round the beechwoods restlessly, smoking. Vanlo followed him, but Sam behaved as if he wasn't there. He'd snapped at one of the other labourers that day, after the man had said, 'You've a long face today. Crossed in love at last?' Caley had silently watched this exchange. Going to the path on the last evening Sam had looked round to see Vanlo some paces behind him.

'What is it, boy?'

'You all right, Sam?'

'Can't say as I am, but I'll live.'

'They're muttering about you back there. They're brewing something up but they don't tell me what. It wunt me, Sam. I never said nuffing.'

Sam stood very still. The boy looked up at him, pleading to be believed.

'Lukey asked me. But I said we just mooched round, you tellin' me things. Like an uncle does.'

'*Dordi!* I'm for it then.'

'I never said nuffing!' said Vanlo again.

'I believe you. Look, I'm going to the village for a bit.'

*

He asked a pleasant-looking middle-aged woman tending her garden the way to the Quainton home. Grace Lambourne regarded him curiously for a moment and then pointed to Oliver's cottage. Encouraged by her courtesy, he said, 'I hear Miss Quainton ain't well.'

'That's right. I saw the doctor call. I can't tell you more'n that.'

He felt her eyes on him as he raised the brass fox knocker on Oliver's door.

Flora answered. Looking up at him, she said, 'We don't need anything. One of your tribe came with pegs only a week ago.'

'Who is it, Flora?' came Oliver's voice from the parlour.

She turned her head. 'Just one of them Gypsies from Surman's Wood. I've tole him we don't want anything.'

'I'm not selling, lady,' said Sam gently. 'I wanted to ask after Miss Quainton. I hear she wunt well.'

Flora uttered a small scream and clung to the door-frame, staring at him like a rabbit before a stoat.

'Send 'im away, woman!' Oliver came stumping to the door and looked Sam up and down. 'What's the matter with you, Flora? Get inside and I'll deal with this!'

With a whimper Flora scuttled indoors.

'You heard the lady. Be on your way, will you?'

'I came about Ellen, sir. Her being sick, I mean.'

The effect on Oliver was electrifying. His face darkened, his side whiskers trembled.

'Know why she's sick, do you?'

'No . . . I came as soon as I heard, sir.'

'Heard *what*?'

'That she was sick, sir,' said Sam in confusion.

'And what has the likes of you to do with my grand-daughter?'

With utter simplicity, seeing his feet and hers on the road waiting for the carrier, Sam said, 'I love her.'

'Get away from my door before I kill you! *Flora!* My shotgun! I'll teach you to come deceiving God-fearing souls – ruining a decent girl.'

'*Ellen!*' shouted Sam. The casement above rattled, but in the same moment Oliver tore his shotgun from Flora's shaking hands and shouldered it.

You're no use to her dead, Sam! He took to his heels, turning his head again to shout out her name. A shot rang out, and he jumped, though the bullet came nowhere near him. He saw Oliver and Flora struggling over the gun, and heard Ellen screaming his name from the upstairs window. It tore his heart to hear her voice, but he took comfort from the fact that only strong lungs could make that sound. Neighbours appeared at the cottage doors; Sam knew he would have no supporters here. *I mun go back and have it out with them, see if Mother will come along of me when I go, then I'll get my things and doss in Horwood's barn. Tomorrow I'll look for that dark girl, see will she get a message to her from me.* He was crossing this bridge earlier than he had expected, but was relieved to be upon it at last.

*

Sam sensed them waiting for him well before he reached the clearing. It was the silence. Even the children and the dogs had ceased their racket. His gut contracted with fear.

The fire was going as usual; the hiss and spit of damp wood was the only sound. They had even gathered in the bantams; he could see them shifting in their wicker cages beneath each *vardo*. Fifteen or more pairs of eyes were looking towards him, most of them belonging to the children peeping fearfully over the half-doors. He glimpsed Sibela's face, streaked with tears. His mother, Lukey, her two elder brothers, their wives stood waiting. Vanlo was further off, looking as if he wanted to merge with the trees. Even at a distance Sam could see he was trembling. His mother was weeping noiselessly, tears making tracks as luminous as snail trails down her seamed cheeks. She still held her pipe in a corner of her mouth but had forgotten to smoke it and it had gone out. Then he saw the weapons Liberty and Caley carried: a stave and a horsewhip. Liberty started to swing his stave from side to side, and taking this as a signal, Caley moved towards him.

'What's this?' Sam asked.

'Liberty here see'd what you did, you and your *gauji lubbeny*[15].'

'She's no *lubbeny!*'

'Shameless, she was,' leered Liberty, 'but you gev 'er your *diklo* like it was your right to!'

'How dared you look at her?'

'She looked like she didn't care who see'd her! And how dared *you* put your *karri*[16] where you did, brother! When our sister has never gev you cause!'

Sam felt sick with rage and fear; he felt as though in looking at her, Liberty had assaulted Ellen in front of him,

---

[15] Prostitute

[16] Penis

and he had done nothing. Without thinking, he moved towards his brother-in-law.

Then his mother cried out, 'Don't argue with your brothers, Sam! Ask pardon! She begged a prayer on you, son, so's you couldn't help it. Tell 'em it warn't your fault!'

'No, mother! That's not true.'

'Get your shirt off!' commanded Caley.

Sam obeyed in silence. A warm day still, but the air felt cold on his skin. He thought of Ellen's gentle hands, Ellen lying sick in a room he had never seen. He put up his fists, the only weapon he had. Caley laughed, flashed the horse-whip in the air and brought it down. Sam screamed as it caught in the flesh of his shoulder; someone had added a metal tip, fashioned from the tin used to make clothes pegs. He tried to grasp the whip as Caley raised it again but the shock of pain made him slow. He staggered under the second blow, raising his hands in helpless surrender, but Caley was relentless. The whip whirred in the air, on and on, and the circle tightened round them. Sam's shoulders and back were bright with blood. There was nowhere to run even if he'd had the strength.

'Enough of your tickling!' cried Liberty at last. 'Let me at him now!'

Sam was by now on his knees, but the first blinding blow of the stave knocked him to the ground. He clutched his head, groaning, and his hands came away sticky. He tried to rise, but tipped forward. *They're going to kill me. They'll bury me under the campfire and I'll never see her again.* He wrapped his arms round his head and stayed down, exposing his bleeding back to a rain of blows. Liberty paused, panting, then with a kick, rolled Sam onto his side.

'Get him in the conkers, Caley!'

Caley's boot was merciless. Sam doubled up, screaming with pain, but the sound he made seemed to come from far off. In his confusion and agony he saw again Whitelam's face distorted with grief.

'Lukey! Lukey!' he shrieked, because she was the only one who could stop them. A stave cracked against his hand, and the pain of the blow made him involuntarily raise it in the air, in a mute plea for mercy. None came. He saw boots close to his face, and closed his eyes in anticipation of another kick, a broken nose. Instead the stave was swung low. Lucretia cried out, 'Stop!' but too late. Sam took the blow hard on the top of his head, and he collapsed and lay motionless.

'We'll fix his pretty face for him now, Lukey,' said Liberty.

'No, killing him's enough!'

'Wait a minute,' said Caley. He walked up to Sam's inert body and gave him an exploratory prod in the shoulder with his boot. Sam groaned faintly.

'We did it for you, Lukey. An' if you'd an ugly husband you mightn't have a 'dulterating one.'

'My Sam,' wept Lucretia. 'Let's get you away from here, away from her. Mother Harmony! Will you help me clean 'im up?'

Harmony kneeled beside her son's head. 'You will not, Lukey. I'll do it myself. You stay in the wagon for now and I'll keep him in the bender till he wakes and decides if he likes living or not. Vanlo, boy, come here and help me move him!'

*

'Lor', Ellen, who'd have thought it to look at you!' Judy studied her friend in frank admiration. 'I'd wanted to get there first, and you beat me to it!'

Pale, sick and frightened, Ellen managed a weak laugh, then got out of her chair and staggered into her friend's arms.

'He's a looker, your Gypsy, ain't he?' whispered Judy in her ear. 'I asked you about brothers, didn't I?'

'There's just him and his old mother – and his wife!'

Judy whistled. 'What a buster, Ellen!'

'Go and meet him again, Judy! Tell him I can't come myself. I'm that overthrown – and I've promised Mother to stay here. Grandfer was all for locking me in otherwise. Tell him I'm his, but not to come here again for I'll not answer for Grandfer.'

'I'll let you tell him your news, though,' said Judy. She could not trust as Ellen did in Sam's joy at impending fatherhood. 'I'll be back as soon as they let me in again – my good deed for the day.'

*

Judy waited nearly an hour that evening, pacing the path and getting angrier with men by the minute. *I'll not go back to her until I've seed him,* she vowed.

The following day she waited again, but for a shorter time, and the day after even less. On the fourth day she determined to face Sam at Horwood's farm, and ask him where he had been hiding himself. *I'll give him such a larruping if he tries a dodge on her.*

*

The hay was piled high in Horwood's ancient barn, its spine as bowed as a seaside donkey's. With a sinking heart Judith watched the men rolling down their shirtsleeves and lifting their jackets from where they lay heaped on a barrel in a corner of the yard. Each man lifted his cap to her, and most of them greeted her by name, greetings she returned absently, though she knew most of them, saving a few itin- erants, none of whom appeared to be Gypsies. Finally she approached Horwood, who was closing the great doors.

'Oh Judy, daughter – you're a sight for sore eyes.'

They stood and looked at each other for a moment, both thinking of what should have been: Reggie one of the team of threshers, Judy living in the farmhouse.

'You've come about Ellen's man, haven't you?' he said eventually. 'I can't tell you where he is, though. Them other Gypsies came by three days ago and said they was clearing off.'

'Oh God!'

'I'm sorry, Judy. I'm sorriest for Ellen – she deserved better. They took their wages and wanted Sam's, but I said I'd only put it in his hand myself. They didn't care for that much but I know what's correct, and I also wanted to give him a piece of my mind – my best hand and just to up and go like that in the middle of the threshing. I wasn't happy.'

'Not half as unhappy as she's going to be . . .'

'Not that I can make sense of it, Judy. He was all of a scram for her. I mean, I didn't know it was Ellen at the time, but if ever there was a man in love, it was him. He got on with his work all right – he always did. But you never heard a man sing and whistle as joyful as he did. We all joshed him about it, but you could see the Bucklands didn't care for it one bit.'

*

'Don't take on so, Ellen,' said Judith. 'You'll lose the poor babe!'

'That would make everyone happy, wouldn't it?' sobbed Ellen. 'Nobody wants it but me!'

'Something ain't right, Ellen. Why'd he have come here looking for you if he didn't care? Most men'd have worked out why you was sick, surely, and run a mile – not come here to get shot at.'

Ellen raised her pale face. 'I want to go to Surman's Wood. I want to see for myself that he's gone. Then I'll believe it.'

'I'm coming with you. No, don't try to stop me. They'll not let you out of the house otherwise. Get your things on and I'll square it with them downstairs.'

'Now?'

'Why not now?'

*

'She's coming out with me,' said Judy to their upturned faces. 'It don't do her any good being cooped up in here with no fresh air and just her own misery to live on.'

'You'll let them all see the shame she's brought on this family,' growled Oliver.

Judy raised her chin. 'The shame ain't exactly as you'd notice just yet. And let them think what they want – they don't know for sure any of 'en that there *is* a baby coming.'

'They all saw that man come here shouting for her!'

'So? They don't all know he left his calling card, do they?'

Flora gasped and wrung her hands in her apron. Oliver opened his mouth and shut it again.

'So she's coming out with me with her head high. After-wards you can think up whatever story you want about why she's being sent away. *Ellen! Come down!*'

*

The cows were in the field as they had been that fateful day but neither girl took any notice when the herd began its lugubrious progress towards them. They reached the stile, Judith insisting on helping Ellen over, and plunged into the wood. No plume of smoke guided them, nor barking of dogs.

'I never got as far as the camp, Judy, but he used to go this way,' Ellen whispered, as if they were in danger of being overheard. Then at last the trees opened out and they stood in the empty clearing. The remains of a fire lay dark from the drizzle. There was a scattering of small animal bones, some sodden rags and twisted bits of indefinable metal – that was all. Ellen prodded the ashes; a spark winked red and died. She saw paired rows of holes in the ground, as of tent pegs. Here were the marks of wheels – the path the wagons had taken out of the clearing.

'What's this then?' asked Judy, picking up an earthenware beer bottle from amongst the roots of a beech tree, 'Thorp – Coley St – Reading,' she read out. 'Worth a penny if returned, this is.'

'Give it me here,' cried Ellen. A wild hope gripped her – a message! She tipped the bottle up, listening for the rustle of paper, then remembered her lover had told her he couldn't write so much as his name. It dripped sour beer. Clutching the bottle with both hands, she sank to her knees and wept.

*

'Come in, child,' said Grace, putting her hands out to support Ellen, slumped against Judy in the cottage doorway. 'I've been expecting you.

'Here.' She led her to a rush-bottomed chair and gently pushed her into it. Ellen leaned her arms on the deal table and rested her head on them. Her shoulders shook, her eyes red and dry and sore. Judy pulled a chair alongside and put her hand on Ellen's back.

'I saw 'em go the other day,' said Grace. 'Three wagons going t'wards the Wallingford road. It was him, wasn't it, Ellen, that has got you in this trouble? That handsome one that used to take Reggie out?'

Ellen moaned.

'Did you think no one knew? You can't but sneeze round here and someone will notice. And if we do then you can be sure his people do too, for they can hear the robin put his head under his wing, I reckon. They've took him away, Ellen, I'm certain of it. They don't like their kind to mix with ours, no more'n we do with them.'

Ellen raised her ravaged face and asked piteously, 'Did you see him go, Grace?'

'No, but don't get your hopes up. To my mind they had him hidden in one o' their wagons. He's gone, Ellen, and you must think no more of 'en.'

'I can't believe it!'

'Oh Ellen . . . Told you he loved you, did he?'

'Oh yes!'

'And now you've lost everything for that – but I don't blame you.'

'Nor him either!'

'Oh, I blame him, child, for all he needed to do was to get up on that wagon and go.'

'If Charlie had been here—'

'I know,' said Grace. ''Tis hard for a maid not to be loved, to be cheated as you and he were. But there are plenty who will lay this trouble all at your door. Listen to me, Ellen. You'll not be let to keep your Gypsy child. If the connexion doesn't find somewhere for you, the poor mite will be born in the workhouse, saving a miracle. And *you* could be shut in the asylum after. Your grandfather loves you, Ellen, believe me, but though he knows pride to be the worst of sins he'll not overcome it now. It'll be stronger than his love.'

'I want the baby, though nobody else does. And I'll do anything to keep it.'

CHAPTER 11

Art thou bound unto a wife? Seek not to be loosed.
Art thou loosed from a wife? Seek not a wife.

John Wesley, 1743

Salvation

'Who is it?' growled Oliver from behind his front door.

'Harold.'

'Brother Chown!' Oliver said, unbolting the door.
'I expect you've come about our misfortin. Everyone else
has.'

'Um . . . I incline to believe that the fault is not mainly hers.'

'That's generous of you, and the sign of a forgiving
Christian mind. But she knew better – brought up as she
has been. Her poor mother is gone all to pieces.'

'I was wondering if we might talk—'

'Forgive me! I'm forgetting my manners with all this
trouble. Come in, come in.'

Harold hesitated.

'Could we walk instead, Oliver? I should find it easier to say what I want to say if we are outside – I would prefer Ellen and her mother not to hear this just yet.'

The door through to the scullery was open on this warm evening, and Flora Quainton, trying and failing to distract herself by paunching a rabbit, did hear, and wondered about the 'just yet'.

*

They took the bridle path across the fields towards the next hamlet. Harold spoke first.

'What do you intend to do about her, brother?'

Oliver stopped, looking away across a gate into a field of cows, anywhere but at Harold. He fumbled in a pocket and, pulling out a clean white handkerchief, blew his nose so fiercely that two sparrows perched on a hawthorn bush took flight. Harold realised that his old friend was weeping, and didn't want him to see it.

'I mun write to friends in the connexion – I think those in Birmingham might be best, so that she may go there. I don't know . . . I've never had to deal with something like this before.'

'You mean until the child is born?'

'And after, mebbe. There is our own orphanage down at Alresford if the right couple can't be found – they do good work there, thank the Lord. But they won't take 'en before five years old. Otherwise there's the poor ward and then the workhouse for the infant. There's others would have her committed to Littlemore. But I wouldn't wish that on the poor silly maidy.'

'Um . . . can the man be found?'

'The man be damned!' shouted Oliver. 'Forgive me, Harold . . . Even if he could be found and . . . and *tamed,* somehow, it would be no use. He has a wife already.'

'Oh merciful heaven,' murmured Harold. 'And she knew it?' He felt cold.

'Oh, she knew it all right. From the start, too. So she must take the blame. He never spun her a yarn, I'll give him that; no promising her a ring to get his hands on her.'

'This is *Ellen*?'

'It is, my own dear son's child. She nearly threw the fact at me. She went running back to that wood where they met thinking to find 'en there. Grace Lambourne and your Judy brought her back. Sister Grace even said she'd wished Ellen had've disgraced herself with Charlie – though she used some other sentimental term, but disgrace was what she was talking about, however you dress it up. I said if she was thinking about that now to unthink it smartish – and she went off home wailing. No, the sooner Ellen's away from here the better.'

'And afterwards?' croaked Harold. His mouth was dry.

'I don't know. But she can't come back here.'

'I might have a suggestion,' began Harold.

'You know where we might send her? Does your Mr Lightfoot deal with – oh, I don't even know what to call 'em – when a man must pay vittles for the child he shouldn't have?'

'Oh no, it's not that. I mean if she could be found a husband.'

'A *husband*! Who'd want her now?'

'*I* would, Oliver. I'd marry her.'

'You'd do that? You'd take my poor soiled girl and make her right?'

'I'm revolted by what she's done – in that man's hands – coupling like the beasts in the open air, they say! But no one can't be saved, Oliver. The man has gone – that's good.' Harold kicked at a tussock of grass. 'She was brought up on the path of righteousness and can be brought back to it now. Judy loves her and I'd always seen her as a good influence. My daughter might learn something, from all this.' He took a deep breath. 'I'd be proud to marry her.'

Oliver turned away, pulling out the handkerchief again. He talked quickly, falling over his words.

'I wonder how we can do it . . . Send her away until the baby is born and taken care of. We tell everyone she has gone to the college, and that there never was no baby after all. She's too clever to be a shop girl as it is. Then you mun come across her – we'll make out you've been specially requested to preach outside the district – and she puts aside the college to marry you as she can't be married and a teacher as well, so why go on with it . . . I think that might work. Oh Harold, you are a true Christian!'

'Um . . . I was thinking to marry her straightaway.'

'Straightaway? But what about the baby?'

'No, Oliver, I meant marry her and take on the baby.'

'And leave here?'

'No.'

'Are you mad, Harold Chown, or a saint?' Oliver said at last. 'I'm sure I don't know which.'

'I . . . I've said nothing to her, of course. But I don't see why she would accept me unless it was for the baby. From what little Judith tells me, Ellen seems determined to find a way to keep the child. If she goes away, and the baby is given up, and she comes back, then all is as before—'

'Nothing is as before.'

'No, not quite, I see. But she'd have no reason to marry me if she had no child to support, would she? I'm not a catch for a girl like her.'

'You are, though! The little fool should count herself lucky!'

'I don't believe she'd have me, though, unless she got to keep her baby.'

'Chown, come back and ask her.'

'Now?'

'Yes. I don't want you to change your mind. But try first if she won't have you without the little cuckoo. I say it for your sake, though I should have pity on the poor babe.'

*

Oliver opened the door to the staircase and called up: 'Ellen?'

She raised her head from the damp pillow. Was it her imagination, or did he sound kinder?

Then she heard her grandfather's voice rumbling down in the parlour. He was talking to her mother. All she made out in reply were murmurs, and an occasional 'my poor child!', but Ellen knew her mother would acquiesce in anything Oliver decided.

Perhaps if I went to my brother? She began to pin her hopes on John, that he would come home on a vegetable cart and bear her away – do what Sam had promised and never done. Her head sank back into the pillow. *How can I saddle John with my problem? He's his own life to lead, and so active in the connexion too – all his work with the poor.* But Ellen had a strong sense of what she thought of as the 'deserving poor'. She was not poor – yet – and she was not deserving. She scurried endlessly round this labyrinth of the mind, looking for a way out and meeting only dead ends. Ellen knew of at least two cottagers' daughters who had got into trouble. There had been the obligatory raging to start with, but in their easy-going and ramshackle homes these inconvenient babies had eventually been accepted, and brought up under the same roof as their mothers as though they weren't their children but their youngest siblings. Oliver, of course, frowned on such arrangements as encouraging a loose and irresponsible way of living, his head deep in his Old Testament for justification.

Ellen tried to take some comfort from the familiarity of her little room: the flower-sprigged curtains, the dark stained boards that creaked so familiarly she knew exactly where she stood even in pitch darkness, the rag rug she had made herself, the patchwork counterpane that her mother had stitched as a girl, the framed exhortation to recognise God's love in all His works.

'Ellen?'

She sat up on the bed. Oliver stood in the doorway. *He's looking me in the eye this time.*

'Harold Chown has called. He has a suggestion to make to you, dear. I think you might hear him out.'

'About the baby,' she said, a statement not a question, thinking of documents she would need to sign, of Sam's child and hers being handed to strangers, of her whole life spent trying to remember what the baby had looked like, imagining what her child would grow into. Would they even let her know if it was a boy or a girl?

'It has to do with the baby, yes. Will you come down? It would be better than him coming up here.'

'Why not let him come up here? I'm a bad girl as it is. Let old Harold see me sitting here on my bed! I've nothing left to lose!'

Waiting downstairs in the little parlour, 'old Harold' winced. Her grandfather grasped the doorframe.

'Come now, Ellen,' he said. 'There is no one who cannot be saved if they want it enough. Will you step down? He wants to speak to you alone.'

Ellen frowned. She had tried to avoid Harold since that day when he had talked of Charlie's death as being a sign from the Almighty. *What can he have to say to me now?* Yet a tiny pinprick of light winked somewhere in her tired brain and would not be ignored. She followed her grandfather down the cramped staircase.

'Here she be,' said Oliver unnecessarily. 'I shall be out the back with my beans along of her mother.'

'Good evening, Ellen,' said Harold. They stood facing each other, he turning his hat nervously, she holding one hand in the other.

'You're looking well,' he added. She wasn't, and she knew it. Her face was puffy and tired, her eyes smaller, her hair dull, her normally neat dress crumpled. He thought she looked older. With a little rush of pity and hope he thought: *That Gypsy wouldn't want her now.*

'Um . . . I have heard about your trouble, Ellen,' he went on, looking down at the hat in his hands.

'You and the world, I expect,' she said.

'I would like to help you.'

'Everyone says that. But no one asks what I want. That's because I've no right to say what that is.'

'You want to keep this child?'

'I do, – you're the first person to ask me that,' she said. 'You!'

'How will you?'

'That I don't rightly know. I shall have to go away, of course. London again, or Birmingham. Somewhere where I am not known. Where I can pretend to be a widow. If I put on my "good face" again I will probably be believed.'

Her 'good face'? Do I really know this girl at all?

'I can sew. I can write a good hand,' she went on. 'It must be possible to find *something*.'

That something hung in the air between them. She looked so undefended. *Good God*, he thought, *if she's lucky, she'll find someone to keep her – but with a baby?*

'Marry me,' he said.

'What did you say?'

'You heard me, I think. Marry me, Ellen.'

She laughed, a horrible, joyless sound. Harold flinched.

'Marry me,' he said for the third time, feeling a fool. 'I'd take you tomorrow, baby and all.'

Ellen reached for a chair and sat down.

'Of course, I quite forgot the form,' apologised Harold, remembering his first wife, his Millie. He began to creak onto one knee.

'*Don't!*' cried Ellen. 'Get up, Mr Chown!'

He obeyed. 'Call me Harold – please – whatever your answer is.'

'Harold, then – but no romantic gestures. It doesn't suit you, nor me, nor this fix I'm in. I thank you for your proposal. This is what you meant, then, when you said it was God's will that Charlie had to die?'

'Forgive me. I was clumsy and thoughtless.'

'I expect you think that what you're doing now is all part of the divine plan too. But it doesn't matter. Would you, though, give me just a little time to think about your offer?'

'Shall I come back tomorrow?' asked Harold.

'No, I meant only a short while. An hour.' *Anything to get out of this maze.* 'You've taken me completely by surprise,' she went on. 'Does my grandfather know?'

'Oh yes. I spoke to him first.'

'Of course, you would do that,' she said. 'What did he say?'

'He was very pleased. But he thought I meant to have you without the baby – to marry you after . . . after the baby is settled. He thought that would be best.'

'Oh he did, did he?' *I shall never forgive him for that.* 'But you didn't agree?'

'I said I didn't think you'd have me unless it was with the baby.'

Ellen stood up. 'All right, Harold.'

'So I may come back in an hour?'

'Never mind that. I'll marry you, Harold. I've no choice, really. Grandfer would prefer his great-grandchild in the poor ward than for me to keep it. I doubt I'll make you happy, but I will marry you.'

'Oh Ellen!' He grasped her hand and drew it to his lips. How Victorian he was! *Oh, but whatever you do, do not kiss my palm!* She felt warm breath on her knuckles, the dampness of his mouth, and gritted her teeth. Then she was released. She saw tears in his eyes.

'Shall we go out and tell them now?' he said. He tried humour: 'Before you change your mind?'

'I shan't do that,' she said, unsmiling.

'Would you take my arm, Ellen? Then we don't need to say anything.'

*

'So you're to marry Pa? Are you mad, Ellen?'

'He's asked me, and I said yes, that's all.'

'There has to be some other way!'

'No, Judy, if there had been I'd've taken it, with all respect to your father. If they took my baby away I think I'd die.'

'It's a cheek of him to ask you!'

'It's not, you know. I should be grateful to him.'

'*You* in the same bed as Pa! I can't think of anything worse!'

'*I* can. My baby taken from me.'

'What'll you do, shut your eyes and think of Sam?'

'Oh, Judy, no, please . . .' Ellen started to cry. 'I'm not meant to love, am I? Charlie gets killed, and Sam abandons me. This poor baby is all I've got now . . . I *can't* lose it too!'

'Oh, Lord, I'm sorry. I didn't mean to upset you. I'm just vexed with Sam for running away, and Pa for doing his holy and righteous bit. Using you to make himself a martyr! He's old enough to be *your* pa. That's not decent!'

'*I've no choice, Judy!* And if you care for me at all, don't mention Sam to me ever again. He's forgotten me, and the only thing to be grateful for is that he knew nothing about this baby. If I'd had a chance to tell him he'd probably have taken off even sharper.'

'I suppose you're right. Oh well, gel, at least you and I rub along well enough.'

'Oh Judy, it's you that'll keep me sane! I don't know what I'd do without you.'

'Ellen, come here till I give you a hug! You'll not expect me to call you ma, will you?'

Ellen collapsed into hysterical giggles. 'Oh Judy!'

'He never talks about Ma, you know.'

'Never?'

'No. Ten years old I was and I'm expected to get over it on my own. A squeeze of the hand and told it's God's will. It's always God's will, but then why don't the bad people get their comeuppance? God's will that poor Reggie came back in bits and too ashamed to see me anymore, though

I'd have taken him in any state, I would indeed. God's will that your Charlie didn't come back at all. I'll tell you something, Ellen Quainton: I've had a bellyful of God's flamin' will! What's that you say?'

'Your mother. Tell me about her.'

'I'd be glad to. He gev all her dresses and shoes away, said there was those that needed them more. I wanted to keep something, something that smelled of her for a bit longer. I saw things I'd loved to see on her and told her so, hanging on other women, with the wrong hat, the wrong stockings – just all wrong, you know. And when I tried to say something I was told: "Don't be selfish, it's what your mother would have wanted", though I'm blowed if *he'd* ever even noticed what she was wearing, so long as it wasn't showy.'

'Men aren't good at these things, Judy.' Though Ellen thought of Sam's grumbling about her dowdy togs, his admiration for her pretty hands, his beautiful words. 'But perhaps he did love her, Judy, and just didn't know how to show it. He's stayed unwed a very long time.'

'I don't know what Dad thinks. All I know is that he's always been set on "bettering hisself", as he puts it. No job out of doors for him! Always a stiff collar and tie, even if he lives in a cottage. Somebody needs to till the earth and make chairs, as long as he doesn't have to. That's not progress, as far as he's concerned. He's always needing to be looked up to, studying – to get to be what? Lightfoot's clerk! Calls it using his talents, like in the parable. Anything but work with his hands.'

'Wedding me is hardly going to help him then, is it?'

'I don't think my father has ever done anything just for the joy of it. He'd consider that sinful, I should think. So he's never put his head in a book unless he thought he was going to learn something useful. I've never known him to read a novel – only those dull ones that come out in instalments in the Prim magazine. He keeps telling me to read them, says they're uplifting. Yawn! He's mortal scared of anything or anyone that's not respectable – as if it's catching – tramps, hawkers—'

'Gypsies. I'm not exactly respectable, am I?'

'Oh Ellen, that's different! I think he thinks he can save you – bring you back to the path of righteousness. And though he won't admit it in a hundred years, I'd bet my last tanner that he thinks by marrying you people will look up to him as a good Christian.'

'So I'm to be his cause,' said Ellen, bleakly, 'him taking another man's leavings.'

'If you put it like that, yes. But I've seen how he looks at you – how he always looked at you. I joshed him for it. Of course, he never got up the courage to ask you before, when he could have.'

'I gave him no encouragement. Quite the opposite.'

'You don't really like him at all, do you?'

'I wish he wouldn't say "um" all the time. I don't like that hat of his, or that he always wears a tie – at any rate,

I've never seen him without one. I hated him for saying Charlie's death was meant. He's a good man, though, isn't he? Everyone says so. And he's my only port in this storm. God help me, Judy!'

*

When Harold called that evening at the Quaintons' cottage, it was in the company of an elderly woman. Flora answered his knock, called Ellen to come, then disappeared back inside.

'I thought, um, it would be helpful, Ellen, if we clarified arrangements in advance. You know Sister Britnell, of course?' Harold said.

'Don't leave people standing on the doorstep, Ellen!' called out Flora.

'Do forgive me – please come in. We could sit in the parlour. Of course I know Sister Britnell very well – a mainstay of our sewing meeting. You taught me tatting.' Ellen put out her hand politely.

'Perhaps you could bring us some tea?' prompted Harold.

'Oh yes, of course. Mother, could you sit with our visitors whilst I make it?'

*

'I've done for Brother Chown, as you know, ever since our poor Millie went to her eternal rest,' said Mrs Britnell, holding her cup an awkward inch above its saucer. 'I did try getting Miss Judy to take over, but I'm afraid without success,' she went on, with a nod and an indulgent smile in Harold's direction. 'Brother Chown does have some lovely things – all lacquered, you know, not like our plain country beech, but they do show the dust. If it's agreeable to you, Miss Quainton, I should like to retire and give more time to the connexion. Perhaps if I stayed on just until you feel able yourself—'

'I should be most grateful, Sister Britnell,' said Ellen, clasping the hands that lay in her lap more tightly, urging a polite smile onto her pale face. She saw herself ten years from now, holding a duster, hemmed in by Harold's pretentious furniture. 'Will you have some more tea, Mrs Britnell?' she asked. 'I should like you to tell me more about Mr Chown's likes and dislikes – so I will know what to do.'

Mrs Britnell's old-fashioned stays creaked as she leaned forward and held out her cup. Harold smiled. This visit had proved most satisfactory.

CHAPTER 12

The general subjects of talk were the Revival, now over, with a superb record of seventy saved souls, the school-treat shortly to occur, the summer holidays, the fashions, and the change of ministers which would take place in August.

Arnold Bennett, 'The Sewing Meeting',
Anna of the Five Towns

The Sewing Meeting

Ellen recognised Grace Lambourne's gentle knock and answered the door herself. Charlie's mother kissed her cheek. 'How are you, child?'

'Oh, you know, people have been very kind.'

'Let's have some tea. I want to ask you something.'

Flora came forward to greet her neighbour, mumbled something about carrots, and disappeared out the back.

'You can't stay shut up in here until it's all over,' said Grace, settling herself in a chair by the kitchen hearth.

'It won't ever be over, Grace.'

'That's what I mean, really. You'll have to face the chapel sometime. You'll not see them again until you go in as a bride if you don't.'

Ellen cried out, as though pricked with a pin, and put her hand on her stomach.

'Ellen! Are you all right?'

'Yes . . . yes, it's just the thought of the ceremony. It's so soon.'

'You are sure you want to marry, child?'

'Oh yes, I'm sure,' and the hand patted.

'Well, I was wondering, as an easier place to start, if you'd come to the next sewing meeting. I'm hosting it, remember.'

Ellen did remember. The calendar had all been arranged in happier times. Before the summer. Before Sam.

'I don't know that I can face them, Grace, not yet! Just think how Hilda Lindow is going to look at me!'

'Hilda can be a little sharp, I know. It's hard for her, that a baby never came. But you have to get the support of the ladies, Ellen, if you're going to have any sort of life in this village – you and baby. They're your best defence against the church people. I'll admit, you might find the men more forgiving to start with—'

'Not Grandfer.'

'Perhaps not him. But Harold . . .'

'Yes, poor Harold.'

'I don't believe he thinks he's poor Harold. How's your dress coming on?'

'Mrs Colton came and measured me. I'm to have a dove-grey costume – very suitable, she said, for a circuit preacher's wife. I'll get a lot of wear from it. And the straight style favours my . . . my situation.'

'That's something to be grateful for, isn't it?'

'It's not at all what I dreamed of – I mean, when I was little,' said Ellen, seeing a white dress trampled into the Picardy mud.

'None of us did, Ellen.'

'I still don't think I can come to the meeting, Grace. I'm terrified. Can't you tell them I'm poorly? I am still sick some mornings.'

'If you don't come to the meeting, you'll still have to go back to chapel before you marry. I could call for you. So there'd be me, and Oliver, and Flora to support you.'

'I shall try. I promise.'

*

Three weeks later, heart pounding and legs weak, Ellen took Oliver's arm, whilst Grace walked on her other side, Flora following timidly behind, glancing over her shoulder as though she expected an attack from the rear. As they entered the chapel, heads turned, then quickly turned back again. Oliver led the little party to their pew next to the rostrum, where Harold and Judy waited, he with an expression of righteousness that curdled Ellen's already churning insides, whilst Judy held her head high, her eyes flashing proud defiance. She and Grace sat flanking Ellen like benign wardresses throughout the service, each with a hand tucked reassuringly under her elbow. Ellen dipped her head and her face flamed, as from the rostrum Oliver hurled Matthew's challenge at the heads of the congregation: 'And why beholdest thou the mote that is in thy brother's eye, but considerest not the beam that is in thine own eye? . . . Thou hypocrite . . .'

*

Afterwards, as the chapel emptied, Grace whispered in Ellen's ear: 'The ladies are waiting for you in the school room.'

'Oh, I couldn't!'

'You've got to, gel,' said Judy, squeezing her hand. 'Trust us.'

Ellen allowed herself to be led into the room, Judy and Grace either side. *As if I was going to the gallows!* Flora cut off escape from behind.

The teacher's desk was invisible beneath a blizzard of tiny white articles. Mrs Lightfoot, wife of Harold's employer, stepped forward and began the inventory. 'There are four of these,' she said, holding up a tiny vest with a lace-edged neckline and back ties, 'same again of petticoats and bootees – Mrs Potter knitted them – and four of these to keep baby's little legs warm. Four is all you'll need of anything apart from these, of course—'

'One on, one dirty, one drying and one clean,' interrupted Mrs Stopps, bursting with excitement.

'You'll need these most of all,' resumed Mrs Lightfoot, holding up a corner of a towelling square. 'That's why there are so many of them. I daresay Sister Flora will show you how to use them!'

'I've never forgotten,' piped up Ellen's mother behind her, prompting a polite titter from the group.

'These are pilch wrappers to keep them in place.'

'I remember,' said Ellen faintly. 'My little sister . . .'

'This was my contribution,' said Hilda Lindow, holding out a cobweb of a shawl. 'I'd made it some time ago, truth be known. I should like your baby to have it.'

Ellen started to cry. 'I don't deserve . . . you are all so kind . . .' She held out her hands as, clucking like hens in sympathy, the chapel women flurried round her.

CHAPTER 13

All our unmarried members are advised to refrain from marriage with persons whose life and conversation are not according to the Gospel.

'Rule 318', *The General Rules of the Primitive Methodist Church*

Vow and Covenant

Tomorrow I'll be safe. No one will be able take my baby away then.

Ellen sat on the bed and faced the wardrobe. Inside, her new suit hung in a miasma of camphor balls. Her best underthings, the ones Sam had been so dismissive of, were folded demurely away in the chest. *I shan't wear them again.* Her small act of rebellion would be to put on the plain drawers and chemise she wore every day to work. Harold was taking her as used goods after all. Freshly polished but not new shoes sat primly paired under the bed. Before going to sleep she would shake the suit out and hang it near the window, even though she knew that everyone else's Sunday best would be stored the same way and the chapel would be redolent of that same scratch-nose smell. The chapel women did not habitually wear scent, but for this occasion Ellen's mother had given her a small bottle of lavender water, on the grounds that it 'calmed the nerves'.

She got up and went down to help her mother with the tea for the last time.

'Where's Grandfer?'

'Gone to Risborough on the trap to meet your brother's train.'

Her heart leaped. 'John's coming!' She darted forward and kissed her mother's cheek.

Flora Quainton fluttered and said, 'Careful, I'll have this tray over!' *Poor child,* thought Flora, *that her brother coming gives her more joy than her wedding!*

*

'Ellen!' John Quainton held his sister at arm's length, his hands on her shoulders. 'So you are to be married, and I am to be made an uncle!'

He smiled, and Ellen burst into tears.

'Oh sis,' he murmured, holding her against his shoulder, whilst their mother hovered ineffectually round them trying to dab Ellen's tears. Oliver had yet to come in; he was stabling the horse.

'I'm taking Ellen out for a walk,' John said. 'Tea can wait ten minutes, can't it?'

Flora Quainton acquiesced, used already to bending to male prerogative, and oddly proud that her son, though only twenty-two, now naturally followed where father and grandfather had led.

*

'Are you sure about this, Ellen?'

'If you'd asked me instead did I want to, I'd've said no, John. But sure that it's the right thing to do – yes.'

'There's no hope from the father, then?'

'None. Better not to mention him.'

'Does he know?'

'Gone before I could tell him,' said Ellen.

'Scoundrel.'

'Don't, John!' Ellen started to cry again.

'I'm sorry. It's just that I don't like to see you tie yourself to a man I can't believe you love.'

'I don't love him. But I love the baby.'

'But you'll stand up there in front of everyone tomorrow and say that you do.'

'That would have frightened me once, John. Standing up in God's presence and speaking a falsehood, I mean. But I'll do my best to . . . to love Harold.'

'I can see from your face you ask too much of yourself, Ellen. Oh dear . . . I wish I could help you, sister. Something for all the times you were there for your little brother. And you were always the one with common sense . . .'

'Not now, obviously.'

'Will they not bend?' he asked.

'Who?'

'Mother . . . Oliver – the lot of them.'

'You know Mother's opinion doesn't count. I think she's afraid to have one, let alone speak it out loud. And you know Grandfer and his principles. He wanted me to have the baby away from here and then come back and wed Harold. Even Harold himself knew I'd never wear that.'

'Does it have to be old Chown, Ellen? Couldn't you and the babe stay here and in time you find a man you like and who likes you – who sees what you're really worth?'

'There are few men as it is, so why would one of them settle for shop-soiled?'

'Could you come back to London with me?' But Ellen heard the doubt in his voice.

'Oh John, I'll be grateful all my life you made that offer. But I can't accept. You've your own life to lead – and besides, it's all organised: dress, minister, party,' and she flung her arm out as though indicating the trestle and the tea urn that would be waiting for them after the service. 'I'll get to live with Judy. With her there, I'll survive somehow. But most of all, nobody will take my baby away.'

*

'You look beautiful, daughter!'

'I don't! I wish I looked plain. I must do from now on!'

Her mother's eyes filled.

'I know this isn't what anyone wanted . . . If Charlie—'

'Oh Mother, leave poor Charlie in peace, today of all days!'

'I'm sorry . . .'

'No, I am! My feet are swollen and everyone will know why . . . I was sick again this morning and I am tired to death.'

'Being sick will pass off soon,' said her mother.

'Well, as long as I can get through the service without disgracing myself any further . . . I couldn't be sick any more than I've been already.'

She pulled down the little veil on her hat and made final adjustments to the plain suit in the mirror, wishing the skirt longer to hide her puffy ankles. Measuring her, Mrs Colton had reassured Ellen that the suit could be altered if necessary. Taking the last pins out of her mouth she'd added: 'And nobody will be able to see what you're hiding in there. I must say you're the last girl I thought would find herself in trouble, Ellen. But I can only wish you well. You're lucky Harold Chown is taking you on, though I don't believe either of you will be happy.'

'Here are your flowers, dear,' said her mother, handing her the spray of hot-housed ivory roses. Ellen bent her face towards them, drinking in through the veil their moist, fresh, innocent scent. She could already see them curled and brown, thrown on the compost heap – what a useless sacrifice, to cut the poor flowers!

Oliver waited by the cottage door, pale and quiet, stiff in his Sunday clothes, the old-fashioned whiskers of which he was so proud carefully trimmed and combed.

'You go on first, and take your usual place,' he said to his daughter-in-law.

Obediently, Ellen's mother took her hat and hymnal and left without a word to either of them. Oliver pushed the door closed behind her and took Ellen in his arms.

'God bless you child, on your wedding morn.'

Ellen started to weep again.

'*Hush,* Granddaughter. "And God shall wipe away all tears from their eyes; and there shall be no more death, neither sorrow, nor crying, neither shall there be any more pain: for the former things are passed away."'

*

Ellen had made that short walk from the cottage to the chapel more times than she could count, but saw her familiar surroundings now in heightened colour and richness. The sycamore tree at the corner would never again have quite that pattern of dying leaves, nor would its shadow fall on the road in quite that way. The lichen on the low wall by the forge would grow and spread, and come the spring, the daffodils would push through the tufts of grass in a pattern known only to themselves. Nothing would ever be the same.

*

When Oliver relinquished her arm below the rostrum, Ellen instinctively reached out to keep him close. She felt utterly alone, standing there with all those eyes upon her. She couldn't bring herself to look at the dark figure next to her, and she caught only murmurs of the words being intoned by the visiting minister – something about 'mutual society, help and comfort'. Panic washed over her. She would be alone with this man for the rest of their lives. What comfort would that be? What comfort could she ever be to *him*? The minister went on and she stared at him through the veil she had forgotten to lift.

'. . . that children might enjoy the blessings and privileges of family life . . .'

There was the ring, now, lying on the service book. And then Harold was fumbling with it and pushing it onto her unresisting finger, and declaring shakily: 'With this ring, a token and pledge of the vow and covenant now made between me and thee, I thee wed.'

A memory as sharp and clear as pain – Sam's mouth on her palm. Ellen looked round wildly, as though expecting him to burst through the tiny chapel door and bear her away. But she knew that she could only pass through that door now as a married woman. She saw the kind faces, the nodding, the satisfaction. Grace sat slightly apart from the others, towards the back, with the expression of someone witnessing an unpreventable tragedy. Ellen's brother was looking down at his hands, his shoulders slumped.

Then the minister was talking to Ellen with some urgency in his voice. Ellen turned back to him and answered automatically the words she had been taught. She gripped Harold's hand so tightly that she felt him wince, and tried to relax her hold. The minister spoke again, urging them to 'a thankful, sober and holy use of all conjugal comforts; praying much with, and for, one another; watching over and provoking each other to love and good works, and to live together as the heirs of the grace of life.'

She was married; she was saved. In a dream she walked back through the assembly on Harold's arm, dimly aware of the faces turning towards her like corn in the breeze, and the little door opened and she and Harold proceeded out into the crisp November day, to be stared at by the other villagers, as the congregation milled out behind them.

'They have a little celebration planned for us in the Sunday school,' murmured Harold, pink with pride.

Ellen looked directly into his tired, kind face for the first time that day, and said steadily but firmly: 'I cannot love you, Harold, but I want you to know how grateful I am.'

'I need no more than that. I am patient; I've waited for you long enough. Let us go to the breakfast, and then I will take you home.'

*

Ellen put her small suitcase down just inside the cottage door. Though she had been in Harold's home many times, she looked at it today as though she had never seen it before. His heavy, glossy, Victorian furniture, polished specially by Mrs Britnell the previous day, was the product of factories in Birmingham, whilst local beech worked by local cabinet-makers served in her grandfather's home. There was a piano she had never seen played, that Judy had told her had been Millie's, with cellulose keys, an embroidered panel and fussy fretwork. Ellen wondered at the length of the hire purchase for such an item. This would be hers now. She would no longer have to play the jangling old Shaw cottage piano that stood in the corner of the Sunday school. A squat dining table with ugly, machine-turned legs stood on a mock-Persian rug of discordant reds and blues. Ellen missed the rag rug on which she had put her feet every morning in her old home.

'Um . . . it's a bit cramped, I know,' said Harold. 'I'd like to provide you with a better home, with an open staircase, and tiles on the roof. Not this old thatch.'

'It's very comfortable, Harold, I'm sure.'

'I don't require much, Ellen. If you can just make sure I have a clean shirt and enough studs for my collar, and my shoes polished. Um . . . I like to go to work on a good breakfast and come back to a nourishing meal – nothing fancy. You see, it all works out rather conveniently, doesn't it?'

'I suppose it does.'

'Um . . . there is something I wanted to say to you, that I was thinking about most of last night.' He cleared his throat and fidgeted with his collar. 'I'll say it now, before Judy gets back from clearing up the hall. I thought it would be best if we were not man and wife, if you get my meaning, until after the baby is born. I think that would be more seemly – don't you?'

'Oh! Yes . . . yes, of course.'

Oh Sam, Sam!

'I'm glad we've settled that.'

CHAPTER 14

A faithful friend, a father dear, an unfortunate husband lieth here.

Tombstone of John Hughes, Gypsy, aged 26, the last man to be hanged for horse-stealing (in 1825)[17]

Reading Magistrates

May 1923

Sam knew he was being watched. He'd only been able to work for the last three months, and though the warmer weather helped, a day spent stooping and rising alongside Vanlo, seeding wurzels in a Berkshire field, left him stiff and sore.

'You could split, Sam,' the boy had told him more than once. 'I'd tell 'em you'd run too fast for me.'

'And get you into more trouble?'

So when, that evening, he put his foot on the first step of his *vardo*, it was with an immense longing to simply lie down and close his eyes.

---

[17] St. John the Baptist, Itchen Abbas, Hampshire

'Not yet, my Sam,' said Caley behind him. 'Me and Liberty are going for a walk. You're coming with us.'

'It's dark, bruv. And I'm all in!'

'There's the moon.'

'Where're we going then?'

'Down there a bit . . . along the towpath.'

'So's you can pitch me in?'

Caley laughed. 'Never crossed my mind! Just a bit of business.'

*

'Wait here.'

'What for, Caley?'

'Patience, Sam!'

I could just go now, thought Sam, as Caley and Liberty disappeared into the darkness, *only I don't know as one of 'em wunt go up there and come back down through them trees.* Standing on the towpath in the moonlight, the water as smooth and dark as treacle to his right, the trees dense and secretive to his left, he listened intently, until eventually the animals and birds that had fallen silent at the appearance of the three men resumed their nocturnal rustlings and whirrings.

Sam stiffened, listening intently, when, a few minutes later, the scuttlings and squeaks in the undergrowth suddenly ceased. He could hear the unmistakeable thud thud of horse's hooves coming along the towpath. The white star on the mare's forehead was the first thing he saw, then that she was led only by Liberty. *I was right then, Caley's in them trees somewhere, watching.*

'That *grai's*[18] bin *chorred*[19]!' hissed Sam.

'Quiet, my Sam. The *gaujo*'ll be along in a minute. He'll give you some coin and then you come straight home. Caley'll know if you don't.'

'I wunt!'

'Is that what you want?' said Liberty, inclining his head towards the canal. ''Sides, you still owe Lukey. You ain't much of a husband to her, are you?'

'I've been a long time mending, bruv.'

'Take the bridle, Sam. Stand under them trees.'

*

Twenty minutes later the horse whickered and Sam saw two figures materialise from the direction of Hungerford.

'Have you the goods?' said a voice.

'I have,' Sam answered. He led the horse onto the path. There was a click of metal, and light flashed straight in his eyes. The mare shied and whinnied. He raised an arm,

---

[18] Horse
[19] Stolen

and in a rush of movement he was too dazzled to see, someone hit him in the diaphragm and he sprawled on the path. A whistle shrilled, and more men came running. At least four held Sam down, though he was too winded to fight back. He was handcuffed before he could catch his breath.

'Ellen!' he whispered.

*

Sam sat helplessly in the dock alongside a man he'd never seen before, listening as the whole sorry tale of the stolen mare unfolded. His companion, an ostler who handled stolen goods from his lodgings above a livery stables in Hungerford, had, the morning of the theft, been informed by a scullery maid that she was expecting. Sam heard the girl's hesitant and tearful evidence, as she stood with one hand on the rail and the other on her belly.

'He gev me jools and rings he couldn't have come by honestly,' she said. 'But when I tole him about the baby he said he'd a child already – in Newbury – and a wife too. I was that upset I ran all the way home and the first person I see'd was the policeman Cook keeps company with, so I tole him everything.'

That 'everything' led to the ostler's lodgings being raided, and the man arrested. In the hope of leniency, he told the police of the deal that he'd made with 'some Gypsies' and told them where he'd agreed to meet them to collect the horse they were to steal.

*

'Sampson Loveridge, you have been found guilty of the theft of a mare belonging to John Jenkins of Avington on the fourteenth May 1923. In recognition of your coop-eration with this court and the fact that this is your first peacetime offence, I am prepared to be lenient. I sentence you to twelve months' imprisonment, and trust that you will take this opportunity to use your time profitably and wisely. We now strive to be reformative rather than punitive in our treatment of malefactors, Loveridge, so I strongly encourage you to learn a trade – or to master reading and writing – so that you may, upon your release, finally become a useful member of society.'

Sam thought of all the horses he had shoed – of plough-ing, harvesting, hedging, ditching, stripping hops, of all the pegs and toys and flowers he had whittled and carved – and said, 'Yes, sir, thank you, sir.'

As he turned to let them take him down, he glanced up at the public gallery. Lucretia was now nowhere to be seen. Liberty and Caley were on their feet, and already making their way to the staircase; Liberty was whispering in his brother's ear, and Caley was nodding. Neither man looked in Sam's direction. A pale Vanlo sat on, raising a timid hand to salute his brother-in-law. Sam smiled back at the boy, until warned to 'look where you're going or you'll break your neck on them steps!' He surrendered himself to the dark descent, the prison van, the search, the shearing, the scratch of the uniform, the enforced camaraderie of fellow criminals. He hadn't understood all of the magistrate's words. Did they still punish those prisoners who, when circling the yard, dared to look up at the sky?

*

'You're booked for Winchester, Loveridge,' said the officer, 'soon as we've the van. I just need a few details first.' He pulled out a form and took the cap off his pen. 'Why'd you say you did it? I know you were taken with the mare, but the solicitor said the fence swore blind there was some other fellow – and you wouldn't even let him mount a defence.'

'You mightn't believe it if I did tell you, sir.'

'You'll have your reasons. Gypsy code of honour, is it? They don't care upstairs, of course. As long as they've got someone for it, it doesn't matter much who he is.'

CHAPTER 15

Thou hast taught us that as man is doomed to a life of toil-some labour, the sorrows of women are greatly multiplied, as a penalty for the original transgression. To these sentences, we bow with becoming contrition and resignation.

George Lamb, Forms for the sacraments and occasional services, drawn by the order of the Primitive Methodist Conference, Newcastle upon Tyne, 1859

Childbed

Chingestone, 27th May 1923

Harold was driven out into the lane by her screaming. It was too much, surely. Hadn't Millie shown more dignity than this? Or did he simply not remember? The little house seethed with women: the midwife sent for from the market town, Ellen's apologetic mother who got in everyone's way, Judith, who refused to miss any of the excitement but who did make herself useful, and Grace Lambourne, Ellen's unlikely and steadfast champion who had won the chapel wives over to her cause, so that all held their heads high in righteousness against the sarcasm and scorn of their church sisters. But could none of them stop her from shrieking like a cat under torture?

It was dusk, and labour had been underway for some nine or ten hours.

'It won't be long now,' the midwife had said, 'but we're being especially careful.'

'Is the baby in trouble?'

The midwife frowned, not liking what she had glimpsed in Harold's face.

'We'll tell him – or her – off once he's born, Mr Chown. Your wife is strong, but she's narrowish in the hips, as you know.'

Harold flushed.

'It'll be all right if you go out for a bit, sir. Not much you can do here.'

So, gratefully, he had gone out. He stood irresolute in the middle of the lane. The cries ceased for a moment and the evening resumed its normal concert of birdsong and barking dogs. Then they started up again, it seemed to him more loudly this time.

What if she shouts out his name? he wondered. *I've read of such things.*

Just then an unseen hand banged the casement shut against the cool spring air. Oh merciful heaven! What might the midwife hear? The peaceable Harold in that moment longed for the Gypsy – any Gypsy – to come sauntering along the lane, that he might rush at him and kill him with his own hands, and tear his face to pieces. Now where to? Oliver's, of course. His daughter-in-law was here, so the old man would be alone. He was the only one Harold thought could give him courage, could bolster him in his conviction of having acted as a righteous man.

He hadn't gone two hundred yards before a panting Judith caught up with him.

'My brother is born, Pa,' she said in triumph. 'You've to come back.'

'And Ellen?'

'Both tired, but doing well. The midwife will show her how to feed him, then she wants to be on her way. She says she'll come by tomorrow to see 'em both.'

Harold winced at the little picture of maternal intimacy that Judith had casually shared. Millie had always modestly fed her daughter out of his sight, and he felt some unreasonable resentment that this unseen, inconvenient child now depended on the breasts that he had never yet seen, much less handled.

'Oh, and she's called him Thomas – but he'll be Tom, she says. I'll run back now to tell 'em you're coming, then.'

Thomas? The name was a decent one, of course, but could she not have asked him what he thought?

'I count for so little, then,' he muttered. 'And he's no brother of Judith's!'

'What's that you say?'

'Nothing, Judith.'

*

Behind the door he heard the murmur of female voices. Such peace had descended on the house, and thus on the lane, that it seemed unimaginable that he had been driven out by noise and agony not twenty minutes earlier. He knocked softly. Some bustling sounds, and the latch was lifted.

'Mr Chown,' said the midwife, avoiding his eye. 'I shall leave you with your wife, but I advise you not to tire her after such a long labour.'

'Thank you. My daughter has your fee and will go for the trap.'

Harold thought: *She's said nothing about the baby.* He went upstairs and, closing the door behind him, stood uncertainly on the polished boards. Ellen lay marooned on the island of the bed he had inherited and in which he had slept with Millie. The bed in which she had died. The new mother was billowed about by bolsters and cushions. Her hair had been brushed and tied back and it looked damp. Her face was flushed; it appeared to him slightly blurred at the edges. Harold aged ten had discovered his terrier in a barn suckling her puppies. The dog had loved him but she'd snarled at the boy before his words calmed her. Ellen's eyes had her same look of triumph and wariness now. Her white nightdress was unbuttoned, and in her arms slept her son, his head capped with glossy black hair. Harold thought him extraordinarily small to be the cause of so much suffering.

'How are you?' he said.

'I'll do. Come and have a look at him, Harold.'

He took two paces forward.

'Judith says he's to be called Thomas,' he said.

'Yes. But Tom for everyday.'

'We should arrange his baptism then,' said Harold.

'Oh . . . yes.'

'What's the matter, Ellen?'

'I'm just thinking of when we stood up to be married.'

Harold shifted his weight, and coughed.

'The worst is over, Ellen. We did what was right; we can hold our heads high.'

'*You* can.'

The baby stirred, mewed, opened his eyes.

'Don't you want to look at him, Harold?'

He stepped up to the side of the bed and made himself lean forward. He thought of Millie, holding Judith up to show to his younger self. Tom gazed up at him, unfocused, perplexed.

'His eyes are blue!'

'They won't stay that way, the midwife says. She held a candle near him and said that blue eyes as dark as his are likely to change – after a few weeks.'

'His skin . . . Judy's was very pink.'

'The midwife thought jaundice at first. Then she looked at the whites of his eyes and said not.'

'Thomas Chown,' he said. 'May I choose his middle name?'

'Of course, Harold.'

'Well, as I said, he should be baptised.'

'I'll leave it to you, then.'

The baby opened his mouth in a thin wail. Harold averted his eyes as Ellen opened her nightgown and guided the little bobbing head, as the midwife had taught her.

'I'd best go, then.' He turned away in relief.

'Harold?'

'Yes?'

'Thank you.'

'Oh yes . . . all right.' He couldn't look at her. 'Shall I send your mother up?'

'Yes, please do.'

She heard him descending the stairs with exaggerated care.

'Tom,' she whispered. 'It's just you and me now.'

*

Three days later Harold walked to chapel with Oliver, who was due to lead the service. A knot of people stood round the porch, and came forward one by one to shake his hand.

'You're a good man, Brother Chown. Congratulations,' said the first. In a daze, Harold accepted their greetings, their immediate turning away. Two or three avoided meeting his eyes, whilst another made a point of holding his gaze. He went in, proceeding to his usual form near the front, though for the first time he would willingly have taken the lowliest position at the back of the chapel. Heads turned towards him as though propelled by a lever; people murmured, hands were held out. He held Oliver's arm to stop the older man ascending the rostrum, and with his back to the assembly, whispered, 'It's like a funeral!'

Oliver patted the hand on his arm. 'Courage, brother. They all wish you well.'

Harold heard not a word of his friend's preaching. His message washed over him and out towards the door as a swell of noise that might have been a foreign language. Yet Oliver was evidently on form. The upturned faces of his listeners reflected his words as if they were light. 'Amen! Glory!' rang out like sporadic gunfire in that narrow space.

The old man accompanied Harold to the door to greet the people as they left, and to exhort the faithful to attend the prayer meeting that afternoon. As they stood on the path both men turned at the sound of a scuffling behind the hedge, followed by children's voices, high and clear and pure as if they were choirboys: 'Cuckoo!'

'Cuckoo!'

'Cuckoo!'

'*Wretches!*' shouted Oliver. 'Come out here till I tan yer hides!'

Silence, but for some muffled sniggering.

'No, brother, offer them no violence,' said Harold quietly. 'It's not them I blame. It's those who've taught them.'

CHAPTER 16

Next to death, gaol is the greatest leveller known to man. To me the flitting shadows of the underworld are not the sinister figures portrayed in the columns of sensational journals or in the pages of popular novelists, but just grown up children weeping in the shadows!

Stuart Wood, *Shades of the Prison House*

Stirapen[20]

Winchester

Keys rattled on the landing; a cell door was being unlocked close by. There was a murmur of voices, then, 'In you go!' and the door clanged shut. Sam lay in the dark, ringing silence of his cell, listening. Then it started: the sound he most dreaded hearing in this place. The man the other side of the white-washed wall was weeping.

---

[20] Prison

He had no idea how long it was before the sound subsided, but it was enough to banish hope of sleep. In the unseen man's tears Sam relived his first days in Lincoln, dank and dripping Princetown and then his time at reception here in Winchester: the stripping, searching, bathing under another man's stare, numbering, processing – at least this time leaving him his hair!

He'd learned to count the time in Lincoln on his fingers with the help of the cathedral bells. Now the hour struck twice. He turned his face to the wall and saw himself leading Ellen under the trees, asking if he might kiss her. Sam's eyes filled. *No, I can't go on thinking of her, not with him sobbing his heart out through there too. It'll kill me.* Yet a sleepless hour later, engulfed in self loathing, he took the only means he knew of making sleep come. In the darkness of his thoughts he pulled Ellen's pliant body into ever more obscene positions. Lack of fresh air, prison diet and limited physical movement had sapped his strength; arousal was harder every time. When at last he was finished he said to himself, *You put her on the streets, thinking of her that way,* and resolved, as before, not to do it again. He waited for the compensation of sleep but it didn't come. Through the wall the new prisoner started weeping again.

*

Standing blearily on the landing as the cells discharged their occupants, each holding his slop-bucket, Sam was able to appraise his neighbour. Middle-aged, a bit seedy, some vestiges of distinction in the slightly too long grey hair, the length of the cheekbones. And scared, very scared.

Sam whispered to him, for though the silent system had been abolished, at Winchester the old ways died hard. 'Just do as I do. I'll show you.'

The man timidly smiled his thanks.

*

Later, they were herded down for exercise, two circles of men, one inside the other, each man the regulation six paces behind the one before. The elderly prisoner in front of Sam started to plead with the warder. 'Please, sir, if I might go in the inner circle today. It's my heart, you see . . . the pain.'

'Then you'll get what you wanted, won't you?' retorted the warder. 'You'll stay in the outer circle until I say otherwise, you old malingerer!'

Wheezing, the old man shuffled back into line. At the blast of a whistle the meaningless, circling shuffle began. Sam gulped down the fresh air, taking breaths as deep as he could make them. They had completed about two and a half circuits of the yard when the man in front of him shuddered, staggered and then silently folded onto the asphalt. Sam stopped short, but the prisoners who followed him, their faces turned to the ground, dominoed into the back of him before the warder had time to get his whistle out.

'Halt! You and you – lift him onto that bench,' he barked, pointing at Sam and the man behind him, his new neighbour.

'You take his legs,' whispered Sam. 'I'll manage his other end.'

The old man's head lolled against Sam's chest, his lips blue, eyes staring. The other warder on duty ran across. 'I'll call for the M.O.,' he said.

'Wait, you two,' shouted his colleague at Sam and his companion, and as the two prisoners held the old man, he lifted the hand that lay across the body, felt at the wrist and called to the other warder, 'Tell 'im he needn't hurry.'

As they laid their burden gently down on the bench, Sam was startled to make out the words the new prisoner was quietly intoning: '. . . the resurrection, and the life, he that believeth in me, though he were dead, yet shall he live . . . and whosoever liveth and believeth in me—'

The whistle shrilled, followed by the order, 'Show's over, back in line, march!' and the tramp of boots resumed. As he passed the bench again, Sam saw the warder who had sent for the medical officer had returned, and was covering the corpse's face with a handkerchief.

'A small mercy,' he muttered to himself. At the next revolution, the M.O. was reassuring himself that life was extinct, whilst two prisoner orderlies stood by with a stretcher, and at the next, it was as if the death had never taken place – the bench was empty.

Turned round to file back up to their landings, Sam was behind the new prisoner. He whispered: 'Are you a parson?'

'Yes.'

*

They met again in the work hall over a heap of mailbags.

'Sampson Loveridge. I'd give you my hand only they don't encourage it.'

'A pleasure to meet you, sir, though one might have hoped for better circumstances ... Cecil Acland – the Reverend Cecil Acland.' Acland passed a trembling hand over his face. 'May I ask what you are in for, Mr Loveridge?'

'Your first stretch, ain't it, Reverend?'

'As a matter of fact, it is.'

'I don't mind myself, but don't ask the others that question. Wait until they tell you. It was horse-stealing, though I didn't do it.'

'Mine was fraud. I did.'

'How long they gev you?'

'Five years.'

Sam whistled. 'That's a curse.'

'*Keep the noise down over there, B2.26!*'

'They said I'd brought shame on my calling, and betrayed the trust of hundreds,' said Acland.

'What's a reverend to do after a stretch like that?' asked Sam.

'Oh, I expect my bishop has some malarial swamp in mind for me, if I survive. I will be expected to be grateful; I would be grateful were it not for my poor Beth.'

'Children?'

Acland sighed. 'Two sons . . . my daughter. She's not long married. I thought my son-in-law might throw her over because of my trouble, but he's made of sterner stuff, fortunately. Her eldest brother gave her away.' Acland wiped his eyes.

'Keep your spirits up, Reverend. Them as love you depend on it. And hold your needle this way – look – you'll find it'll come easier. People must write a powerful lot of letters to need all them sacks – you've got to make your number, or they'll put you on report.'

'Thank you. They're the ones I've let down most. I told Beth not to visit me. It's no place for a lady, this. Nor my sons.'

'What d'they do?'

'The elder is a barrister; the younger is in theological college. I couldn't have done them more harm if I'd tried.'

'You med regret that – your wife not coming, I mean. Mine won't, but I don't mind that. And the one I love don't know I'm here and I've no way to tell her.'

Acland scented a cause.

'Can't you write to her?'

'Me? Can't even write my own name!'

'I can. I could write for you.'

Then Acland looked up, too late, at a point above Sam's head.

'I warned you, didn't I, B2.26?' shouted the warder. 'On your feet! You're on report, disobeying an order to keep quiet. And you, B2.27, you'd be as well, only we know you've been led astray, but I'll not be so lenient the next time.'

'Sorry!' mouthed Acland.

*

'Are you sure you don't want me to come with you, dear?' Flora Quainton was pummelling nappy squares against a washboard.

'No, Mother,' said Ellen. 'We won't be long. Just once round the village for fresh air; it helps him sleep.' *And it helps me think. I'm half stifled in here.*

Nevertheless, Ellen's heart thumped as she set off up the lane as though wading into a choppy sea.

I have to get this over with.

*

Frank Newcomb stood near the window of the dining room of his manse whilst Rose laid the table for tea, and watched Ellen's stiff-shouldered progress.

'The witches!' he exclaimed.

'What is it, Frank?' asked Rose.

'Ansell and Larden, matrons of this parish. Staring at the Quainton girl with her baby until her face caught fire, poor girl.'

'Mrs Chown, you mean,' said Rose.

'Horrible, such a pretty girl being sacrificed to an old man like that.'

'She should count herself lucky. There are girls locked up in Littlemore for what she's done.'

'Locked up for frailty, Rose!'

'She could have waited for some decent young Englishman, not gone with the Gypsies in the woods. Oh, I've forgotten to bring the sugar.'

'You have, haven't you?' muttered her husband, as Rose left the room.

*

'I should have come with you,' said her mother, seeing Ellen's face.

'It's all right, Mother. I can take the baby for an airing on my own.'

But in the privacy of the bedroom she laid Tom down on the counterpane and watched him kick his legs at her.

'Oh my little man, you don't know what's in store for you!'

*

The following day she manhandled the pram onto the bridle path and met no one but old Mott.

'He's a handsome boy,' said the old man, peering in at Tom.

'Thank you, Brother Mott,' said Ellen, fighting tears. 'I think so too, but there aren't many that say so.'

'Every child is a gift of God, daughter. My mother always said that. It was just her and me, see? It was hard, very hard.'

'I never knew!' said Ellen.

'Not many do these days. I've lived longer than the scoffers. You've been lucky, daughter, even if old Harold ain't as handsome as the other one.'

Ellen's hand went to her throat.

'I thought to warn you then, but what maidy would listen to old Mott? Well, I mun leave you now.' He raised his cap and shuffled away.

Ellen pushed on, refusing to glance into Surman's Wood.

*

'It's all right,' said Sam. 'We're allowed to talk at association, within reason. The politicos told me that.'

'So what happened to you?' asked Acland.

'Three days on short commons in chokey – the punishment cells.'

'For *talking*?'

'It's better than it was. It used to be that you couldn't talk at all – even the screws couldn't talk to you, except to give orders. And all your jobs you'd to do on your own, in your cells or in pens. You'd be out of your cell most days for less than an hour, save Sundays.'

'Good Lord . . . If the outside world only *knew!*'

'What makes you think they'd care? They don't see or don't want to . . .'

'It's a Christian's duty to visit the imprisoned, Sam.'

'We don't know many Christians, then, you and I. But did them musicians come on Sunday?'

Acland's face brightened. 'They did. Oh, it was marvellous! I wish you could have heard them.'

'The guv'nor's one of the old school. He don't really like them new reg'lations, and nor do the screws, most of them. But he can't refuse people like the musicians when they offers.'

'I'm sorry you got penned up like that. It was my fault for making you talk.'

'You didn't – I chose to. And besides, if the screws want to put me on report, anything will do.'

'You missed a good sermon yesterday. About Psalm twenty-three. It's so often talked about, but not as meaningfully as the chaplain did – after that poor wretch's collapse. He didn't dwell on the green pastures and still waters, but comfort in the valley of the shadow of death. That man was here for attempting self-murder, and never got a kind word!'

'He was begging for his life just before he fell, Reverend.'

'So he'd wanted to live after all. The chaplain asked us to pray for him – and he sounded as though he meant what he said, so I wish now I'd been kinder to him that time when he came to see me. I'm afraid I sent him away with a flea in his ear.'

'The chaplain's a good man – the best of 'em in here. He'll give you another chance. I'd bet he's waiting for you,' said Sam.

'All right. I'll try to put myself in his way. I'm learning that you need friends in here if you're not to finish up in the padded cell.'

'That you do . . . I was thinking, whilst I was downstairs. Did you mean it about writing a letter for me?'

'Of course. I'd be glad to. But how does one get paper and pen in here?' asked Acland.

'I'd try the chaplain.'

*

Sam and Cecil sat opposite each other at association, a blank piece of lined paper on the table between them.

'"Ellen, I love you,"' said Sam.

'All right, Sam. I'll just start it in the normal way. "Dear Ellen" would be customary.'

'"Dear Ellen, I love you", then.'

'Straight to the point – why not?' said Acland.

'I don't know how much of a good idea this is, Cecil. I don't know what I'm doing.'

'You've not much of a choice. The girl thinks you've abandoned her.'

'I'm sorry. It's only that I'm sitting here talking to you. If I had her in front of me I'd know what to say.'

'Try this then,' said Acland. 'Take that chair and turn your back on me.'

A warder stopped his strolling up and down between the tables and stared at them. Then he shrugged, and went on walking.

'Good . . . Now close your eyes,' said Acland. 'Look at her instead. Can you see her, Sam?'

'Oh yes.'

'Now tell her. Slowly, if you can, so I can get it all down.'

'And you'll make it good?'

'I'll make it good, without taking any of you out of it.'

'All right then . . . Dear Ellen, I love you and I hope you love me still. You'll be thinking I run off and left you when you are the best thing I ever seed but I was taken off by main force by Lukey's brothers. They gave me a whopping such that I thought to die but kep' alive because my mother is a clever woman and because if I didn't I wouldn't see your face till judgement. Two of my ribs got bust and they still bother me, especially on cold nights, which is when I miss you most, though we never had nights only days and those too short. My hand is not right either but fortunately it's not the hand I use the most. I got my mother to leave you a *pattrin—*'

'What was that, Sam, a pattern?'

'No, it's our word meaning something you leave so the next person knows where you've gone.'

'I'll put "sign", shall I? She might not know your word either.'

'All right, then – I got Mother to leave you a sign but I don't know would you understand it. It was to say I was gone to Reading, though maybe they'd've not let you to go there. Now I am not in Reading, but in Winchester, in the prison, with twelve months for horse theft. But I didn't do it, Ellen. Liberty made me say I did or otherwise he would thump me better the next time and nobody ever thinks to dig under where there's been a campfire, so here I am with all this time to think about you and miss you more than I know how to say.'

'Wait a minute, Sam. I need to put more ink in this . . . That's it, go on.'

'There is a kind reverend in here what has writ this down for me. He is also going to teach me so next time I write maybe I can manage a bit myself. The reverend misses his books. I miss you, Ellen, and saying all this to you makes it worse as well as better because I can see you more clearly now as if I am talking to you, but I can't put my arms round you and show you I love you the way I did in the woods. I miss your smile and your gentle words and the way you look up at me and a lot else besides, but that is private. I don't mean that against the reverend, who is my friend, but because he tole me all the letters that go out are read by the governor's men. You are a real lady and my lady. I will be out in May and I will come looking for you even if Caley and Liberty are waiting for me, as they can't do much to me in a town in front of a prison. So for now all I can do is kiss the paper when the reverend finishes writing all this and put my mark on it, and if you kiss the paper too we can remember what that was like until I can kiss you again and not let go of you ever. I love you, Sam Loveridge.'

*

Ellen was singing quietly to herself. A perfect wash-day Monday, dry and blowy. She didn't hear Harold's approach across the grass to where she pegged out nappies and sheets. Tom lay sleeping in a basket under the plum tree, tiny fists gently furled, his bud of a mouth open. Ellen eased back her shoulders, stiff from turning the mangle.

''Tis much work to change three beds, I think,' said a voice behind her.

'Oh Harold, you gave me quite a turn! I never heard you coming! No, 'tisn't so bad, for Judith and me work it out between us.' She spoke gaily, still warmed by the fine weather and the pleasure in hoisting fresh laundry into the breeze.

'Your child is three months old,' said Harold.

'Yes. He does well, don't you think?'

Harold glanced in the direction of the plum tree.

'It's time I came to sleep in the marriage bed,' he said. 'As we'd agreed. I'll come tonight.'

Ellen's busy hands stilled. The breeze still ruffled her hair and flapped the sheets, but the light had gone out of the day.

'Yes, Harold.'

'I'll be back at teatime.'

'Goodbye, then.'

Ellen went on with her task, now in silence.

*

The warder's whistle shrilled, and the pacing men stopped. No one dared look round, or anywhere other than at the back of the neck of the man in front; even the most recent prisoners had learned quickly the wisdom of passively waiting for the next command, for it was bound to come, and obedience was simplest. But Sam had expected something unusual. Out of the corner of his eye he had seen a group of screws massing on the far side of the yard.

'*Outer ring – bath-house!*'

They were formed into pairs to march off the ground.

'It's not bath day!' whispered Cecil.

'Dry bath,' Sam whispered back. 'Just remember you're a man, and don't let them take a rise out of you.'

*

'Clothes on the side of the bath, and quick about it,' ordered the warder.

Sam stripped, shivering with cold and shame.

'Nippy for you, is it, sweetheart? Sorry, I forgot to warm the towels!'

The screw stepped up to him, so close that Sam could smell the pomade on his moustache, and see the bristles in the creases of his neck. He was breathing heavily and smiling, ruffling the prisoner's hair.

'Nothing there, then. It was easier when you lot were kept cropped.'

He stepped back. 'Take your hands off your prick and put them on your head!' he barked. Similar shouts, and some laughter, reached Sam from the other stalls. The screw quietly pushed the door to with his foot. A trickle of sweat ran from Sam's left armpit, despite the cold.

'Feet apart.'

The man appraised the prisoner slowly, from head to foot, until Sam had to look away.

'Lift your prick up,' hissed the screw.

'What?'

'You heard, darling. Finger and thumb. Keep your other hand on your head.'

Sam obeyed.

'*Very* nice. Both hands on head now, and turn round.'

Sam shuffled round to face the bath-tub. The warder ran his hands lightly along Sam's sides, as though patting down a dressed man.

'Bend over the tub. Hold onto the rim,' he said, loudly again.

Heart pounding, Sam at last found his voice, though it came out hoarse.

'Shouldn't there be someone—'

'No need for that,' murmured the screw. 'Want to earn some baccy, dear?'

The man's hands landed on Sam's buttocks, and in a rustle of clothing and warm breath he bent to look more closely. Sam raised his right foot and, planting the sole firmly against the warder's chest, pushed hard. The man staggered back, roaring for assistance, and within seconds the small cubicle was heaving with uniforms.

*

The governor settled his glasses on his nose and looked up at Sam in the adjudication dock.

'Obstructing a routine search and assaulting one of my men,' he said. 'These are serious charges. Have you anything to say?'

Sam stood silent.

'Well?'

'He took a liberty, sir.'

'Adding calumny to your list of misdemeanours, B2.26. Do you think that's wise? It's not what the other officer says.'

'With respect, sir, what other officer? We was alone.'

The governor stiffened. He glanced at his clerk, and said: 'For the obstruction it'll be three days downstairs, usual bread and water. For the assault, fifteen strokes of the cat.'

'What?'

'You heard. Go on like this and I can see no remission for you. You'll have a few days to think about what's going to happen to you until we get the necessary permissions. We do things by the book in this gaol. All right, take him away.'

*

Ellen lay between clean sheets in the bedroom she and Tom had inhabited as their private, secret world. She had wanted Judith's company, but unable to cope with Tom's cried demands night after night, the girl had chosen to roll bedding on and off the divan in the parlour, whilst her father slept soundly and alone in the room that had been Judith's since childhood. Often Ellen had woken to find the baby still beside her, having fallen asleep as she fed him in the darkness. He was feeding now.

'You'll have to stay in the cot from now on, my little man,' she murmured, stroking the dark hair. How beautiful he was! Ellen tried not to search too closely for his father's likeness. It was there in the dark hair, the olive tinge to his skin, the alertness of his eyes, but when she looked for it in the shape of his mouth, or nose or chin, she feared losing what memory she still had of the man.

'My dear Tom!' she whispered.

Finally the pressure on her nipple ceased, and the baby sighed into sleep. Very gently, she eased off the bed and laid him in the wooden cot that had sheltered Judith and who knew how many Chowns, Harold included. She buttoned her nightgown over her breasts, small and soft now after the feed. Harold was to be her husband this night. He would have the unbuttoning of her, then. She turned down the oil lamp and waited in darkness.

*

Harold came in, wearing his old-fashioned nightshirt and carrying a candlestick. His lower legs were spindly, almost hairless. He held the candle above the bed as Ellen looked at him mutely, then turned his back on her to place it on the dresser. She saw his reflection in the mirror as he bent to blow out the flame; his face looked pursier, older than when he was dressed for his clerking.

The bed creaked as he lay down, but he said nothing. From his breathing she realised he was already aroused. With a muffled grunt he turned to her and pulled back the blankets, then lifted up her nightdress as far as her navel. The night air on her skin made her shiver. Then, as the cool flesh of his belly flopped onto her stomach, she bit back a cry, but he gave no sign that he felt the involuntary recoil of her body. Then fatly, wetly, clumsily, he was in her, his breath hot against her neck. It hurt. Ellen tried to recall the urgency of Sam's sinewy embrace, but it had nothing at all in common with poor Harold's silent heaving. And thinking of Sam as she lay beneath Harold made what was happening now feel like an act of infidelity to the man she had loved. She put her hands tentatively on Harold's back over the cotton of his nightshirt, closed her eyes and told herself: *You do this for Tom! It's for Tom!* Her husband speeded up momentarily, then groaned as though someone had hit him hard on the skull. His face was buried in the pillow as she felt him shrink and leave her. He eased off her and lay down on his back alongside her, feeling for her hand, which he took in both of his, patting it.

'All right, Ellen?'

'Yes, Harold.'

'It's been a long time. I thought it would be forever. Thank you, dear wife.'

Seconds later he slept, pushing air rhythmically through his open mouth as though blowing bubbles. Ellen wept silently, hot, fat tears pooling in her ears.

A little before dawn she woke up with a cry, feet thrashing. The last image she scavenged from her dreams was of Sam's face emerging from beneath her skirts, laughing, wiping the back of his hand across his mouth.

*

Sam had lost count of how many days he had lain in solitary confinement, waiting for some *rai*[21], who didn't know him and never would, to put a signature to a document that would sanction his judicial flogging, when keys rattled in the lock and two men entered the cell.

'Stand up, B2.26, and take off your shirt,' said the warder.

'Time, is it?' asked Sam, unbuttoning.

'Time, is it, *sir,* if you don't mind. No, medical officer's come to clear you for the cat. It'll be tomorrow morning.'

The M.O. gave Sam a cursory inspection, grunting as he saw the soft white pits left by Liberty's whip, then hooked his stethoscope to his ears and listened to Sam's heart.

'Strange work for a doctor,' muttered Sam.

'Hold your tongue!' barked the warder.

The doctor continued his prodding, then told Sam to sit, and proceeded to test his reflexes. Finally he said to the warder: 'He's sound'. Turning to Sam and looking him in the eye for the first time, he said, 'You won't be given breakfast tomorrow. I don't advise it.'

*

Sam's lips were parched and cracked. In the silence of the night he pulled his lower lip under his teeth and raked it from side to side until he tasted blood. Then he tugged at the bleeding flesh between his teeth and shredded it, bringing

---

[21] Gentleman

tears to his eyes. With the tip of his tongue he explored the crevice he had made. He stared out at the near impenetrable blackness as the blood cooled and crusted.

*

'Get up, and take that shirt off.'

The two warders led Sam, unresisting, down the length of B Hall. Warders stood at regular intervals on either side. *It's as if they're taking me to the scaffold,* he thought; *they might just as well be.* There was the silence of a solemn ceremony, almost religious in its patient intensity, but Sam sensed the listeners behind every cell door, the pounding of prisoners' hearts – some in fear and sympathy, some in a state of sadistic arousal. Behind one of those doors the warder who would shortly inflict pain on Sam was hiding, but he would never be permitted to see his face.

In front of him loomed the altar to which he would be bound, a high frame of wood and iron and leather straps. The governor stood, sweating in his serge suit, avoiding meeting the prisoner's eye. Sam noticed the sheen of his recently polished shoes. The warders stepped aside as a male nurse came forward and bound a broad leather band round Sam's back, just above the waist, buckling it in front.

'Too tight?' the man whispered.

'No,' murmured Sam.

'That's for your kidneys.'

The rest of me is fair game, then.

He wondered if they might blindfold him, so strong were his thoughts of execution. But no blindfold came; instead he was told to lean against the frame, his feet planted wide. Leather straps were buckled round his ankles. A canvas sheet with a hole for his face was tied onto the upper part of the frame.

'Tall, ain't he?' muttered one of the warders to his colleague.

'Your face goes in there, and don't go trying to look round,' he was told. 'Raise your hands.' His wrists were buckled to the contraption.

'Hold the frame tightly. You might find that helps,' said one of the warders as they withdrew.

Sam could not move. He decided to keep his eyes open and fix his gaze on the pale light coming through the high panes at the end of the hall. *You're a big bird, Sam,* he told himself. *Stretch out your wings and fly right up there till all this looks no bigger'n a child's toy.* Instead, the medical officer's face appeared, inches in front of his. He frowned at the prisoner's bloody mouth. Sam merely raised his eyebrows.

'I've to see how you take it,' whispered the doctor. 'I advise you to yell. Governor might call it off earlier.'

I'll not make a sound. I'd not give them the satisfaction.

Behind him Sam heard the familiar sound of a cell door opening, then a soft tread approaching. He clenched his teeth and tried to stop quivering.

'*One!*'

A whirr – then a hot, tearing pain. Sam felt his skin part like an opening mouth. No moment to draw breath.

'*Two!*'

He opened his mouth wide in a silent scream. He glimpsed the doctor's face damp with sweat.

'*Three!*'

Sam shrieked, his fingers curling, clutching at the cold metal of the frame.

'*Four! – No!*'

He heard the cord pass through the air and braced himself, but it never fell. He badly wanted to pee. He heard the governor say in an irritated, high-pitched voice, 'You know the rules, man! No running up to your target. Maintain your position and lash him from there.'

Can't they get on with it, for the love of God!

'Yes, sir!' Sam strained to recognise the warder's voice.

'Again then: *four!*'

Another split in his skin, and Sam felt blood dribbling off the leather kidney strap and into the band of his trousers.

'*Five!*'

Sam screamed again. The doctor's face was a pale oval blur. Far off, he became aware of a swell of noise, a wordless, shapeless murmur. It seemed to be coming from above him, but he didn't know if it was the protest of his fellow prisoners or if it was sounding within his own head. Another face bobbed and swayed in front of him, and a tear-smarting chemical smell burned his nostrils. The faces of the doctor and the orderly swam into focus; something ammoniacal was being waved beneath his nose.

'*Six!*'

Fully aware now, the pain was more excruciating than ever. The swish of the silken cord and his cries blended. There was no pause, no moment to drag together even two words for heaven.

'*Seven!*'

Again Sam screamed, eyes screwed shut.

'*Eight!*'

No respite, no numbness. A memory. Sam saw a soldier on a stretcher being carried back behind the lines, a leg missing. Yet the man didn't make a sound until one of the stretcher-bearers told him he was an amputee.

'*Nine!*'

Sam's eyes rolled up in his head. He could hear from a distance the medical officer calling, 'Governor!' but what he saw in his mind's eye was a woman, fully dressed, lying across a bed and sobbing, before he slumped into oblivion.

*

Sam came to lying on his stomach on a cot in the cell he'd been brought from that morning. His mouth tasted of vomit and his back was aflame. Someone was splashing it with disinfectant; the cold liquid gave momentary relief, and then his flesh burned worse than ever.

*

Pale and twitching, the following day Sam took his place opposite Cecil and reached for his pile of mailbags.

'Dear God, Sam, what are you doing here? Why aren't you in the infirmary?'

'Fit for work, they said.'

'*What*? I heard your screams – we all did.'

'Keep your voice down.'

'But who did that to your mouth?' whispered Cecil.

'Oh, that? That was me.'

*

Ten days later they sat in the peace of the library.

'We're only here thanks to the chaplain, ain't we?'

'That's right, Sam. *Now* will you tell me what happened? That row in the bath-house – was that you?'

'The screw came on to me.' And as simply and plainly as he could, Sam recounted the story.

'Hell fire! What are you going to do about it?'

'*Do*? What can I *do*? They've punished *me*. It's what the screw will do now that worries me.'

'Hell hath no fury and all that?'

'I wondered was it him what did it – flogged me, I mean.'

'Surely they would not be so perverse as that. Have you seen him since?'

'No. If it weren't for *her*, I'd deal him the same card again. But if they put Puss to scratch me another time, I don't know how I'd bear it.'

'He's most likely been transferred to another hall,' said Cecil.

'So he'll fix on some other poor wretch.'

'Of course. Someone who is more desperate for tobacco than you are. Does it hurt as much now?'

'It stings, and itches something terrible. Weeps too. I sleep – when I can manage it – without my shirt on or it'd be stuck to me and the devil to peel off.'

'Will you let me see?'

'O' course.' Sam stood up and unbuttoned. Then he slipped off the coarse putty-coloured shirt and turned round. Cecil could not suppress a cry.

'Oh merciful Jesus!'

'It could have been worse, Cecil. The governor called a halt after ten, the orderly told me.'

'It's bad enough!' whispered Cecil, staring at the half-crusted wounds with greenish, stiff edges that scored Sam's shoulders and back, and snaked onto the more tender skin of his sides and armpits.

*

'What is it, daughter?' asked Oliver.

Flora Quainton held an unopened envelope in her trembling hand.

''Tis a letter. For Ellen. Someone who don't know she's married.'

'I'll take it,' said Oliver. 'Hmm. I see they don't know this place either. "Chingston", they've written. Boil the kettle, would you?'

Flora watched her father-in-law as he read the steamed-open letter, saw his mouth tighten. He crumpled the paper with such sudden violence that she jumped.

'You are to say nothing about this, daughter. To no one. Never.'

He tossed the letter and envelope on the fire, leaning against the mantel until they were entirely consumed.

CHAPTER 17

What means, quoth he, this Devil's Procession
With Men of Orthodox Profession,
Are things of Superstitious Function,
Fit to be us'd in Gospel Sun-Shine . . .

Samuel Butler, *Hudibras*

Skimmington

Ellen ignored the whispering and giggling and pressed on.
Then she heard the pad of footsteps behind her. She paused,
without looking round, to let whoever it was overtake her.
The footsteps paused also. She walked faster. At least three
others were following her now. She pushed harder against
the handle of the pram; it bounced on the uneven path, and
Tom woke, eyes widening.

'Ssh, my baby, we're nearly home.'

Someone sniggered as a clod of earth hit her in the back.
Ellen turned, putting her back to the pram. Her tormentors
fled, laughing.

Children! She trembled. *I'd swear that little girl was in my Sunday school.*

*

'They'll stop in the end,' said Grace. 'As soon as someone else's misfortune gets their attention.'

'So I've to pray for that, have I?'

'No, Ellen. They torment you because you didn't follow their rules. If you'd given Tom away, or even if you'd kept him and brought him up on your own—'

'Which I would have, if they'd let me!'

'And which would have been the hardest and loneliest way in the world, Ellen!'

'I know – I'm sorry.'

Grace softened. 'It was easier for me, though. Being a young widow. They could pity me. What they don't like is that you didn't hang your head – and you had the cheek to marry, even. It's that they can't forgive. If they could have dressed you in sacking and paraded you round the place facing a donkey's tail, they'd probably have been satisfied.'

'They can do their worst but I'll not give up my baby.'

'Well, don't be proud, Ellen. I'll talk to the sewing meeting again. We'll take it in turns to walk out with you and Tom.'

*

'We must be grateful for small mercies, Sam. That man in forty-eight was spared the cat, I heard.'

'Him that had torn up his cell, you mean?'

Cecil leaned forward, trembling, his hands over his ears. 'How shall I ever get through it? How will *he*? I'll never forget the noise he made, a soul in torment. I'll hear him forever – as I'll remember your screams.'

Sam looked round to see where the screws were, and slipped an arm across Cecil's back, thinking: *This is what a father does*, recalling a distant memory of his own.

'You remember I told you how I got a whopping in Lincoln?' said Sam.

'From the warder who'd lost his sons, you mean?'

'Well, the pain of the cat was sharper than that, but of course they weren't trying to kill me – which I'm pretty sure Whitelam would have, if they hadn't stopped him. The cuts Puss gave me were bad enough, but mebbe the worst of it was being made to wait days for them.'

'Sanctioned torture, Sam!'

Since his flogging, Sam could often smell fear on his companion. To encourage him, he said: 'Thank God you're here, Cecil.'

'*Me*? I cannot stand what happens here, not as a man should.'

'A man who is a man and not a beast should not stand them. You're a decent fellow, Reverend, and you show it.'

'Well, at least they've taken forty-eight to the infirmary, poor devil. Anyone shrieking and raving as he was couldn't be sane.'

'He hit a screw. They have to punish that. But he's not in the infirmary. He's been packed off to Broadmoor.'

Cecil gaped at him.

'You see,' said Sam, 'why you mun do all you can not to go under, Cecil.'

*

Sam leaned against a stack in the prison library and said, 'Nothing today, neither.'

'It may not mean what you think,' said Cecil. 'The warders mayn't have sent it. Letters can get lost. The wrong person could have got it from the postman. They might be holding her reply in the governor's office until it suits him.'

'Would you write another for me?'

'Of course I would – but the schoolmaster won't give me more paper for one for a good few weeks yet. He said you're only allowed to send a letter once in three months.'

'*Three months!* I'll only get one more chance, then. First time in my life I've ever wanted to write letters and now they don't let me!'

'Sam, don't despair – or if you must don't let them see you like this; they'll take advantage of it.'

'You're talking like a lag at last, Cecil!'

'Sam, if it hadn't been for you I don't know how I would still be alive in this place. My own despair would have done for me . . . If you hadn't told me to go to the chaplain I wouldn't have got that librarian's job.'

'And we wouldn't have this place to talk in.'

'Without you – and these books here – the utter, dreary hopelessness of this place would destroy me . . . the monotony of days that never diminish.'

'Except that they do.'

'They do, but each day takes me further from what I knew. I fear that too. Now I don't know how I will cope – outside. I don't know how I'll cope when they release *you*, Sam. I'm sorry. This is very selfish of me. Let me read what Beth says and then we'll have your lesson.'

'You should let her come, you know.'

'I can't. Not here.'

'Is that because of you, or because of her? She med be stronger'n you give her credit for. And you ain't the only one doing a stretch, are you? She is, out there. Maybe she wants to tell you what *her* days are like? Which friends have stuck by her.'

'You may be right . . .'

'You need to keep her picture clear in your head, in your dreams, Cecil. That *biti*[22] photograph won't do. Otherwise the bad stuff will get in instead. Anyway, I'm stopping you

---

[22] Little

reading her letter. We don't need to bother about a lesson today. I can't say I'm in the right mood for it, myself.'

'But I am, Sam. I need to teach you, for my sake.'

'All right then. But let her come. You've much longer in here than me, though what I'll do when they let me out I don't rightly know. If Ellen wunt write to me, I'll have to find her and see if she'll forgive me leaving her there, once she knows it wasn't my doing. But I've seen some of 'em as have a long stretch to do and what happens to them. I'd bet they don't even see a woman when they're dreaming now, whatever way they're made. It even gets to screws in the end. That Barker wore a wedding ring. Stay here long enough and even you med feel that lonely that you'd forget who you were for a bit, and then . . .'

'I wouldn't . . . for if I did, I could never look Beth in the face again.'

'My point exackly. Look her in the face now, and you'll manage.'

*

Without knocking, Ellen nudged open the door of Oliver's cottage, her fingers curled round the handle of Tom's baby-carriage, and for a moment savoured the familiar smell of what had been her home.

'Mother?'

'Hello, Ellen. What brings you here before chapel? Bring my Tom in so's I can see him properly.'

Flora leaned in over the sleeping child.

'You're lucky, daughter. Such a good baby!'

'Well, let's hope the new one'll be as easy!'

'Oh Ellen! Are you? Oh my dearest girl!' Flora put her arms round her. 'Ah, mustn't squeeze too tight, must I? You see? Everything has worked out, hasn't it? You can be happy now, can't you?'

'I can be content, I think . . .'

'Well, yes, but—'

'I wondered, Mother, would you mind bringing Tom yourself? I wanted to get to chapel early to lend the ladies a hand setting up for afterwards – and tell them my good news. They have been so kind. I am so loved, Mother, more than I deserve.'

'Will you stop and tell your grandfer? He's out the back.'

'I'll wait for him at chapel and tell him going in.'

'All right. I'll not say anything. And of course I'll take Tom. I wish you'd let me out with him more often, if I'm honest.'

'I know I protect him too much, Mother. It's just that I'm still afraid.'

'You needn't be, not now, Mrs Chown.'

*

Four or five men were clustered round the chapel porch. Lightfoot the solicitor saw Ellen first and hastened forward.

'Mrs Chown, I would urge you not to come any closer. I fear . . . there has been some unpleasantness . . . not something a lady should see . . .'

She heard Oliver at her shoulder. 'If Mr Lightfoot says come away, come away, child,' he said, taking her elbow almost roughly. 'What brings you here so early anyroad? Without your husband too!'

With his curt words, something gave way in Ellen. *How long am I to put up with this? Catcalling, mudslinging, stares – and now goodness knows what? Have I not paid?* She twitched Oliver's hand away and strode forward. In appalled surprise the other men gave way, revealing what lay propped against the chapel door.

She heard Lightfoot's voice: 'It's a matter for the constables.'

Oliver was pulling at her sleeve. 'Come out of it, Ellen!'

White-lipped, she stood over two entwined effigies.

'The devil finds idle hands,' said someone.

They were crudely but accurately made, straw-stuffed sacking dressed in scarecrow rags, posed obscenely. She saw what she immediately recognised as her own face, the mouth a red slash of paint, blue eyes, stiff arms sticking up round the male effigy pinning her down. Trembling, Oliver pushed past her and seized Sam's dummy by its filthy shirt, flinging it to one side. Its brown painted face leered above a tattered red neckerchief. Oliver wiped his hands feverishly on his trouser legs, as though he had just handled something dead.

An old hat came to rest at Ellen's feet. *Oh, that hat!* There was a ringing in her ears, a tightening of her throat. She gasped, and collapsed back into waiting arms.

*

'They've burned 'em,' said Oliver, perched awkwardly on Harold's divan, convinced that if he moved it would collapse. 'You're not to think on 'em anymore.'

'Easier said . . .' Harold found it hard to pay attention, for he was straining to hear the murmuring from above – the doctor's voice, and Flora's.

'You mun listen to me a minute.'

'Go on,' said Harold.

'I remember when I was a boy – long before I was converted, this was. There was a man and wife here, not long wed. He was what you might call well set-up, by way of fields and cattle and that, a bit older than her. It was said that the maid had had an understanding with another man, but that she married the richer one just the same, him being the safer bet – not the first nor the last to reason that way. Now, I don't know if it was truth or not, for I was too young then to understand properly, but there was murmurings that after she was wed she'd been seen on the path there with her old swain. Next thing happened was that she and the young man were got up in effigy and tied back to back on a donkey, and paraded up and down for all to see, afore they drove the beast to the house where she lived along of her husband, with them all banging saucepans together, and shouting, and hitting the ass so he brayed the louder. My mother said as it was a shame, but it didn't stop 'er going to the spectacle all the same – Mother and Father never did convert. Nobody came out, o' course – I spied a hand trying not to be seen closing the curtains. They went back the next evening with those figures on the donkey, but the morning after I saw the pair of 'em go away on the carrier earlyish – I had work as a bird scarer then and was up with the lark. The man was all grim-like and his wife weeping, sitting there amongst their bits of things. Your Mr Lightfoot's grandfer sold the land for them, for less than it was worth, but wouldn't say where they'd gone except that it was one of the big cities – them as had had family round here for centuries. I never thought to see again such shameful goings on.'

'And the other man?'

'Joined a regiment and went to the Crimea. I don't know what happened to him but he never did come back. But what would you do if that Gypsy showed his face round here again?'

'He wouldn't ... he wouldn't dare!' Harold's face cleared a little. 'His tribe should be back by now – and they aren't.'

'He don't have your sense of shame, brother. He med just be staying away this year to avoid the consequences of what he's done. Don't mean he couldn't come back and cause trouble again. You've saved my poor girl. Take her away; take her where neither of you are known. Start anew.'

'Perhaps you're right. I want no more trouble for her. She is to be a mother again – that is, if this doesn't— 'What's the matter, brother? You've gone pale as a sheet!'

*

Towards evening, Ellen woke to a gnawing pain in her belly. She opened her eyes.

'Is anyone there?' she whispered. A chair scraped on the floorboards, and Judith leaned over the bed.

'Will I do?'

'Judy! Help me sit up – thank you. Oh, my head feels as if it's stuffed with rags.'

'The doctor said he gave you a bromide, that's why.'

'*What?* Didn't Mother tell him?'

'Tell him what, Ellen?'

'Oh, get me the pot, Judy . . . though I seem to have wet myself already.'

As Ellen swung her legs over the side of the bed, Judy quietly closed the bedroom door and went to sit halfway down the narrow staircase. From below, Oliver and Harold's voices reached her, something about 'the connexion would help . . . Lightfoot will know about openings', until Ellen's cry sent her thumping back into the room without knocking. Ellen was squatting over the pot, her nightdress tenting about her. Even in the gloom Judy could see it was spotted – as was the bed.

Ellen raised her stricken face. 'I've lost it, Judy. I've lost my baby.'

*

'Sam. Listen. Look at me. Write to her again.'

'She never wrote back!'

'We've been through this – all the things that could have happened to your letter. Do you really think she would have ignored it if she'd got it – a girl that must otherwise have thought you the worst kind of rotter?'

'I don't know, Cecil . . .'

'So what's your plan?'

'To go and find her, o' course.'

'So you'll just turn up after all this time, and then expect her to come away with you? Put yourself in her shoes . . . Write, man! You can do it yourself by now!'

Sam looked up at last.

'You'd help me again, I mean, to find the right words?'

'I won't need to. Whatever your heart wants to tell her heart will be right.'

'I'll make mistakes, use up all the paper – your patience.'

'That's all right. Thanks to you I get to see Beth. I'm in your debt.'

'Will you put the address on the envelope, though? In case I get it wrong and it doesn't get to her – again.'

'Of course.'

PART TWO

CHAPTER 18

Well may he pause who comes to Canterbury. The meanest flower that blows brought thoughts too deep for tears to William Wordsworth; this proudest shrine of all our Motherland stirs thoughts too deep for tears in us.

Arthur Mee, *The King's England: Kent*

Nesting

Canterbury, January 1924

Ellen sat disconsolately on the trunk and looked round at the scuffed packing cases and tea-chests, at the dingy panes of the sash window, and the little grey yard beyond.

'So this is to be our home, Judith?'

'It ain't so bad, Ellen. There's a bit of life about the place at least. I've never been to London so I've never seen so many people all together in one place. I even heard furriners talking out there on the high street this morning when

I went to find a baker's. When we're shipshape we can do our own baking but for today I thought we could allow ourselves that little extravagance.'

'Foreigners?'

'Furriners – not Gypsies,' said Judith. 'They looked just as you and I do, though I couldn't understand a thing they said. French, perhaps – we're just about as close to France as we ever shall be, here.'

'Oh, Judith! I promised poor Charlie I'd go and find his grave over there, to put a handful of earth from our village over him. And I forgot, I forgot, and now I can't go back there anymore to get it!'

Judith looked at her steadily. 'You've had plenty else to think on since then, Ellen.'

'Betraying his memory, you mean.'

Judith hesitated, for once not knowing what to say. Then eventually she said, 'I can go back sometime. And I'll get the earth for you. I'll go to Grace's garden for it, but I'll tell her it was your idea. And then you and me can go together.' Judith became more animated. 'I've never been on a boat – just think of it, water all round! And sailors!'

'Judy!' But by now Ellen was smiling.

'Not any old sailors, *French* sailors!' said Judith, warming to her theme.

'Aren't they all Romanists?' asked Ellen. 'Charlie said that's what the French people are. Your father wouldn't like that much.'

With the mention of Harold they fell silent for a moment, but Judith was irrepressible.

'Not all!' she sang out. 'I went spying at the cathedral today. They have meetings – services, I mean – in French too, for the French Protestants. So some of them *are* saved. Maybe Providence has saved one specially for me!'

'Oh, *Judith*!'

'At least I've made you laugh, Mrs Chown! Now let's be stirring or my father will be home and nothing put right.'

*

By late afternoon Ellen had managed to unpack most of the boxes. Activity had momentarily helped her suppress her growing fear that life would forever after be defined by the limits of that humble Victorian brick and mortar.

'The house will do very well, Judy,' admitted Ellen, 'but having strangers through that wall,' she stretched out her right hand, 'and that one,' stretching out her left – the terraced house was only one room wide – 'makes me feel I'm in a crowd with people pressing in on me from all sides. I have to sit halfway up the staircase where I'm safely boxed in to get away from them. And all these houses look the same, and so straight and sharp at the angles. If they turned the corners of this room inside out I'm sure I should cut myself on them!'

'But there's water indoors, Ellen! There's a tap out there in the scullery and you turn it and out the water comes like magic – it's Moses striking the rock under our own roof! And gaslight! Let there be light!'

'Don't let your father hear you talk like that!'

'As if I would. But try to see it this way, Ellen: God provides, so let us be thankful. And you've paid your dues.'

'Harold is angry with me.'

'Oh Ellen, he's only unhappy.'

'He can't see why I couldn't keep his baby when I had no problem keeping Sam Loveridge's. It's easier for him to blame me than blame God.'

'Blame those beasts that tormented the baby out of you. Your grandfer does. But how much do you want another one?'

'I need to have one. It's not about *wanting* – at least not only, though I'd have loved the poor lost babe, of course I would. If I don't get another one, Harold will hate Tom. But if I do manage another one, I'd feel like I'd let *him* down.'

'Him?'

'Tom. Having less time for him, I mean,' said Ellen.

'Oh Gor, who'd be a woman! And you, Ellen, always worried about what you ought, not what you want!'

'If I'd had this other baby I'd have my hands too full to think of anything else.'

'Then get yourself another one, Ellen, and the sooner the better. I'll try not to think of you and Pa at it. And here was me thinking you could advise me how I am to get a man and not die of boredom and ... of wanting one. Oh well, must get on! At least there's less work to this house. My favourite is that privy. You've only to go out the back door and there it is on the end of the house, and the bricks inside all painted shiny. Now, how shall we organise things? Upstairs you and Father in the room at the back, with the little room beyond it for Tom, and me at the front so I can see the men going to the tannery of a morning?'

'You're a terror, Judith Chown!'

'Seriously, Ellen, I should be thanking you. I was going to die a thousand deaths of loneliness in that village with always the same faces to talk to, with everyone knowing if you so much as sneezed and how often you went to the privy – and the young men what were left shrugging their shoulders and making for London or Birmingham and me not allowed to go too ...'

'You could have gone before now, Judith. The missions are always in need of willing hands.'

'Yes, well, I *wasn't* willing! Not for the missions!'

'No, I suppose you weren't.' Ellen looked at her step-daughter standing there, hands on hips, dark bobbed hair coming out of curl, the red laughing mouth. What had Millie Chown been to produce such a girl? Harold was present in the line of her jaw and in the shape of her eyes, but some of the thoughts that lay behind those eyes would turn him pale if Judith had been foolish enough to let her father hear them.

'Will you look for work, Judy, once we're all settled?'

'Oh, not half! I wouldn't care if it was just accounts, like at Boddington's, just to get me out of the house a bit, even if Pa don't like me working. I'll see if they need anyone at the tannery. I think I could bear even the stink of the place for the company I'd have there.'

'I'll back you up. Your poor father does love you, though, Judy,' said Ellen.

Judith frowned. 'I know. But I know I'm a disappointment to him. Everything he does is just Christian duty to him. Even being married to you, Ellen, though I was the first person to see that he really was gone on you. But he'd rather the world thought he wanted to help a young widow than that he was beside himself with love.'

'What young widow?'

'That's what he wants to put about. You had a husband. An Italian stone-mason, apparently – he had an accident at work. Accounts for Tom's lovely dusky skin, you see. Stops the gossips.'

'So Sam never existed. What am I to tell Tom?'

'Cross that bridge when you have to.'

CHAPTER 19

I thought of the men I was leaving behind, of those men who had become my friends.

Wilfred Macartney, *Walls Have Mouths*

Freed

Winchester, May 1924

'Take your boots off, B2.26, and stand here.'

The screw was shorter than Sam, and had to stand on a box to bring the crossbar of the yardstick down on the top of his head.

'Five feet eleven,' the man sang out.

'Taller than most of his tribe,' commented the warder, who was sitting at the desk, filling in a chart.

'On the scales, prisoner ... Place your feet square ... Ten stone four! All right, get down, and take your shirt off. Hands on your head. What age are you?'

'I'm not rightly sure. Twenty-eight, p'raps.'

The man at the desk looked at him directly for the first time. 'You don't know how old you are? Well, what am I supposed to put here?'

'I don't know, sir. What about putting what it was a year ago, plus one?'

The man's eyes narrowed. 'Less of your lip.' Yet he quietly consulted the record and did as Sam suggested.

'Continue.'

'Black hair, slight curl, going grey at the temples. Skin swarthy. Eyes dark brown. Clean-shaven. Open your mouth, prisoner. Teeth look sound, far right incisor broken.'

A tape measure was passed loosely and rapidly round Sam's chest, then dropped to his waist.

'Forty . . . thirty-four.'

The clerk glanced up at Sam's thin frame. 'Really?'

'More or less.'

'All right. Corresponds to what he came in with. Scars?'

'Through left eyebrow, about one inch.'

'How sustained? Speak up, B2.26!'

'Lincoln.'

'Well, as long as it wasn't here. Any others, George?'

'Hallo! Back and shoulders full of them. Puss has been at him. But there are lots of older ones – not cat scars. Little white pits all over the place – fifteen, at least, or more like twenty. What's this then, prisoner?'

'Family argument, you med say.'

The screw whistled. 'Are you sure you don't want to stay in here?'

His colleague laughed. Sam said nothing.

*

'I'll miss you, Sam, more than I can say!'

'I'll miss you too, Cecil. I cannot remember a man who has shown me kindness like yours. Teaching an ignorant fellow to read.'

'The debt is on my side. You've helped me find meaning in my life. Before I came here, I never really considered who my fellow men were. This place is as much a leveller of men as death. I thought there were learned men, and ignorant ones – but I know now the ignorant ones are often the wiser. For me there were good men, and then there were felons – like pure women, and fallen ones. I can never say this to Beth, but had I not come here, I would never have found my calling. I wouldn't go back to the genteel boredom of a village rectory now even if they'd have me. I hope it won't be the malarial swamp, though. The chaplain says he will speak to the bishop when the time comes. Perhaps I could be useful in the East End.'

'Now that'd be twice as dangerous as the swamp, Cecil!'

'Write to me, Sam.'

'My writing ain't much good yet, as you know.'

'Not true. But if you like, I'll bring you the corrections later!'

'Ain't you cleared your cell yet, Loveridge? *Move yourself!*'

'I mun go.'

'Bless you, Sam! Promise me that I shall meet your Ellen one day!'

'She ain't my lawful wedded, Cecil. Nor can be.'

'Let God be your judge, not men.'

*

The cell was soon emptied of Sam's pitiful possessions: a prison-issue Bible he was allowed to keep, a pair of canvas slippers, several pages of painstaking exercises done for Cecil, and a regulation toothbrush. Sam had never owned one before, relying on apples to keep his teeth in his head. Now those teeth were clean, but felt loose. In a year he had not eaten any fresh fruit, nor vegetables other than those boiled to slush. By some perverse logic of the prison system, his last night was to be spent in a punishment cell.

P'raps it's to remind me not to come back. He descended the clanging stairs of B Hall for the last time.

*

After Sam had eaten his last prison breakfast the following morning, sitting on his blankets in the furnitureless, featureless cell, a screw stuck his head in and handed him a bedsheet.

'Strip, Loveridge, and wrap this round you.'

Oh dordi, *what now?*

Instead, he was instructed to walk out barefoot on the cold, waxed stone floor of the hall and into the neighbouring cell. Here he found a forlorn, limp pile of clothes, unmistakeably his own, but stale and crumpled, as though all the fight had been beaten out of them. He dressed slowly. His boots felt too big. Only his hat felt familiar. He picked up the small canvas bag containing his few belongings, and found the two shilling pieces he had had on him when he was arrested, along with an envelope containing some coins earned sewing mailbags and a further shilling from the Prisoners' Aid Society. But his writing exercises were gone. He was searching for them when the screw came back for him.

'No written materials to be taken out of the prison. Regulations,' said the man. 'Now just your photographs and you'll be out of here. We hope *not* to have the pleasure of your company again.'

'Thank you, sir. Just one question. Was there any letters for me?'

'Letters? No. Everything is in that bag.'

*

Two other men were released with Sam. He didn't know either; they were from other halls, and both were met, one by his mother, another by a bedraggled wife and four small children, whom he barely acknowledged despite their clamour. The light and the noise stunned Sam and he leaned back against the great door. He had counted weeks, days, then hours up to this point. He could now write a simple, if somewhat ungrammatical, letter, sign his name, and with some effort read straightforward notices, and whilst he could copy these exactly when they were in front of him, found that his memory did not always oblige when away from them. He had also learned some basic arithmetic, which he took to readily, enjoying the idea that there was always an answer, and one only. But that numeracy was also now a burden. It parcelled up the world for him. He could count the strokes of the prison bell and know what time it was, and what he was supposed to do when, and how long he had to do it in, none of which necessarily coincided with either how long the task in hand actually took, nor his desire to do it. And now he had time of his own. It crashed over him, as overwhelming as a tidal wave.

He looked at the flow of people, each one a world to himself: going to work, taking the baby for an airing, leading a horse. He saw with astonishment what he had not been able to see a year ago – that signs painted on the sides of carts, on the façade of the pub opposite, meant something. Words spoke to him as loudly and distractingly as noise – so many of them! How long would it take him to see the world normally again?

These togs smell like grave-clothes, they've been put away so long. He fidgeted. *Stop shivering! The sun's warm enough!*

He looked at the pub. A pint of ale, air thick with tobacco smoke – perhaps someone would oblige him with a cigarette? It looked like a simple enough place. He creaked his legs into a walk and set off towards it, then – '*Oi!*' – he had to jump back to avoid a brewer's dray. How could he have missed something so large? And had cart-horses got bigger since he'd been inside? He pushed open the door. The familiarity of the warm, beery fug that greeted him brought tears to his eyes. But there was no greeting in the landlady's face. She looked him up and down, took in his crumpled, ill-fitting clothes, the prison-patina of his skin, the little bag on his shoulder. She raised a hand from the bar and her forefinger ticked back and forth like a metronome. The three or four customers in the place watched him in bored curiosity as he backed out of the door and back into the merciless sunlight.

What now? Where now? He stood outside and watched the mass of people and carts. Instinct made him want to go where there were fewer of his fellow human beings to see him, but he knew that a man is less visible in a crowd, so he followed the drift of people until it led him into the town. He walked as in a daze, shambling, and was dimly aware that others stood back to avoid him, for the noise, the light, the colours still disorientated him. Finally, panting, he turned off the maze of streets into an alley and came on a little white-washed church with a patch of garden before it. The noise behind him diminished as though someone had closed a door. The door to the church, however, stood open.

They can't turn me out of here, can they? he thought. There had not been much to look at in the prison chapel; he had gone there to hear the words spoken in that gaunt place, and to follow the tracery of the windows, high and luminous, unlike the barred rectangle of light in his cell, but he had never been able to go there alone, or when he chose.

The space in this church was also light and airy, but some of the glass was coloured, and of such joyful brightness that it brought tears to his eyes for the second time that morning. Here was the scent of beeswax and incense, life-size benevolent plaster statues frozen in the act of blessing or of offering flowers, and best of all the silence of reflection, not fear. A rack of candles shimmered at a side altar, and three or four shawled women huddled separately in the pews. An upright wooden structure, as sombre as a coffin, yet hung with little red curtains like a *Punch and Judy* booth, stood against a side wall. For a moment Sam struggled to breathe; it looked exactly like the condemned pew in the prison chapel. He heard a bubble of childish laughter and a little girl in a gingham dress ran in below one of the curtains, followed by the clang of her father's nailed boots on the tiled floor.

'Don't strike the little maid,' he muttered under his breath. Some muffled giggles and the child was lifted out; he heard the slap of her sandals as she was placed upright. The man bent over her, his hand on her back. She looked up at him and took his hand. Sam saw them approach one of the candle racks, heard the clatter of a coin against metal, and watched the rapt face of the child as two candles were lit in front of her.

If I'd been a father it might all have been different.

He sat forward, his face in his hands.

Help me find my way back to her.

Someone scuffled in the pew behind him, and cleared his throat ostentatiously. Then a loud whisper: 'Sam!'

'*Vanlo!*'

'I'm supposed to be following you.'

'Well, you aren't now. How did you know it was today?'

'I remembered from the court. And then when I knew a year was almost up, I pestered any *gaujo* I could get a hold of to tell me what date it was.'

'You're a smart boy. I can't tell you how glad I am to see you again. You're quite the man now. You *rommered* yet?'

'No! Nor want to be.'

'All right, don't take on so. You're wise enough, anyroad. But why didn't you just come to meet me?'

'Lukey wanted to know where you'd go first.'

'Where is she now? Lukey, I mean.'

'That place. Surman's Wood.'

'*Dordi!* What's she about?'

'I'm not s'posed to have tole you that. Lukey wanted to see where you went first – if you looked for us or for the other lady. That's why they're in Surman's Wood. If you goes to that village, she'll know – she'll have catched you.'

'Well, I'm going to walk right into her trap, then ... Why do you look so pleased about it?'

Vanlo puffed out his meagre chest. 'I'd do the same, Sam.'

'Oh Vanlo, you shouldn't go looking up to me, *chavvi*,[23] 'twill only get you in trouble.'

'Again! You med say this is me gettin' another chance. See if I do right this time.'

'Have you seed her then? Did you stop in Surman's Wood last harvest?'

'No, I ain't seen the lady. We went up Banbury way instead, but the place wasn't so good. It was her that decided – Lukey, I mean.'

'All that time I was inside, Vanlo, I thought about being in the wood with her. But I med as well have been outside there in the street with the world watching us.'

One of the shawled women turned round and held her finger to her lips.

'So why *did* you keep quiet?' Sam went on, whispering now.

''Cause I never saw Lukey kiss you the way that maidy did. I'd not leave someone who liked me that much.'

---

[23] Boy

'Come on, then. We'll work out what to say on the way. I'll make sure you arrive after me – so they still think you've been following.'

'How was it, Sam? In there, I mean?'

'Horrible. But it wasn't so much being in there that was bad, as not being out here, if you see what I mean.'

*

'You know I can't take you on now, Sam, much as I'd wish it.'

Horwood rested his elbow on the back of the cart, and looked away.

'That's not why I came. It's Ellen Quainton I'm after. Could you at least tell me where she's gone?' said Sam. 'I made sure the old man was out of the way first, but then her mother shut the door in my face and told me from behind it to leave them all in peace, on her Christian soul.'

''Tis as well you didn't see Oliver. He's a peaceable man most times, but a stern one and a slave to his principles. And he's vowed to horsewhip you should you ever show your face round here again. I swear he was waiting for you to turn up last year.'

'I would have come, only I was prevented.'

'Prevented? Or were you 'fraid to come? You've caused a good family no end of trouble and shame, Sam.'

'*Who is that you're a talking to, Father?*'

'Reggie!'

'No, don't you go in there, Sam! He wept when you went away without a word, but he always talked fondly of you—'

'*Who is it? Will you not bring him here for me to see?*'

'Please go, Sam. He'll try and struggle out with his chair on his own in a moment. Don't raise his hopes again.'

'All right, I'll go. But thank you for talking to me, sir, when no one else will.'

Sam set off slowly along the dirt track away from Horwood's farm. He was almost at the road when he heard the thud of running feet behind him. He spun round, instinctively raising his fists, then lowered them at once on seeing it was Horwood.

'Sam – your wages. I never got to pay you last time.'

'No . . .'

'Come on, take 'em, you earned 'em. And for Reggie's sake I'll wish you well.'

'Then thank you. I'll take the money, for God knows I'll need it. But don't wish me well, wish all good on her, if you may.'

'Sam, I can't tell you where she is and I'm not sure I would if I did know. But she's wed, Sam.'

'*Wed?*'

'The husband took her as a favour, being a friend of her grandfer's and not far off the same age as her father would have been had he lived.'

'Who is he? Not Chown?'

'That's him. Any port in a storm, as you might say. Sam, you look as you've seen a ghost. Come back with me and take something – and speak to my poor boy after all.'

'I can't, I mun get back, an' have words with them that took me off, if they don't kill me first.'

'There's more, Sam. Ellen's had a baby boy. But outside the chapel they was so mocked that life here was impossible for them and they took themselves off.'

'A baby?' said Sam, white-lipped.

'I'm sorry, it didn't oughter been me to tell you so. Look, the only person as might be able to tell you more is Grace Lambourne. But I don't know as she'd welcome the sight of you.'

*

Sam trudged back past what had been Ellen's door, averting his face. He saw the cottage Horwood had described but paused at the little gate.

What you doing this for, Sam? She's wed, with a baby. Better if I'd never come round from that floggin'.

He was about to turn away when the cottage door opened. Grace was wiping her hands on her apron.

'Come in,' she said quietly, 'before them across the way sees you.'

*

Sam put his hat on the floor and took the cup of tea held out to him. Whilst Grace was in the little scullery he'd glanced round the room, taking in the plain beech furniture, the wall clock, the embroidered tract he could now read, the mantelpiece with the photograph of the young soldier in pride of place.

'That your Charlie?' he asked gently.

'Yes. How did you . . . ?'

'Ellen spoke of 'en. Often and often. I was at Arras too, Mrs Lambourne. Not that time – the second battle. With Remounts.'

'I've always wanted to go. Ellen and I . . .'

'Me too. To Verdun, I mean. My brother's there.'

Grace hesitated. 'Mr Loveridge, would you like to share my supper?'

*

They finished their simple meal with an apple each; Grace watched as Sam stripped his down to the core.

'You look as if you've not had one of those in a long time.'

'I haven't. Not where I've been.' He couldn't bring himself to say the word prison. 'I couldn't get back. I was ill – and then I was prevented, see.'

'You broke her heart all over again. Just like when she lost my poor son, only he couldn't help it.'

'I'm heartily sorry for your loss, lady. Believe me, though, that I never wanted to hurt her either,' he said, staring down at his plate. 'They've a baby, though – mebbe that'll make her happy.' He looked up at Grace's sharp intake of breath.

'What's the matter?'

'Tom's a handsome child, Mr Loveridge. Dark as a 'Talian.'

'Tom, you said?'

'That's right.'

'But she ain't dark. And nor's old Chown.'

'That's right too.'

Sam stared. 'When d'you say he was born?'

'I didn't. It was in the May. I don't remember the exact date.'

Sam scraped back his chair and stood up. 'Where are they? You got to tell me where they are!'

'I can't, Mr Loveridge! Only the Quaintons know. I would if I could, believe me. All I know is they've gone out of the county.'

'Don't cry, Mrs Lambourne,' said Sam, dropping on one knee in front of her, and taking her hands. 'I'll find them. Her and my son. However long it takes. And I'll remember your kindness to me as long as I live.'

*

His long stride took him quickly through the wood. It was just as he remembered it. *One of them times in this wood made me a father. But where on God's good earth are they?*

Finally Sam stood at the edge of the clearing, waiting to see who would look up first and notice he was there. *Liberty and Caley ain't here – that's a mercy, anyhow.*

Lucretia was crouched by the fire with her back to him, stirring the pot, talking to Caley's wife. Sam's dog Fred pulled on the string that tied him to the wheel of his and Lucretia's *vardo*, whickering. Opposite his wife his mother bent over the fire, feeding in twigs. Then she straightened up and looked directly at him, and her pipe slipped out of her mouth. Harmony Boswell wiped her hands down her skirts and, saying nothing, walked past the others and into his arms.

'Sam, my Sam!' she wept into his chest.

He stroked her head, looking over her to the group by the fire. All the faces in the encampment were turned towards him now. He smiled at Sibela, who had lengthened out, a shy young colt. Lucretia stood with her head on one side, hands on hips.

'Where've you bin all this time, then?'

Sam stared at her. It was as if the last year hadn't happened, and he'd merely been for a walk. *Oh, those walks!*

'You know well where I bin. Stir.'

'I know *that,* boy! But you've been out days.'

'I bin looking for work. There ain't any for me. Not here.'

'What do you mean, no work?'

'None of 'em would hardly speak to me, let alone give me work,' said Sam.

'Not even Horwood?'

'Civil enough, but said it was more than he could do.'

'So me and the other gals'll go *bikinin*[24] the pegs in the morning, whilst you sits here? That's how we're to live? 'Tis as well, Sam Loveridge, that you could put no child in me.'

Sam shouted, ''Tain't me! 'Tis you, Lukey, the cause of that misfortin, always was! So help me God, but I could raise a fist to you now, though I never have to any woman, whatever her provokin'!'

'You try it, Sam, just you try and see how my brothers serve you next! You've a short memory for how you left here!'

'I wunt be here at all only I can't leave Mother alone with you longer'n you've made me do already. An' I remember well enough what happened here – I've a fine *biti chavvi,* Lukey! She gev me a fine boy!'

Lucretia paled, but recovered quickly.

'What makes you think the *chavvi* is yourn, then? Your fine young lady mebbe makes a habit of showing her *minge* to other women's men in the woods!'

'A curse on your filthy mouth—'

Putting his mother to one side, he lunged towards Lukey, ignoring the tightening circle round them. Then at the sound of a whistle somewhere in the trees, the circle shattered as when a stone hits the surface of a pond.

'The *gavvers!*' The bobbing helmets of four constables came into view.

---

[24] Selling

'Out of here now!' bellowed the first of them, a shiny-faced man whose reddened neck flesh curled over his tight collar. 'Now, or you'll all be summonsed for trespass! Come on, hop it, look alive!'

'Please, sir, have pity on an old body who means no 'arm, and has been a coming here nigh on thirty years and never troubled no one,' cried Harmony, grasping his sleeve.

'Out of my way, old woman! And get this fire out before the trees catch alight!' Before anyone else had a chance to move, the policeman kicked over the fire and the kettle on its crane, sending hot sparks everywhere. Two of the smaller children who had been closest to the flames screamed and beat down their ragged clothing, more from fright than actual danger. The tethered dogs set up a universal howl, and the horses stamped and reared in response.

'This is your doing, Sam!' hissed Lucretia. 'I don't know where we'll find as good an *atchin' tan* as this. Nothing before Wycombe as we know of, and that twelve hard miles with the ridge in the way, and only an hour left of daylight!'

*

Deer Cecil,

I promised to send you news but it is not good at least not all. I wish I cud be back in the gaol and still wating as it would be better than nowing what I no. I got a baby boy on Ellen but she has wed an old man becos she never seed me to tell me and he has taken her away I doant no where to. I am back with my wife for I have no place to go tho I hate her for it near as much as I hate myself and I doant no how I should mannidge on my own for work is short and I must go with my wife's brothers where we are alreddy nown or starve or go back inside. In the hole world I have only my old mother and you if I hav lorst Ellen but Mother says I am not to despare for I will find her but I think she says this so I do not go mad. I went to her villadge but her mother shut the door agen me but a kind lady sed was she was gorn and wed with a dark baby but not where. Then the police was sent and we was turned off our stopping place so we are at Wycom it is not a good place. I have no plan for where I mun start looking but I will never stop looking.

I hav no adress for you to write to me but you shud not for they doant let you write when you want and you shud write to Beth not me. I hope they hole back my letter and gev you hers in sted.

Your friend Sampson Loveridge

CHAPTER 20

The Lord hath sought Him a man after His own heart.

Samuel 1:13–14

David

Canterbury, February 1925

'Easier this time, wasn't it?' said Judith.

Ellen stared down at the baby's crumpled face. 'Oh yes – in all ways, and worth waiting for. I shall learn to love him.'

'Ssh, silly. Of course you will! He's a dear little baby; how could you not love him?' said Judith.

'I'm afraid of him taking Tom's place. Tom has only me.'

'He has a sister too and I'll not hear different!'

'Dear Judy. Will you go for Harold?'

'I'll go now. I'll get the midwife another cup of tea and see if she'll stay a few minutes longer. If not, there's always next door.'

'Oh no!' Ellen sunk back into the pillows. 'Not old Clerk. I don't think I could cope with her just now.'

'I'll do my best.'

'Bring Tom up before you go.'

*

'Oh Tom! How big you are!'

It was true. Ellen marvelled at the toddler's sturdiness, his size and solidity against the frailty of the little bundle in her arms.

'My brother?'

'Yes, Tom. If you two are friends you'll never be lonely.'

'But your tummy was very big. He isn't,' said Tom sceptically.

'He'll grow. You did. Look at you now!'

'Did it hurt?'

'A bit.'

'Like doing big browns?'

'Yes, but not so smelly . . . Get up here properly so's I can cuddle you.'

'Are you going to have more babies?'

'Oh, I don't know. We'll need to ask Pa that.'

'Will Pa like this baby more than me?'

'Oh Tom! Of course not!'

'And what about you?' asked Tom.

'Me? Well, I'll love you more, Tom, because you'll be a big brother. Big brothers need love so they can love, you see.'

'He'll want my toys.'

'We'll get more toys for him. But some you can share.'

'I'll decide,' said Tom.

'All right. What if you help me choose the toys for him?'

'Yes. There's Pa coming up now.'

Harold loomed in the doorway, still wearing his overcoat, bringing with him the coldness of the day and a miasma of soot and yellowing paper. Tom scrambled off the bed and stood warily to one side.

'I've a brother,' he said.

'I've a son,' said Harold, looking at Ellen and the child. He stepped forward and sat heavily on the side of the bed.

'Oh Ellen, you have made me so awfully happy!'

Poor man, thought Ellen; her eyes moistened with pity.

'May I?'

She held out the bundle; the baby mewled and bubbled.

'David,' said Harold. 'The second son.'

*

'What's the matter, Ellen?'

'Would you pass me that Bible, Judy?'

'What do you want with that now?'

'Please!' said Ellen.

She riffled the pages, trying not to displace Harold's numerous markers. 'I used to be much quicker at this, Judy. I even won prizes.'

'Sunday school prizes! Books no child would want to read!'

Ellen found the text and read it to herself, her lips moving.

And when he had removed him, he raised up unto them David to be their king; to whom also he gave testimony, and said, I have found David the son of Jesse, a man after mine own heart, which shall fulfil all my will.

'Ellen, what is it?' said Judith. 'You're all pale. I'm going to bring you that stout like the midwife said, whatever Pa says. You need building up. And sit up a minute whilst I sort those pillows.'

'No, Judy, listen. Saul – the first born. His place is taken by his brother David.'

Judith stopped punishing the pillows.

'Don't, Ellen. I can't think he means it like that. And whatever *he* thinks, makes no difference to how I love Tom. Just don't take against the poor baby for it.'

*

Harold got up from the floor. Ellen had said her prayers kneeling up in the bed.

Standing looking down at her, he cleared his throat. 'I was thinking, Ellen, to do as we did before. I shall continue to sleep downstairs until—'

'Until I am fit again to receive you?'

'Vulgarity does not suit you!'

'It's what you mean, though, isn't it?'

'I don't know what I've done to annoy you so, Ellen, other than my continued existence. I had hoped, now that we have this child . . .' He tailed off, sitting down on the bed and reaching for her hand. She let it lie inert in his.

'Do I revolt you so much, Ellen?'

'No.'

'Did you think I never notice that when we embrace – as husband and wife must do – that you turn your face away whenever you think I want to kiss you? And you're angry with me. I came up this evening wanting to tell you, my dear, that today has made me the happiest I think I have ever been. Happier than the night Judith was born – though you must never tell her that. I thought – now that we have David – that our circle is complete. That we can live out our lives in peaceable companionship, do some good perhaps. I know that you do not love me, Ellen, and that you cannot be made to. It's enough for me to love you, even if I'm not very good at showing you I do. I suspect you'd like me no better if I were.'

'If you love me,' said Ellen energetically, 'then you must love my son too. I only took you for him!'

Harold flinched.

'Tom? I do. He's a fine little boy. A credit to you, and I hope, in some ways, to me.'

'But you'd put David above him. You'd remove him to make way for David.'

'What do you mean?'

'You should know. You're the preacher!'

'Do keep your voice down! Nobody's removing Tom.' And then the penny dropped. 'Oh Ellen, David was my father's name. That's all! And he *is* a second son – our second son.'

'He's waking up. I shall need to feed him.'

Harold stood up and lifted the baby from his crib, handing him to his mother, but he turned away as Ellen unbuttoned her nightdress.

'You can choose some other name, if you prefer,' he said.

'No. I'm sorry I lashed out.'

'Why did you choose Tom? I've never asked you.'

'Sam's grandfather.'

'Oh God . . . I never knew the man's name.'

'Sampson, not Samuel.'

'Sampson. Please, Ellen, do not mention him again.'

'I won't. But it doesn't matter now, Harold. He never knew about Tom. The man means nothing to me, and he hasn't for a long time.'

*

'Oh Mother, I wanted you here!'

'Why? I wasn't much use to you the first time.'

Ellen brushed this aside. 'It's usual, isn't it, for a girl to want her mother? It wasn't so bad, you know . . . Quicker . . .

though David was bigger. And Judy was here all the time, so I think he came faster for all the laughing.'

'Have the chapel people been good?' asked Flora.

'Oh yes. They've been most generous. Harold is very respected here, you know. I sit below the rostrum now. He's kept very busy on the circuit. He's away half the Sundays in the month. And Mr Deakin – the solicitor – says he can't do without him.'

'Are you happy, Ellen?'

'Happy? You've asked me that before. Why shouldn't I be?'

'Well, I hope you are. Now that everything has worked out so well.'

'I suppose it has.'

'But you look so sad.'

'Oh Mother . . . I shall live – for my babies, I mean.'

Flora leaned forward to take her daughter's hand, and something crinkled in her pocket.

'What's that?'

'Oh, only a letter I've forgotten to post, dear.'

'It'll be very crumpled. I hope it's nothing important.'

'No – not important at all.'

CHAPTER 21

The rustic dwellers in our villages, as well as the inhabitants of the large towns and cities, are better able to appreciate the truths of the gospel when they are presented decently and in order, and accompanied with the gifts and graces of a cultivated mind, than when they are flung pell-mell from the voluble mouths of ignorant and totally unlettered men.

Primitive Methodist Magazine, 1871

John

'Oh, John! It's been far too long.'

Ellen embraced her brother.

'Look at you, sis!' He held her at arm's length.

'I'm respectable, John. That's what I am, if nothing else.'

'Oh Ellen . . .'

'Never mind me. What's your news? It must be important if you've come all the way to Canterbury to tell me. And look how smart you are! You've filled out nicely, little brother.'

'I am to be married.'

'John!'

'But not just yet. I've other news. I've got through my probation and I've been accepted for training for the ministry. I'll be going to Hartley.'

'But that's in *Manchester*!'

'I know. It'll be a long haul, but the connexion has been generous. I won't even have to pay half the fees as most men must. It'll be tough for Amy – my fiancée – more than it will be for me; I'll be too busy to think.'

'Grandfer must be pleased.'

'I'm not sure that he is. I think he feels that education and evangelism get in each other's way, that it's what a man feels more than what he knows that counts. I wonder sometimes if he really knows the difference between a banner from Mr Arch's union and one for the Band of Hope. Whatever helps the working man is God's work.'

'Isn't it? What about George Edwards? Peter Lee? They preach, and stick up for the poor man's rights.'

'And well. That is their mission. Mine's more like Dr Peake's. We must know our religion to bring its riches to the people. We're not a sect of ranters anymore. You know things have changed. Don't tell me you don't feel a bit uncomfortable when the older people shout out at services?'

'Of course, though I'd never admit it,' said Ellen. 'I envy them a bit, if the truth be known. They're the ones who come all pink and shaky to get their tea after the service. They've seen something, felt something, sitting in that chapel. I don't feel anything. I live a lie, John.'

'But you do so much good work there.'

'Do I?' She looked at him wildly. 'Sometimes I think if I were not busy – not just with the children, I mean with tea meetings, soup-kitchens, Sunday school – I should go quite mad. I resent it all – no, not all, not the Sunday school. But I do none of this for the right reasons. I do it for me, not them.'

'I think you are too hard on yourself,' said John. 'You always have been. Whoever you have done good for, regardless of what was in your heart when you did it, will have been glad of it.'

'I'm a lost cause. But that's enough about me. I'm forgetting your news entirely – tell me about Amy, John!'

'You'd love her. We must do everything to make sure you are truly sisters. I can think of no one better suited to be my help-mate in the life I've chosen – though of course that's not the real reason I'm marrying her.'

'I should hope not, John. You ought to be hopelessly, ridiculously in love with her.'

'I am!'

'So how did you meet her?'

'Through the connexion, of course. She teaches Sunday school, just like you. But not only that, she's a school-teacher.'

'Oh!'

'Ellen, I wish things had gone differently.'

'But they didn't. Don't think that I'm jealous of Amy's fortune, John, for I'm not. I am happy for you – and she's a lucky girl. Go on, then, show me her photograph.'

Amy Kernick was a dark, unostentatious girl of about twenty-one, her photograph taken hatless, in three-quarter view. There was nothing remarkable about any of her individual features, but the straight nose, the clear forehead, the kind eyes came together to give an impression of indomitable patience, and reassurance. Her neck was bare; she wore a plain linen blouse, and no jewellery.

'She's beautiful,' murmured Ellen.

'Oh, she is, you know! But most people wouldn't see it, though I'd expected you would. They'd see it more in her movements, perhaps, and her voice.'

'She's right for you, John. You're lucky too.' Ellen leaned forward, resting her forehead on her brother's shirtfront, and started to cry.

'Oh Ellen, I was afraid of this!'

She sobbed uncontrollably.

'I shall be three years in Manchester,' he said. 'And when I marry at last money will be tight, for we won't have Amy's salary anymore. But could you and the boys not come to us then?'

As suddenly as the turning down of a gas lamp, Ellen stopped crying.

'No. Absolutely not. If you and Amy are to be happy you must live your own lives. You'll have a new ministry, a family, probably, and then a sister with a spotty history turns up with two children that the world can see aren't properly brothers. Don't even dream of it.' But as she said this, in the depths of Ellen's thoughts a heavy iron door clanged to, and keys clunked in the lock, once, twice over.

'Is Harold good to you, Ellen?'

'Oh, he's *good,* certainly. He provides for me and the boys. He's even-handed with them, which most men wouldn't be, I'm sure. I wish sometimes he would ill-treat me, like poor Mrs Figg – you remember. Then I'd have some justification for how I feel about him.'

'You can't mean that.'

'No – of course I don't. No child should see his mother struck. I'm respected here; I don't know if I'm liked. I have a name. But, oh, I hate it when he comes near me. I hate the sound of his voice when he's being solicitous. I hate the way he rolls up his napkin after eating, the way he places his fingers when he's holding his fork. I hate the way he puts on his cuff-links, and the way he breathes when he's brushing his hair. I wish – oh, I wish sometimes he was dead, John, God help me! Or that I was – if it weren't for the boys, and if it weren't for Judy. She's a lifesaver.'

'Oh Ellen! Does that man—'

'Tom's father? Never heard from him again. A pebble thrown in a pond. He broke my heart, John, so I couldn't love Harold if I tried – and I have tried, believe me. That man could have charmed the birds out of the trees. Couldn't read or write but what a way with words! He's probably doing the same, right now, to some other poor girl. I hate him, John, and all his kind. Thieves, parasites, shirkers . . .'

'That's not you speaking, Ellen. Hate *him*, then. Hate the cad. Even your Mr Lee is part-Gypsy, they say.'

'One day I'll have to tell Tom. How can I tell him his father is worthless?'

CHAPTER 22

. . . my brother had fallen into the water and the poor Gipsies had got him out and had started to dry him and give him a hot drink. But my cousin had mistaken what they were doing and thought they were taking him away as the Gipsies got the blame for things like that.

R. Vaughan, hopper, Hilary Heffernan, *Voices of Kent Hop Pickers*

The King's Mile

Canterbury, October 1926

Ellen had one last errand, to the ironmonger's at St Dunstans. But passing under Westgate Tower with the children in tow she encountered waiting crowds three deep either side of the road, and two constables walking expectantly up and down between.

'What is everyone waiting for?' she asked a middle-aged woman with her shopping basket resting on her feet.

'It's the tinkers,' said the woman. 'They have their parade here when they've finished in the hop fields. They come down the hill and then go out to the watermeadows, where they'll build their fires and drink with the circus people. You could get your fortune told, dearie, if you're so minded. Mind you, looks like you know where your life is going, seeing as you've already your family. You've no need of tall dark strangers at any rate! Lovely children you have, though you'd never think they were brothers, would you?'

'He *is* my brother!' interjected Tom, fiercely.

'*Tom!* Don't be so rude to the lady!'

'He's not rude, dearie, bless him!'

'You're right in a way, though,' said Ellen. 'I was a widow and then I remarried. So I have one boy from each husband.' She now barely felt a twinge of conscience, for she had repeated this lie so many times. She thought if she said it any more she would start to believe it, and think of the light through the trees dappling Sam's skin not as a memory but as a dream. Nevertheless, she felt her heart beat faster as the wagons came into sight, rolling down from the junction. She stared at the couple on the first *vardo* to pass her. The man held the reins limply, letting the big shire find his way forward, unfazed by the closeness of the people gathered on both pavements to watch their progress. Ellen stared at him, trying to see Sam, but the Gypsy was a stranger.

'Just a word of warning, dearie,' murmured the woman, nudging her arm, 'they are fine to look at but as thieving as the day is long. And they'd go for you, they always do like the innocent-looking ones, and that's what you are, for sure. So make sure your purse is well out of reach of their prying fingers! 'Tis the children are the worst, I believe, for they train 'em up to it early.'

'Indeed,' replied Ellen, absently, then looked at her own children, one either side of her, in their lovingly mended and pressed cotton shirts, short trousers, lisle socks and carefully polished lace-up shoes. Both were transfixed by the noise and the spectacle, Tom trembling with excitement, his little brother open-mouthed with awe. A second caravan was rolling past, this one with a gaggle of children peeping past the couple who held the reins. Then a third – *no, surely not – it's only that hat.* She felt herself swaying, as though the ground beneath her was shifting, and then the man's face turned towards her. She saw his eyes widen, his mouth open, and she cried out, grasping the woman's arm to stop herself falling.

'Are you all right? You're as pale as a sheet!' The commotion sent a shudder through the crowd.

'I'm sorry, I didn't mean to startle you,' babbled Ellen. 'The heat, you know, odd for this time of year . . . We really must go!'

'Well, if you're sure . . .'

'Boys, come *along*!'

'But *Mother*!'

Head down as though against a strong wind, Ellen pulled the protesting children along. Tom dragged against her hand, demanding to know why, grizzling that it 'wasn't fair'. Poor toddling David stumbled, and she pulled him up sharply, too sharply. He started to cry.

'*Quiet!*' Ellen caught the note of hysteria in her voice. People were staring, but then their attention was drawn away to something going on behind her – a horse's protesting neigh, a woman's shrill curse, shouts.

'Down here,' she commanded the children, and pulled them into a sidestreet.

'Mother! That man is calling you!' Tom tugged at her hand.

'Take no notice!' she cried.

'*Ellen!*'

She let go of the children's hands, so abruptly that little David staggered. The man ran towards her.

'Ellen, at least look at me!' said Sam.

'Not here.' She didn't raise her eyes, speaking instead to the gleam of sweat on his collar-bone. Her heart felt as though it crouched at the base of her throat, making it harder to breathe.

'Boys! See that shop on the corner? Here.' She fumbled in her bag. 'Go in there and buy yourselves some sweets, as many as you want and can pay for. I'll be with you directly. Go *on!*'

Tom stared at her in astonishment.

'Ellen, wait . . .' Sam's hand hovered uncertainly over Tom's head.

'Go, boys! Please!' She was frantic.

Finally it was David who pulled his brother away. 'Thweets, Tom!' They went.

She looked up at him at last. 'What do *you* want?'

'What I've been looking for, all this time. You.'

'*You* looking for me? What a nerve!'

How beautiful he was, and how sad! The face was leaner than she had remembered it, the eyes darker, etched round with tiny wrinkles, faint creases of disappointment running from his nose to the corners of his mouth. To her horror she realised that she was crying. He pulled out a clean white handkerchief and gently, gently dried her tears, but at his touch she lost all command of herself and struck him in the chest with both fists.

'You ask me that?' he said, grasping her wrists. 'If you hadn't shifted in that crowd I might never have seen you today. The horse noticed something – they do, you know, – and turned his head, so of course I looked too. I might have passed by and never known you was there, looking at me.'

'Sam, let go of me! I can't be seen talking to you!' She made as though to follow the children, but though he let go of her wrists he put a restraining hand on her arm.

'I *have* been looking for you someways all this time! I wrote to you – the second time all by myself!'

Brisk nailed boots rang out their approach on the cobbles.

'Hey, you, Gypsy fellow! What are you doing bothering this young lady? Your fairground tent is that way, so shift and get down there now before I think of something better to do with you!'

'Oh, Constable, what excellent timing. Yes, these people are a bit of a nuisance.'

'*Ellen!*'

'Go on, I said hoppit, you!' said the policeman. 'Unless you want to be taken in charge. And take that hat off when I'm talking to you.'

Humbly, Sam did so, revealing hair shorter than Ellen remembered, its gloss dulled, touched with grey at the temples. She felt a tiny stab of pity, and of shame, aware suddenly of her own dowdiness, the limp cotton blouse, the sensible shoes and stockings too heavy for this weather.

The policeman turned to Ellen. 'I'm sorry you've had this trouble, and if you want to make a complaint – oh, it's Mrs Chown, isn't it? I recognise you from the chapel . . . Now push off, will you, or I'll put you in chokey, and that's my last word on the matter!'

'I'll find you, Ellen, I promise!' Sam walked off slowly in the direction the boys had taken.

'Gor, that one's persistent, ain't he?' said the policeman. ''Ow does he know your name, then?'

'Oh . . . he came to my village – where I lived before, I mean. I suppose there's no harm in him, really – he just presumed on a childhood friendship, that's all.'

'Presumed a bit much then, for you to have to take your fists to 'im. Are you sure you don't want me to take 'im in?' The policeman looked back up the lane to where Sam now appeared to be looking in the window of the sweet shop. The boys erupted out of the door, waving their purchases in small paper bags. Sam made a move as though to speak to them but saw the policeman eyeing him.

Tom took David's hand and half-dragged him back to Ellen. The Gypsy was already forgotten; they had a policeman's uniform to investigate now. As its owner was explaining his whistle and notebook to them, Ellen saw Sam wave at her once and turn the corner out of sight. She had to fight down the urge to run after him.

'Well, I'd best be off, Mrs Chown . . . boys. I'll see you on Sunday probably.'

The policeman touched his fingers to his helmet respectfully, and walked off. Ellen stood there breathless, as though she had been running.

'Come on, boys, let's go home. Best not tell Pa about the sweets.'

Tom shrugged. 'He won't ask,' he said, as though he were a much older child.

Best not tell them not to mention Sam – makes too much of it. And if they do, I'll just say it was someone else, not him. But what if he has *been looking for me all this time?*

*

Judith practically skipped home from the tannery, bursting with news for Ellen. But outside their front door, she paused, listening. Ellen was pounding the keys of Millie's piano. As Judy's key turned in the lock, the music stopped dead.

'Lor, Ellen, it's a pianner, not a runaway horse! You don't have to murder the poor hymns!'

Ellen turned round on the piano stool.

'Oh God, whatever is the matter?'

'Oh Judy!' Ellen held out her arms.

'Ssh!' said Judy, holding her. 'It's all right – whatever it is. Judy's here now. Where are the boys?'

'Playing upstairs. I've not even started tea, and your father'll be here any minute!'

'Never mind that. Come upstairs and lie down. I'll tell him you're poorly and afterwards you'll tell me everything.'

*

Later, Ellen asked: 'What did you tell Harold?'

'Women's problems. That shut him up. But you can't stop Tom talking, though. Sweets and Gypsies and policemen.'

'Oh, Judy, he says he's been looking for me! He sent letters . . .'

'What letters? Thought you said he couldn't write.'

'Could I have got him wrong, all of this time? Oh, I didn't need this . . . I thought I'd buried it all as deep as poor Charlie.'

'Instead you want him with every nerve in your body, don't you, Ellen? You remember every word, every look, can't get enough of the smell of his skin. And there's no one else in the whole world who can make you feel the way he does.'

Ellen sat up. 'You're in love yourself!'

'I am! Mind you, he smells better after a good scrub. He's a tanner, my Walter.'

'Oh Judy!' They clung to each other, weeping and laughing.

Hearing the noise, Harold called up the stairs: 'Everything all right up there?'

'When can I meet him?' whispered Ellen.

'Soon. We shall want your help, maybe. But I'm not going to let you meet him until you've written to Flora about those letters . . . Stop shaking, Ellen, and let's go down now, or Pa will think we're plotting.'

'We are.'

*

Dear Cecil,

Mother was rite I would find her agin for I have seed her today at Canterbury and my son to he is a fine looking lad and another littel boy she have of her husband only a policeman came and sent me packing. You were rite she did not get my letters. I made her cry which I dunt want to but maybe this is a good thing as she at least thinks something of me which even if not good is better than nothing at all. She is bewtiful but mortal sad my pore girl. I am sorry my riting is not good.

Your friend Sampson Loveridge

*

Dear Mother,

I hope you and Grandfer are both in good health, as all of us are here. Tom looks as though he will be tall . . .

Ellen nearly wrote 'like his father' . . .

He is up past my waist. David talks a lot now, though he still has a lisp, but everyone tells me he will grow out of it. He has had the whooping cough, which was an anxious time, but is now out of danger and is not a risk to anyone else, though he still coughs occasionally, but the doctor says that is the illness working its way out. He gave me medicine for him but I also gave him coltsfoot and thyme tea as you'll remember it did so much good to Mrs Hempton's Joan. Forgive me for not telling you but I did not want you to be alarmed and would have sent a telegram had the danger been greater but praise the Lord it was not.

We have had a very successful cake day for the Chapel Aid Association and Judy has also agreed to sing in Iolanthe in aid of the great work done in Fernando Po but I do not know what part. She sings loudly when she wants to, as you know, but I think does not like to be told she might be more tuneful. I believe I told you we have two young men from the congregation going for training in Hartley; I have written to John that he may make them welcome.

Please give my love to Grace Lambourne when you see her next and to all who remember me with kindness and tell them I will never forget them.

Your loving daughter,

Ellen

With this letter Ellen enclosed a smaller piece of paper folded over many times. She experimented with different ways of putting both into the envelope, envisaging the folded paper falling out in front of Oliver.

Mother, I have lately discovered that letters have been sent to me that have not been forwarded. I can guess why this is but I am sure you will agree that it is wrong to withhold them and perhaps not legal. If you know about them tell me, and if you have them forward them as soon as you can for they are mine.

Ellen had no idea whether keeping letters back did amount to a crime, but she knew enough about her mother to know that 'perhaps not legal' was enough to frighten her into action. *Poor soul – but I must know if he is telling the truth.*

*

Three days later Sam was doing what he had once enjoyed most in life: sitting atop the steps of his own *vardo,* holding the reins lightly and watching the breeze lift the horse's mane. Lucretia sat beside him as she had all their married life, but stiff and silent. When she had first joined him on his *vardo* she had chattered ceaselessly about the people they had met at their last *atchin tan,* or the sales that she had made at the houses – which *gauje* ladies had driven a hard bargain, and who had been gullible. Her wit had made him laugh to begin with, but after a while it wore him down – there was no kindness in it.

Now he could hear uninterrupted the sound he loved, the regular clop of hooves, and feel beneath him the swaying rhythm of their progress, following the gentle list left and right of Liberty's wagon as it moved on in front of him against the sweep of blue Kentish sky. Caley's wagon followed Sam's, as if the brothers needed to keep him hemmed in. *Not much risk of me making a break for it, with her alongside me*, he thought. But these familiar sensations didn't comfort him as they once had. Every pace of the horse took him away from where he most wanted to be, he who had never wanted to stop in one place for longer than the task in hand.

'Canterbury,' he murmured.

'What's that you're muttering?' asked Lukey. 'Can't hear you, Sam, you miserable *mush*. Face as long as a coffin, you have!'

'Nothing, Lukey, nothing you'd care about.'

'It's the old gel you're worryin' about, ain't it, Sam?' she said in a more conciliatory tone. 'We'll get her a *drabengro*[25] at Maidstone if you like.'

'No *drabengro*. Ma knows what she's doing – knows herself best.'

*

'We've to meet him at the bandstand,' said Judith. She and Ellen were walking along the avenue of lime trees in Dane John Gardens. The boys had already veered off onto the grass, where they kicked up drifts of fallen leaves and took possession of the space like birds freed from a cage.

'What is it, Ellen? You look all wobbly.'

'It's just that this is a lovely thing to do, Judy – a girl to meet her young man in the park on a Saturday afternoon. No need to worry about who might see you. Just to walk under these trees in autumn and be glad you're both alive!'

---

[25] Doctor or apothecary; *drab* can mean medicine, or poison.

'He's found you, Ellen. He's sure to be back. Oh look – there's Walter!'

A man strode across the grass towards them. Ellen saw a broad face, eyes spaced far enough apart to give him a candid look, a slightly snub nose and a mouth that seemed perpetually amused. He smiled, revealing clean, crooked teeth. Walter was sturdily built and scrubbed; he wore a Sunday suit, with a fresh collar on a shirt that had seen a little too much blue-bag, and he smelled of tar soap, which didn't quite mask an insistent whiff of sour animal fat. Ellen thought him not handsome, but attractive, vivid.

'Walter Graves,' he said, putting out his hand to Ellen. 'You don't look much like a wicked stepmother to me, if I may say so! I hope you'll excuse me a moment.' And, releasing Ellen's hand from his reassuring grip, he slipped an arm round Judy's waist and kissed her neck. She giggled and pretended to push him away.

Ellen felt suddenly much older, overwhelmed by their exuberance – dull Harold's wife, not the girl who had cried out in Sam's arms in Surman's Wood.

'Boys!' called Judy. 'Come and say hello to Walter!'

Tom and David had given up on the leaves and were shrieking their way round the Boer War memorial, but without slowing up they veered and ran towards the little group, faces uplifted, shining. Ellen began to relax at last. *Their dear little coats . . . and those chubby knees!*

Walter ruffled Tom's hair. 'You're a fine young shaver! Heard all about you! And this little fellow must be David . . . want to come with us for pop and buns?'

*

'I like him, Judith,' said Ellen as they began to walk home, the boys tired out by fresh air and ginger beer. 'I think he's just right for you.'

'I knew it was him, Ellen, from the first time he came into the office for his pay and he looked over the counter to where my place is and asked Miss Edwards what my name was, but so's I could hear him. Pa won't like him, I'm sure of it. A man who works with his hands, enjoys the odd smoke. Lives with his mother – a char. But I did want him to meet you. Good with the boys, ain't he?'

'Yes. I think they don't get enough fun with just us, Judith.'

'Well, I'm glad you like him. I hoped you would, not least because I want you to help us.'

'How?'

'Oh, just tell the odd fib about where I am – should you be asked, of course.'

'I don't find lies easy, not even little ones, Judy. But if someone *does* come back again—'

'You'll need to get used to them. He'll come back all right. Our secret, Ellen.'

'Our secret, Judy.'

'The boys, though . . .'

'About Walter?' said Ellen. 'We'll just say we met friends from the tannery. That'd be true. But you know Harold doesn't ask them much. As long as they are neat and clean, and have good table manners, and say their prayers . . .'

'I expect you're right. I used to get away with murder because he'd never think to ask what I was up to. Oh Ellen . . . look at that South African obelisk.'

'What about it?'

'Doesn't it remind you of anything – a man's thing?'

'Oh *Judy*!'

CHAPTER 23

The community whose operations penetrate most deeply through the lower sections of the people is the body called Primitive Methodists ... their rough, informal energy is best adapted to the class to which it is addressed ... for every convert added to their ranks, society retains one criminal, one drunkard, one improvident, less.

Horace Mann, Census of
Religious Worship, 1851

The Borough Chapel

Canterbury, November 1926

That Sunday, Harold led his family to one of the forms placed sideways to the rostrum.

'Why are we sitting up here, Harold?' Ellen whispered.

'You know. They've made me Treasurer. It's an honour.'

'Aren't we equal before God?'

Harold sighed. 'Must you find fault with everything I do?'

'It's not that. I just don't like everyone being able to see me, that's all.'

'I confess, Ellen, it is a source of pride to me that they *do* see you.'

Ellen shut her eyes.

The chapel was full, for a circuit preacher of some notoriety was due to speak. He took as his subject the Lord's undying forgiveness, but a forgiveness that was both merciful and uncompromising. He looked like quite an ordinary man, perhaps a book-keeper or a bank clerk, with his fussy little moustache and neatly side-parted hair. He wore a dark suit, shiny with ten years' use, a plain woollen tie, and a wing collar that would not sit symmetrically. But in spite of his unprepossessing appearance, Mr Ellis was a gifted orator, with a voice that rolled over them and carried his audience as though on a wave.

'And John tells us that "the scribes and Pharisees brought unto him a woman taken in adultery" – taken how, brothers and sisters? We must imagine this wretched sinner dragged naked into the public square! "They say unto him, Master, this woman was taken in adultery, in the very act." Did they seek her, knowing what they should find? Did she sin beneath the sky, like the beasts of the fields? And what did the author of her shame do? Run from her, abandoning her to her fate? For the Pharisees knew the law of Moses, that such as she should be stoned to death – and her partner in sin, though he had fled to leave her to face her merciless judges alone.'

Tom sat on Ellen's left, his thoughts far from the sermon, out on a field in Harbledown with a kite. Little David leaned into her right; by the weight of him she knew he would soon be asleep. David's father sat the other side of his son, but now he reached a large soft hand across the boy and patted Ellen's clenched hands. She felt his gaze on her, but refused to look his way. She wanted to cry out against him for his kindness, for she revolted against him with every cell of her body.

*

Later, standing behind the tea-urn, Ellen hated herself for the impatience she felt with these people dressed in their creaking Sunday best, their hair smoothed down with soap and water to make immobile caps round their heads, their collars starched and their clothing smelling of camphor and fusty presses. But as always, she made the effort to smile, telling herself that this was the high point of their week and she had no right to despise them for it, though if she could have done she would have walked swiftly out of the hall and into the open air, to walk until the houses petered out amongst the fields, to muddy her good shoes above Harbledown, to strike out towards Whitstable, or simply to sink into the woods at Blean. Who knew what she might stumble upon there if she looked long enough.

'Are you all right, Mrs Chown?'

Ellen looked sideways at Miss Sole, who'd paused in her self-appointed work of laying out the cups and saucers in neat rows. There was concern in the little puckered face, but curiosity also in her glossy black eyes.

'Yes, indeed, I am very well. Just a little distracted, you know, thinking about what the boys have been up to,' she gabbled.

'Oh, it's just when you laughed like that . . .'

'What a splendid job you've made of those crocks, Miss Sole. Makes my task so much easier.'

'Thank you, my dear. Whatever little I may do, you know . . .'

Ellen continued to mechanically slip milk into the empty cups and to follow up with the dark orange brew of tea, murmuring her acknowledgement of the polite thanks of the people who queued up for it. No one else but Miss Sole had apparently heard her unconscious laughter, for the conversation in the room was animated and noisy. So Ellen sensed rather than heard that she was being discussed. A momentary lull in the dignified press against the tea table gave her an uninterrupted view across the room to where Harold was talking with the visiting preacher. Her husband was flushed, proud and unusually lively, his hand frequently touching the other man's arm for emphasis, or to prevent him from leaving. But something in what he said had grasped the preacher's attention. His head inclined closer to Harold's, and a moment later he turned and looked straight at Ellen with some interest – and then looked her swiftly up and down, taking in as much as he could of what was not obscured by the table and the tea-urn.

'Miss Sole, would you mind taking over for a moment?' said Ellen. 'I think I need some air.'

'Oh, but I'd better come with you. Let me just get Enid to help—'

'No – please – I shall be quite all right. Judith is sure to be outside.'

Judith was. She leaned sulkily against a shop window a few yards down, smoking a rebellious cigarette.

'Blimey, Ellen, you look like you've seen a ghost. Sam wasn't in there, was he?'

'Oh Judith, your name is tact! No, of course he wasn't. But Harold is, and he's telling that preacher all about me!'

Judith dropped her cigarette and ground it out without looking.

'Go on! As if he'd dare!'

'I'm sure of it. He couldn't resist it, not after that sermon. All that bit about the man leaving the adulteress to face the music alone—'

'Sam hasn't, though. He said he'd be back.'

'I'll believe that when I see it,' exclaimed Ellen, on the verge of tears with anger and humiliation. 'I can barely think about Sam now, for being so angry with Harold. That man stared at me, Judith, and there was no man-of-God in his look either. I wonder how long it's going to be before he finds he's got to tell other people of my misfortunes just so he can show them how God moves his wonders to perform! Judy, would you go in and get the boys from the playroom and let's go home? Promise them anything to make them come quickly – I'll take them to see the cattle auction Saturday morning, they always like that.'

'What'll I say to Pa?'

'I don't care what you say to him but I won't go back in there.'

CHAPTER 24

'Have you got the old gipsy blood in your veins?' I asked the other day of a gang I met on their way to Quenington feast. 'Always gipsies, ever since we can remember,' was the reply. 'Fathers, grandfathers were just the same – always living in the open air, winter and summer, and always moving about with the vans.'

Joseph Arthur Gibbs, *A Cotswold Village*

Outcast

Medway

In a hastily erected tent in a copse near Maidstone, Sam crouched beside his mother.

'*So's mandy to ker, daiya, to ker tutti feder?*'[26]

'*It is my Duvel's kerrimus, and we can't ker kantch.*[27] I s'll stay here now, boy. No, I'll not go in the wagon. I was born

---

[26] 'What must I do, mother, to make you well?'

[27] 'It is my God's doing, and we can't help that.'

in a bender and I'll die in one. Now, all I'll want here is a bit of carpet to lie on, and my best togs. Don't worry about my shoes – they'll be good for someone after. You go get my bits and pieces, and then when I'm ready sit with me. There are things I want to say to you. Don't let the others near me. And don't forget a candle for my head.'

*

'My pipe.'

'Here, Mother. I'll light it for you.'

'You won't! I'm not dead yet! I shall want it by me – something your father made to take with me. Baccy always tasted better to me in wood, not clay. Tell Jenner to put it in my right hand. He was good with his hands, your father, better'n he was with the horses. You've got that gift from my side.'

'How do you know it's now, Mother?'

'How do I know I'm going? I know. The money is here for the laying out of me,' and coins chinked in a pocket. 'Go to Otham with it, and go to Jenner's cottage. He'll be expecting you, though he didn't believe it when I tole him. I gev his lady something for the rheumaticks. And ask him to see the sexton for a place for me, as close to the hedge as can be managed. Then I want you to promise me something. Come closer . . .' she whispered. 'I don't want any of 'em Bucklands hearin'. I should've said this long since, best child of mine. I could never have said it when your father lived. I think you mun *go*, Sam,' she said fiercely.

'*Go?*'

'Ssh! You're all I've left since my Miselda took off. I don't know where she is nor how she does, but I think of her every day and hope she's happy. I'll die and my own daughter not know she was all this time in my heart. And your *biti tickner* the *gauji* girl have gev you – I'll not see his face either but in my dreams.'

'He's handsome, Mother, handsome and brave.'

'And I've seen you thinking of him and his mother all this time. My own child, the only one I have left, the saddest man on earth! This life ain't going to last as it is – them cars and tractors and whatnot will push us off the roads, I can see it. But it's me that has kept you from her. You could have gone straight back there when you was better. Then them lot put you in the gaol, and who is to know they won't do it again? What is there for you here? Promise me you'll go, for I want to go to my rest knowing I don't leave you with them as don't love you. Lukey and them others made you pay hard enough for what you done, in front of me, so there'll be nothing will stop them doing whatever they want when I'm *mulo*[28] . . . Don't look at me that way, Sam. I'm only sorry to leave Lukey the *vardo* your father gev you, but it can't be helped, and you mustn't be there

---

[28] Dead

when they *yag*[29] it. Take your cup and plate, and then when she finds they're gone, she'll know and you won't have to tell 'er anything. I never thought I'd say this, Sam, but I don't see another way.'

'You want me to leave the road, Mother?'

'I've wanted that ever since they *ladged*[30] you.'

'They'd say I *ladged* Lukey, Mother, and they'd be right.'

'Maybe so, but it's her pride you hurt, not her love. That one don't love you nor has for a long while. But the *biti gauji rakli* does, and has your child, and that's good enough for me for I'm your mother afore I'm anything else.'

'She has a husband, Mother! And a little boy with him.'

'She might do, but he's older'n her, ain't he? That's what I see, anyroad. 'Twas you that made her bleed, weren't it? She be yours, Sam. And her other *biti* boy, you make sure you treat 'en right. He's your boy's brother and a son is always more his mother's than his father's, this I know. Now are you going to promise me, Sam, so's I can go content?'

'Yes, Mother.'

'So bury me, burn everything of mine whilst you're still a travellin' man, say a prayer for me from time to time and remember me often – and go to her.'

*

---

[29] Burn

[30] Shamed, humiliated

Sam lay awake most of that last night in his customary place on the far side of the bed, carefully not touching his wife, watching the familiar things in the wagon take shape in the pale dawn. The bedding that had wrapped his mother on the bunk below had been taken out and burned along with her remaining clothes in the bender tent in which she had died. Her crockery he had smashed himself, and twisted her cutlery out of any recognisable shape, and then he had buried the lot behind the wagon. He had cried over that little funeral more than at the graveside. He looked at the curve of Lucretia's mouth as she slept, as if assessing a stranger, and felt pity move in him like a physical pain, pity he knew she would dispel the moment she opened her eyes and mouth. *Did I love you, Lukey?* he wondered. *Would love have stayed with us if a* biti tickner *had've come too?* And then he thought of Ellen.

Sam feigned sleep, as he always did, as soon as he heard an alertness in Lucretia's breathing that meant she was close to waking. This was not idleness on his part; a Gypsy wife was expected to go to bed after her husband, and to rise before him. If he had done otherwise she would have taken it as a personal affront.

He opened his eyes as she stepped down from the wagon. Over and over during the night he had listed in his head what few items he would need to take with him and now he looked round the interior checking everything was where he expected it to be, thinking about the order in which he planned to gather them up. Though no longer illiterate, Sam had retained the sharp visual memory of the intelligent man who has never learned to read and write. Hearing Lucretia clanging the kettle on the crane over the fire, and cursing as she tried to coax the embers into life, he moved swiftly to gather his plate and cup, knife and fork, his shaving things.

Lucretia didn't turn round as he climbed down the steps so she didn't see that he carried a small sack over his shoulder, the same one he had carried out of the prison. He considered speaking to her, but didn't want to rouse her suspicions, so walked off into the trees as nonchalantly as he could, as if this was a morning like any other, and he was going to relieve himself. He had to force himself not to look round the encampment or to acknowledge the other wives emerging from their wagons or the children from the bender tents. The children – *oh I'll miss them!* The only beings to whom he had whispered his good-byes had been the animals: the patient drayhorses and Fred, the elderly lurcher who slept beneath his wagon. He would see none of this ever again, and if he encountered any of these people who had been his family, the best he could hope for is that they would look through him as though he were not there, for he would never be able to mix with other Gypsies again, and the fact that he had chosen that path did not make it any easier. He walked on in the direction of the road that would lead back to

Canterbury, but this time he would walk all twenty-seven miles of it.

Oh, I should've taken the dog! He knew Lucretia disliked it and would think nothing of telling Liberty to get rid of it. But he marched on, at a swinging pace, through a film of tears. Sam hadn't considered yet how others, not only a mere dog, might suffer as a result of his flight. He couldn't think that far yet. His horizon was bounded by Farmer French's fields, and his need of willing hands to lift the turnips and swedes, and the mangolds that would feed the cattle in the cold months.

'You're a *chorredi gaujo*[31] now, Sam Loveridge,' he said to himself, wondering when he would get used to the greatest insult a Gypsy could suffer. He kept his back turned on his world and went on.

*

'How *could* you, Harold? How could you humiliate me like that?'

He had never seen Ellen like this. He had believed he had married a girl who was docile, submissive and, finally it occurred to him, *broken*, her young romantic dreams shattered, first by death and then by the Gypsy's desertion. Now that same woman shook with vexation. He recognised

---

[31] A poor non-Gypsy

in her something of Oliver in his most exalted moments, those times when his voice carried clear from the rostrum whilst his congregation shouted and sobbed. Her slender figure seemed to fill the little front room. She didn't shriek, as he had observed with distaste that angry women – or drunken ones – often did. The force of her voice was lower in register than usual – it was an older voice, he thought. Nevertheless he muttered, 'Could you keep your voice down – the neighbours . . .'

'*I. Do. Not. Care!* Why should I? You didn't give a damn—'

'Language, Ellen! A woman should never foul her mouth!'

'Oh, shut up! You didn't give a damn about what I thought when you told that preacher everything! You are a *hypocrite*, Harold Chown! "For they love to pray standing in the synagogues and in the corner of the streets, that they may be seen of men." That's what you are, Harold, a *Pharisee*!'

'I am sure Mr Ellis will be the soul of discretion, Ellen . . . All I wanted to do was to compliment him on the strength of his preaching – that scripture speaks to us whatever the day, whatever the season—'

'*How dare you! How dare you justify yourself to me!* Do you really think your precious Mr Ellis will keep that story to himself? No, no, no! He'll tell it every time he speaks of that scripture. My troubles, my poor Tom, will get them all listening and witnessing to God's glory, but oh, won't the husband be quite the Christian! *I should never have married you, Chown.* I should have waited for Sam to come for me!'

'He never did, Ellen! He left you to face your accusers!'

'*That's what you think!*'

Harold paled. 'You've seen him?' he whispered. He felt as though the floorboards shifted beneath his feet, and caught at the mantelpiece for support. Ellen stared at him, stony-faced.

'Where is he, Ellen?'

Silence.

'Ellen, you must tell me.'

At last she sagged, the fight gone out of her.

'I don't know. I have no idea where he is.'

Harold put his hands to his forehead in relief. *It's just bluster, then, that's all!* Hearing what he wanted to hear, he didn't then realise that she had not answered his first question.

'Why do you hold a candle for him still, even though he abandoned you, Ellen? Every inch that Tom grows puts more distance between him and you – more distance in *his* mind too. Can you not find some way to love me instead, even a little?'

'I think you're a good man,' she said quietly.

'A good man! Oh, what an epitaph!' he said. 'I am going to go out for a while. I want to walk and pray, and seek guidance. Then I will come home and I will beg your forgiveness for having asked too much of you.'

He took his coat and hat from behind the door and stepped directly out of the room into the street. He walked away briskly, head bowed, in the direction of the tannery and the fields beyond. He didn't see the twitch of his next-door neighbour's curtains.

Judy came through from the scullery, where she had stood silently throughout the argument. She'd shooed the boys out to play in the yard ('Poor little beggars have had enough God for one day, even if it is Sunday!') when Harold had come through the back door asking, 'Where were you all?' and walked into the storm.

'Lor, Ellen, that was close!' As Judith held her, Ellen let out the tears she hadn't wanted Harold to witness.

'It's true, though, I don't know where he is, Judy!'

'You told me he said he'd be back. He wouldn't have jumped down off that wagon and come running after you in front of all those people if he didn't want you, Ellen. I'd trust him if I were you.'

'But what should I do if he does come back?'

'I know what I'd do. Sit down now, girl, and I'll get you a cup of tea. I don't suppose you got one for yourself you were that busy serving those old tabbies.'

Ellen sank down into a chair, wondering what would happen next.

*

The following morning they took breakfast in strained silence, after Harold had spoken a hurried grace that the children joined in with but the women ignored. Tom looked questioningly from his mother to Judith, whilst his younger brother, oblivious to the atmosphere, drove a finger of toast round the edge of his plate where glazed lines made for him an imaginary railway line. The spout of the teapot chinked loudly against Harold's cup.

'Any letters, Ellen?'

'Just Mother. I shall read it later,' she answered, feigning indifference, squeezing her left hand into a fist beneath the table.

*

I hope you can forgive me. I thought I was acting for the best, her mother wrote. *There was another, but Oliver burned it. I have something else to tell you if I can find the courage, so next time I see you my dear girl. I haven't read it I promise.*

Ellen merely skimmed this letter, sniffing instead the crumpled envelope it enclosed. Tears came to her eyes; it smelled of her mother's lavender bags. Had she been too hard on her? No, the postmark was more than two years old. She opened it with shaking fingers. *My God, it's from a prison!* She read the round, childish handwriting, and Sam Loveridge stood pleadingly before her.

. . . so now you no I did not abandon you but I am feard that you have fergotten me. I have nothing to do here but

305

think about you and that I have lorst you. I go round in circles like in the exsercize yard all in my head at night and curse myself for a weak fool who did not fite for you. I am feard now to leave this place becos when I come for you maybe you will shut the door in my face thow I will die like a rat in a trap if I stay here longer with no grass to walk on nor no more than a hangkerchif of sky to look at. I love you Ellen. I always will. I am your servant.

Sampson Loveridge.

There were faint pencil marks on the page; Ellen looked more closely and saw that his spelling mistakes and punctuation had been neatly corrected in a smaller hand. She wondered if he had not had enough paper to make a fair copy, or had otherwise been prevented from doing so. With those marks, the letter looked like Sunday school homework; the corrections could have been her own.

Ellen carried the letter upstairs, and opening a drawer in her dressing table, reached in and took out a package awkwardly wrapped in brown paper. Inside lay a stoneware beer bottle, and folded within tissue paper, a tattered man's neckerchief, which she lifted out and kissed. Then with reverent care she placed the envelope with these and tied up the parcel again. *Oh Sam, come back, come back!*

The bedroom door edged open, and Tom peered round it, followed by David.

'Don't cry, Ma!' said Tom. She put her arms out to her sons, resting her burning face against one boy's cheek and then against the other's. David began to cry without knowing why.

*

'Where's that useless *dinilo* got to?' muttered Lucretia.

'More full o' shit than ever!' laughed Caley. 'All the tea will be drunk if he don't get back here soon!'

Lucretia had a presentiment that something was different, that Sam wasn't just late at the campfire, but that his presence in the clearing had somehow been cancelled out. She got up, went into the wagon and bent over to open the low cupboard nearest the door. Her hand went in but didn't encounter the items that had been there for as long as she had lived in this *vardo*; it froze in the empty space. She remained bent over, deciding what face she would present to the tea-drinkers a few feet away.

Eventually she stood up and called out, 'You drink his bleddy tea, brother!' But all she needed to say when she joined them by the fire was, 'I'll get his togs. They're for burning.'

She brought them out later, but not before pressing her face into them one last time.

*

'How could they have been so cruel, Judy?'

'Don't blame your mother – the poor soul is afraid of her own hiccups. She sent you it, didn't she? She could have pretended there'd never been a letter.'

'She couldn't. I'd've got it out of her next time I saw her. She couldn't lie to save her life. It's him – Grandfer. Judging a man he's never met. And doing that to me – I thought he loved me!'

'Ellen, do you think Pa knew?'

'That they were in it together? Oh Lord, what if they were?'

*

Sam calculated that Canterbury was nine or ten hours' walk away, but he didn't want to go there by the most direct road. *I don't think them Bucklands will come after me, but if they do, I'm not going to make it easy for them.* True, he would hear a man on horseback more readily on the main road than in a country lane, but even here he'd have enough warning, his senses attuned by a lifetime outdoors to the slightest sound or vibration of the ground beneath his feet. And to his infinite thankfulness, he was now not making the journey alone. By the time he'd turned onto the village green at Bearsted, pausing to consider which of the pubs might serve a Gypsy, at least at the back door, he'd heard a scuffling and a whining behind him.

'Oh Fred, Fred, you followed me, old fellow!' He squatted down and held the dog close enough to smell the sweet mustiness of his pelt. The animal was unused to such an obvious sign of affection and overjoyed at having found his master, so pressed home his advantage by nuzzling Sam's face. Sam automatically stopped him, for no matter how much he loved the dog, he knew that as a dog, he was *mochadi*, impure. *I ain't so clean myself,* he thought, and looking round first to see if there was anyone who might object, he washed his face and hands at the village pump, shivering in the cold air. He told himself it wasn't to wash off Fred, but because he had not gone to the stream that morning and was dusty from the road.

A woman of about thirty, aproned, with her sleeves rolled up, emerged from the door of the White Horse and stood watching him, hands on hips.

You're in their world now, he thought. *Can't put it off any longer.* He shook the drops from his hands and walked towards her.

'Good morning, lady.'

'Morning. What might you be wanting here?'

'A glass of ale, if you'd be so kind.'

She looked at him in silence as he braced himself for a refusal. Then Fred gently padded over and sat on his haunches, looking up at her. At last she smiled.

'Your dog looks hungry. Come round the back, the two of you,' and she turned and went back into the pub.

'Bless you, Fred!' whispered Sam. He walked behind the pub and stood at the back door, waiting to see if he'd be invited in.

'Come in, then, you look clean enough,' she called out. 'Stay in the back bar – the men'll come in by the front for their dinner soon.'

She put a pint glass in front of him, and held out her hand for payment.

'I've some offal if the dog wants it.'

'Thank you kindly.'

'Where are the rest of you then? How long will you all be staying?'

'There's no one else, lady, just me and him.'

'Go on, you Gypsies always travel together.'

'Then I can't be a Gypsy, can I?'

She frowned, and said: 'You've had some bother, I suppose.'

'You could say that.'

'So where are you bound for?'

'Canterbury – but I thought I'd go in the Ashford direction first, see if I can't find some work there.'

'Funny way to get to Canterbury. Throw 'em off the scent – is that the idea?'

Sam laughed. He wanted to say, 'Spoken like a Gypsy', but didn't want to push his luck.

'That's about the size of it!'

'The law after you?' she asked.

'No. Family trouble, you might say.'

'I'll give you some bread and cheese, if you like. So you can keep him company when he's eating them lights.'

Sam sat quietly, considering what the road might immediately bring if he sidled up to Canterbury from the southeast. That way if Lukey's brothers did pursue him, they were a lot less likely to find him. He was almost certain the Bucklands had never really swallowed his excuse for jumping down from the *vardo* the day of the fair, saying he'd wanted to avoid someone he owed money to. He was sure, too, the unwillingness with which he took part in the preparations for leaving the city and heading west had been noticed. Lukey had twice urged him to get a move on. There were other considerations too. Sam didn't want to meet other Gypsies. He'd encountered a *pattrin* before Bearsted, but as he had expected at that time of year, it indicated west. Nor did he want the *gavengros* to take him up for vagrancy, which they might too readily do were he on a wider road. If he ran into a rural constable he had decided to say he was Tom Boswell; he didn't want any conscientious policeman linking him to the Sam Loveridge who had done time for horse-stealing. He rummaged in his pockets; he'd been able to pay for his ale but there wasn't much left.

'Do you need any help with anything, lady?'

'I thought you said you was moving on,' she called back.

Stung, he said, 'I am. I meant for giving Fred and me our dinner.'

'You could bring up another barrel. My husband's supposed to have done it, but he's still upstairs. Recovering from the barrel he put away last night, you might say.'

*

The decision to take a meandering route was to be far-reaching in its effect, not least because it brought Sam back to Canterbury far more quickly than he had anticipated.

Two days later, on Saturday afternoon, Sam approached a farmhouse in search of work. He calculated that he had walked about half the distance he had to cover, and had spent the first of what he thought of as his '*gauje*-nights' in a corrugated-iron wheeled shepherd's hut where rain kept him awake, but Fred kept him warm on a heap of straw and sacking. Now Sam had some money, for that farmer had needed some hedging done, and wanted him to stay the next day for a few hours' more work. Fred had needed some persuasion to get inside the hut, for it evidently looked to him, as it did to Sam, like a small *vardo*, and so the dog had rustled about underneath it looking for somewhere to lie down, as he had done his entire life. No animal was ever allowed in a *vardo*; even the caged songbirds hung outside.

The second night was better, in a barn near Lenham Heath, but he and Fred had needed to work to make it habitable: the farm buildings were overrun with rats.

Sam busied himself, to the mystification of the farmer, in making rudimentary traps with old treacle cans and rags of stockings from a pile of flotsam awaiting the rag and bone man. He blocked as many rat-holes as he could find so that their occupants had to leave by those that ended in the can and stocking traps, whereupon they were fired on with a catapult. Fred finished off those that managed to escape the traps.

'I've never seen anything like it!' said the farmer in admiration.

'It'd have been much faster if I'd had my ferrets,' said Sam.

'You come back this way next year or whenever you want, with your ferrets, and you'll always have work here.'

'Thank you, sir, but I'm expected for a permanent place at Patrixbourne,' Sam lied.

'Well, if that don't work, you make your way back here,' said the farmer, and stumped off to dig a hole to throw the corpses in.

But Sam's employer laid down another condition to fulfil before he would be paid. Sam had some intimation of what was coming when he was offered lemonade with his supper, rather than the customary ale. But he had been asked to eat that supper at the farmer's table, with his taciturn wife, two teenage sons, a younger daughter, and a gnarled and bent farmhand of about seventy, who looked on Sam with some suspicion until he understood that he was only passing through. Natural courtesy made Sam wait before reaching for his food, so that his hosts might start first.

'Bless, O Lord, this food to our use and us to thy service, and keep us ever mindful of the needs of others. In the name of Jesus our Lord, Amen,' intoned Farmer Piper.

The two boys were nearly as silent as their mother, but the girl, an awkward fourteen, could not keep her eyes off Sam. Every time he looked in her direction, drawn by her furtive gaze, she would look down at her plate.

It's that earring she's staring at, I'll bet. Probably she's not let to wear any geegaws herself, poor maidy.

On the dresser behind the farmer's wife Sam could see two framed studio portraits of unsmiling men in uniform, propped amongst the willow pattern plates. The farmer noticed his glance, and said quietly, 'The Lord giveth, and the Lord taketh away.'

'I'm sorry, sir.'

'Have you a family yourself, Mr Boswell?'

'No . . . not now. I've just buried my mother. So it's just me . . . and the dog.'

The woman glanced at her husband then, as if asking permission. 'I'll make you a bed up in the house. You'd be more comfortable.'

'Ah, no, thank you all the same. I'd not want to put you to that trouble, and if the truth be known, I'm used to sleeping out of doors, so to speak, so the barn will suit me fine.' It was not that sheets and pillows did not appeal – they did, for straw is noisy to lie on – but to be enclosed within four walls was too like the prison cell. Yet Sam knew that sooner or later this too was something he would have to adjust to.

After the meal the woman gave him some horse blankets and the farmer said goodnight.

'Tomorrow is the Lord's day. We would be glad if you would give Him thanks for this day's work by accompanying us to our chapel tomorrow. There is a preacher from Canterbury coming out special for us and we should make him welcome. Will you join us, Mr Boswell?'

He hesitated. It would be churlish not to.

'It is just that . . . I cannot read that well, sir. I won't know the words of the hymns you sing. And I have only the clothes you see me in now.'

'I wonder how many of our Lord's disciples could read. It is enough that you can *hear* His word. Mary has some clothes that belonged to my late brother who was more of a size with you than with me. You can wear them and then we can parcel them up for you.'

'Thank you for your kindness, sir,' said Sam. 'Of course I'll come tomorrow. If I could just borrow a mirror in the morning to shave in?'

'I shall lend it you tonight, Mr Boswell, if you don't mind, straight after I have used it myself. It's better not to perform such tasks on the Sabbath. Whilst I have my shave, Mary will get the clothes to see if they fit you.'

They did, more or less, though they would have benefited from another inch on the sleeve and one less round the waist, but they came with braces so he didn't need to use his customary length of twine. Sam especially liked the crisp starched feel of the shirt, but was flummoxed by the tie.

'I shall have to ask you for help with this tomorrow, sir,' he said humbly. 'I have never worn one.'

'That's all right,' said the farmer. 'Mary will get you fresh water to shave in, and if you put the mirror here and turn up the oil lamp, you'll see what you're about. I daresay you know your own face well enough. You might want this too,' he said, rummaging in a drawer of the dresser and pulling out a battered steel comb. 'You can keep it – I've another.'

Sam wondered if it had also been the brother's, or had belonged to one of the boys in uniform.

'You've been very generous to a stranger, sir.'

'I do only my duty. "Be not forgetful to entertain strangers: for thereby some have entertained angels unawares."'

'I am no angel, I'm afraid, though I think no devil either.'

'Devil no, for you are created in His image and so I pray you may be saved. Goodnight, Mr Boswell.'

*

Sam shaved carefully in the now silent kitchen. He was about to turn down the oil lamp when he looked again at his tired, lean face in the mirror and decided on one more step to *gaujo*dom. He worked the thin gold hoop round in his ear lobe until he could locate the join.

Ow! No need to rush, Sam. He had forgotten to turn it since his mother died, and he felt the pull on his flesh. Then carefully he prised the thin loop apart, and eased it out. He looked at it lying forlornly in his palm, then back at his face in the mirror. With some grimacing he pulled the comb through his unruly hair, aiming for a parting like the one the farmer himself had. *You'll need to find a barber in Canterbury*, he told himself, remembering that the last time he had put his head beneath another man's hands had been in Winchester. Since then Lukey had inexpertly scissored away when he'd asked. His hair thus partly tamed, and his ears naked, he didn't immediately recognise himself.

'Make the best of it, *gaujo*,' he muttered, 'there's no turning back now.' His past years, his whole life, seemed weirdly to telescope. The earring had been removed twice before, the first time when he was in Lincoln. Within a few weeks the hole in his lobe had closed up, leaving barely an indent. When he had been demobbed and returned to his old life, his mother had taken him into the *vardo* alone and bored through the lobe again with a needle passed through a candle, and he had gritted his teeth with the pain, so that neither Lukey nor her brothers might hear him cry out. Nor had it been easier when he had left Winchester and had to repeat the process.

Shall I give it to the rakli? he wondered. *The little maidy spent long enough gazing at it – but I don't think her father would like it. No, gold is gold. I'll take it to the pawn in Canterbury and that'll be the end of it.*

Curled in the straw beside Fred, Sam slept better than he had for months, exhausted by his long tramp, lack of sleep in the shepherd's hut the night before, and the tearing about killing rats. But most of all the sense of desolation he had felt when he set out on his journey was lifting. He would be able to keep himself – and maybe more than that – and he was halfway to Canterbury.

*

Ellen feigned sleep as Harold undressed. He always removed his garments in exactly the same order. She heard the swish of his tie being pulled undone, the quick, repetitive movement as he rolled it round his fingers and then dropped it into the top left-hand drawer of the dresser, the rattle of his collar studs in their wooden box, followed by his cuff-links in theirs, the unclipping of his braces, the folding and hanging of shirt and trousers, the shoes lined up with military precision in the foot of the wardrobe, his pyjama jacket buttoned – on coming to Canterbury he had abandoned his old-fashioned nightshirts – and their trousers tied before his sock garters came off and the socks were balled up. Ellen did not know what her husband looked like without his clothes but could have described all these sounds minutely. She dug her nails into her palms as she listened. Millie's bed creaked as Harold sat down. Ellen shifted, turning her back.

'I have to be up early – on the circuit. Barton's lending me his trap.'

Ellen made a small sound, as though disturbed in her sleep.

'I know you're not asleep.'

'What was that, Harold?'

'I'll turn out the light, then.'

He lay on his back silently for a few minutes. She could tell from his breathing what was coming next. She saw herself scrambling out of her side of the bed and running downstairs, to lock herself in the outside privy. He reached for her, taking her shoulder and easing her onto her back. She felt a scream rising in her throat. It was Saturday, a fortnight had gone by since the last time, and Harold was as predictable in his approach to sex as he was to undressing.

'No,' she heard herself say. 'I can't.'

He withdrew his hands as though she burned him.

'What's the matter?' he eventually asked. 'Have you your . . . monthlies? No, you can't have . . . so why?'

'Don't ask me, Harold. I'm sorry.' *Because doing this with you would betray the man I love.*

'I'm not a brute, Ellen. I shan't force you.'

Wordlessly, both turned their backs. An hour later Harold spoke into the silence.

'You have always taken me on sufferance, Ellen. I shall try not to importune you again.'

*

The family looked approvingly at Sam when he appeared at breakfast. He had risen early and stripped to the waist before washing himself at the pump, his body tingling at the shock of icy water on his skin on a misty November morning. He wondered if already he was being softened by the prospect of a journey's end, by food provided at a farmhouse table that he had not had to trap, shoot, or beg himself. It was as though his imperviousness to the elements was leaking out of him through the tiny puncture left by the earring. He found himself more than once with his fingers to his ear, feeling that what had been part of him was missing. It felt odder this time, because he had chosen to take the hoop out himself.

Sam smiled back at the farmer's family, taking his cue from the way they reached for the bread baked the evening before, how much of the pale creamy butter they spread on it, how quickly they drank down the generous mugs of tea. Fasting didn't figure in these people's lives, evidently; simple, plentiful food and kindness to strangers, however, did. The farmer's daughter had got over her curiosity of the night before – either that, or one or other of her parents had taken her aside and told her off for rudeness. Sam hoped not the latter. All she had to look at today was a worn, thin agricultural labourer who felt old beyond his years, dressed decently and warmly for Sunday observance. Or was it that his clothes hadn't belonged to her uncle but to one of her brothers and she couldn't bear to look at them?

*

The farmer walked with Sam just ahead of his wife and children.

'If you like, Mr Boswell, you can sit at the back of the chapel, so's you don't feel you stand out, like. You'll still hear all that's going on, for today's preacher has a fine, clear voice, without deafening anybody. My Jemmy has said he'll sit with you. There is quite a bit of singing and that, and as you said, you'll not know the words, but I wouldn't let it worry you. The chapel folk sing as a way to pray, so they won't be looking to see if you're praying too.

'There's a bag comes round, not a plate, so whatever you put in will be up to you. We don't judge a man by the size of his offering, for did not the poor widow's mite please our Lord more than all the abundance of the rich man?'

'Indeed, sir,' said Sam politely, remembering one of the sermons at Winchester.

'Sometimes the converted will come forward to the penitent form, or them that want to atone for their sins and ask forgiveness. But that depends on the preacher. The ones who preach what I call high, that really pull the soul out of you so's you'd do anything, they get many to come forward.'

Sam shivered inwardly. What was this they did? A court where the wrongdoer was tried before all his community? Momentarily distracted, he didn't immediately follow Piper's talk, until a name shocked him into full alertness.

'There are times I wonder if they think they're more successful the more tears they get a body to shed . . . But this Mr Chown, he's a quieter sort of man entirely. I like when it's his turn in the district to come out here. He says things very calmly, like, that you think on a lot after. And then you think he must have been saying it directly to you, but that you had to consider it first and weigh it up before you can understand what you must do with it: "For now we see through a glass, darkly; but then face to face", as you might say.'

'Your preachers, can they have wives, same as parsons?' Sam managed to get out.

'Why, of course,' said the farmer, his eyebrows raised in surprise. 'We ain't like them poor Romanists, shut up in a house without so much as a cat for company, if not another songless blackbird like themselves, when. Didn't the Lord God himself say: "It is not good that the man should be alone"? Mr Chown has a wife, though he's not been long in these parts so I haven't met her. He has a young family so no doubt his lady will be taking them to the chapel in Canterbury instead. His first wife died, they say, years ago, and in another part of the country. But he bore her loss for many years and the Lord saw his suffering and provided him with another helpmate – a widow lady herself. So they have each other to love and comfort now.'

'He's a lucky man, then,' said Sam bleakly.

'Well, yes, I suppose he is!' The farmer looked sideways at his guest, and wondered what unhappiness of his own made him speak in those tones, but he didn't dream of prying.

'I've had a thought,' said the farmer. 'If Mr Chown hasn't come with a full load, you could go back on the trap with him to Canterbury.'

'I wouldn't want to trouble the gentleman.'

'What trouble would it be? "As we have therefore opportunity, let us do good unto all men." You leave it to me. If I'm honest, I'm already sorry to lose you, but if things don't work out with your Farmer French at Patrixbourne, I could use another pair of hands here – all those turnips to pull in the long field, for one. Old Ted is more rheumaticky by the day, and I'll give him whatever he can manage to do for as long as he's able, for I won't have him in the workhouse if it can be helped. That's where he was born and he deserves better than to go back there. You're young, but not too young, and strong, and you've a nice, polite way with you . . . I'll be honest with you, Mr Boswell, I haven't always had such a good experience of your kind – I mean, there's been good 'uns and bad 'uns . . .'

'They're not my kind, Mr Piper, good or bad. I don't belong with them now.'

'Well, I wish you well whatever you're a going to do now. And the offer is open. Only –' and here he smiled, to take the edge off what he was about to say – 'don't think of casting your eyes on my Esther! I saw last night as she couldn't keep hers off of you!'

'I wouldn't dream of it!' exclaimed Sam, in genuine alarm.

'Yes, well she's not such a bad-looking girl as all that, is she?' said Piper, nettled.

'No, I didn't mean that! She's a fine girl and will turn into a finer woman. I mean one like her could do a lot better than a fellow like me who has nothing to call his own but what others are kind enough to give him!'

'You've your hands, Mr Boswell, and the willingness to use them well. Those are riches,' replied the farmer, mollified. 'We're here now. Jemmy! You go in with Mr Boswell, like I said, and you've permission to sit in the back. I'm going up near the rostrum.'

At the junction of three roads stood the little brick chapel. Sam pulled off his hat, and crushed it in his hands. He was fond of it, but knew it looked outlandish with the respectable countryman's suit and tie that he wore now. He wanted to make himself as inconspicuous as he could, for

he was shaken by Piper's news that Ellen's husband was to
be the preacher, and if there had been a way of avoiding
the farmer's kindness in organising this lift to Canterbury,
he would have taken it. What if Chown invited him back
home? He could hardly make the excuse of getting over to
Farmer French's early, when his supposed employer had
been expecting him later, and on foot. He would have to
think of something. It was a cold day, but Sam sweated
inside his new clothes. This collar was surely too tight, the
tie a noose . . .

*

Sam had never seen a place so plain and stripped, yet called
itself a church. Here there was no stained glass, nor any can-
dlesticks. There was no altar, just a pulpit made by a village
carpenter, the steps up to which made Sam think of a gallows.
And here, arranging his notes, was the middle-aged man who
laid his soft, pale, God-fearing flesh next to Ellen's every night,
and who fed and clothed her dark-haired child.

I wonder does my boy call him father?

Sam began by studying Chown, who looked older and
more care-worn than the man he had glimpsed through the
trees that day when jealousy sank its teeth into his heart.
But gradually he became absorbed by what he had to say.

'Remember, brethren, how we met as multitudes in the
fields, and listened to the Word of the Lord spoken from

the back of a farm cart, and how His plan was revealed by the rudest of vessels fired with the Spirit?'

Sam felt hemmed in by the congregation in their dark, damp clothes, a study in grey, brown and black, lightened only by the whiteness of shirts starched and pressed into respectability by the heat of many spat-on flat-irons. Perhaps a sermon in a field was kinder; no need to dress up for it, and the opportunity to slope off without being noticed. Young Piper sat close by him on his right. To his left were two old women blocking his path to the narrow aisle and the door. Chown was grey-pale from a life spent indoors, slightly, almost apologetically, stooped, as one who passed long hours bent over a desk, but without the bright eye and energy of a scholar. His voice was firm and modulated, and just strong enough for this small space and its docile audience. Sam tried to imagine this man seated opposite Ellen at the tea-table; he couldn't bring himself to try to imagine him with her in bed. *That* rai *is bringing up your own* biti chavvi! he reminded himself. This felt even more unreal than the idea of Chown crying out against Ellen's skin.

*

'I can take the reins if you wish, sir,' said Sam. He wanted to do something with his hands.

'Oh, would you, Mr Boswell? That would be most kind. I can manage to guide a horse, for I'm a countryman born and bred, though I labour now in a town, but I don't have a gift for the handling of our dumb friends. I had thought to come with the owner, but he is in bed with the pleurisy, poor man, so I had to trust to my own feeble skill to get myself here. And I am rather tired, though the people do their best to welcome one. Fortunately the pony is a docile one – and your dog seems to be most biddable.'

'Old Fred? Yes, he's all right.'

'You've been staying with Brother Piper, I hear?'

'That's right, but I've work to go to in Patrixbourne.'

'He'd've kept you, probably. He lost his two eldest.'

'He offered me, but I had already given my word to the other man.'

'I see. You're not from these parts, are you, Mr Boswell?'

'I'm not from anywhere in particular, sir. And I goes everywhere.'

'Ah yes – the tribe of Egypt. I'm an Oxfordshire man, myself. Ever been that direction?' asked Harold.

Something of Sam's tension communicated itself to the pony. He soothed her with a few muttered words and the sound of the Romani in his own ears had the effect of calming him too.

'I bin all over, but I don't remember the names of all the places,' he said warily. 'We was reg'lar at St Giles's fair up in Oxford.'

'We? You're on your own now, Mr Boswell?'

'My mother died, sir, not a fortnight ago. She told me I should settle.'

'I'm sorry to hear of your loss. No one can replace a mother.'

'Nor a father . . .'

'No, indeed. But why Patrixbourne?'

'It's a good farm and the farmer a decent man. Mother knew she was going, and wanted to see all the places she'd been before she went. So I took 'er round first, and now she's gone, I'm going back, since I've promised the farmer.' Sam found he disliked lying to Chown, especially about his mother. Whilst it was true that Harmony had urged him to leave the road, there had been no customary tour for her round the old stopping-places; there had not been enough warning of her end. And he'd left the Bucklands out of his account altogether. Ellen's husband was no doubt sitting beside him imagining a devoted son and an old lady travelling in their lone wagon to visit the places she had loved one last time.

'Canterbury looked a neat enough town to me when I was there,' Sam added carefully, 'and I like how the name sounds on the ear – like the ringing of bells.'

Chown looked at him in pleased astonishment. 'You know, it does. I'd never thought of it in that way.'

'We've a name for Canterbury, in our way of speaking,' said Sam. 'We call it: *mi develeskey gav*.'

'Sounds nothing like it!'

'But it means "my God's town".'

Chown laughed; he did so, however, as if the muscles of his face were not accustomed to it. 'Let us hope that it is!' he exclaimed.

Oh dordi, *I like the poor fellow. He's different entirely when he laughs like that.*

'What did you say your Christian name was, Mr Boswell?'

'I didn't – 'tis Tom.'

'A fine name, for an apostle and for an archbishop, and for my stepson, as it happens . . .'

'Oh?'

'My wife was a widow, Mr Boswell. The boy never knew his father – so he thinks of me as one.'

'No doubt you're right, sir,' said Sam, staring fixedly at the pony's ears. *You can lie as well as I when it suits you, Mr Preacher!*

*

Harold walked round the back of the terrace and in at the scullery door.

'Hello, Harold,' said Ellen. 'You look pleased. It went well at Lenham Heath, then?'

'Um, I believe it did, rather.' Harold handed her his hat and started unbuttoning his coat. 'No, don't worry, I shall hang them up myself.' He walked through to the back room. 'I'd be grateful for some tea.'

Ellen went to prepare it, saying over her shoulder: 'How did you manage with the pony?'

'She was very biddable. Barton said she would be. No doubt your grandfather would have had something to say about how I drove her, but she got there. I had a stroke of luck on the way back, though.'

'Oh?' She came in with the cups and saucers on a tray.

'Yes. There was a young fellow who had work to go to at Patrixbourne. He took the reins for me. Likeable chap ... I hope you don't mind, Ellen, but I encouraged him to call here – I gave him our address. It was the first time he'd been to the chapel, you see.'

'Why would I mind, Harold?'

'Um ... he's a Gypsy.'

A teaspoon clattered in a saucer.

'Name of Boswell,' said Harold, watching her.

Ellen swallowed, then said shakily: 'Forgive me, Harold, you startled me.'

'You don't know him, do you?'

'I know no one of that name. But if he should call, I shall of course make him welcome.'

*

That night, lying as still as he was able, the mattress heaving as for the umpteenth time Ellen turned over and sighed,

Harold wished he had never mentioned Tom Boswell. *If just naming one of that tribe makes her react like this, I have no right to feel content.*

*

Yet by breakfast time he noted that Ellen seemed to have recovered her equanimity, though she was pale, with dark shadows beneath her eyes. At the door, she handed him his umbrella and hat, as she always did, and asked, casually enough: 'That Gypsy, Harold, the one you said might call here. What did you say he was called?'

'Boswell – *Tom* Boswell. If he should call, do make him welcome.'

'I will. Tom's an easy name to remember, anyhow. Have a good day at work, Harold.'

She closed the door behind him, and leaned against it, closing her eyes. *He's come back for me! Will it be days – or hours?*

*

Harold knew his way to work so well now that he was left free to think as he walked. *That wasn't the name. Sam – Samson, she said it was. And the wretch had a wife – and there was a whole tribe of them in those woods. It must've been only a trick of the light made me think her pupils got bigger.*

CHAPTER 25

An ignorant man ... lately led his wife, a decently dressed well-looking woman, about 30 years of age, into the public cattle-market, Canterbury, to sell her! ... the "untaught knave", insensible to every sense of shame, engaged a pen ... to which the poor creature was led by a halter. She was soon, however, disengaged from this vile station, by a young man named T. Fuller ... who purchased her for 5s.!

Annual Register, 1820

Cattle Market

Canterbury

Holding onto the railings of St George's Terrace and swinging back and forth like pistons, Tom and David looked down on a maze of pens and gates in which cattle seethed and bellowed as corduroy and moleskin-clad men moved swiftly back and forth, directing the livestock from one enclosure to another with a logic that made as much sense to Ellen and Judith as it did to the cows themselves. Finn, the auctioneer's man, presided over the whole proceeding from atop a cart turned backwards, just as though he was a preacher at a camp meeting, though what came out of his mouth was a demented monotone, punctuated by gestures that miraculously made sense to the cattle-hands and the little knots of brown-suited farmers. He never missed the almost imperceptible signs these bidders made. Up on the terrace behind the railings, Ellen was afraid to make any gesture in case she found herself the unwilling owner of a herd of these shifting, fractious animals. *Poor things*, she thought. They were beef cattle.

'Horses, Ma!' Tom had at last let go of the railings and was pulling at Ellen's sleeve.

'Don't tug so, Tom. Take my hand instead.'

The little group moved slowly along the terrace. Here below the walls horses were being put through their paces. This, for the small Chowns looking down, was as good as watching a race – something Ellen had never done, for the Prims racecourses were the haunt of gamblers, men – Gypsies amongst them – fortifying themselves from hip flasks. Here they saw buyers pushing the velvet, whiskered lips back to inspect teeth of horses wide-eyed with indignation. Others ran their hands over legs in search of spavins. A boy led a young roan pony in a canter along a channel roped out for the purpose. A tall cloth-capped man in a shapeless old jacket stepped forward and nodded approvingly. Some words were exchanged and the animal was quickly saddled. Ellen watched as the boy joined his hands as a step for the man to swing himself into the saddle, and saw him reject the offer with a gentle motion of his hand. He was up with the effortless swing of the practised horseman, and the little horse trotted obediently and elegantly down the track, his rider loosely holding the reins. As he turned back again Ellen saw the rider's face and clutched at the railing to prevent herself from crying out.

Judith was at her elbow.

'Him, ain't it? I told you he'd come back.'

'Yes!' whispered Ellen.

'Now stay here, Ellen Chown. I'm taking the boys up the other end to see the pigs.'

'Don't go!'

'Don't be silly,' said Judith, as though talking to a child.

'I'm coming with you.' Ellen turned her back on the railings. 'You see? He's here, Judith, but he's not been to see me. I cannot be made a fool of again – I don't think I can bear it!'

'Ellen, you haven't the wit you were born with! The hopping is long over – what would he be doing here if it weren't for you? You've read his letter – he's been true to you all along. You can at least speak to him!'

'But it's so public here!'

'Exactly. If you try and run off hundreds'll see you. It's too late, he's seen you and he's coming anyway. I just saw him pay that boy to hold the pony.'

Judy waved her arms at Sam, pointing. In a panic Ellen saw him nod and start to weave his way through the crowd of buyers.

'What have you done, Judy?'

'He can't climb this wall, can he? We'll walk down to Burgate and you can talk to him there. Come along, boys! Oink oink!'

*

Ellen left Judy and the boys further on, leaning over the railings to look at the pigs. She'd panicked at the thought of seeing Sam and now panicked at the thought of missing him, and almost ran the last part of the terrace. He was waiting for her. She stopped a foot in front of him.

'My Ellen.'

'Sam!' Her body prickled with desire, and she fought the urge to put her hands out to him. She took a deep breath. 'We can't talk here.'

'Nine o'clock by them big towers, then.'

'The Westgate?'

'If that's what it's called. I'll be there. I'll wait all night for you if I have to.'

'I can't promise anything. But Sam, I got your letter finally – one of them. They'd kept it from me.'

He took a step forward and grasped her shoulders. He was smiling.

'*Don't,* Sam. Someone might see,' and she extricated herself.

'So you do believe me, Ellen?'

'Oh yes. I believe you.'

'You're mine then. If you still love me.'

A pause.

'Yes . . . I never stopped.'

He smiled again, delighted as a boy. 'Go and look at them pigs then. I'll take the pony home and I'll be back after supper. You'll be kissed this night, Ellen.'

*

The tea things tidied away and the children in bed, Ellen was trying hard to concentrate on the tablecloth she held in her lap.

'Ow!'

'What is it, Ellen?'

'Oh, nothing, Harold, I pricked my thumb again. I just can't get this mending to come right.'

Harold lowered his newspaper and stared at her over his spectacles.

'You've been distracted for weeks now. Ever since you had woman's trouble that time Judy put you to bed. But I've seen no doctor's bill. When are you going to tell me what's the matter?'

'Oh, I don't know.'

'You're not, um . . . ?'

'Oh my, oh goodness me, no . . . no . . . I mean, not this time.' Aware that she sounded too relieved, she added, 'I'd like to go out for a minute, Harold. My head hurts a bit; maybe the air will clear it.' Her heart thumped so loudly that she thought he must hear it.

'Why are you asking me? We've a back yard, haven't we?'

'Yes . . . well, the children are sleeping, and Judith is already gone up, so . . .'

'Go on, then. Just don't catch cold. We've that temperance meeting coming up and much to do for it.'

'I'll wrap up, then.'

Harold grunted, and went back to his reading.

She closed the door as quietly as she could, and looked through the window at Harold's jowly face and neatly brushed hair illuminated by the oil lamp. *I'll let Sam kiss me tonight and you won't know!*

Harold stared fixedly at the page and didn't see a word.

*

The back entrance to their terraced house was reached via a narrow passage cutting through between neighbouring homes. To reach that tunnel she passed by other kitchens, other back parlours. She scuttled by Mrs Clerk's window with head bowed, not wanting to be waylaid. At the back of the next house she glimpsed a homely gaslit tableau, a young husband reading in his shirt sleeves whilst his wife prepared a child for bed, and thought, *I shall be a different person by the time I see my children again.*

As she passed the Black Griffin, the door of the public bar opened and shouts and laughter reached her, some of it raucous and female. She didn't look round, but heard a drunken argument continuing on the cobbles, too involved for the participants to take any notice of a plainly dressed woman walking swiftly by in the near dark, face eclipsed by a soft hat. Ellen was convinced others would smell fear on her. This nocturnal Canterbury was one she didn't know, for darkness for her meant turning up the gaslight, sitting opposite Harold over the dying fire, mending or reading, or listening to him telling her what he would speak about the following Sunday, so that by the time she heard his sermon all the brightness had gone out of it.

The Westgate bulked massive against the clear night sky. Even in daylight Ellen didn't like the little passage that ran alongside it, much less going through it in darkness, in spite of there being a police station close by.

I'll go under the main arch instead as there are no carts passing through at this hour, and I'll come back through the passage; the light's better this side than that. And if he's not there . . . I should count myself lucky, she told herself, thinking again of that moment when she had walked into the deserted clearing, and found only the empty beer bottle. Head down she walked swiftly through the arched darkness, when behind her, silent as a cat, a shape detached itself from

338

the black wall, an arm slipped round her waist from behind, and a hand muffled the shriek that rose in her throat.

'Quiet, Ellen! You'll have me *lelled*!'

She twisted round in his grip.

'What, Sam?'

'I'm sorry – you'll have me taken up, I meant. I couldn't resist coming up to you like that. You were walking so purposeful I thought you'd walk right away and up the hill.'

'Let go of me.'

'All right, but give me your hand at least. There's that little park by the river – let me talk to you in there.'

'It'll be locked.' But her hand in his, she allowed herself to be led.

'So we'll go over the railings,' he said.

'I can't climb over that.'

'But I bet you don't want to be seen talking to me out here. What if your policeman friend comes by again? Come on, it's not high. I'll lift you over.'

Ellen put her foot into his linked hands, and as he eased her up and over, leaned into the old suit jacket and collarless shirt of the labourer. Oh, how she had missed the smell of him! All evening, through tea, through Harold's little account of his day, through preparing the boys for bed, she had thought only of Sam's promised kisses. And now he was hooking himself over the railing after her, and failing to stifle a groan.

'Sam, what is it?'

'Oh, I shouldn't go at these things so fast. They broke two of my ribs in that beating . . . Here, come under this little arch.'

'What beating? Where are you taking me? I can barely see a thing!'

'You're not so used to the dark as me . . . You bin too long out of the country. Keep hold of my hand.'

'Sam, I can't go further. He thinks I'm in the back yard!'

'Let him think what he likes! I shan't let go of you again. Let me hold you, to know that everything of you is still where it was . . . My lovely girl. Kiss me, Ellen.'

'I have to go!' she whispered, twisting her face away, but letting him lean his weight into her, pressing her against the wall, nuzzling her neck. 'I can't be your girl!'

'You are, and I want you, my love, but not here, not where I can't see you. Not in a rush.' He raised his mouth from her neck and kissed her – all her loneliness, pain, humiliation, tears wiped out by his nearness.

Eventually he said, 'Best get you home – for now.'

'What beating, Sam?'

'The one that stopped me coming back for you. I'll tell you next time.'

'How can we have a next time, Sam?'

'Trust me, we'll have one. I knew that when I kissed you just now. You as good as told me. I've left them, Ellen. I walked off and came back here – don't go all stiff like that! I've got work; the farmer trusts me enough to go and buy that little roan for his daughter . . . Just tell me, though, I want to hear it from you. Your dark boy, the one you called Tom. He is mine, isn't he – ours, I mean?'

'He treats Harold as his father. He's been told his real one is dead.'

'Let me see him at least. I'll be where those children's swings are, Wednesday afternoon.'

'Are you mad? It's always full of people there.'

'Best way to hide.'

'I can't promise anything. And don't come back with me!'

'Just to the corner. I saw you didn't like going past that pub.'

'Oh!'

*

Harold looked up, fishing in his waistcoat for his watch.

'You've been a while. Is your head better, then? You're all flushed, Ellen, and your coat undone – you look feverish. It's not wise to go catching a chill when others are relying on you!'

'It's still mild out, Harold. All I wanted was air and a chance to gather my thoughts.'

'Well, if you think you've gathered them sufficiently, perhaps we can go upstairs and say our prayers.'

*

The seesaw and the swings stood abandoned. Tom and David squatted intently over an ant hill. Ellen turned round suddenly.

'How long have you been there?' she demanded.

'I bin in amongst them trees over there watching you three,' said Sam. 'I bin there a while – I wanted to see who he is like.'

'For me he is like you, in all his little ways. From the first smile he gave me. In the length of his fingers.'

'It's like seeing my own face in a pond for me. And he has my father in him – that little gesture he makes with his hair. I wish my old mother had known him. A fine Gypsy *chavvi*. No need to look scared, Ellen. It's what he is,' he said. 'Did you think I was going to take him away? They say we steal children, but we don't, never have, though it's easy to blame us for the horrors others do. It'd be too tough a life for a child what hasn't been brought up to it. We love our own, though, and all of us bring them up. I have nephews and nieces I love – I'm forgetting myself. I should say I did have, for I'll not be getting to see them again. But it's not the same as one of my own. Without a child, I wasn't a proper man.'

'He's a bright, quick boy, and a loving one.'

'I can see that. I can see how he talks to the little fellow. Does Chown love him?'

'He's most of the time with me, not with Harold.'

'He provides for him, but he dunt love him, then. Why should he?'

'That's not fair on Harold.'

'You're right, it ain't. It's just he's in my way, that's all.' Sam walked across to the children. She followed him slowly. Sam crouched down beside them. He laid one hand gently on the top of Tom's head, and with the other was softly stroking David's back.

'Now tell me about this little fellow,' he was saying to Tom. The boy looked to Ellen for reassurance and said, 'He's my brother. I look after him for Mother!' David gazed wide-eyed at Tom, his mouth open in an effort to understand.

Ellen saw that in the arc of Sam's arms there was no place, no hope for Harold Chown.

*

Harold and Ellen kneeled either side of the high bed, intoning the Lord's Prayer in unison; she pressed her hands together and let the familiar words run their course, but the plea she sent to heaven was: *Don't let him touch me tonight!* Harold didn't – he hadn't done since she had repulsed him that time – and Ellen lay in the darkness remembering over and over Sam's mouth, Sam's hands.

*

They stood in a corner of a churchyard, hidden from the road, by the most recent graves. 'If someone comes, we're visiting family,' said Sam.

'I don't like it.'

'No more do I. Because I can't kiss you here.'

'I shouldn't have let you anyway.'

Beginning to cry, she pushed his hand away and rummaged for a handkerchief. 'Try to understand what my life has been. My marriage is a sham – right from the start. I've not even tried to fool poor Harold. I've gritted my teeth when he's been . . . with me. I couldn't, I daren't, think of you. I've been driven out of the village I'd lived in all my life and cannot ever go back there. The only person I trust in the whole world is Judith – and my brother John, but I hardly ever see him. I love my mother but she goes through life afraid of everything and everyone. My grandfer says he loves me, but not near as much as his principles. My two boys are what saves me. I don't understand the law, and can hardly ask Harold to explain it to me, but what would happen to them if I threw all that pretence aside and took your hand and went with you? Believe me, Sam, when I tell you every nerve in my body wants to do exactly that. But I can't abandon them.'

Sam looked down, scuffing the toe of his boot in the grass. Then he said, so quietly that she strained to hear him, 'I'm uprooted too, so believe me, I understand you. I've no business calling myself Romani now, though for everyone else I'll always be a dirty Gypsy all the same. I've left the travelling life, and there is no way for me back into it, even if I gave you up – which I won't. I can't do anything but come after you. You were all I thought about when I was lying in the gaol. You're all I have, and all I need – and without you I'd be nothing. And there's our son. Nothing changes that fact. We mun do what we can with what we have, though what I want is to have you with me always. An' you love me, an' I you.'

'Oh God!'

'Our Tom, whose name does he have?'

'Whose do you think? Chown's, of course, that poor fool of a husband of mine.'

'It was Horwood tole me you'd a husband. An old man, he said. I knew I'd reason to be jealous of that old *mush*.'

'Jealous? He was my only chance to keep your child, Sam! And he's not old, only older. He strives to be a good father in his own way. The boys are fed and clothed and educated. Harold wants them to have a profession. He doesn't want them to have to work with their hands.'

'He wouldn't, would he? And you, Ellen? You only tell me how *good* Harold is. How do you live with a man you don't love?'

'Because I must.'

'I don't know how much *he* loves *you*, but even supposing he does, he doesn't know how to show you he loves. Was it him as made you cut your hair?'

'Harold *asked* me to. He said long hair was for girls, not wives.'

'At least let's make the best of it.' Sam carefully took out her hair-grips, Ellen holding her breath as she felt the warmth of his fingers near her skin. Then with both hands he tousled her hair about her face.

'There, that's a bit softer. Your face looks happier now too. Beautiful hair and your eyes brighter for your crying.'

'They're not. They're red and swollen, you know they are.'

'Chown's never told you that you've lovely hair, has he? How could he and then cut it all off? Ellen, remembering you that day at the stream with your hair all over your shoulders has kept me going in my blackest moments. Does that man know how lucky he is?'

'I don't think he's lucky at all. And anyway, he's never even *seen* my shoulders, Sam! He's not seen any of me uncovered. He just pushes up my nightgown in the dark.'

Sam winced.

'That's not how to treat my poor girl, but I'm glad he hasn't just the same. I know you better than he, Ellen.' He took her hand and kissed her palm.

'That woman who was on the wagon with you – that's your wife, is it?'

'Yes, that was Lukey.'

'She came looking for me, you know.'

'I do. Tole me after I got taken off.'

'Then I went looking for you, and you were gone – no message, nothing! I was done for. When poor Harold offered me a way out, what else could I do? Believe me, it has not been easy being his good deed!'

'I did leave you a message. But I was afraid you wouldn't see it nor understand it if you did, but it was all I could manage. We leave *pattrins* when we move on, so other Gypsies know which way we've gone. They're sticks and leaves arranged in a certain way, but for us they're sign-posts. Caley was having a new wagon made for him in Reading, so we were due there next—'

'The beer bottle!'

'So you did find it? I got Mother to put it there, for I couldn't do it myself, I was in such a bad way. All them little stoneware bottles are a bit different one from the other, and I knew where that one had come from by the shape and the colour and the way the letters were made out on it.'

'I kept it, Sam. I have it still.'

'They gave me such a whopping that day. Her broth-ers laid into me so hard that I was bruised for weeks; they cracked two of my ribs and bust my hand – it ain't so strong as it was. If poor old Mother, God rest her, hadn't nursed me, I don't know as I would have made it.'

Ellen wept. 'I'd thought you'd abandoned me. Oh Sam!'

'Sssh! It's over now.'

He held her, unresisting.

'The beating finished what little was left between Lukey and me but they went on making me pay for making a fool of her. She took to passing between me and the fire when-ever she liked. No Gypsy woman should do that to her man – we think that a great insult. And then there was Winchester – lost a year of my sweet life in Liberty's place, a year I should have spent with you, being by you when our son was born. Winchester was a worse place than Dartmoor, and that was damp and cold enough – though it was better than Lincoln. Perhaps any gaol is better than your first. But this time I had you to remember, and time to remember you better. I used to dream of holding your face between my hands – and a bit more besides. It was in there that I learned to read and write a bit,' he said shyly. 'There was a parson in there for stealing to feed his gambling. That man kep' me from *jawing diviou* – from going mad, I mean. I couldn't do much to pay him back except to tell him not to place another bet on the nags unless he could get my advice first. There, after all this time, I've made you smile again. I thought I never should!

'But prison stopped me going to look for you and that was the worst of all. So when I was let out and Vanlo tole me the wagons were all in Oxfordshire again for the harvest, I went asking for you. I was treated with silence or curses – I think I liked the curses better. There was only two people took pity on me with all my bothering – Horwood and the widow lady, Grace. He sent me to her to see if she might know more, though he said she'd mebbe not welcome the sight of me. I went all the same, for I couldn't not do. Yet she was very civil with me. She said the chapel people made much of your Harold for what he'd done, being all holy and everything and forgiving the sinner – like he was a reg'lar St Joseph! But he went away in the end because the other villagers laughed at him for a fool and a gull.'

'He at least could take their sniping for proof of what a good, suffering Christian he is . . .'

'Don't cry. I am never going to let you go now!'

'That was Charlie's mother you spoke to. Of all the people . . .'

'She's your friend, Ellen. She asked to be remembered to you if I ever found you.'

'Poor, kind Grace. What you had should have been Charlie's, Sam. He and I should have been living quietly with our babies alongside her in that cottage, not hiding in the corner of a churchyard hoping none of the chapel people see me and getting my husband's own daughter to lie for me!'

CHAPTER 26

Frederick Anderson, a publican, was summoned at St Augustine's petty sessions at Canterbury on Saturday to show cause why he should not contribute towards the maintenance of the illegitimate female child of Jane Jarvis, of which he was the alleged father . . . the defendant keeps the "Flying Horse" public-house at Canterbury.

Whitstable Times and Herne Bay Herald,
14th October 1905

The Flying Horse

'We'll go in the back way. No one will see us.'

Ellen hung back. 'I've never been in a public house, Sam.'

'You won't be in one. We'll go up the back stairs and you'll be nowhere near the tap-room.'

'The room must cost you a bit.'

'What have I to spend my money on? I get it cheap for helping the landlord unload the dray on Wednesdays. I'll go up first, so if you want you can run away and I won't chase after you.'

'Go up, Sam. You know I won't.'

The room was small and shabby, but clean. He drew her in and closed the door, locking it and leaving the key in the hole. Flimsy faded curtains hung at a window overlooking the yard. He crossed the room quickly and closed them. They kept little light out but he sensed Ellen felt safer that way, even though they were not overlooked. Dark green linoleum covered the floor, and where it had cracked over an uneven floorboard, someone had repaired it by glueing over another piece that didn't match. To the left of the window stood a rickety wash-stand, one leg propped up with a folded beer-mat. On this stood a dented tin jug and basin with an ironed tea-towel covering the mouth of the jug. There was a small smudgy oil painting of an oast house hanging from the picture rail on one wall, whilst opposite, on the fireplace wall, was an old spotted engraving of Canterbury cathedral. The only other furniture was a narrow iron-framed bed.

Ellen stood by the door, irresolute.

'It's not much, but it's ours when we want it,' he said.

'I like it. It's simple. It's clean.' She thought of the little front parlour of her house, and how Harold's pretentious

Victorian furniture crowded its narrow space. Then she asked, 'Does anyone else use it?'

'I don't think so, unless the landlord has given out other keys.'

'What did you tell him?'

'Nothing. I didn't need to. I just asked him if he had a room I could use sometimes and he took me up here. He just patted me on the back and smiled and wished me luck. Old Percy's all right.'

'Oh Sam, I don't know . . .'

'I'll do no more than hold your hand, if that's all you want. That would mean a deal to me, you know, just for you to put your hand in mine and no one to tell you not to. And if we hang our coats on the back of the door here, it will be as if we're at home.'

Ellen fumbled with the buttons of her coat. Sam eased it off her shoulders, hung it up and lifted off the little bell hat shadowing her face. Then, as he had done in the churchyard, he took out her grips and fluffed her hair round her face. His jacket followed Ellen's coat, and the cap Farmer French had offered him in place of his old fedora, with the kindly meant words, 'Take it, lad. You'll look less of a Gypsy than with that other one.'

'Oh Sam! Your hair!'

'I'm doing my best to be respectable, you see! First time at a proper barber since the prison . . . I'd to get up the courage but it wasn't so bad in the end. Him not being another con helped. He even called me sir.'

She ran her hands over his head, and up the stubble at the back.

'You're quite different. You've even a bit of grey here.' He looked poorer, denuded somehow of more than his hair, but she didn't say so.

'Do you like me less for it?'

'Oh no, Sam. It makes me think I've known you for longer – because you look a bit older, I mean.' She lifted her face.

'What a tender way you have,' he said, and cupping her face in his hands, he kissed her, pressing her against the coats hanging on the door. Finally he drew back, and held her at arm's length.

'Ellen, I want to court you all over again. I want to be sure – of you, I mean. There is nothing I'd like mor'n to strip you of every stitch and lie you down on that bed and love you as if our lives depended on it – well, mine does, at any rate. But I want to win you.' He took her hand and led her over to the bed.

'Sit down, my girl – it'll have to be here as that's all there is, and you weren't brought up to sit on the ground like me.'

Ellen sat meekly, but then turned away from him to pull the thin bedspread back from the pillow and bolster.

'You don't need to do that! I said I wunt going to make you—'

'No, I just wanted to be sure the sheets were clean. They're old and mended, but yes, they're clean.'

'Oh Ellen,' he laughed. 'You could be talking about me! But what would you have done if they hadn't been?'

'Brought some from home, of course . . . the next time. And you're not old, Sam.'

'Not as old as poor Chown, you mean?'

Ellen leaned against his shoulder. 'Don't let's talk about Harold. Don't let him come between us – not here.'

Sam stroked her hair.

'We'll have to talk about what we're going to do – sooner or later,' he said. 'What I mean is I'm trying to get used to staying still – and with stopping, decisions have to get made. Now I've fixed myself in this place, it feels like the world is rushing on round me faster than it ever did before. I mean, when you grow up always moving from place to place, you feel as you're keeping pace with time. You know what season you're in because you're bent over picking peas, or you're selling a horse at St Giles. When the harvest is over, up you get again and come down here to Kent. It's like being a bird that knows he must take wing on a certain day, with all his pals, even if he don't know why. And now I've done the strangest thing. I'm in Canterbury when most of me thinks I'm supposed to be somewhere else by now. I've stopped for two months or more in one place before now, depending on work or weather, but in Farmer French's hopping hut I've got a little home that's rooted to the ground and won't move. The couple of sticks I have in there that are mine might as well be nailed down. No, Ellen, don't draw away from me – I'm not complaining. I have only to get used to it. When I met you in the corner of that field, you were part of the turning world just like Horwood's cows. I saw you and thought you were the best thing my eyes had ever lit on. When you live in a wagon, you're always moving on, either because it's time to go, or because the *gavvers* make you, or because there's trouble – a gamekeeper usually, or the attendance man wanting to know why the *biti chavvies* ain't in school, even if when you send 'em the teachers don't want 'em, and no more do the other children nor their parents. So you hitch the horse to the shafts again and off you go. That little world of mine stopped turning the first time I kissed you, though I didn't know it at the time. I wish I had, for I'd've got you to come away with me then and there and we'd have had a settled life somewhere – might even have been here – and nobody any the wiser. Tom might have got names shouted at him at school but he'd have had a father to defend him. Instead his father is this dead fellow nobody knows the name of.'

'If we'd done that there wouldn't have been David. I can't wish him away.'

'Nor should you. You've been clever, my Ellen. Our Tom is the mirror of me and David of you. I wonder how Harold never saw it when we were on the trap that time.'

'He didn't see you. He saw a Gypsy and they all look the same to him.'

'*Dordi,* that's hard, Ellen!'

'It's as well. He talked about you for days, kept hoping he'd hear from you. When he didn't, I knew that this Tom Boswell must be you and not some other man who really had that name.'

'I told you I'd be coming back, and I have.' He kissed her gently. 'Do you trust me now?'

'Oh yes.'

'But you know that whatever you and me do in this room, now, or next week, or as long as Judith's willing to cover for us, means that some day you'll have to make a choice?'

Ellen looked steadily at him for about a minute, then put her hand to the back of his neck and drew his face down to hers. When she felt his touch upon her knee her legs gently parted as though of their own accord; she was surprised at the strength and speed of her arousal. His roughened fingers found their way gently under the lace edge of her drawers and worked blindly yet accurately at the quick of her. With his other hand he cradled her head against his shoulder, muffling the hot force of her cries against the skin of his neck. As he felt her sex soften and relax he carefully withdrew his hand and held her close, rocking her gently and kissing her damp, flushed forehead.

'Next time,' he murmured, 'I promise to strip you as bare as you were in the wood, and worship every inch of you. I love you, Ellen.' He straightened her skirt. 'Will you see me next week?'

'Oh, yes, Sam.'

'Come and stand on the Burgate where we met that day of the cattle market. I'll walk by and touch my cap politely to you, as though you're a lady I've mebbe done a job for. Let me get twenty paces ahead of you and then follow me. I'll be standing out in the yard below having a smoke. I'll nod to you, polite-like again, and then you go in and up the stairs – I'll have unlocked the door here. If there's no one in the yard, I'll be up at once. Otherwise I'll have another smoke and come up after.'

'You've thought of everything, Sam.'

'Not quite. But you've had enough trouble on account of me already. So I'll do whatever I can to save you more. Now you go down, and walk out through the yard, and go along the lane. Don't turn out by the front. You'll not meet any chapel people out the back unless they've a mind to go preaching in the lion's den.'

He put her into her coat, but before letting her button it he slipped his arms round her underneath it and held her close.

'Oh Ellen, if I died right this minute I'd die happy!' he murmured into her hair.

'Don't talk so!'

'All right. Now out we go, until the next time.'

He stood at the head of the narrow staircase and watched her descend, head bowed and eclipsed by hat and coat collar. What neat little feet she had, and she walked as elegant as a pony!

As Ellen reached the last few steps, the noise of voices and the fug of ale and tobacco smoke rose up from the corridor to the public bar to meet her. The sound grew suddenly louder, as someone pushed open the glass-panelled door on his way to the privy in the yard. Ellen didn't turn round.

*

She found Judith on the steps of the bandstand. Tom and David were chasing each other, as excitable as puppies, in an endless and unregulated game of tig. With a twinge Ellen wondered if they preferred to spend time with Judith rather than with her; Judith worried less about the state of their clothes.

'Well, I thought you'd look happier! You're back early.'

'Oh Judy, I don't know . . .'

'Go on, aren't you going to tell me all about it? Still handsome, is he?'

'I've nothing to tell you, really . . .'

'He must've kissed you, at least! *Go on!*'

'We talked. I can't say more than that. He looks tired, Judy, that's all. Like he has the cares of the world on his shoulders. He's different.'

'Not so Gypsy then?'

'That's it. No neckerchief, no earring, no hat on one side. He's not . . . he's not cock of the walk the way he was, Judy. If you saw him you'd just see a poor labouring man, but you might ask where his father came from.'

'Not disappointed, are you?'

'Oh no, not at all.'

'So he's poor but honest, in love with the respectable lady,' said Judith, who devoured novels from the circulating library that she didn't let her father see.

'Respectable? Oh, Judy!'

'Remember what we agreed. You cover for me and Walter Saturday afternoon.'

'What if it rains?'

'We'll deal with that if it happens! Now stop worrying.'

'What's your father done to deserve this, Judy?'

'Don't care a button about him, do I?' she said, with a toss of the head. 'If he had his way, I'd never see no one, never have a laugh, never have pretty clothes, not read anything but scripture or that dreary paper he writes for that's supposed to be so "uplifting" and "improving". I'd have no life!'

'Judith, he trusts us both.'

'Well, more fool him then!'

*

Sam's instructions had worked perfectly. Ellen sat on the bed in the room above the Flying Horse, her head light with a peculiar floating feeling of relief at having reached the shabby little sanctuary, after counting the days, the hours, the minutes.

'The fire's already laid!' she said.

'I came early and did that,' said Sam. 'There's no travelling man who don't know how to get a fire going.'

'And the rag rug? I used to make them when I was a girl.'

'You're still a girl – my girl. It's clean. Mrs French gev it me for my hut, but I wrapped it up careful and kept it for here.'

'It's warm as toast in here!'

'O' course it is,' he said. 'I meant what I said last time. I don't want you catching cold, but I want every stitch off you – if you'll let me.'

'Oh Sam!'

'I can't tell you how many times I've thought about this moment, Ellen . . .'

'I've thought about it too,' she answered, looking down.

'So many buttons, though! No, don't help me . . . undo my shirt instead . . . Oh, this is pretty!' he exclaimed, running his finger along the edge of her chemise.

'Don't you recognise the lace, Sam?'

'Mother's!'

'I didn't want anyone else to see it but you. It's too pretty and I didn't want questions about where it came from. I made that chemise, and my drawers,' she added shyly. 'I've not worn them before, apart from last week.'

'My girl! You came prepared even then. You're blushing, but you've no idea how much I like that. My braces, Ellen – and the fly buttons. Oh dear, that fellow can't wait much longer. Unhook them stockings, I'm afraid of tearing 'em.'

'Wait,' she said, as he was about to take off his shirt. 'Let me.'

She ran her fingertips down his body, from shoulders to navel, her nails catching his nipples, and then circling his back.

'*Sam!* What's this? Turn round!'

He did so, and said over his shoulder. 'Lukey's brothers. Then the cat – in Winchester. I'm sorry, Ellen, I should've warned you.'

She started to cry, laying her wet face against the stippled skin.

*

'You're beautiful, Ellen.' He propped himself on an elbow, and with his right hand caressed her breast.

'Your pretty *birks* are softer'n I remember, but these are bigger and darker,' he said, circling her nipple with his forefinger. 'Makes your skin all the whiter.'

He shifted down until his face was level with her breasts, and gently stroked her stomach, easing a fingertip into her navel. 'That little rabbit hole ain't the same.'

'You're tickling!'

'It looks like a button hole – or a tiny letter box.'

'Babies did that, Sam.'

His hand stopped moving, then tapped her skin lightly.

'I want my son. I want to know him and him to know me. I want him to love me.'

'He loves Harold, Sam, in his own little-boy way.'

'And what does Harold do with his little cuckoo?'

'Not cuddling and kissing and all that babies need – not with David either. He sees that as womanly. I think the boys fear him a little, though they've no call to. He never beats them, but he can make them feel guilty with a frown – and a sermon if needs be.'

'Leave him. Come away with me.'

'How can I, Sam? What about David?'

'I'd take him along too. I'd love lots of kiddies.'

'Look at me, Sam . . . Can you really mean that?'

'I want to put more babies in you, Ellen. He'd have to give you up then.'

'Have you any idea what you're saying?'

'I'll dig under this parsley patch again now, if you don't believe me,' he said, moving his hand gently between her legs. She shifted, aware of a slight soreness, that salty aching tenderness of prolonged love-making after long abstinence.

'I don't know that I can, Sam . . .'

'I'll never make you if you don't want to.'

*

She watched him as he stood naked by the corner of the opened window, where he had been sent to smoke ('Not here – I can't come home smelling of tobacco'). She'd pulled the covers up against the draught, but he didn't seem to notice the cold.

'Sam?'

'What is it, lovely girl?'

'After us . . . did you still go with Lukey?'

Sam turned back to the window.

'Just once. She was all I had – I thought I'd lost you. She was my wife – *is* my wife. I cried after; I hated us both.'

'Did you ever have other girls?'

'No. That's not our way.' He threw the cigarette butt out of the window, closed it and crossed the room. 'Let me in.'

Ellen turned back the covers. He got in and lay on his back.

'If I'm honest, there very nearly was one once – before I met you, I mean,' he said, staring at the ceiling. 'In France. One of the boys said we needed cheering up – we did, of course, we always did. Joe said he knew somewhere. I thought he meant a *kitchema,* an inn, and I liked the ale they had over there. It was a poor enough place we went to. There was five or six girls – you paid an old woman at the door and then you went in. They were sitting round, waiting, all *nangi,* of course.'

'*Nangi?*' asked Ellen, flushing.

'Naked. But they wore their nakedness like a blacksmith wears his apron, or a nurse her uniform. There was a good fire going in the place because of it. My chums chose their girls and followed them upstairs . . . I was tempted, I'll tell you. I was so bloody lonely – lonely there, and lonely at home. But I knew Lukey wouldn't have served me that way. Joe took the prettiest one, I remember, but I went outside and smoked coffin nails till they all come out again. For a man that had gone to be cheered up Joe had a pretty long face on 'im. He said the girl had a picture in her room, a little boy, her *putty feess* she called him. When I heard that I wished I'd gone up with her just to talk – or try to, with my mumbling French.'

'What did she look like – that girl?'

Sam paused, thinking about lying.

'She looked . . . a little like you.'

'*Oh!*'

'Listen, Ellen, I could've told you she was dark and skinny, but then you'd think the kind of girl I liked was more like Lukey, and that ain't so. And she wasn't really like you at all – much more joking and laughing, not quiet and peaceful the way you are, though o' course I don't know as that wasn't the way they taught 'em to be in that place, or whether she was like that to hide what she really felt about herself inside, poor girl. I couldn't pay a woman to love me – I'd never know if she meant it – but I wouldn't think badly of one who had a child to feed, or for helping a man to forget the hell round him for a minute. For even if I wasn't waking every morning to kill a man, I was helping those that did every time I got some poor horse ready for battle or to move their infernal kit about.

'You've no cause to be jealous, Ellen. It's poor Lukey I've treated like a *lubbeny*, a whore, like one who didn't care much if it was me or some other man – which was not fair to her, because she'd never played me wrong that way. You've gone with your Harold. You could go away from me now and he might come bothering you for his rights tonight, whilst I'm lying in the dark in my hut burning up for you and not being able to do a thing about it – because that's what I do, every night. I'm living for these afternoons, being in this room with you for two hours at a time when I'd like to lie beside you all night and hear you breathing, and bring you your cup of tea in the morning. We've only got this – for now – so let's not let either of 'em come between us here. I've left her for you, Ellen – she'll never get me back! Now it's you I'm waiting for.'

Ellen was silent for a moment, then said: 'You thought I'd gone with Charlie before you.'

'O' course I did. It was the war made me think that way, for I'd hear the other lads talking about their girls. Some of 'em married fast just to have a chance of it before a bullet got 'em. Some persuaded their girls without. Some I'd say was just boasting. Our first time, you know, when I made such a *dinilo* of myself, thinking you'd got your sickness . . . that's because with you being a *gauji,* I thought you *must've* been with poor Charlie before me. For me that didn't signify that you was a bad girl. We're taught the *gaujos* don't do as we do, so if a travelling man has to do with a *gauji rakli* then the same rules won't apply, so he'll do with her as he'd never do with a Romani *chie.*'

'We'd call that the letter not the spirit,' said Ellen coldly.

'I don't know about letters and spirits – I'm a bit scarce when it comes to the first,' he said uncomprehendingly.

'I mean that it's like obeying the rule as it's written down, but not what the rule is trying to do.'

'Oh, that's deep, Ellen. I never had the Sunday school like you.'

'And if I'd been a Gypsy girl?'

'Well, yes . . . I wouldn't have thought you a good girl if you'd been Romani. You weren't one of us,' he rushed on, 'but I was your first all the same. That binds me to you. It's Harold that's in our way, not me in his.'

'I'm his wife. I've made him promises.'

'Only 'cause you didn't know different! You did what you had to do so that you and my Tom would be fed. Now kiss me, will you, and tell me you still want me.'

*

The following week, Sam was again banished to the window to smoke, when he spotted the bag Ellen had brought with her.

'What's this, then?'

'Some books, Sam, but I don't know if you'll like them.'

He kneeled and rummaged.

'They're books for kiddies, surely? What's that cat doing wearing them clothes?'

'They're the boys' books. I shall have to take them back with me or they'll miss them.'

'The pictures are very fine ... Oh, I recognise this. A keeper with a gun! I've had enough run-ins with them – and that was after a rabbit usually, same as here. Oh look, he's shot off his tail and his whiskers but the *shoshoi* gets away all the same!'

'Just try reading them. See what you can remember from the man in Winchester. If I know how much you understand I can get you better books next time. These are the ones the boys like me to read to them. I'm using them to teach Tom before he goes to the school in September.'

'Is he good at his learning?'

'Oh yes! He's quick – fast as a flea. Always asking questions – and the sharpest memory! He misses nothing.'

'Our boy. He should be sitting here between us now.'

'He shouldn't see his father without his trousers on!'

'And that parson didn't teach me in his chemise! But you're so much prettier than him—'

'Stop it, Sam, and tell me what it says here.'

'Sorry. You distract me, that's all, when you look down with your head on one side like that, all serious. I do want to learn, Ellen. The reverend helped me more than he knows, and not just with the reading and writing. I want my boy to be proud of me – his little brother too. I want to read to him, not him read to his poor ignorant father. What tales does he like the most?'

'Of these little books, there's one where a badger gets the better of a fox – and another one where a kitten is rescued from a pie. I have to read them over and over, and never change a word or he'll notice.'

'I wonder what *I* can do for them. Something I can make with my own hands, and give to them.'

'We must be careful.'

'But for how long? How long mun I wait?'

CHAPTER 27

Why unbelieving? Why wilt thou spurn,
Love that so gently pleads thy return?

Primitive Methodist Hymnal no. 252, London, 1887.

Dipty Man

Canterbury

'Why don't you go up and say your prayers yourself, Ellen? I want to finish this article for the *Review* tonight but I don't want to keep you up.'

'All right, Harold. Goodnight, then, but don't tire yourself out.'

Harold's papers lay strewn across the table. His Bible lay open on top of them, but the cap of his fountain pen was firmly screwed on. The article was already written and sealed in its envelope. He thought of going out to post it but couldn't summon up the energy. Always prudent, he stood up and dimmed the gas, then reached for the oil lamp and turned down the wick, and sat in silence and near darkness. That little train the boys had been playing with, hand-carved and cheerfully painted, was more beautiful than any toy he had ever possessed as a child.

'Where did this come from, then?' he'd heard himself asking. His own son, his David, had looked up smiling with his mother's eyes and said, 'The nice dipty man.'

'Dipty?' repeated Harold, as a cold hand reached round and squeezed his heart.

'He means Gypsy, Father,' said Tom. 'Mother got it from a Gypsy that came up to her in the park. He said we were fine boys.'

'And so you are,' croaked Harold.

'What's the matter? You look all funny.'

'Oh, I'm all right. Just tired. You go on with your game.'

*

In the back room of the Cricketers, Walter lifted Sam's empty glass and said, 'Another one?'

'If you will too, Wattie, then thank you.'

They knew Walter in this pub. Sam watched the confident roll of Judith's young man's shoulders as he went to the hatch to refill their glasses, and felt his sense of adventure at being part of their subterfuge. Walter, in his own way as forthright as Judy, had wanted to know was Sam 'all right'. Having decided pretty quickly that he was, he'd declared with clumsy frankness that: 'You might be a gippo, but as far as I can see, you're a pretty straight sort of fellow', and the conversation had turned to horse-racing. Three pints later, and Walter had become more confiding, declaring his intention to marry Judith if he could.

'Well, what does she say about it?' asked Sam.

'I can't say as I've ezackly arst her yet. I need to find the right moment, you see. She's a bit of a handful,' he said, a proud smile breaking over his face. 'You'd not be sure she wouldn't cuff you or laugh at you if the idea didn't please her. But I've never met anyone I liked even half as much.'

'Just ask her. Be grateful you have that chance.'

Walter raised his eyebrows. 'Gor, sorry, Sam. I'm forgetting . . . Truth is,' and he leaned in and lowered his voice to give his story greater importance, 'I did get mixed up with a married woman a couple of years ago – husband a commercial traveller. Thought I was on to a good deal there! Then I found she was just getting me to tag along of her to annoy some other fellow she had her eyes on. A bit different for you, though, with your kiddie and all.'

Sam flushed. *But I want the world to know Tom's mine!*

'I'm married too,' he muttered into his glass.

'Blimey! You're quite the sheikh, ain't you?'

Sam looked up sharply, but faced with Walter's open, somewhat befuddled face, it was impossible to be angry. If any other man had said this to him, Sam would have got up and left in order not to take a swing at him, but Walter was so artless in his manner, admiring, almost, that he could only smile back, feeling himself to be much older. Judy's man was a well-meaning, not very perceptive *gaujo*, but Sam saw him with absolute clarity, in this same pub, surrounded by his work companions, waving his glass about and saying, 'You say that about the gippos, but I'll have you know that a good friend of mine is one and he's as honest as they come – trust him with my last shilling, I would.' Walter might not question any of the assumptions of his upbringing, but would be loyal in defending a friend, whoever he was.

Sam said, 'No, for me there's only Ellen now.'

*

Laying his papers down on the table, for he couldn't concentrate, Harold dimmed the oil lamp and went at his problem again, as if picking a scab until it hurt. Maybe it wasn't him. Wasn't there a whole encampment of Gypsies out by Thanington? No doubt Ellen had bought the toy from a hawker and hadn't wanted to say anything because she knew he thought the boys already had too many things. *Heavens, she can buy them as many toys as she wants – she's a careful enough housekeeper, after all – anything but accept gifts from that man!* What if it *was* him? Anger bubbled up in Harold and displaced his fear. Surely she was not in danger from someone who had treated her so badly? But doubt crept back; Harold turned up the oil lamp again and pulled the heavy Bible towards him. Where was that terrible passage? Ah yes, here . . .

> *And a man lie with her carnally, and it be hid from the eyes of her husband . . . and the spirit of jealousy come upon him . . . then shall the man bring his wife unto the priest . . . and of the dust that is in the floor of the tabernacle the priest shall take, and put it into the water . . . the bitter water that causeth the curse . . . and say unto the woman . . . if some man have lain with thee beside thine husband . . . this water that causeth the curse shall go into thy bowels, to make thy belly to swell, and thy thigh to rot . . .*

Harold wept. *If only there was some bitter water that could ease my mind or tell me she makes a fool of me.*

Ever since his conversion, as a seventeen-year-old at a camp meeting, he had found in scripture both comfort and guidance, and had marvelled at the way that there was always something in that book to guide him with any challenge or trial. He'd said so always to those who came to him for advice, and his knowledge of where to look had impressed in ways his preaching had sometimes failed to do. But there was no comfort in his agony now, only the confirmation that there had been husbands before him who had faced this terrible dilemma. *If I denounce her, I must put her aside. If only there was something else that she could drink that would make her love me . . .* He put his head in his hands and a distant memory swam up before him. He was a boy at a village fair, in love with the colour and noise. He preached against the dangers of such events now, though much of what he remembered was quite harmless: prizes for the biggest vegetable, or for guessing the number of stitches in an enormous knitted golly-wog . . . apple-bobbing, coconut shies, the vicar greeting people in the sunshine. Yet he had also found the Morris dancers sinister, the fool, the blackface, the raggy men. And whilst other children had laughed, he had covered his eyes when Punch beat Judy to death. A group of older girls had been clustered round a tent advertising fortunes, egging each other on to go inside. Harold had stood there fascinated when an old Gypsy woman had come out, fantastically dressed in an old plaid skirt and a Paisley shawl, a wide-brimmed hat groaning with artificial flowers crowning her grey curly hair. She had spotted him staring and called out to him: 'Want a love potion, dearie, to make one of them pretty ladies thine?' He had run off with the laughter of those girls stinging his ears.

Harold groaned. He would say his prayers now rather than upstairs in the bedroom where Ellen was, and put the matter in God's hands. He kneeled, and with the well-tried words, sought safe harbour from the storm. Eventually he rose to his feet and went reluctantly upstairs. From the regularity of her breathing, he knew that Ellen was already asleep. Her soft breath sounded so innocent. Perhaps, he thought, with a little joyous spurt of hope, perhaps she was completely blameless, and there was some harmless explanation for the presence of the wooden toy.

He lay some minutes, bathed briefly in relief, sending silent thanks heavenward. Then he turned on his side, and gently patted her sleeping shoulder. Ellen made a low, indistinct sound, and rolling towards him, embraced him, fitting her body to his. She slept on whilst Harold lay stiff with despair. Never had she held him in that way. He eased her sleeping arm away and turned his back, mouthing silently into the darkness, 'Let the day perish wherein I was born, and the night in which it was said, There is a man child conceived,' but like Job, he refused to curse his God.

CHAPTER 28

What makes you leave your house and land?
What makes you leave your money, O?
What makes you leave your new wedded lord,
To go with the wraggle taggle Gypsies, O?

Traditional

Hosea

In the narrow scullery Ellen clinked the crockery onto the tray with as little noise as possible. She could see Harold through the doorway, staring at the open Bible. He was preparing for preaching that coming Sunday. There would likely be no more than the usual congregation, she thought sadly, for though Harold's sermons were diligently prepared, perceptive and thoughtful, he couldn't compete with the fire of the famed circuit preachers. The fare would be plain, ungarnished, but she would do her best to listen attentively.

Why was he so still? Normally he attacked his sermons briskly, with much lifting of pages, running his finger down concordances, muttering the quotes he would use under his breath. Now he seemed transfixed by what he saw on the page. She was not close enough to see whether his eyes moved. The boys played quietly on the rag-rug with the wooden train. They would have preferred to run it smoothly across the linoleum where it could get up speed, as they did when Harold was out, but were obedient to the command to be respectful of their father's work. She lifted the tea-tray. He looked up at her, stricken, but asked her an apparently harmless question.

'Um . . . is Judith at the temperance meeting still?'

'So far as I know.'

Harold stared at her.

'She isn't, is she? You both deceive me. Do you think I don't know, Ellen?'

The tray shook in her hands, the willow-pattern crockery shivering. She put it down, but could not look at him. He went on quietly.

'I am an unimaginative man. I don't know how to show what I feel, but do not assume that I do *not* feel. Do not assume that I cannot be hurt, humiliated. And never think that I do not love you.'

This was the worst of all. Had he raged at her, thrown the tea-tray against the wall, struck her, even that might have been better.

'I should ask your forgiveness, Ellen.'

'*You?*'

'Keep your voice down. Next door has ears.'

'Let us eat something if we can, Harold. Then let me put the boys to bed.'

'Did you think your children didn't know? Were you bribing them to secrecy? Their understanding isn't perfect, but I found out because of them. I said I should ask your forgiveness, and it's true. Nobody like me should have aspired to one such as you, Ellen. I took advantage of your situation. I took advantage of you in my own way as much as that Gypsy did . . . knowing that you really didn't have much of a choice. You thought I was proud of what I'd done, for looking saintly in the eyes of our brethren – don't deny it, I've always known it, always seen your resentment, and yes, I *was* proud. Walking out of the chapel with you on my arm was the happiest moment of my life – more than when I married poor Millie. And you were honest with me. You told me you didn't love me, but you were grateful to me. I thought we could start from there, and make something of it all, if I watched over you, and that we would do good work for the Lord together, that in time all His gifts would be granted to us. Then David came, and I thought we might both be content at last. I did believe that, Ellen. You took me for a hypocrite. You told me as much, and I was guilty of that, I admit, in that business with Ellis, but the reality is much simpler than that. I love you, Ellen. I'd always admired you from afar, but the seed of love was planted when your grandfather came to me weeping—'

'He never wept!'

'He did then, believe me. I saw my chance – I thought – and I took it. I don't know as I should do any different, even now, knowing that you have loved that man all this time and you see him again whenever you can. I'm sure you don't manage your meetings without the help or the connivance of my own daughter – I am betrayed and made a fool of on all sides. I don't know which way to turn. I even ask myself was it the workings of Providence that brought him and you together.'

Then Harold's poor jowly face worked, creased and gave up the battle. He put his head in his hands and wept. The two little boys looked up, puzzled. Ellen tentatively patted his shoulder. It was like trying to comfort a stranger, someone she barely knew.

'Ellen!' He spoke into the cup of his hands. 'I must speak to him. Arrange it, will you?'

The fork in the road was reached at last.

CHAPTER 29

Rejoice for a brother deceased,
Our loss is his infinite gain;
A soul out of prison released,
And freed from its bodily chain.

Primitive Methodist Hymnal no. 973.

Denne's Mill

'Judy! Wake up!'

'What's the matter, Ellen?'

'Harold hasn't come home.'

'What time is it?'

'Gone midnight.'

Judith sat up in bed. 'So he has been out three hours. They could still be talking. Or maybe he's gone for a walk.'

'In that rain? I want to go and look for him. I'm frightened.'

'I'll come with you then. Just let me get dressed.'

'We can't leave the children alone, Judy.'

'I'll get next door in.'

'At this hour? I don't want to make a fuss—'

'Oh Ellen, you never have, and look where it's got you! There'll be no fuss. Mrs Clerk hasn't a job to go to in the morning and she'll get a bit of excitement from it. Maybe Pa has got into trouble at last – breach of the peace by night-time preaching or something.'

'Oh please don't joke now, Judy! He went to see Sam!'

'Oh, Gor! Look, Ellen, I'm getting my clothes on. I'll get old Clerk organised. Go out the front door meanwhile and see if you can't see him coming along the road. Take the gamp. Did you never get ready for bed then?'

'How could I?'

*

'So where are we going, Ellen?'

'The bridge at Denne's Mill.'

'It's a funny thing being out at this hour.'

'I don't care for it, Judy! I wish there were more constables about.'

'Well, you're in luck. Who do you think that is coming along there with the torch? I don't like the way he's shining it right at us, though, up and down like that – what's the matter with him?'

'Ssh! Judy, he'll hear you!'

'In this downpour? He's got a river running off that cape of his.'

'Right, you two – stop there!' called the policeman. 'You look like you're new round here. A bit wet for business, isn't it?'

'Will you stop shining that into my eyes!'

'*Judy!*'

'What, no paint? No geegaws?' the man exclaimed.

'Constable, could you help us please . . .'

The policeman shone his torch briefly under Ellen's umbrella, dazzling her. Then his manner changed abruptly.

'I do beg pardon, ladies – it is rather late. I'd see you home myself only there's been an incident back there. Don't suppose you've seen anyone acting suspiciously, running but not trying to get out of the rain, for instance?'

Ellen caught Judy's arm.

'I'm looking for my husband – this is my stepdaughter – he went to meet someone by Denne's Mill, and he's not come home.'

'There's no easy way for me to say this, ladies, but they've just pulled a man from the mill race. I think you'd best come with me. We'll need to get a description of your husband – no point putting you through an unpleasant experience unless it's absolutely necessary.'

He looked directly into Ellen's ashen face.

'Identifying the deceased, I mean. If it's not him, nor the man he went to meet, then we'll at least have the description of your husband if we're to look for him.'

'Deceased?' whispered Ellen. She'd been clinging to the idea that a drowning man had been saved. But which of them was dead?

*

Half an hour later, having refused the small brandy the kindly desk sergeant offered her, Ellen tried to give a description of Harold Chown.

'It's hard to say what he looks like, really. He's quite . . . ordinary.'

'Start with his age, then.'

'Fifty-six.'

'How tall?'

'Oh, about middling.'

'Well, if Ernest and I stand up here, who is he closer in height to?'

'Maybe a little less than Ernest, sir.'

'Hair colour?'

'Grey.'

'Got all his own hair still?'

'He's going a little thin on the crown, but yes. He uses a bit of pomade but just to keep it tidy. He parts it about here . . .'

'Eyes?'

'Hazel.'

'And how would you describe his build?'

'Oh dear ... middling again. He stoops slightly, on account of his work and ... perhaps because he doesn't like people to notice him too much. He's got a bit of weight round the middle.'

'Any distinguishing marks?'

'Oh ... I don't know, really. I never ... saw any. He complains about his bunions. His shoes always pinch him.'

'And what about his clothes?'

'He always wears a collar and tie – a dark one, but I can't remember which one he was wearing today. I've never seen him without, even by his own hearth. Plain collar studs always – not silver or mother of pearl or anything like that. The suit he wears for work – it has a very fine stripe in it – a waistcoat, and his father's watch on a chain. I think it has something engraved inside it. Dark grey braces. He didn't take his gamp with him; I noticed it by the door when Judith and I went to look for him. Black shoes, oldish ones but with new soles, a homburg hat.'

'Thank you. Is there anything *you* can add, Miss Chown?'

Judith shook her head.

The policeman sighed, and replaced the cap on his fountain pen.

'I'm afraid, ladies, the man they have in the mortuary at Longport more or less answers this description.'

Ellen shut her eyes, appalled at the relief she felt, and gripped Judith's hand. *It's not Sam!*

Misunderstanding her, the policeman went on.

'However, we shouldn't despair just yet. There are probably hundreds of men in Canterbury would fit that description. It's a possibility that the man you'll be asked to identify will be a complete stranger.'

'Perhaps he's at home by now, wondering where we are?'

'We can rule that out. An officer has gone to your house and is being looked after by your Mrs Clerk at this moment. If he *is* your husband then we shall need to ask you what, if anything, you know about the man he went to meet. But, first things first. There's a car ready to take you to Longport.'

*

The brightness of the light in the white-tiled mortuary hurt Ellen's eyes and a stench of ammonia made them water. She had never been in anywhere quite so clean. The body lay under a sheet on a marble-topped trestle, but the feet protruded, pale, creased, pathetically helpless – and bunioned. An aproned orderly led her to the head of the trestle. She could smell the pomade he used on his hair and moustache despite the ammonia reek. The orderly took the sheet in both hands and murmured: 'Are you ready, ma'am?'

She took in the torn forehead, the jowls slack and pale, the teeth visible through the parted blue lips, but also the delicacy of the skin over his collarbone. She heard Judith sniffling at her shoulder, and thought: *Sam, what have you done?*

*

By the time Canterbury petered out amongst swaggering Victorian mansions, Sam was drenched through. Once the street lamps ended he guided himself by the blur of the moon beyond the heavy clouds and by the grit of the road. By Milestone Farm, where he turned left towards Patrixbourne into the tunnel made by looming hedgerows, his boots were squelching and he began to feel light-headed, wound-up, the desperate circular conversation with Harold repeating itself in his brain. He missed his footing, landing clumsily with one knee in the rivulet bordering the lane; someone had recently scythed back the hedge, and the snapped twigs scratched his face and plucked off his cap. He retrieved it, sopping wet, and went on bare-headed beneath the storm.

French's farm loomed up, closed and dark, after what had felt like a journey of four hours, though he had come only five miles, which at his customary swinging pace usually only took him an hour and a half whatever the weather. The rain had at last eased off, and the flagstones of the yard between house and barn glittered in the moonlight. Two indistinct shapes skittered towards him, and first Fred's shaggy face pushed at his hand, followed by the softer nose of French's collie Ben. Neither barked: they reserved that for tramps.

'Oh, boys, I'm done in!' he murmured. Both escorted him silently to his hut, Ben then leaving to go back to the barn. Sam collapsed in exhaustion on his mattress, though Fred butted at his boots, wondering why he didn't take them off.

An hour later Fred nosed open the door of the hut and loped across to the porch of the house, lifted his head and howled. Ben trotted over and joined in. French opened up eventually, his sou'wester over his nightshirt. He held an old miner's lamp, and picked up the shotgun propped up inside the door. His wife hovered behind him.

'Wake Algie,' said French, referring to his other farm-hand.

Following the dogs, the two men could hear Sam's muttering before they reached his hut. Pushing the door back, the farmer lifted the lamp above a sweating, putty-hued face.

'You take his legs, Algie, and we'll get him into the house.'

Meg French, her long grey plait flicking back and forth, took over. 'Algie, lay the fire now – we'll need the warming pan.'

'He can go in my bed,' said Algie. 'The other room'll be too cold.'

She glanced at him. 'Good man. Let's get his boots off and then take 'im upstairs. I'll sit up.'

'Ellen,' murmured Sam.

'So he has got a woman,' said Algie.

*

Three days of broth and nettle tea, and sponging with warm water and vinegar (Meg French stifled a cry when she first saw Sam's scarred back), three days of damp sheets and tossing and yelling, and the fever abated. Finally Sam was able to sit up in bed and thank his nurse with lucid eyes.

'Oh Sam,' she said. 'What have you done? There's two policemen downstairs wanting to talk to you.'

Matthew French's exasperated voice carried up the stairs.

'I told your men yesterday he couldn't do a thing like that. He'd not cause pain to any living thing if he didn't have to, much less a man – or a woman, for that matter. He'll bag a rabbit for the pot, of course. And he'll shoot down a crow rather than let 'im pluck the eyes out of the new lambs. The only creature he hates like poison is the rat. I've been talking to him at the door of the barn and seen him shift so's an old tabby who's found herself a place on the straw where the sun hits ain't in shadow.'

'What do they want with me, Mr French?' said Sam, stepping slowly down into the room. The older of the two policemen got to his feet.

'Sampson Loveridge? Wednesday night Mr Harold Chown was found drowned at Denne's Mill. His widow says he'd gone to meet you. You've to come along of us. The coroner'll be sitting in the morning.'

*

Though it was still daylight, Ellen, Judith and Walter sat in the back room with the curtains closed. Harold's Bible, bristling with page markers, his inkwell and the paper on which he wrote his sermons were just as he had left them, tidied away into the alcove to the left of the chimney breast. On the table lay the receipt for the telegram Judith had sent to Chingestone that morning. Nobody had remembered to get tea ready, though before too long the boys, driven by hunger, would come downstairs and ask for it, and when Pa would come home, and why could they not play outside?

Walter had slept on Millie's settle in the front parlour since that rainy night, telling them that they and the boys could not be left on their own: 'Too many nosey parkers poking about the place.'

White-faced, Ellen looked at her hands and said for the sixth time that evening: 'It must have been an accident – mustn't it?'

Instead of answering this time, Judith got up and said, 'Kettle.'

Ellen turned a pleading face to Walter. 'What do *you* think?'

'I think you did right telling them where to find him – Sam, I mean. If you hadn't, they'd've found him anyway and thought you was in it together.'

'"In it together"? Oh, Walter!'

'Ssh. I don't mean it like that!' He looked through to the scullery where Judy was crashing the tea things onto a tray. 'I think,' he said, without looking at Ellen, 'if Sam ain't done anything then he ain't got nothing to worry about.'

CHAPTER 30

... about twenty years since at the Assizes at Bury [St. Edmunds] about thirteen were condemned and executed for this offence, namely, for being Gypsies.

Sir Matthew Hale 1649

King's Coroner

Canterbury

'Mr Loveridge, will you tell this court when you last saw the deceased?'

'I met him by the mill race at Denne's Mill by St Radigund's, on the second of August, about half past nine at night. I can't be exact about that time, for I have no timepiece, but it was a little after Bell Harry chimed.'

'Was this an accidental meeting, or by arrangement?'

'By arrangement.'

'On whose part?'

'Mr Chown's, sir.'

'And who decided the place?'

'I did.'

'Why there?'

'I knew he'd have something to say to me that he wouldn't want others to hear, and the water runs hard there.'

'Did you know Mr Chown before that time?'

'Yes, I'd met him once. He came preaching in a village I passed through on my way to Canterbury and I went back on the cart with him.'

'So he knew where to find you, Mr Loveridge?'

'He sent a message by Mrs Chown, sir.'

'By *Mrs* Chown? And what did he want to see you about?'

'On account of my seeing Ellen – Mrs Chown.'

'You were having an affair with Mrs Chown?'

'I was, sir, I am.'

'Tell the court what happened when you met him.'

'He ... he was greatly upset, sir, about the business I had with Ellen – with Mrs Chown. He told me he loved her, in spite of everything. He said he would do anything to convince me to give her up, that she was the world to him.'

'And what did you say to that?'

'I told him 'twas the same for me, that I couldn't give her up, that I loved her too and she me.'

'And how long is it that you have been engaged in this adulterous liaison with Mrs Chown?'

'I can't think of it as 'dulterating, sir, for I knew her before he did. To my mind he was 'dulterating me, for she was mine first.'

'May I ask you to clarify, then, Mr Loveridge, exactly how long it is that you have known the lady?'

''Bout five years on and off. I was encamped about half-way 'tween Oxford and Wycombe, but I got forcibly took off by my wife and her brothers and by the time I got back there she was gone, wived with Mr Chown, and I never see'd her again till nigh on a year ago, and that was accidental, and here in Canterbury.'

'You have a wife, Mr Loveridge? And where might she be now?'

'I can't say as to that. She may turn up again with her relations for the hopping next month, as I work now on the same farm as we went to for the last lot of bines. If she do, I shall need ask Mr French can I not make myself scarce until she and they be gone away again. But I don't think she'd care much to see me anyroad.'

'I think it would be advisable for you not to "make your-self scarce" until the means by which Mr Chown met his death have been determined, and I am sure the constabu-lary will agree with me. So you resumed your liaison with Mrs Chown last year?'

'I went back to loving her reg'lar, if that's what you mean, yes, sir.'

'Yes, I expect that is more or less what I mean.'

'I didn't kill him, sir, to get her to myself, if that's where you are a going with this.'

'Nobody has yet suggested that you did, Mr Loveridge. Perhaps you will let me continue ... You said of Mrs Chown that – let me consult my notes here – she was "mine first". I had been given to understand from the deceased's friends and colleagues that Mrs Chown was a widow when he married her, a widow with an infant son.'

'She wunt no widow, sir.'

'No? So do you know, then, who was the father of her elder child?'

'That was me, sir.'

'I . . . see. So you met Mr Chown by the mill race that night by his invitation, you being the father of Mr Chown's wife's first child and now once more her lover. Tell us what you judged to be the deceased's state of mind when you met him.'

'As I said, he was mightily upset.'

'Disturbed, shouting?'

'Oh no, sir. That was not his way. I mean, I didn't know him well, that being only the second time he and me ever spoke, but I heard him preach and even then he was quiet-like, though what he said was what you'd remember for there was no bluster about him so you listened hard instead. He seemed angrier with me for not having told him my true name before.'

'Indeed. Are you in the habit of using false names, Mr Loveridge?'

'It wunt really a false name, sir, it was my grandfer's.'

'I see . . . And how would you describe Harold Chown's manner towards you that night?'

'He was sorrowful, I would say. Not angry, more despairing. He asked me would I leave off seeing Ellen, and I said I couldn't.'

'Try to remember exactly what he said – what you both said.'

'First thing he said was: "Boswell! It's you! I did wonder," or something like that. He'd taken a bit of a fancy to me on the way into Canterbury that time – the first time I met him. That happens with the preacher men, I've found. He said he was disappointed I'd not come to see him in Canterbury but now he knew why. He thanked me for meeting him – I remember him as being very polite. Then he said he knew Ellen had been betraying him with me, and that what hurt him nearly as much was that she couldn't have managed it – not with the children to take care of – without the help of his grown daughter. He begged me to leave off, for he didn't know how to bear such a cross – those were his words, sir. I said how I was sorry, but that I couldn't let her go, and how by rights she was mine for I had made her bleed and not him—'

The public benches rustled and muttered; the coroner cleared his throat and stared straight ahead.

'Please continue, Mr Loveridge, but do recollect that there are ladies present.'

'Well, he gev a bit of a start when I said that . . . just as them people up there did . . . but you did ask me to tell exackly what we said. Then he said he'd married her before God and she was his wife in the Lord's eyes and what we did

395

offended his holy law, to which I said what I'd said before about being her first and that if the Almighty had brought us together again it must be for a reason. He got the closest to being angry then, and said she wasn't a tree I could steal apples from whenever I felt like it, and that every man could rise above his baser instincts, but sir, I dunt think of the lady in any base way. I just love her and she is the mother of my child, the only one I have, and there is no sermonising or law can change that. That being a Wednesday and my free day I had met her as usual that afternoon and she was still all about me, if you understand me, though I didn't say that to him.'

Sam paused and looked round the room, but Ellen wasn't there. She too had been kept in a side room, so that she would not hear his evidence. He caught sight of Walter, sitting on the public benches, who nodded and gave him a wink of encouragement. Yet he still felt very alone.

'Chown offered me money then but I could see he was defeated and didn't like the business of the money, but it was almost his last go, not because he was afraid of giving away his gold, but more I think because he was afraid I might take it, and then he'd feel he'd bought her and I hadn't thought much of her all along if I could let her go for a bit of coin. I said no, and that I wished he'd not talked about money at all. Then I said he couldn't keep me from my Tom, that anyone with eyes in his head could see he was mine, and that I would see him, come what may. And he said how he'd been the real father to Tom – for he had fed and clothed him and loved him like a father should and why could I not leave alone. He said that Tom was bound to love his little brother, him that is Chown's child, more than he'd love me, even if I was his father. He asked me would I come between them two brothers, and I said I'd take 'em both on if he'd let me, for David is a fine little fellow. I saw him clench his fists then but I don't think he thought to strike me, it was just him trying to get the better of his feelings. He said I'd no right to say that, for David was his boy, just as Tom was mine, and I had no argument to that but to say that a child should be with his mother. So you see we talked round in circles and got nowhere. I can't give up Ellen and he couldn't give up his boy. I said we should ask Ellen but he cried at that, poor fellow, saying he had done all he could for her, but he said quiet-like that I should never have David too and then we'd see what choice she'd make, for it would be an unnatural mother would desert her child, even if she were a false wife. And it's the truth that I don't know which way Ellen would go.'

'So how did your meeting end?'

'It being a heavy hot night, such as would give a man a headache he hadn't deserved, it came on to rain plentiful. I said I would have to get back to Patrixbourne and that it was a relief most of the harvest was already got in. He just looked at me then with his face all wet from rain and tears and told me to go for he needed to think how to face this trial. So I left him then. I looked back before I turned the corner and he was still standing there with the rain running off his hat, staring into the water. I got home eventually, but caught a chill, and Mrs French had to nurse me. If she hadn't then most likely Ellen would have had neither man left to love her.'

'And you didn't see Harold Chown again after you left him there in the rain?'

'I didn't, sir.'

'Thank you, Mr Loveridge, you may step down.'

'Sit there by that officer, Loveridge, you've already given evidence,' said one of the clerks. 'You can hear what the doctor has to say about it.'

Aware that as many eyes rested on him as on the speaker, Sam listened to evidence of 'a significant blow to the head', 'bruising throughout the body', and 'caught against the mill-wheel'. He closed his own eyes and saw Harold, like a poor broken doll, tossed on the great dripping blades. Then he heard the doctor's closing words: 'Harold Chown drowned, but I cannot say how he came to go in, whether he slipped, jumped, or was pushed.'

*

There was a murmur of eager expectation as Ellen's name was announced. Sam tried to get up, to go to the slim pale figure in black, but the policeman's hand on his arm restrained him.

'You are Mrs Ellen Chown, widow of the deceased?'

'Yes,' whispered Ellen.

'You will have to speak up, Mrs Chown. All those present must hear your evidence. We want to know where you were and what you were doing on the night your husband died.'

'I was at home with my stepdaughter, and my two children.'

'You knew your husband's errand?'

'Yes. He asked me to arrange the meeting.'

'And when did you do that?'

'That afternoon, when I met Mr Loveridge.'

'And where did you meet Mr Loveridge?'

'I . . . we . . .'

'I will remind you to speak up, Mrs Chown. It is imperative that we get all the evidence, regardless of how uncomfortable you may find it.'

Ellen gripped the sides of the witness box until her knuckles whitened.

'I met him in an upstairs room at the Flying Horse.'

'Were you in the habit of meeting Mr Loveridge in that room? Speak up, Mrs Chown, don't just nod your head. The recorder needs to get all this down.'

'Yes, Wednesday afternoons.'

'And this was for the purpose of committing adultery with Mr Loveridge? No, don't nod, Mrs Chown, please. We need you to speak up.'

'Yes, we met as man and wife.'

'Mr Loveridge has told us he is the natural father of your child Thomas, who goes by the surname of Chown. Is this true?'

'Yes.'

'We have heard that Mr Loveridge made your acquaintance again after the space of three years and that he succeeded again in seducing you.'

'Seduced, no. I went back to him.'

'But your husband found out.'

'He did. But I was going to tell him anyway, before he realised about the baby.'

'What baby is this, Mrs Chown?'

'The one I am carrying now, sir.'

Sam gasped, and made to rise again.

'*Quiet, you, or I'll take you out!*' hissed the policeman.

'Loveridge's child?'

'Yes, sir. Only I wanted to tell Sam first. And it was too early. I wanted to wait until I knew the baby was for keeps.'

'Mr Loveridge has told this court that in the course of his conversation with the deceased that he, Loveridge, had said that the choice between the two of them had to be yours. That being so, whom would you have chosen?'

Ellen started to cry. 'I would have taken Sam. I couldn't do otherwise. Even though Harold threatened to keep my sons – not only David. I'd have had to find a way to get them with me, or to see them with Judy . . . I don't know.'

'I think you might have found that courts do not look kindly on mothers with characters such as yours, Mrs Chown, when they need to decide who best can bring up a child. But your husband's death has of course spared you that obstacle. I suggest you try to compose yourself. There is a little more I must ask. I want you to tell me what you thought your husband's state of mind was when he went out that evening to meet Mr Loveridge.'

'He was very pale, very quiet. Harold didn't find it easy to say what he felt. The only time you would really see what he was thinking was when he was up on the rostrum, when he was preaching.'

'This was as a district preacher with the Primitive Methodist chapel?'

'That's right. When Sam came back, for him it was the suffering of Job. He struggled to understand why he was being put to the test when all he had wanted was to be a just man serving his God.'

'Mrs Chown, would you please try to tell us as well as you can the actual words he used?'

'I will try. He said, I think, "Goodbye, Ellen. I'm going to meet him now" – he said 'him' because he would never address Sam by name. Then, something like, "Whatever is decided this evening, I think we must live apart. But I will remind you that legally I am the father of both your sons." I started to cry then, but he didn't look at me and never said another word. He went out and closed the door.'

'I see. How did you interpret those last words, Mrs Chown?'

'I thought he meant that he would put me aside and keep the boys, even if I was to give up Sam or him give up me.'

'Would Harold Chown have been the kind of man who would have taken his own life?'

'No, no! Never. It wasn't his to take.'

'And is Sampson Loveridge the kind of man who would have taken it for him, Mrs Chown?'

'No! Not Sam! No . . . !' Ellen swayed in the witness box, clutching at the sides, then bumped down out of view.

'*Ellen!*' cried Sam, getting to his feet, pushing away the policeman.

'*Silence!*' the coroner shouted into the ensuing tumult. 'Someone help the witness. She appears to have fainted!'

Two hefty policemen struggled with Sam. 'I warned you, Sunny Jim! Out you come!' And he was bundled out of the courtroom, still calling Ellen's name.

Sam was pushed into a chair in the bare room where he had been kept before being brought to give evidence, with the warning to 'hold your peace if you know what's good for you!'. An officer stayed, standing guard by the door.

'She's in the family way, my Ellen, she'll have to come with me now,' Sam said.

'Well, that's what you wanted, drowning her old man,' said the officer.

Sam stared at him in disbelief.

*

He didn't know how much later it was that he heard a door bang open somewhere down the corridor and a voice shout: 'Verdict!' followed by a roar of noise as the court emptied out. It subsided gradually into sporadic conversation he could not make out, bursts of laughter, the tapping of women's heels on the marble floors.

'Where've they put the proud father then?' called a man's voice.

'Here, George!' shouted Sam's gaoler, unlocking the door. Two of his colleagues came in. Sam stood up.

'How's Mrs Chown? Can I go to her now?'

One of the policemen laughed. 'Hardly! It's murder, Loveridge. And they've named you.'

*

In a room further down the corridor Ellen was being tended to by the doctor who had carried out Harold's post-mortem.

'Well, if nothing else you've been spared the scribblers. They'll have gone off home by now. They'll have their fun at the assizes, of course.'

'What fun?' asked Ellen. '*What fun?*'

'Do try to stay calm, Mrs Chown, if you want to keep your child. I'm afraid that chap of yours has been arrested.'

'*Sam! Sam!*'

'Nurse, go and find *Miss* Chown, would you? I think we'd best arrange a car to take them both home.'

*

'Ellen, the doctor was right, even if he was a clumsy oaf,' said Judith. 'Try to stay calm. You're home safe now and the boys are playing upstairs.'

'They wanted to go outside.'

'Not wise.'

'*Sam might hang!*'

'Ssh. Don't give old Clerk the satisfaction.'

'She's gone out. I heard her door go. She had her clacky shoes on, and was in a great hurry.'

'Let's be grateful for small mercies. Now, Flora and John will be in on the 4.19. As soon as they're here I'll go looking for a legal man. I'd have gone earlier only Wattie had to go on shift.'

'My brother's coming? Oh John!'

'See, he'll know what to do. Hot sweet tea in the meantime, I think.'

But as Judith got up to go into the scullery, there was a thunderous knocking at the front door. She went to answer it, looking through the window first. Trembling in the back room, Ellen heard a rumble of male voices, and Judith's exasperated response.

'You can't just barge in like that! She's had a terrible shock, you know. *Hey!*'

The little room was suddenly full of uniformed men. As if from a distance Ellen heard one of them say, 'Mrs Chown, you're wanted for questioning in connection with the murder of your husband Harold Chown. Come with us, please.'

*

A police matron stood behind Ellen's shoulder.

'An accessory to murder?' stammered Ellen. 'Sam wouldn't murder anyone.'

The older of the two policemen sitting opposite leaned forward. 'Neat, though, isn't it? This is how we see it, Mrs Chown. There's your fancy man with no money of his own, sleeping in a farmyard no better than a dog, and you in a neat little house standing to get whatever your husband has if the poor fool can be got out of the way. He wants his kiddy for himself, but you couldn't just run off and leave Chown because he's the father of your lawful child and who says you'd get to keep him? And what innocent man comes out with "I didn't kill him" when nobody'd said he had done?'

'An honest one – a scared one!' cried Ellen.

'Your house is being searched, Mrs Chown. We've sent a man to the Flying Horse as well. We've had a witness tell us about you shouting at your husband. You'd be as well to tell us all you know, if you want to see your kiddies again. Forget your gippo. Think about them – about yourself.'

'There is nothing more to tell,' she wept. 'Nothing.'

*

'What are those men doing, Judy?' cried Tom.

'Are they taking our toys away?' chimed in David.

'Where's Mother?'

'She'll be back soon – and nobody's taking your toys away!' Judith listened to the thumps and bangings from upstairs. What on earth were they expecting to find?

'Has Papa finished his big sleep yet?' asked David.

'Oh Lord . . . I wish Wattie was here.' Judith covered her face with her hands.

CHAPTER 31

We feare to wrong the law,
We live in servile awe,
Yet wheresoere we goe
We seldome find a foe:
Wheresoere we come, we find
For one that hates, an hundred kind.

'The Brave English Jipsie', broadside ballad, 1570

Witness

Sam sat with his head in his hands after the sergeant had left. The man had actually smiled when he said that Ellen was in custody. Nothing else mattered, not the drop, not a life of sewing mailbags, but that they let Ellen go. He'd sign anything they wanted for her sake, never mind that he'd struggle to read it.

Keys clattered in the lock and a younger policeman came in, carrying a cup of pale tea rattling in its saucer.

'Thought you might need this, Sam.'

He looked up suspiciously.

'It's not poisoned.'

'Don't think I'd care if it was,' said Sam. He pulled the saucer towards him and drank.

'They've nothing on her,' said the policeman. 'She's here but they're going to let her go. So don't go signing anything.'

'What are you telling me for? Why should I trust a *gavver*?'

'A constable, is that? No reason, but why would I tell you something they don't want you to know?'

'Yes, why would you?'

'Maybe because I think they're wrong.'

'About me pushing poor Chown in the drink?'

'As to that, I don't know – I meant keeping the poor lady here. I can't see as there is any proof against you myself, but what they're looking at is motive. You'll need to get your-self a solicitor, counsel, all that sort of thing.'

Sam laughed scornfully. 'How can the likes of me pay for a *rokrengro*?'

'That other young woman – her stepdaughter – she's going to get you a legal man. I could see them letting your lady go just to stop her worrying at them. But take my advice and leave off the Romani cant.'

'It's all I've got left. I still don't understand why you want to help me. Or have you come to soften me up for them?'

'I haven't. You'll just have to believe me. My grandfer . . . I was very fond of him. They called him Tony but his name was Tornapo Hearn. Having family born in a Gypsy wagon won't help me get my stripes. Now do you trust me?'

'I do. But what about the kiddies?'

'Miss Chown has left them with some chapel people – Deakin, I think the name is – but she's going back for them as soon as Mrs Chown is discharged. Now try not to worry more than you have to. Don't sign their papers without your legal man; in fact, until you have one, don't sign anything they give you. If I can, I'll let you know if your Ellen gets out. You'll be going to the gaol this afternoon, but I've pals there who'll take a message. If you see one of the warders scratch his nose at you – like this – you'll know but no one else will be any the wiser. I'd better go now, if you've finished that tea.'

'I have, and thank you. *Kushti bok, prala!*'[32]

The policeman smiled back, uncomprehending.

*

Sam was grateful that this time he was the only man in the van taking him to the prison. But so much was the same as before – the clanging shut of the mighty doors as the vehicle was driven in, the sudden expectant hush of the prison yard, that enclosed world within the living, breathing, free city.

Processing was simpler. He was told he would have more privileges. He was only being held until trial.

---

[32] 'Good luck, brother!'

'Innocent until proven guilty, eh?' said the warder.

It might not be for long – yet . . . *where do they hang 'em?*

*

His first visitor came the following morning.

'And who might you be?' said Sam warily, as he was brought into the room. He nudged the table as he sat down. It was screwed in place. His chair wouldn't move either.

The sober-looking grey-haired man pushed his spectacles up his nose and extended his hand.

'I am James Deakin. Sampson Loveridge?'

'That's me. You'll be the *rai* – the gentleman what's taking care of them two boys, ain't you? Mrs Chown's children, I mean.'

'The very same. And a credit they are to her, I might say.'

'And what business does someone like you want with someone like me?'

'I'm your solicitor – that is to say, at the moment I am what goes for your legal team.'

'You are? I've no *wonga* to give you, more than a pawn ticket for an old earring.'

'That's being taken care of. Now, with regard to the charge laid against you, Mr Loveridge, how were you intending to plead?'

'I never laid a hand on Mr Chown. I left him by the mill race and I dunt know how he came to be in the water. But that jury said I pushed him in, and I'd say yes to it if it got Ellen out of trouble.'

'I strongly advise you not to. If you say you didn't drown Mrs Chown's husband then you must plead not guilty. And sign nothing that is put in front of you without my being present. But I think you should not be overly concerned about a coroner's jury. They can only express an opinion, even if that is finding for murder and naming you. They cannot themselves send you to the gallows, but only to the assizes.'

Deakin pulled some papers out of his briefcase and took the top off his fountain pen.

'A coroner's jury, Loveridge, will sometimes hand down a murder verdict because they are unsure as to what happened, and want a higher court to try the case. If they'd said misadventure, or suicide, then the matter would have stopped there, and even if you had killed him, you could not have been tried. If they'd handed down an open verdict, then the police might have weighed up whether they had any evidence at all, and proceeded accordingly. As it is, they will proceed as they cannot ignore the coroner's jury, but unless other evidence appears, all the police have is a supposed motive, and circumstance. And a real jury in a capital case are, in my experience, *less* likely to convict than a coroner's if they have any doubts. Sometimes it happens that they will convict with a recommendation to mercy, but usually only if they are both sure he is guilty and they feel sorry for the defendant, and think if he puts in some years of hard labour and then takes himself off to Australia everyone may sleep with a quiet conscience. However, if the judge has rowed with his wife that morning then *he* may not feel like being merciful to anyone. You have told me you didn't kill poor Harold, so let us go forward on that basis. Most of all, Mr Loveridge, I would urge you to keep a cool head.'

'You called him poor Harold as if he was a friend of yours.'

'He was. He was my clerk.'

Sam swore, and stood up, swinging himself round the room. Deakin sat on, apparently unperturbed.

'Do sit down, Mr Loveridge.'

'*What do you want with me?*'

'Keep your voice down or the warders will come in. Believe it or not, it's justice I want. I want it for Harold's sake, not just yours. Are you familiar with the Ten Commandments?'

'Course I am. I was taught 'em by the chaplain – in Princetown. And the *rashai*[33] in Winchester was forever preaching on 'em too.'

'Ah yes, of course. They told me you'd had prior experience of our penal system.'

'I'm in this trouble for number seven, I know, the 'dulterating one. That's how I hurt Mr Chown, but not by number six. Seven was bad enough for him, and that's on

---

[33] Clergyman

my conscience, though I swear I couldn't stop myself and don't know as I would do anything different if it was all to come round again. But them commandments ain't so different from how my old mother taught me to live. And I've never stolen, apart from bagging the odd rabbit when there was too many of them for the man as had the land to eat anyway – though people will say otherwise of us. You'll know I went down for horse-stealing but that was to cover for my brother-in-law seeing as I had a debt to pay his sister for the 'dulterating.'

'I try to live by the commandments too, Mr Loveridge. I don't believe it's right to kill a man, even if he is guilty of the most dreadful crime – and I do not believe that you are – because each one of us, no matter how lowly, how debased, how corrupted, is made in God's image and therefore can be saved—'

'You want me for God, then?'

'I'd want any man for God, Loveridge. But that is your choice, though open to you only for as long as you are alive to make it. If you are dead, your hope of redemption – or, to use the language of the world, of reform – has been dashed, utterly dashed. I don't want you hanged. That would be the most terrible inheritance for your son – and the child yet to be born – besides everything else. I would not want you hanged if you *had* drowned my clerk, and because I don't believe that you did, I will do all that I can to save you – and her, of course.'

'I should thank you, then.'

'I should like that, of course.' Deakin smiled at last. 'Now, perhaps we can talk about your defence. I shall have to find you a barrister, of course.'

'A what? I never had all of this when I was took for horse-stealing.'

'Indeed not. The magistrates can put you away for that, but murder is quite another thing. It's the barrister who will stand up for you in court, and argue your case against the Crown's – the prosecution.'

'Like a bare-knuckle fight, but with words?'

'A little like that, I suppose, though the spectators may not cheer anybody on, and the placing of bets is to be most strongly discouraged.'

'I'm in your hands then, sir, and I'm grateful to you.'

*

Ellen pressed her hands against the tiled walls of her cell as if trying to push them back. Their clinical coldness reminded her of the mortuary where she had gone to identify Harold. She remembered that ammoniac reek, and the mere thought of it caused her to gag. Breathing deeply, she strove to master herself. *My baby – Sam's baby!* She sat on the bed frame, next to the folded blanket, and cried.

Ten minutes later there was a rustling at the door, followed by the clank of a key.

'Here, Chown,' said the matron, holding out a book. Ellen flinched at the peremptory use of her surname. 'There's a bit of time before lights-out. This might help.'

Ellen tried to concentrate, following her grandfather's practice of finding guidance by opening the pages at random, but quickly gave up, her eyes blurred and her tears dropping onto the flimsy pages. She laid down the Bible, but kept her right hand on it as she leaned back against the tiles. She shivered: she could feel their implacable cold through blouse and chemise. She looked at the blanket again. *Is it clean?* Holding her breath in case it smelled, she wrapped herself in it, and huddled on the bed. Someone outside turned out the lights, and she slept fitfully, until, she didn't know how much later, she was woken by a cramping pain – a pain she knew. Dragging herself upright and throwing her shoulder to the door, she pummelled it until her fists hurt.

*

Two matrons came, and Ellen found kindness where she had not expected it. The elder of the two, the woman who had brought the Bible earlier, immediately understood. 'Go for the surgeon, Anny. And tell 'em upstairs to bring a clean pail.' She pushed Ellen's hair back from her clammy forehead. 'Wouldn't be respectful, would it, to use the one you've done your water in.'

The woman kneeled beside her and put her arm round her shoulders as Ellen sobbed, her body bleeding Sam's child out into the zinc bucket, with a sound as loud in that space as rain on a tin roof. Brisk feet marched down the corridor.

'A *fait accompli,* evidently,' said the doctor, standing in the doorway to the cell. 'Best get her a stretcher and bring her upstairs.'

'I'll say this,' answered the matron. 'Chown ain't no murderess. There's no hardness in her.'

*

'You have all been most kind,' Ellen said later, looking up into the matron's face, outlined against the bright whiteness of the sick bay.

'That's all right, dear. Your mother and brother came to see you.'

'You told them?'

'Yes. But I couldn't let them in. You weren't ready for visitors.' The matron took her hand. 'Maybe it's better that way, dear.'

Ellen sobbed. She was back in Surman's Wood after the telegram from France, back in the clearing holding Sam's beer bottle, back in the Coroner's Court crying out, no, Sam could not have done such a thing. The doctor loomed over her, and she felt a needle enter the crook of her arm.

*

John got to his feet as the door opened and put his hands on his mother's shoulders.

'Oh my poor little girl! Your poor little baby!' wailed Flora, the moment Ellen was brought into the room. She got up to embrace her daughter, but the matron intervened.

'No touching the prisoner, ma'am,' she said, not unkindly. 'Sit down, Chown.'

'Prisoner!' wept Flora.

'Now, Mother, remember what we talked about,' said John gently. 'We're here to help Ellen, to get her out of here. And him if we can. You know scenes don't help. You look very pale, Ellen.'

'I am better, though. There wasn't quite so much . . . I mean . . . it was earlier this time. I keep being told it's for the best, but I can't see it that way. Another little life has had to pay for my folly.'

'She's done very well, poor thing,' murmured the matron.

'Oh, but you don't know how glad I am to see your dear faces,' Ellen went on. 'Tell me all the news. How is Grace? The ladies from the sewing meeting? Tell me about the world out there – how safe and normal and good it really is. It feels so far away. What about Grandfer?'

Her visitors exchanged glances.

'Go on, Mother,' John prompted.

'Grandfer ain't coming,' Flora said eventually. 'He's waiting back there, for Harold to be brought home.' Then in a rush she added: 'And I ain't going back.'

'*What?*'

'I'm going to lodge with John – in Manchester. And when his mission starts, I'm going with him and Amy wherever he's sent.'

'Leave Chingestone?'

'I can't stay there no longer. I should've spoken out when you lost your other babe. Or when that first letter came, the one he read though it weren't addressed to him. It was because of the dibber, you see.'

'The *dibber*?'

'I'm all muddled up with the sermons, Ellen. I can't hear Oliver preach the scriptures but I get angry with him. Wasn't it our Lord who raised up the paralytic on the Sabbath? All I wanted to do was seed my nasturtiums – I know it's not quite the same thing, of course. Only I'd kep' forgetting to ask Oliver for the dibber and then Sunday was round again.'

'Mother, what have nasturtiums to do with it?'

'I'm just telling you. Your grandfer went out for the class meeting and then I went into his shed. He never likes it if I move his things, so I'd to be careful to put everything back as it was or he'd have known. Only when I went to push the tool box back under the counter it went against something soft. They was old trousers, stuffed with straw. I couldn't think why he couldn't make a scarecrow outside instead of making a mess in there. I got my seeds in and him none the wiser. It was him did that Skimmington, Ellen, that wicked thing that he blamed on our church neighbours, because he wanted you and Harold away. He mun have known from that letter the Gypsy was going to come back.'

'Oh Mother!'

'But what if he had, Ellen? What if he had?' Flora's voice rose, querulous. 'You'd've gone with him. Better that than losing your poor babe. Better that than Harold lying in his coffin. Better than you bein' here! But not for 'en, not for Oliver!' Flora wept. 'I've been no mother to you.'

Ellen grasped Flora's hands. The matron opened her mouth, but looked at John and shut it again.

'And then, of course, he did come for you, your Gypsy. And I shut the door in his face, tired and ill as he was! He pleaded with me through the letter box, and I didn't dare even look him in the face – Tom's face. And Judith's Mr Deakin told me the poor man loves you so much he's ready to put his head in a noose to get you out of here!'

*

'You've the curtains already pulled, Judy! It won't be dark for two hours or more yet.'

'I know, Walter. It's to stop them looking in, not me looking out – Ma Clerk and all the other old biddies. I've heard 'em next door, keeping their voices down so I can't make anything out. And I've to bring my bicycle through the house because if I don't go out the front door then

I've to pass behind my neighbours. You wouldn't believe the washing they're doing and the fussing with their potted herbs and all. But it's the boys I'm most worried about.'

'How are they managing?'

'Mr and Mrs Deakin are very kind. But today David asked me again when his pa is coming home. Ellen hadn't known how to tell them so she said the usual flannel about falling asleep in Christ, and of course Davy didn't understand, though Tom did fast enough. He thinks it's all his fault and cries himself into a puddle because of it, which sets off his brother, of course. Doesn't miss a trick, that lad, and knows all the trouble started when he let slip that his little train came from the Gypsy man.'

'What does Tom know?'

'About Sam? Nothing yet. But he'll have to be told – before someone else makes it their business. Oh Wattie, what's going to happen to them? What if Ellen never comes home? What if—'

'*Ssh*, girlie!'

'They'll not let me keep 'em, not me on my own, even if Pa has left me something. I don't think we could stay here as it is. Mr Deakin has already said he could find places for them, though he couldn't guarantee they'd be together – though I saw Mrs Deakin start when he said that. I think she'd half a mind to keep 'em herself.'

'Better than separating them!'

'Deakin was trying to comfort me – he was telling me not to worry about them, but I can't help myself. But if Deakin weren't there I don't know who would fight for Sam – or Ellen. I have to trust him.'

Walter cleared his throat. 'We could take 'em, Judy, if you wanted.'

'How'd we manage that? We ain't even married.'

'We could manage that, though, if you'll have me. I've got work. If you don't mind having the washing of my stinking clothes, of course. Mother never can quite get the grease out, no matter how much she tries.'

'Oh Wattie, is that a proposal?'

'If you like. I 'spect you'd want to get married in that chapel, wouldn't you?'

'Never! Not now . . . Not that Pa would like the parish church, of course.'

'Your pa's not here, girlie. How could I be otherwise?'

'Oh dear – I keep forgetting. Poor Pa. I should be crying for him, like those two little beggars, but I can't. He deserved better'n me!'

'Hush, Judy, you're crying now. You've just been strong for the boys, and for Ellen, so you've had no chance to even think about him.'

'Who'll give me away?'

'Ah, so you will have me! Don't think about the giving away just yet. Your father ain't even in the ground.'

'Maybe Sam,' sniffed Judy distractedly. 'To give me away, I mean. If they let him go.'

Walter took her hands. 'Now you're not thinking right, Judy. Don't ask him to do something a decent man would find awkward. Whatever happens people will still say that he came in and took away Ellen from your pa and that cost your pa his life. He took Harold's place as a husband. He'd take on Davy as a father along of Tom if he's given the chance – but should he take Harold's place leading you to the altar too? That wouldn't be right, would it?'

Judy shook her head.

'All right, I'll call by the parson tomorrow on my way home.'

'I could ask Mr Deakin, even if he is chapel.'

'That's better.'

*

'Get up, Loveridge, you've another visitor.'

'Deakin, is it?'

'Not this time – a lady, of sorts.'

'You're letting me see her? She's free?'

''Oos "she"? The cat's mother? Nope, this one says she's your wife and has been kicking up a ruckus. Wife like that, I'd feel safer shut in here! There's a man along of her I wouldn't want to meet on a dark night. Says he's her brother. But we're not letting him in.'

*

'Sit here, Loveridge, and put your hands on the table. Jim, here, will stay with you and he's handy enough with his fists should she try to scratch yer eyes out.' The warder left, still laughing at his own wit.

'I've a message for you from a mate of mine at the station,' said Jim quietly. He scratched his nose.

'She's *free!*'

'Ssh! Sit down and calm yourself. Not just yet but she will be, soon as she's well enough. Boss will be back in a minute with your other lady.'

'What do you mean, "well enough"?'

The man hesitated. 'Being locked up don't agree with most people – but 'specially not a lady like her. Quiet now, that's them coming.'

*

Lucretia looked positively garish in the drab setting, a life force in red and yellow. The guard raised his eyebrows at his colleague as he backed out of the room and locked them in. Lucretia rustled and jangled into the seat in front of Sam and smiled.

'Before you start, you've to talk in English here or you'll be taken out,' came Jim's voice over Sam's shoulder.

'Don't you worry, precious!' laughed Lucretia, then fixed her dark eyes on her husband. 'It don't look like the food in here agrees with you, Sam!'

'The food don't bother me,' he muttered. 'So what is it you're after, Lukey?'

'Me, oh, I'm just curious. It's a good life, is it then, being a *gaujo*? Worth it, was she?'

'Don't you talk about her!'

'I can talk about her all I like. She took you off of me. Going to hang you, are they, Sam?'

'I didn't do it.'

'Course you didn't,' she said soothingly. 'But they've only a gippo's word for it.'

'How'd you know I was here?'

'Went back to French's as usual, an' he tole us. But he wouldn't take us on. That's more trouble you've caused us. That was a good place. But everyone's talking about you out there, and nobody wants us Gypsies 'cause of it.'

'We wasn't exackly popular at the best of times,' said Sam, 'but I never thought this would make it bad for the rest of us – for you, I mean.'

'You're a bit of an innercent, ain't you, Sam?' she said contemptuously. 'You and that brother of mine both.'

'Vanlo?'

'Gorn off, hasn't he? Same as you, without telling nobody. Took off when we was in Wandsworth last. And you can't track anyone in a city.'

'Don't suppose you tried.'

'Why would we? Can't find anyone if they don't want to be found.'

'Poor Vanlo. So, seen enough of me now, have you?'

'For a lifetime, Sam, however long that's going to be – maybe yours won't be so long after all. Want me to tell your fortin, Sam, so's you know what to expect?' She reached for his hand, but he pulled away sharply.

'No touching the prisoner!' shouted Jim.

'Thank you, sir,' said Sam, glancing round. He placed his palms flat on the table. 'You can't tell my fortin anyway; we're too close for that.'

'You don't need to tell me that. It's you that forgot it.'

'Lukey . . . I don't know how, but I want to marry that girl.'

'Oh *dordi*, that's funny! Cuts his hair, takes out his earring, finds himself a *gauji* and has to make her respectable. Want me out of the way too, do you? You've spent too long with lawyers, Sam. You want them to get you out of one noose so's you can go and find another to stick your head into. Oh, let me out of here afore I die laughing and save you the trouble!' She stood up.

'Wait, Lukey!'

'What?'

'I'm sorry.'

She stared at him for a moment. 'I 'spect you are. Seeing as you're in here.'

'I didn't mean that. I'm sorry I wasn't a better husband.'

'I'm sorry you wasn't too. I hope they don't hang you, Sam.'

She turned away. The guard rapped on the door and keys rattled outside. Lucretia glanced back as she went out.

'You always was a soft *mush,* Sam. But I never see'd a man I liked the look of more. Goodbye, then.'

*

The desk sergeant leaned over the counter of the police station and did his best to breathe shallowly. 'You again, Tanner. What have you *not* done this time? We're busy. Cells are full.'

'I'm here in my capacity as a responsible citizen!' said the tramp.

'You? Well, get on with it then. I haven't got all day, even if you have.'

''Tis about that 'orrible murder at St Radigunds. I didn't come earlier as it was only yesterday as a nice lady gave me some coppers and I could get meself a few hot chips what was wrapped in an old copy of the *Gazette* and I read about it there.'

'I didn't know as you could read, Marty.'

'They 'ad teachers in the werkiss, Sergeant. Anyways, it wasn't.'

'What wasn't what? The *Gazette?*'

'*No!* Murder most foul!'

'All right, Marty. I give up. Two sugars, isn't it?'

'What, no biscuit, Sergeant?'

'And biscuits . . . Come along with you, then,' said the sergeant, lifting the flap of the counter.

*

' . . . I was quite settled under that tree,' said Marty Tanner, 'when it came on to rain and woke me up, and seeing the landlady at the Millers sometimes takes pity on me I thought I'd see if her 'eart would be moved on this occasion by my wet and miserable state.

'And that's when I saw him – Chown – on the little bridge over the lock. He was staring down into the water and his shoulders was shaking. First I thought he was laughing, but I was starting to sober up by then and asked myself who would stand in the pouring rain like that and stare into that dark water and laugh if not a madman. I didn't want to pass by him, but then he looked up and I saw his face in the lamplight and it was all screwed up. It gave me quite a turn to see who it was, with his clothes wet through and him not minding.'

'How did you know it was Chown?'

'In my line of business you get to know all the god-botherers. I remembered him particular because he'd such a pretty wife used to give out the soup. Most of 'em religiousy ladies is about as pretty as the coal-house door, but not her. Anyway, he wasn't laughing, poor fellow. But though I wasn't meaning to ask, when he saw me he reached in his pocket and gev me a handful of coins. I thanked him and asked him did he not want to be getting home seeing what a bad night it had turned into? "Home!" he exclaimed, all sharp. Now for me home is the best word there is in the English language, and it means a lot to me seeing as I've hardly ever had one of my own my whole life long, but he said it in such a bitter way as if it was something hateful, and perhaps it was, if what the papers say is true and the pretty lady with the soup was carrying on with the gippo. I'll bet he's a young and handsome one like some of 'em are to gev her more joy than an old husband full o' sermons. Anyway, I asked him another time if I could help him home, thinking I'd get a glance at the pretty lady again and maybe something to warm my bones now the ale was wearing off, but he just shook his head and went back to looking into the mill race – muttering something about "bitter water", he was.'

'Are you sure that's what he said?'

'Sure as I can be. It put me in mind of more ale, you see. So I went on my way, though I nearly ended up in the drink myself for them boards on the bridge was all wet and greasy with the rain and I'd to grab for the rail.'

'What time was this?'

'I'm just coming to that. I got to the Millers but they was already shutting up shop. Must've been half past ten or just after. But they let me into the stall in the yard and I got a good sleep on the hay.'

'Did you see anyone else whilst you were talking to Chown?'

'No, who would want to be wandering about in that weather?'

*

'You can go home, Mrs Chown,' the sergeant repeated patiently. Ellen stood with her back to the door and daylight, twisting her handbag. He leaned towards her.

'What's that you say?'

Ellen murmured something.

'No, we won't be wanting you back. There are no charges. You're free. Shall we send for your brother?'

'Oh, don't go to that trouble . . . it's not far.' She turned towards the doors, hesitated, and turned back again. The sergeant and Tornapo Hearn's grandson exchanged glances.

'Are you sure she's all right, Sergeant?' whispered the younger man.

'Matron seems to think so,' said the sergeant gruffly. 'She's a bit pale, right enough. If you're not busy you can go with her.'

The constable didn't wait for his superior to change his mind.

'I'll take you home, Mrs Chown,' and he took hold of her elbow gently and led her unresisting out onto the street. She shrank back in the glare of daylight, tucking her chin into the collar of her coat. Only as they crossed the road with the arch of Westgate to her right did she hesitate, and peered under the arch, as if looking for something or someone. The constable couldn't see anything out of the ordinary, but noticed that the woman had somehow got some courage from somewhere. He felt her arm stiffen; she straightened up, and then looked directly into his face and asked clearly: 'What will happen to Mr Loveridge?'

'He's in the prison, Mrs Chown.' Seeing the spasm of fear cross her face, he hurried on: 'I don't think he'll be there long, though I'm not meant to tell you that. So don't say anything or I shall cop it.' *Poor little thing*, he thought. *It'd be worth the sergeant shouting at me just to see her a bit happier.*

'There's new evidence, see. A witness has come forward, which washes your Mr Loveridge out. The coroner has reconvened for tomorrow morning. I can't see as how they could find for murder again – no, don't you cry, Mrs Chown, there's no need for it!'

Moved by pity for the exhausted face hanging on his words as though life depended on it, he plunged on. 'I've seen your Sam. He'd have swung for you, Mrs Chown – oh, he won't, he won't. He'd have agreed to anything to get you out is what I mean. But he didn't have to. Your stepdaughter – lively girl, ain't she? – she got him his lawyer and he told him fair and square not to agree to anything and not to sign anywhere.'

Ellen smiled faintly, remembering the effort that had gone into Sam rounding out the letters of his name for her in that room above the Flying Horse, staring down at the page as though at a tangled sum – *That's me, then, Sampson Loveridge, in black and white! Will my teacher kiss me now, do you think?*

'And I told him that too – when the sergeant wasn't there to hear it, o' course! But you should be a bit pleased, knowing he'd have done anything for you.'

'Thank you, sir, from the bottom of my heart!'

'My sincere pleasure. Now, do you want me to see you to your door or shall I watch you go in from here?'

'Oh, I think I should go in myself . . . to not have the neighbours talk, I mean.'

'All right, I shall bid you good day, then. I'll just give you one piece of advice: even if all goes well tomorrow, you might need to be careful about who you open the door to over the next few days. There are plenty of nosey parkers as'll want "your story" but you'd best keep out of their way. Give them a fortnight and they'll've forgotten about you – or pray that some other scandal comes up that they can go sniffing round instead. And try to rest easy about Mr Loveridge.'

He watched Ellen cross the road and go straight to her door, without looking round her. Sharp-eyed, he also saw the shudder of the curtain in the neighbour's window.

*

'Come on, Loveridge, off your arse. Get your things together. You'll not be getting breakfast from us this morning.'

'Where are you taking me now?'

'Deakin's downstairs waiting for you. Come on, get your things together, I said. You'll not be coming back up here.'

Sam followed the warder down the clanging stairway; another walked behind him. The galleries hummed with contained silence. Sam didn't know what time it was, but guessed from the skylight far above that it was about half an hour before slop-out. He was afraid of what they would do next, but clung to the thought that Deakin might indeed be waiting for him. Otherwise, what? A rattling ride in a prison van to another gaol, where Ellen, wherever she was now, would not be able to visit him? Or would it be the humiliation of another search, with their laughter crashing round the cell – 'Now we can see what the lady saw in you, Loveridge!' Sam hadn't been able to eat much for days now, yet the reminder that he was empty only led to the thought of the food they brought him in here and that was enough to dispel hunger. Ah, but to crunch on a fresh apple! And to think that the orchards in Kent were groaning with the weight of them now.

The warder's keys clunked and crashed at a lock. Then they were marching forward again along a brick-walled corridor, painted a shiny custard yellow; here the ceiling was lower, oppressively so. The cells were spaced further apart; he could sense their inmates listening. The place smelled of carbolic, disguising a whiff of urine and the unmistakeable scent of pacing men in ill-ventilated spaces. Again they paused, again the flash and crash of the keys. Another corridor, much like the previous one. Were they still moving in a straight line? Sam wasn't sure, and the lack of natural light heightened his disorientation. Would they go round in a circle and then upstairs again, in a cruel game, like a man who is about to be shot hoping the delay may mean a pardon, a pardon that never arrives? No, the door at the end of this corridor had a fanlight, though iron-barred like every window here, and through that fanlight he could see pale daylight. Then another thought crossed his mind, and he stumbled. In some prisons, he'd been told, the gallows shed was outside, not deep within the building.

'Mind your step, Loveridge,' said the guard behind him, but his words sounded kinder than he had heard in here before.

Dordi, was this the end then? Not quite, or not yet, perhaps. The doors were open on this corridor, and glancing from side to side without moving his head he could make out empty desks, bookcases with bulging files. Someone was smoking, and Sam felt a longing for tobacco that was as strong as hunger.

They stopped outside one of these doors, the only one that was closed. The warden knocked, then opened the door.

'Morning, Mr Deakin . . . In you go, Loveridge!'

Sam entered. Deakin was getting to his feet the other side of a table, which, with two plain chairs, was the room's only furnishing. He was stretching out his hand to Sam. The door closed at his back. He looked round. They were alone.

He shook Deakin's hand.

'Sit down a moment, Loveridge. Congratulations. You're free.'

'Say that again, sir.'

'Free. Insofar as any of us are, this side of the grave.'

Sam put his face in his hands. 'I thought I was for it, Mr Deakin,' he said indistinctly. 'I thought I'd never see her again.'

Deakin leaned across, squeezing Sam's shoulder. *The first thing he needs is a square meal.*

'Mrs Chown is at home. She's been there a few days now – I've returned her sons to her. I told her not to try to see you here, as she's been through a lot and both Miss Chown and I thought it best she didn't have to contend with somewhere like this.'

'No, the company is not the best,' said Sam.

'Chown was seen after you'd left him. The Coroner's Court sat again yesterday to consider that new evidence. They found for accidental death.'

'Do *you* believe that?'

'You mean do I think Chown could have done away with himself? Frankly, I don't know. In the normal way of things I'd've said not. It goes against all religion, of course. The jury was taken to the spot. They saw the space below the rail, which a grown man could easily slip through. It's only a surprise that it hasn't happened before, especially with those rolling home from the Millers Tavern. They were shown some scrapes that might or might not have been Harold's, or might indeed have been the witness's; he spoke of slipping, and it was a wet night, as you remember. That bit of evidence told on the jury. In my view they'd rather bring in a verdict of accident than suicide – unless there's a letter, of course – and that's what they did. Kinder to the family. The wood of that bridge is always damp with the spray from the wheel. The coroner's clerk also obliged by procuring a bucket and sluicing the bridge with water, for them to all test the boards after. They did that very gingerly, I must say, but nevertheless the whole proceeding did strike me as properly scientific.'

There was a discreet knock at the door.

'They'll have brought your things. I'll wait outside. There'll be something to sign, then I'll take you wherever you want to go. But there's something else I have to tell you. I've known it for a while but you had enough on your plate.'

'What is it, sir?'

'I'm afraid Mrs Chown lost the baby. I'm very sorry, Loveridge.'

'Oh, oh Ellen . . . oh.' He sagged. 'Mr Deakin? I know you med think it wrong, but we made that child out of love.'

*

Sam blinked and swayed in the fresh air. His clothes felt loose, as though they belonged to someone else – as they had once, a Gypsy's clothes being begged for the most part. He looked to his left, and marvelled at a farmcart descending into Longport, a placid shire horse ambling gently between the shafts. The sight gave him immense pleasure, a sense that normal life perhaps could be resumed, just as it had continued in his absence. Though he had only been in Canterbury prison a matter of weeks, it had felt so much longer than his time in Winchester. Opposite, two old men sat on the low wall in front of the almshouses, watching him with interest. *They must do that every morning*, he thought, *sizing up what the prison don't want anymore.*

'Where do you want to go, Loveridge?' asked Deakin.

'Ellen,' he whispered, then, 'Ellen,' more loudly.

'May I make a suggestion? Let me get you something to eat first, and somewhere you can shave.'

Sam's hand went to his chin. 'O' course. I'd clean forgot. I always asked 'em for a razor after breakfast – whether I'd eaten anything or not. They never left me one of my own.'

'They wouldn't. Not with what was hanging over you – if you'll forgive the unfortunate choice of words. Have you one in that bag?'

'If they've not took it. And I'd be glad of your offer. Truth is, I do feel uncommon faint. The last time this happened – I mean, when I was let out of Winchester – it wasn't like this.'

'There was a bit more at stake this time, Loveridge. Come, then. Broth, bread and strong tea.'

CHAPTER 32

A man must love, for all his wit;
There's no escape though he should die for it,
Be she a maid, a widow, or a wife.

Chaucer, *The Knight's Tale*

Respectable

Deakin waited until Sam had devoured the soup and bread before speaking.

'You're a free man by law and right,' said the solicitor, keeping his voice low, 'but remember that Canterbury is not much more than a village. People talk. You will want to consider what would be best for Mrs Chown – what about a new start where neither of you is known?'

Sam looked up, wiped his mouth on his napkin, and said: 'I've wandered all my life, and that was normal for me, though sometimes it could be hard – the not knowing of it, I mean. Not knowing if you'd be moved on, sometimes at all hours, sometimes when you had just got the fire going and the meat spitted. There's them as think it's a romantic way to go on – firelight and the night stars above an' telling stories and all that – but they don't live like that year round. They don't have to catch – or beg, which is harder – whatever goes in their bowl. I'm in this place here because I'm with you and they knows you here. I doubt I'd be let in otherwise. I saw that respectable lady over in the corner there,' he tilted his head almost imperceptibly, 'draw herself in when she saw me, though I don't know her and she don't know me, much less that I wish her no harm. That mother there with the little girl eating all them buns – she's been watching me ever since we came in the door, though she pretends not to. That's how her girlie has eaten mor'n she should. Those that knows me, Mr Deakin, generally treats me well. You, fr'instance. Without you, I don't know where I should be, but probably not in a good place.'

'I can't take that credit. It was all made easier when that tramp came forward.'

'You say that, but if you hadn't been there, they could have sent him and his evidence packing if they'd wanted to, and I'd've been none the wiser.'

'You can't say that, Sam.' For the first time Deakin spoke with irritation. 'I think we have a constabulary and a judicial system to be proud of.'

'P'raps I'm too hasty. There was one young one who was a perfect gent with me. I couldn't trust 'em when I heard they'd took Ellen, that's all. Anyways, what I meant to say is that I've always wandered, except when I've been stopped, as you might say, by main force. I can't go back to that life, and even if I could, I wouldn't take Ellen there. She's never asked me, right enough, but I've let on to her how tough it is to live that way, impossible for a girl not brought up to it. But you're right, sir, even though it's me now as wants to stay in one place, let the ivy grow up my legs, if you like. I mun pack up and move on again somehow – this time with my family.'

He looked at Deakin proudly, repeating the phrase as though he had not long learned it and needed to fix it in his memory: 'My *family*, Mr Deakin!', his thin face transfigured by his smile.

'I s'll make them boys all the wooden trains – and cars and wagons and horses – they could ever want,' he said, his voice growing louder and more confident. 'And Ellen can fill 'em with broth as good as this one – but I'll never be so distracted as to let 'em eat all the buns!' Out of the corner of his eye he saw the mother with the little girl flinch and reach for the sugar bowl.

*

Sam raised the knocker but paused before letting go. *I've stared at this house often enough*, he thought, *but I've never see'd how she lives.* He saw her again smiling up at him, lying on a blanket in Surman's Wood, amidst shimmering green leaves, birdsong and the chattering of the stream, and in the shabby little room in the Flying Horse, which her presence had made a sanctuary. When he'd been given back his own clothes he had found the key in his pocket, a talisman.

A shadow moved behind the net curtain of the neighbouring house. Sam stared pointedly in its direction, until he sensed Mrs Clerk's retreat.

My family, he thought, as he let the brass knocker fall.

A curtain twitched in the window and a moment later the door opened three inches, with Judith almost hidden behind it.

'Quickly!' she hissed, and pulled the door back.

Sam stood in the little parlour, feeling large and awkward and crowded by Millie's overstuffed armchairs, their embroidered antimacassars, the treacly veneer of the Chappell piano, the framed flowered texts and the tinted photograph of a young Oliver Quainton, already magnificently bearded. He stepped back from the garish red-blue-gold of the carpet that covered the centre of the floor, preferring the firm feel of the varnished floorboards round its edge. *Thump, thump* went Judith's feet up the Brussels matting of the staircase, noisy as a donkey on a dirt track. He heard murmured words above, then Judith thundered down again, threw a rapid 'just going out!' over her shoulder and disappeared through the scullery.

'Lock up after me!' she shouted, before rattling the bolt and crashing through the back door. Sam crossed the rear room, smaller than the parlour, and obediently secured the door.

'Hello.'

He turned round to see two small faces looking up at him from the hearthrug.

'Dipsy man!' crowed the youngest in delight, his fat hand proprietorially on the tender of the little train.

'Can you make us a farm, sir?' said Tom, without any preamble. 'I'd like the cows painted black and white, for they'll be the ones to give milk. And some brown ones I can take to market. And a horse and cart, one where you can take the horse out of the cart so he can do other things. And a big barn for putting the hay in.'

Sam kneeled beside them.

'I'll make you your farm. I can take you to see one too, if you like.'

'Can we go in a horse and trap?'

Sam met Tom's candid gaze. Davy was jigging with excitement. Sam knew he mustn't make promises to them unless he could keep them. He thought of Sibela and Righteous, and wondered what the little girl's wooden flowers looked like now, and of the village school in Patrixbourne, the children there, their parents, who could so readily teach to bait, to persecute. Yet Tom was so confident, and the bond between the two brothers itself made them stronger. Perhaps . . .

'I shall have to see about the horse and trap,' he said. 'It might take a little time to organise.'

'Tomorrow, then,' said Tom, as though that settled the matter.

'Sam?'

At last! Ellen stood in the doorway, her hands clasped, remote. He had not heard her come downstairs.

'Mother needs to talk to Mr Loveridge, boys.'

Mr Loveridge, is it? Sam felt a gnawing at his stomach that was nothing to do with hunger.

'He's going to make us a farm, Ma!'

'That's very kind of him. I hope you thanked him.'

Will she not look me in the eye?

'Would you come through to the front parlour?'

'Ellen . . .'

'Better that we talk privately, I think.'

Sam touched the boys' heads briefly, and got stiffly to his feet.

'I'll make you your farm, no matter what,' he told them, then meekly followed Ellen. She stood in the middle of the room, her joined hands a barrier.

'Mr Deakin told me not to visit you,' she began.

'He was right, Ellen, it was no place for you.'

'You look thinner.'

'I couldn't eat in there – nor sleep much, either.'

'What will you do now?'

What will I do now? 'I don't rightly know. I s'll go back to Farmer French for a bit, I expect. Deakin said he wanted me back, and I'll need to fetch Fred, and anyway, I don't have anywhere else to go . . . apart from the Flying Horse, of course.'

He watched for a reaction, but none came. He went on. 'They turned my hut inside out, you know, the constables.'

'They did the same here.'

'Oh. I'm sorry, Ellen. I'm sorry I brought all this trouble on you. But I'm sorriest about our baby,' he said.

Ellen looked down at her hands. He took a step forward – she retreated.

'Oh Ellen,' he said piteously. 'I'd have swung for you!'

Nothing.

'Ellen, believe me. I didn't kill him.'

'No, I know you didn't, Sam. *We* did. We killed a good man – sent him out of this world in misery.'

'I love you, Ellen. I'll always love you,' he said helplessly across the chasm.

As if he hadn't spoken, she went on.

'Judith is to wed her Walter. Then we'll move. Wattie says he'll look for work elsewhere.'

'You'll leave Canterbury? You'll run away from me again?'

'I never "ran away". I had no choice, if you'll remember. And I don't this time, either. I'd to clean dog mess from the door yesterday. And on Monday there was soot thrown over the washing. The neighbours shun us and stop talking when

I go past. Judith shouts at them, of course, but it makes no difference – or makes it worse.'

She looked straight at him.

'Did you expect to stay here?' she asked coldly.

'No. Never that. I couldn't be here,' he waved his arm vaguely in the direction of the piano, 'amongst all his things. We . . . they . . . the Gypsies, I mean, when one of us dies we *yag* – we set fire to everything he's owned: togs, wagon, bed, tools. Them that's really strict will destroy a man's dog and his horses, even, and bury 'em. When I walked off that day they'd've done for poor Fred if he hadn't upped and followed me, because as sure as I stand alive in front of you I was dead to them. I was always taught that the *yagging* was to set the soul free, to cut it loose from what had tied it to this life. Now I see it's more than that – it sets the living free too. Ellen, when I was in the gaol not knowing what they would do with me or if I'd ever see you again, I'd've done anything to have held you in my arms one more time, but I could no more lie with you in his bed up there than I could cut my own head off.'

'It was Millie's bed before I slept in it.'

'You see? That wunt right either, Ellen, not for you, nor for poor Chown.'

'They'll let me have his body back now. He'll be buried with her.'

'Will you go back?'

445

'No. I was driven away from there and now I'm not welcome here. Mother went back with John this morning – to Manchester. Even *she's* lost her home now.'

'*Dordi,* I've made a Gypsy of you,' he said bitterly. 'I'd best go before I do you more harm. But I mean it about Tom's farm. I'll stay long enough at French's to do that for the boys. But promise me one thing, Ellen. Promise me that one day you'll tell Tom that he's my son and that I'd've done anything for him – and his little brother. Tell him his father wanted to know him and to love him.'

She looked away.

'Will you tell him, Ellen? Just nod, and I'll leave you in peace.'

She nodded.

He turned away from her, taking hold of the latch on the front door. It was then that he lost his head at last. He dropped his hand, and faced her.

'*Have you any idea what you've done to me?*'

'Please don't shout, Sam – the neighbours!'

'*Damn you all to hell!*' he yelled at the wall where he was sure Mrs Clerk listened. '*Put a glass up – they say you hear better that way!*'

He turned to her again, his voice quieter now but more menacing.

'You talk to me about neighbours shunning you, do you? Ellen, I've passed my life – *my life* – having cottage doors slammed in my face. My mother being chased off like she was some mangy dog. The *gavvers* coming and turning us off a stopping-place – after dark, sometimes, when we'd no place to go and no lamps to get there if we did. As if God's good earth was made for everyone but us! Got smuts on your washing, did you?' he jeered. 'You say that – you, a *gauji* who thinks getting clean is sitting in her own dirty bath water? Who'd scour the pots in that sink out there where you'd washed your drawers not half an hour before?'

'I don't . . . I—'

'Don't interrupt me! We made Harold's life a misery and yes, in one way or another we killed him—'

'Sam, *please*!'

'What're you afraid of? The *gavvers* at the door again? Would it satisfy your Christian soul if I was hauled off again and sorted proper this time? An eye for an eye? I can't count the number of times that was given out from the pulpit in all them gaols – remember, lady, I was in Winchester 'cause of you. When I was strapped scream-ing on that frame it was you I saw before I blacked out, same as it was when Liberty and Caley near murdered me – 'cause of you. Well, it wunt just Harold we ruined, Ellen, remember that! A man I liked, by the way – not that I let that make any difference. Too sick for you, I was. My poor Lukey's shamed for life. Couldn't keep the man who'd promised he'd be with her always. She thought me a soft *mush*, right enough, and didn't care who knew it. Made my life a misery for it. Well, she was right – soft for you and look how you treat me – no better'n her, 'cept you dress it up different.'

He grabbed her hand, ignoring her tears.

'Let go, Sam!'

'Or what, Mrs Chown? Here, feel this.' He bent his head and forced her hand upwards. 'Feel the back of my neck.'

'Yes . . .'

'Feel them bumps? I used to run my fingers over 'em in the dark, when I was in stir this last time. Wondering where the crack would come – that's if I was lucky and they didn't get it wrong and leave me strangling in their pit.'

'Stop, for pity's sake, stop!'

He flung back her hand.

'All right, then. I'll come back with the farm. I've promised my son – our son! But you wunt have to clap eyes on me. I'll get it to Judy, or Wattie.'

He lifted the latch and slammed out the front door without a backward look. As Ellen sank to the floor she heard him snarling: 'What're you lot staring at? Mind your own bloody business!'

Sobbing, Ellen didn't hear the tentative footsteps, the patient breathing, raising her head only at a wary touch on her shoulder. She looked up into Tom's face, which wore an expression she recognised as Sam's. David stood beside him, his face wobbling as it did just before tears came.

'Mother,' said Tom. 'Why was Sam shouting?'

'Because I've sent him away. Because I was cruel. But he'll bring you your farm, boys. He keeps his promises.'

Still crouching, she put her arms round the solid little bodies, and thought: *Hearts do break.*

*

Sam tramped in a daze all over Canterbury. He went past St Mildred's, where they had once met amongst the tombstones. Then he went into the fields, striking upwards towards Harbledown, before going deep into Blean Woods until he smelled the smoke of a campfire and retreated out again to look down on the city shimmering in the pale sunshine of that autumn afternoon. Descending by Hackington, he stood for a while in the cool, damp air of the parish church, transfixed by a stone skeleton carved upon a bier. Turning away from it at last he caught a glimpse in his mind's eye of an aproned undertaker's assistant leaning over Harold's corpse on a metal gurney, palpating the right side of his neck for the artery, raising in his other hand the fluid-filled pump that would preserve him for his journey home to lie atop Millie's coffin. He cried out to dispel the image and sank into a pew, covering his eyes, and found himself looking down on Harold's dead face, his sutured mouth.

'You have the gift,' Sam's mother had told him more than once. 'No, I'm just a bit of a dreamer,' he'd laughed back. Whatever it was, Sam didn't want it now. He heard his mother's voice warning him, 'He's not at peace, Sam!'

'I'm all in!' he exclaimed aloud. 'If I could only get some sleep!'

He staggered out into the slanting sunshine. The light, the grass, the birdsong and the gently weathered graves lifted his spirits. He thought of the tomb he'd just seen within the chancel. *Why would that fine rai want to be cooped up in the dead air of a church when he could have the sunshine and the rain fall on him out here?* A pied wagtail, the Gypsy bird, flitted across the path in front of Sam. *Are you an omen, or just a little bird?*

Crossing the railway line he saw to the right Denne's Mill rearing up, and veered away in a cold sweat, tangling himself instead in a cluster of narrow streets just beyond the line of the city walls. He knew that he should be making his way to Patrixbourne, but couldn't tear himself away from where he knew Ellen sheltered with her sons, afraid to open the door to more insults. *If she'd only let me at least protect them.*

Finally, inevitably, with the impassive mass of the city walls at his back, he crossed the road to the Flying Horse and made his way down the corridor into the back room, thankfully empty. He could hear a buzz of voices from the public bar at the front and waited patiently for someone to come through.

'Sam!' exclaimed the landlord's wife, wiping her hands on her apron. 'Oh, it's good to see you back!' The warmth of her words opened the floodgates dammed by Ellen's coldness. Sam sank onto a bench and his face crumpled.

'Oh, you poor boy!' she said, holding his shoulder. 'You poor, poor thing! Wait a minute till I close up out there.'

She bustled off to bolt the back door.

'Now drink this. I've a slice of cold pie in the larder if you'd like that. You look done in. I always knew you was innocent. It was all in the *Gazette* what you said, and as I said to Percy, no one would be so honest and trusting if he really was to blame.'

'He's dead along of me, Letty!'

'It was an haccident, Sam! The Crowner said so! It's a marvel that no other poor beggar has fallen in that mill race before now. That rickety rail wouldn't hold back a dandelion clock. It's one thing taking railings away from the front of fine houses to make 'em into guns but quite another when a poor Christian slips in the wet – when we thought the war had done its worst. Oh, someone's wanting served through there. Now don't run off. I'll bring you that pie.'

She returned and put plate and cutlery in front of him.

'Now you can tell me it's none of my business, but give the lady time. I can see from your face you're not the happy man you should be on a day like this. I've never seen your girl, for you was always careful and respectable – considerate of this house, I might add – but she must love you, Sam, or she'd never have risked everything a woman has to have met you the way she did. And it said in the *Gazette* that she lost her kiddie – *your* kiddie, I mean, Sam – and that makes a woman, if she's a woman at all, not like herself. Those chapel people will have told 'er it's divine punishment but she mustn't believe that – what sort of God is it that would hurt a poor baby what's done nothing wrong? Oh Sam, you're all in! Have you still got the key to upstairs? Well, up you go now and get some sleep and then you'll know better what to do after. I've not touched anything up there so it might be a bit dusty, but I'll come and change the water on the wash-stand.'

*

I don't know as I can bear this, he thought, turning the key in the familiar door. From down below came Letty's cheerful voice talking to someone out the back.

'Oh dear, 'ave you bin there long? I clean forgot to open up! And here was me wondering why I never had no custom but out front!'

Inside nothing had changed, but the little room was unmistakeably deserted. The rag rug he had brought from Patrixbourne was still there, soft with dust, the bed made neatly as Ellen had always insisted it should be afterwards. He let his canvas bag slip to the floor, and shrugged out of his jacket. Hanging it on the back of the door he remembered with terrible clarity holding Ellen, his arms round her under her coat, and telling her that if he died in that moment, then he would die happy. How long ago was that?

His memories were interrupted then by the thunder of feet on the stairs, followed by a tap at the door and Letty singing out his name. He let her in. She bustled across the room and picked up the tin ewer.

'I'll have this filled and back in two minutes.'

'I can do it if you like?'

'No, you sit yourself down and rest, and let me take care of it. The constables came, of course, but there wasn't much here for them to upset.'

He watched her leave, shaken by the strangeness of another woman being in that room, displacing the air with her movement and her noise.

*

It was a fine evening, so after work Judy and Wattie walked under the trees at Dane John, talking about their own future, about the life Ellen and Sam would have.

'Let's stay out a bit,' she said. 'Get ourselves a pie and a sweet stout for me. Deakin's new clerk called by the office and told me Sam is out. Let's give them some time to themselves – they've waited long enough.'

Returning home, Judith announced her presence by slamming the back door. The kitchen and back room were in darkness. *Must be upstairs – where else!* She stiffened then – something rustled in the gloom and gave a muffled sob.

'Lord, Ellen, what are you up to?' Judith kneeled down and put her arms round her. 'Where's Sam?'

Huddled together on the floor, Ellen told Judith everything they had said.

'You're a fool, Ellen Chown. You're blaming the wrong man. Blame your grandfer for chasing Sam away with his shotgun. Blame them two brothers for near enough killing him. Blame your mother for not speaking up when she could have done – and all of them holier than thous that said you couldn't keep your baby unless you had a husband – *any* husband. None of this is going to bring Pa back, is it? Nor give those little blighters upstairs a father. Let alone make *you* feel any better. Did he say where he was going, at least?'

'No . . . Back to her, maybe.'

'Don't be silly. That's the last place he'd go. He'll be in Patrixbourne – or what about that room you had?'

*

As the light faded Sam undressed and washed automatically. Pulling back the covers of the bed and looking closely at the pillow and mattress, he sought the impress of their bodies, but found none. He buried his face in the sheets in search of her scent, but no trace was left. He felt cold, though Letty had lit the little grate for him, saying he looked like he needed warming up, even if the day had been so mild, but nevertheless it was a small relief to go to bed naked: prisoners had to lie down dressed. Finally he slid under the covers, and lying on his back, wept silently. From downstairs a murmur of voices rose and fell, punctuated sometimes by laughter and occasionally by shouts. Someone dropped a glass and he heard Letty scolding. His world had stopped here in this drab little room, whilst the rest went on turning as it always had.

Pull yourself together, Sam, he told himself. *You ain't dead. Not like poor Harold.* Yet that thought plunged him deeper. The man whom he'd begged Ellen to leave had taken himself off, by accident or intention. A good man no one really wanted – not his wife, nor his daughter, even – but who, by dying, had driven Ellen away from him.

Tom and David are young enough, and loved enough by them two girls, that they'll grieve, but they'll get on all right in time. He remembered their faces when they'd set eyes on the wooden train. *I'll make their farm. I'll stay just long enough at French's to collect enough elder wood. Something to do – that'll make me feel better, for a bit, anyway. But I can't see her. I can't bear her coldness again. And she wunt see me, not after I've spoken to her like that.* But was Letty right? Was it losing the baby that made her not herself? Surely he was to blame for that too – the baby he'd wanted to be her ultimatum to Harold.

Sam thrust his feet from under the covers, and turned the pillow to the cool side. He fidgeted, getting hotter and more restless. Downstairs the noise had dropped to a murmur. Then a hand-bell was rung, followed by a last flurry of movement, another bell, and then the passage below filled with sound. Sam shut his eyes and listened to the wave of voices washing out of the back door, dispersing in the night air in farewells and the uneven tread of boots. Some thumps and bangs followed, the stacking of stools on tables, the cellar trap-door closing. These were sounds he had missed in the clanging and echoing of the gaol.

Round in circles he went. In his head over and over again he made the toy farm, counting and recounting the cows, the sheep, the sheepdog. He'd make a farmer, and his wife – and two boys painted to look like Tom and David. The farmer's wife would be Ellen, of course. Who would be the farmer? Some man she'd find after he'd gone. Sam groaned.

Bell Harry boomed out midnight. In his mind's eye Sam turned the little figure of the farmer's wife in his hands, but could not get her to look at him. He must try to sleep. Soon it would be wake-up, the slat in the door pulled aside, the turnkey crashing the keys on the door. He was leaning against the white-washed wall, looking at a man prone on a bed, utterly still, a corpse with a sheet pulled over its head, a label attached to a protruding toe. Water puddled on the floor. Sam cried out, but no sound came, but the turnkey did, knocking at the door, not loud, but insistently. Why did the screw not just open it?

Now awake, Sam sat up in the bed, wondering where he was. His jacket was hunched against the door, in the shadows looking like a figure leaning with its head against its arms.

'What do you want?' he screamed. But the figure didn't move, though the tapping faltered.

He scrambled to his feet, pulled on his trousers, hooking the braces onto his shoulders, and fumbled at the lock. At last the key turned.

I must have been shouting. I'll say sorry and tell Letty I'll be gone in the morning.

But this slight female figure with the hat pulled down over her eyes wasn't her.

'Sam?'

'*Dordi,* Ellen, it's you!'

He pulled her to him in relief and tenderness, and kissed her forehead, her cheek, her nose, her mouth, her neck, and *mi dearie Duwel*[34] – she responded!

'My Ellen!'

She nestled against him, her cheek resting on his bare chest. 'Judy said I was a fool, Sam.'

'It dunt matter what you was, or are. And I shouldn't have taken on as I did. What matters to me is that you're here. Take off that coat and sit down. I'm locking you in with me now.'

---

[34] My dear God!

He kneeled in front of her and with awkward fingers unfastened her shoes.

'Take off your things, Ellen,' he whispered. 'Get in here with me. I've dreamed of this for so long – to fall asleep in your arms and find you still there the next morning.'

*

Sam woke early, conditioned by the senseless rhythms of the prison. Ellen lay curled on her side. He wondered whether she had moved at all in the night; his body still followed her shape, knees tucked under hers, his arm over her. He had opened his eyes once in pitch darkness, but he hadn't wakened her then, telling himself that yes, she would still be there if he fell asleep again. So he had put his fingers near her half-opened mouth to feel the heat of her breathing, kissed the fine skin of her shoulders, run his hand in wonderment from the cap of her arm to her hip, and closed his eyes.

*

He saw that the fire had sunk to embers, so he got up and poked it into life, adding a log from the little basket Letty had left for him. Without uncovering Ellen, he wriggled under the bedclothes and set about kissing and nuzzling her into wakefulness. The answering tremor came soon, then a cat-stretch of her back and shoulders, and she turned onto her spine.

'Love me, Sam,' she said, and put her hands up to his face.

*

He wouldn't let go of her even when they stood on the landing and he turned the key in the door, so they went awkwardly down the narrow staircase and out through the passage with his arm round her waist. At the back door she hesitated.

'Here's my arm, Ellen. I'll take you home.'

'No. Not yet. Walk with me, but don't touch me, Sam. It's too soon.'

'You're not ashamed of me, are you?'

'No, no!' And she grasped the front of his jacket with both hands and kissed him rapidly, but then held her palms pressed against him, holding him back.

'I'd be proud to walk with you anywhere, Sam. I'd hold my head high to be seen with such a fine man as you. I've dreamed of it, us going together along an avenue, my arm under yours, David on my side and Tom on yours. But not yet.'

'Deakin warned me what we might get. But I want to see my son. Then I'll take myself to French's – he'll be wondering where I've got to if he's seen a newspaper.'

'All right. But we mustn't . . . flaunt.'

They walked, then, side by side but a foot apart along the High Street, as the waking city flowed towards and round them: ponderous farm carts and hooting self-important cars with goggled drivers wove their way through milling messenger boys, imperious women in fox-fur stoles, brisk bowler-hatted men, shouting sandwich-men, a shawled woman selling heather, boys in Eton collars with their hands in their pockets, a slew of flat-capped labourers on bicycles. A moustached policeman as smart as a guardsman stood at the junction with St Margaret's Street, deciding with a flick of his right hand to give precedence to an omnibus. Shops drifted past Ellen as though they moved, not she: gunsmiths, chemists, piano showrooms, bed-linen stores, butchers, wine-merchants. Sam more than once protectively caught her arm to draw her out of danger, then wordlessly they separated.

Finally they stepped out of the maelstrom, entering the alley that led to the row of terraced houses.

'Thank you, Sam.' She wondered, absurdly, if they should shake hands. Except he wasn't looking at her, but down the street, and frowning.

'I'm coming with you. Something ain't right.'

And at last he did pull her arm under his, in spite of her murmured protests. His grip tightened as they got closer. Walter was standing before the front window, his mouth full of nails, hammering a board into place. His feet crunched on broken glass. He knocked the last nail home, tested that the board was firmly in place, and spat the remaining nails into his palm.

'Hello, Sam,' he said. 'Before you ask, everyone is fine. But it looks like the house'll have to be given up.'

'Not just that. Looks as if we'll have to give up Canterbury,' said Sam.

'Come in and see Judy, then. I'm to wed her, by the way.'

*

A subdued Judy kneeled by the fireplace in the gloom of the back room; the curtains were still closed. The two little boys cowered beside her.

'Ma!' shouted David, and grabbed Ellen's knees.

'Oh my darlings, I shouldn't have left you.'

Tom got to his feet and looked up at Sam. Unlike his brother, he hadn't cried; he was expectant.

'Have you brought our farm?'

Instead of answering, Sam kneeled and pulled the boy towards him. The child was stiff and unyielding in his arms. He ruffled the dark hair, and kissed him.

'I'm going to see about it direc'ly. I have to get my tools. I'll make you anything you want. Whatever will make you happy, *chavvi*.'

'There's a telegram come,' broke in Judith. She rose and got it from the mantelpiece and handed it to Ellen. 'I'm sorry.'

'Oh!' said Ellen, staring at it.

'What is it?' asked Sam.

461

'"Coming Wednesday fetching Harold home. Won't see Ellen. O.Q." He's sent it from Chingestone, so they'll all know what he's put. I'll never see any of them again, Sam.'

*

'Sam! We was wondering where you'd got to. You look like you want a bit of feeding up.'

He stood in the porch of the French farmhouse, wary, not quite trusting the welcome.

'Everyone says that, Mrs French. But just to be out in the fresh air makes me feel better – knowing I'm free, I mean.'

'Are you, though? Are you free?'

Sam turned his cap in his hands, hesitating. 'In a manner of speaking. But a decent man is dead, Mrs French. There are those who'll always lay that at my door, and they'd be right, in one way. There are two women in Canterbury, and two innercent children that are afraid to be seen in the street and afraid inside their home. Tom, that's Ellen's eldest – my son, I mean,' and Sam's face lit up for a moment before lapsing into its earlier anxious expression, 'won't be able to go to school for fear of the other children, or more rightly their parents.'

'I can't say myself that I approve of what you done – looking at it on its own, I mean,' she began, picking her words, 'but I hope you'll stick by the lady.'

'She's my life. I want to do right by her. I've got to show her she can depend on me – that I can keep her, I mean, and the little boys.'

'You'd best come in.'

*

'You know I'll give you work, Sam,' said the farmer. 'It's where to put you is the problem. The huts'll be empty again soon, but you can't keep a woman and children in 'em through the winter.'

'I don't want to. She's not been brought up to that life. Ellen is respectable, you see, a lady.'

Matthew French shifted in his chair.

'I'm sure she is, Sam. But people mayn't see her that way, even if the first ones to cast stones med be them as has the biggest secrets.'

'I can't leave her where she is, even if she don't come and live along of me. She hides in the house for fear of what'll happen if she goes out. She daren't even peg out the washing. Her stepdaughter can stand up to people, and the man she's marrying is a sturdy enough fellow you'd not want to put your fists up to.'

'Will they come here too?'

'Might do. That house has to be given up anyway. The landlord wants them out before any more windows get broke.'

'There is one possibility,' said French. 'I can't promise but I can put a word in for you. It's a tied house, belonging to him at the Manor. The family that was in there has shifted up to London. His Lordship is an odd fish. He'll either take to you or get his gamekeepers to send you on your way, depending on his humour.'

*

'Loveridge!' said Deakin. 'I trust you haven't come to tell me you're in some other trouble?'

'No, sir. I only want some advice.'

'Go on.'

'I want to know, can I marry Mrs Chown?'

'Ah! You've a wife already, so I don't see how, frankly. I can tell you why that's what I think, and you can decide how much you like the advice. Divorce is a rich man's privilege. What I'm about to tell you would normally cost three or four guineas – do sit down, Loveridge, I have no intention of charging you – and there'd be much more to come. The evidence Mrs Chown would need to give would be in public and wouldn't be kind to her reputation. My advice would be that you and she quietly make your bed as best you can. Your only hope otherwise would be if we could establish some irregularity about your marriage. How long ago did it take place?'

'Twelve, thirteen year since, maybe.'

'Don't you know? Your marriage certificate will tell you that.'

'I don't have one, sir. The only certificate I have is the one they gev me when they let me out of the army.'

'You must surely have had one. What was the nature of the ceremony – before a clergyman or a registrar?'

'It was on Wycombe Common.'

Deakin stared at Sam. Then eventually he said, 'Tell me what happened, exactly. I am not familiar with your customs.'

'I saw her. I liked her. She seemed to like me. I asked for her. She said yes. Then we went off together a few days, and when we came back, I put up a bender – that's a tent, sir – and she came in it with me and we was man and wife, and everyone there knew it was so.'

'And that was all?'

'All? What else should it be?'

'It's very biblical, I must say. I think they may see it a bit differently in Scotland, where they're more robust about such matters, but for the law of England, Mr Loveridge, you have never been married at all.'

'Not married? But I promised her, and her me.'

'Legally, that means nothing. Nor to any man of the cloth either, since you did what you did without involving them.'

'Poor Lukey . . .'

'Your wife? A little late to think of her, Loveridge.'

'There wouldn't be another Gypsy would want Lukey now, not even if I was dead and she a widow, Mr Deakin. She'd have to find herself a fellow as isn't a travelling man. I haven't treated her right, no more than Ellen and me did poor Harold. And now you say she was never my wife at all.'

'There is a part of me, Loveridge, that finds this discussion distasteful, if I may be as honest with you as you are with me. My employee – my friend, I should say – is dead because of you, and not so indirectly. Some of our chapel marriages also fall by the wayside, though we enter into them with every intention that they should not. And professionally I see men who come to me asking how they can rid themselves of a blameless wife, usually because they have got a younger woman into trouble or are in a fair way to doing so. But I seldom hear regret for the hurt all this causes – as to your credit I hear from you. The most some feel is some compunction at the idea of their new love having to give evidence in open court about matters which are best left private. You and Mrs Chown will be spared all that. There is nothing to stop you marrying the lady if she wants you, apart from scruples, possibly – perhaps after a decent interval, and perhaps in another town. Yet you express regret where one might have expected relief.'

'I thought I was tied, Mr Deakin. I *am* glad, more than I can say, for I can do right by Ellen. I'm sorry only that our ways, the ways of my people – a promise honestly made – count for nothing at all.'

'There is something else I think you should know, Loveridge. Mrs Chown's eldest boy . . .'

'My Tom?'

'Yes. Tom Chown. I don't know what difference this may make in practical terms, Loveridge, but his birth certificate gives Harold as his father. It was that or no father recorded at all. So legally he is Chown's son.'

Sam crumpled in his chair. 'I dunt understand your laws at all, Mr Deakin.'

'I must confess that I too sometimes have that problem. I'm sorry.'

*

'I don't know, Sam.' Ellen stroked his arm. They sat side by side on the bed in the room in the Flying Horse, the only place they felt safe together.

'I thought you'd be pleased.'

'It's only that, what you described . . . it's very beautiful. A boy and a girl standing beneath the heavens, making a promise and needing nothing else to make them keep it.'

'But in your world it means nothing, Ellen. It's as if it never was, just because it never got wrote in a book somewhere. So don't you see, I cannot do that with you. The promise I made to her never counted for nothing, so the promise I'd be making to you wouldn't either. It would have to be another way. It'd have to be the *gaujo* way. But there's something else too, Ellen, I wanted to ask you.'

'Yes, Sam?'

'Wattie and Judy was talking about going away, once they're wed, I mean. Well, if they was agreeable, and you of course, I thought we med go too, with them, I mean – be with them. Could be England, or New Zealand, or wherever it was – though Wattie's old mother isn't mad keen on him emigrating, o' course. But to be together. You see, apart from the boys, you've lost just about everything along of me.'

'And you because of me.'

'It warms me that you see it that way too, Ellen. You know I can turn my hands to most things – carpentering, soldering, smithing – and most beasts. If my teacher is willing, I'd like to get better at my reading and writing. And I can gather food – fruit or hops. I don't know yet how or what I should grow ... I have learned to sleep under a roof, even the ones I was made to sleep under. But whatever we do, it isn't going to be an easy life for you, Ellen. You'd be a poor man's wife, for the law or without it. We might have many more kiddies – maybe ten, eleven of 'em. I wouldn't be able to stop myself getting babies of you! P'raps you'd like a little girl next ... I would. Like that little maid I saw with her father in that church in Winchester ...'

'You'd still love me in the middle of all that noise?'

'O' course I would! All I'm saying is that it would be hard. The way I was brung up was always a struggle, but I was never alone, even if sometimes I med have wanted to be. You, me and the boys, well, we'd have each other, first and foremost, but for me, a family is a bit more than that . . .'

'Like the chapel was for me. Kindness to a sister in distress.' She saw herself again in the Sunday school, looking at the little clothes prepared for Tom's arrival.

'That's it exackly, Ellen. I rub along with Wattie well enough, and Judy – well, she's the boys' sister as well as your best friend. Anyway, that's why I'd like it, I think, if we was to stick along of them.'

'Oh Sam!' She kissed his cheek, and he turned his face, seeking her mouth.

'Just a minute,' she said, putting her fingers to his lips. 'There's something I wanted to ask you too. That time when you said about the hip-bath – and my drawers in the kitchen sink—'

'*Dordi,* I'm sorry, it oughtn't to have come out that way – I didn't mean you was dirty, not in the way you'd think—'

'No, Sam, don't be sorry. What I mean is, if you wouldn't mind, would you show me what I should do? I think I could learn.'

'Teach my teacher? My Ellen, oh my Ellen!' and he kissed her all over her face.

CHAPTER 33

In a talk I had with a gipsy . . . he said to me: 'You know what the books say, and we don't. But we know other things that are not in the books, and that's what we have. It's ours, our own, and you can't know it.'

W.H. Hudson, *A Shepherd's Life*

Gypsy Lore

Patrixbourne

'Wish me luck, Ellen! Wait for me in there.'

They stood under an elm tree in Patrixbourne's little churchyard. Ellen watched him go off to the interview, shaved and brushed and wearing the clothes Mrs Piper had given him. Once he was out of sight, she turned and pushed open the heavy church door. To her relief, the building was empty. She sank into a pew and looked round. *It's plainer than I thought it would be, but that coloured glass is very pretty.* She shut her eyes and delivered herself up to the old habit of prayer.

She couldn't have said how much later it was when she heard the door open again and footsteps – not Sam's – strike the flagstones. A working man – a labourer's boots. *Welcome to the house of God, whoever you are, sir.*

She kept her eyes shut as the steps passed her, then hesitated, then stopped. Her heart knocked in her chest. Whoever he was, he was watching her, she knew it. He was close enough that she could hear him breathing.

'Miss ... sorry ...' A young man's voice. She opened her eyes, then opened them wider. How long since she had seen that face? He was taller, his face thinner. He still looked frightened. Ellen smiled.

'That's the first time you've said anything to me, Vanlo.'

He looked too abashed now to say anything else.

'Why don't you sit down? I'm waiting for Sam. Will you wait with me?'

*

At last, the door opened, and the two heads murmuring in the pew turned together to see Sam, rather flushed – and stunned – standing by the font. Vanlo got up.

'*Bruv!*' Sam embraced the boy, exclaiming over his shoulder, 'He's too thin, Ellen. Where've you bin, my Vanlo?'

'London, mostly. 'Orrible places. Rooms with rows o' beds still warm from the last men to sleep in 'em. Labouring.

Factries. I tole the lady. Don't suppose she wants to hear it all over again. Says you've seen a man about a *kenner*[35].'

'I have. We've got it!'

'How big is it?' asked Ellen, smiling, her eyes indicating the boy.

'Oh! Big enough, provided we all rub along all right, my girl. Come here till I kiss you, if Vanlo don't mind.'

'Oh Sam, you've been drinking . . . in the morning!'

'I'm sober enough for what I've got to say. Don't go all Band of Hope with me, Ellen! They'd have taken it for rudeness if I'd refused their hospitality. The house'll need a few days' work. But it took some getting. I've never seen a place like that *rai's*, Ellen. A creaky gate and an overgrown garden, and then there was this rusty old manservant came to the door and tole me he'd see was the master available. Then he turns round and shuffles away down the hallway. He didn't say nothing else to me so I just stood there, turning my cap on the doorstep. It was a grand house, all coloured brick on the outside, but the windows needed cleaned, and inside so dirty, all ponging of dust and dogs and tobacco, and full of things I could see no use for – a big brown stuffed bear with a grett grin on his face, holding out a plate and losing sawdust from 'is knees. There was plants in pots gasping for daylight, and a huge black stair-case going up into the dark. Then the servant turns round

---

[35] House

472

and says, "Well, come in, then. Don't hang about out there
. . . and shut the door behind you. You weren't born in a
field, were you?" Of course, I never said I was . . . but I did
have a look for somewhere to scrape my boots afore I came
in, though the matting they had down couldn't have shown
more dirt had it tried. "Wait there!" he said, so I stopped
between that bear and a man with a wig on in a painting
that looked ready to fall out of its frame. I waited ages,
expecting the old *mush* to come out from the back again,
but there must've been some other way up because instead
he comes down the big staircase, picking his way like a cat,
there being so much stuff – books and papers and things –
on every step.

'"He'll see you now," he says. "And as you don't appear
to be hawking anything, he assumes you to be a gentleman
and says to come up the main staircase."

'There was gaslight on the landing, and the place needed
it, for there was just this one long window full of red and
blue glass like in a church, so not much daylight got in. The
man knocks quiet-like on this big panelled door and opens
it for me, and then he says, "He's got the parson with him."
Well, I couldn't turn back then, so I thought I'd just take the
talking to and get out of there. And I'm being announced
with my Sunday name – "Mr Sampson Loveridge, m'lord" –
though I'm sure I never tole him it; Matthew French must've
done. Then off he goes and I'm left with them in a room that
made me feel as near boxed in as the gaol.'

'Oh Sam!'

'You've not heard the best of it yet. It was all dark pan-elled like a courthouse, a good size of a place but full of books and broadsheet things more than the staircase, all over the place in little towers I'd to pick my way past. There was some sort of carpet in the middle of the floor but so dusty I couldn't tell you what colours it was meant to have. And there's this horrible big fireplace as red as raw beef, but no fire laid, and a sofa losing its innards and these two old codgers sitting there smiling at me, got up in togs Farmer French wouldn't wear even to clean out the pigs – the kind we'd have turned down when we went *monging*[36]. I couldn't say which of 'em was the parson and which my lord, for they looked to me like twins. But they had this dicky little table in front of them, with a cut-glass jug with a stopper, and three glasses, and they looked clean enough. I didn't know who to greet so I just nodded and one of 'em says, "Come in, Loveridge . . . Get down, sir!" and I didn't know was I supposed to fall to my knees, but then this snuffly old Labrador dropped down from an armchair and that's where they told me to sit. You can help me brush my trousers in a minute. Then one of 'em looks at the other and says: "I think we have a pure-bred."

'It was only about half after ten when I got there, but they gave me this sweetish wine out of that jug and then they

---

[36] Begging

drank my health and I'd to concentrate hard on what they said for I never drink so early in the day but they were well used to it. Turns out they aren't twins but they are cousins, and the parson has his living thanks to my lord. The strangest thing is the parson has a bit of Romani – the words, I mean. I thought that wine must be powerful stuff for it to have gone to my head so fast, but then he starts asking me do I take the Gypsy Law Journal, and I said I'd never heard of it and where was I to take it, for I tried to keep clear of the law, be it Gypsy or *gaujo*, but that it had a habit of coming after me. They laughed like drains at that and said it was *lore* they meant, stories and wisdom and that – so then I knew what tack to take with them. My lord said something about a "true child of nature", which I didn't like the sound of but said nothing as I knew French had put a word in for me and I wanted that cottage.'

'Are there neighbours?'

'There *are* neighbours, but not through the wall – not like in Canterbury. Now stop crying, you should be pleased.'

'I'm sorry, Sam,' she said. 'It's the relief of it all.'

'Anyway, the parson talks about this Gypsy lore business a bit more and says that the most eminent Orientalists write for it, but I'm sure being born in a field near Oxford doesn't make me Oriental. He asked then had I read my borrow or barrow or something, and I said I neither took nor borrowed whatever other people said, for I'd rather pay for it fair and square. This made them laugh again but I'm damned if I know why and didn't care for it much. I told them I could only read a little but enough to know what was written on a cart's end and to write my own name—'

'Not true, Sam, you've come on so well.'

'But I did say that I was learning fast and had a good teacher; I didn't want the parson to offer to learn me, and I could see that's what he was thinking about. Then he said something in an important voice about the "oral tradition" or some such, and asked about campfires and story-telling and violins but I think I disappointed him because I said we'd always been too hard at work with trying to get food, or making things, or just being too bone-tired for stories and fiddles, but I got out some of Mother's tales and he seemed happy with them. He'll want some more, though, and if I don't remember I'sll have to make something up, I suppose.

'Then m'lord asked about how I found the prison and bit by bit got out of me all about Lincoln and the conchies on Dartmoor. The wonder was, he was pleased with me for not going to fight as he'd have been a conchie hisself only he was too old to take a stand, he said. He listened too when I tole him about France and how I'd seen more than once a poor nag drown in mud and manure. He filled my glass again then, though I tried to stop him.

'Then he clears his throat and looks at the parson and then asks me about you. I said you'd suffered on my account and lost near all your friends—'

'Not all. A letter from Grace came today.'

'Oh Ellen, that's hope, ain't it? And p'raps the old man will come round in time.'

'He won't. But I'll manage. So what about me?'

'The parson asked – in his professional capacity, he said – was I intending to make an honest woman of you. I said that in my opinion you were honest already but that I wanted to do right by you but I'd still to persuade you. He asked a bit more about that and did I have any marriage lines from before and I said no, and I tole him what I tole Deakin. He looked disappointed when I said that and went on about hand-cutting and blood-mixing and leaping over fires. I said I didn't know anything about that unless it was something they did in the fairgrounds because it sounded like that kind of show. Then he looked at his cousin and shook his head and said something about the sad loss of the old traditions but I'm sure I don't know where he got all that from, because I never see'd any of that tomfoolery.

'He asked me then what age I am and I said I didn't know exackly but that I reckoned to be about thirty when I think of the places I've been and when. He asked did I not have a certificate to say so and I said no, the only certificate I had was that demob one, same as I said to Deakin. He looked a bit happier at that and puts his hands together in a steeple then and looks at his cousin and says something about Somerset House. I said where's that, was it on the road to Dartmoor, and he laughs and says no, in the smoke right on the banks of the Thames.

'M'lord then says: "If they have nothing on you in Somerset House, Loveridge, you probably don't exist!" and they both laugh then. Anyway, the long and short of it is that it says in Somerset House when you was born, Ellen, and when you wed, and when the boys was born, and when Harold died. But me and Noah and my mother and her dead babies and Vanlo here won't be there anymore than old Fred would be. So – Vanlo, would you mind stepping out a minute?'

'Like last time, Sam?'

'Oh . . . not for so long this time, I hope. Don't go wandering off.'

Vanlo went.

'So when are you going to marry me?'

'I'm not sure, Sam.'

'Oh Ellen, the *rashai* talked about letter and spirit, same as you did with me, that time. He said children shouldn't marry as they don't know what they're about, but by the time Lukey took me I'd long had to stop bein' a child. They're only prompted by their trousers, was what he said. Then the *rai* went on a bit about some artist he knows what lives like a Gypsy – he says – but like no Gypsy I know. This man has two wives with him and has children all over the country, wherever he takes his *vardo*. I said, I can only think this is a rich man and no Romani if he can have two wives and paint all the time, for he can't be getting his own food. Honestly, Ellen, a lot of the time I didn't know what they was talking about and I don't know that they wasn't making fun of me, and I was hard put to it to keep listening to 'em through all that sticky wine, only that I wanted that cottage. But finally they took me to see it, and gev me the keys and the parson said to come to him if you and I wanted to be wed. But I've thought about that, and though I want you so's nobody can say ever again that you aren't mine, there's only one man I'd like to stand up in front of with you, him being Cecil Acland, if you'll come with me and help me look for him if he ain't still in Winchester – I don't know how I'd find him otherwise.

'It's a strange thing, though, Ellen, that I walked away from my old life, just as you've walked away from yours to be with me, but that's the one the two *rais* want to know about, not what I want of life now. It makes me feel as I'm my lord's dancing bear, an' him calling the tune, that's all. Pure-bred, indeed!'

CHAPTER 34

. . . blessed are the dead which die in the Lord . . . Yea,
saith the Spirit, that they may rest from their labours;
and their works do follow them.

Revelation, 14:13

Stopping Place

Chingestone

'"Persecuted but not forsaken, cast down, but not destroyed."
That was my friend Harold Chown; great is his reward in
heaven. Let us go and bury his poor mortal husk, brothers
and sisters, and be grateful that we knew him.'

The new minister had listened to Oliver's tribute with
interest and some grudging respect. Now, standing back
from the grave as it was filled, he wrung the old man's
hand and said, 'We had excellent instruction in homilet-
ics in the college, Brother Quainton, but I don't think
I have ever heard an address as sincere and moving as
yours.'

Oliver regarded him suspiciously for a moment, unsure he wasn't being patronised, but the young man held his gaze. 'Thank you, Brother Chapman,' he said eventually. 'Ye're the poorer for not having known Harold.'

'But *you* will help me, won't you? I shall need your help – many changes are to come the way of the connexion.' For the minister, 'connexion' was now an archaic term, but instinctively he knew it was one Oliver would use.

'I live alone now, sir, so my time is at your disposal. My little birds is all flown. My grandson to Hartley.'

'*John* Quainton?'

'That's him. You know him then?'

'I regret only by repute. The best Moral Science man of his year. You must be very proud of him.'

'Of John? Oh yes, I'm proud of *him* all right. I'll be glad to help you, sir, in your mission. You'll be coming back to the tea, won't you? I think you've still to meet Mr Newcomb – the Wesleyan man. 'Twas good of him to come . . .'

*

'So, my Vanlo. How are they all? I seen . . . I don't rightly know what I should call her now – your sister, I mean – when I was in the gaol, but we couldn't say much,' said Sam.

'Lukey, I'd call 'er. She's the same, or was when I took off. Bossy – you can't pull Lukey down for long. There was this parson turning up after 'er sometimes. Always asking questions. Writing in a notebook all the time. Had a forehead that big and wide he looked like a baby. He made 'er laugh one time when he said, all timid-like, that he'd like to get hisself a wagon of his own and come along of them – don't know how he'd do that and still be a parson, mind. They were travelling with some Lees the time I went; Nelson Lee was sweet on Sibela but Caley said she was too little yet.'

'Why'd you go in the end, my Vanlo?'

'Missed you, s'pose. Didn't like that I couldn't even say so.'

*

Sam and Ellen embraced in the early dawn of a damp Sunday morning, listening to the cockcrow.

'Tom's last day of freedom, today,' said Sam.

'No! I think he's looking forward to school. He says he wants to show them all he's learned already. I'm only sorry he didn't start when the other children did . . . All that commotion . . .'

'That's one way of describing it, I s'pose.'

'David is going to miss him.'

'Vanlo said he wants to take him nutting tomorrow.'

'He's good with them, isn't he, Sam? They were tearing round yesterday afternoon with a ball he'd made for them – rags stuffed with sawdust. They liked it so much

I thought I'd get a proper one for them, next time I can get to Canterbury.'

'No, Ellen, don't do that,' said Sam gently. 'Not after Vanlo went to all that trouble.'

'Oh – yes, of course, I see what you mean.' She was silent for a moment, mortified. He held her tighter.

'About us being wed, then . . .'

'It's enough for me that you want to, Sam. I've told you that I'll always walk with my arm in yours.'

'Marry me so no one can ever say you mayn't. Do it for the boys, then. And for the others that come.'

'Everyone knows our story here already, Sam. They'd talk anyway.'

He shifted his position, putting an arm behind his head.

'Let them. There are seven of us under this roof. Enough to defend ourselves if we do stay on here. And I'm the *rai's* favourite performing monkey, remember. But sometimes I'd like to sleep out in the open air – or in something like a shepherd's hut, a shed on wheels I could roll about a bit. Would I be able to do that, do you think?'

'Of course. But mightn't you be lonely out there?'

'Not if my *rakli* came along of me too, and gave me a hand to undo all them buttons of hers!'

'I'll come! But first I'll help you find Cecil.'

'You will? You'll be my lawful wedded, Ellen?'

'Yes. But there's something you must do for me.'

'Anything!'

'Where's your old hat?'

'That? It's in that box of tricks under here.'

He got out and kneeled by the side of the bed. Ellen traced with her forefinger the ladder of his vertebrae. The little white scars from Caley's gouging whip gleamed but the longer marks of the cat were fading. He tugged the trunk out and rummaged through it.

'Here it is. A bit the worse for wear but some use in it yet.'

Ellen took the hat and gently smoothed the nap, then placed it on the head of the kneeling man as though crowning him. She looked at him, head on one side, then pulled the brim forward over his right eye.

'Oh Sam, I'd die for you.'

'Kiss me first.'

HISTORICAL BACKGROUND

British Romanies

The term 'Gypsy', derived from the English term 'Egyptian', comes from a misappropriation of identity that is three centuries older than the Romani language. In the eighth century, Greek Byzantine fortune-tellers claimed to have received ancient Egyptian wisdom from the Persian Magi, who had been dispersed by the Muslim conquest. It became a general name claimed by fortune-tellers, dancers and entertainers, amongst them probably Dom (Indo-Aryan ethnic group), who arrived from India three centuries before the ancestors of the Roma. The Romani language assumed its modern form, probably as a military command language of a Hindu militia of diverse Indian origins in eleventh-century Turkey, and as its speakers looked and sounded like Dom, were seen by Greeks and Turks as another set of Egyptians. The Romani language is part of the Prakritic group, of which Sanskrit is an ancient example.

The destruction of any independent military organisation of Roma led to various groups fleeing the Ottoman empire to other parts of Europe. They are first recorded in the British Isles in the early sixteenth century – first in Scotland and subsequently in England. After decades of peaceful trading, the gathering economic depression and unemployment led to foreigners – Jews, Africans and Gypsies – being made scapegoats. In 1530, the Egyptians Act demanded the expulsion of 'the outlandish people calling themselves Egyptians'; the penalty for staying was execution and hangings simply for the offence of being Romani were recorded at Bury St Edmunds and York. This legislation (along with further acts) was not repealed until 1856 (though meanwhile other legislation was enacted, such as the Vagrancy Act of 1824, which specifically outlawed fortune-telling). Under Cromwell, Romanies were deported as slaves to plantations in the Americas; later, transportations were to Australia.

In the period in which this novel is set, Romanies who remained nomadic worked as itinerant agricultural labourers, peddlars, horse-dealers, metal-and woodworkers, although many in each generation settled and assimilated. The industrialisation of agriculture, particularly from the 1960s onwards, along with legislation such as the Caravan Sites Act of 1968, severely restricting access to stopping places, has had a major impact on this way of life.

In nineteenth-century literature, Romani people were represented notably by George Borrow (1803-1881) in his semi-autobiographical novels *Lavengro* and *The Romany*

Rye, by Matthew Arnold in his pastoral poem *The Scholar Gipsy,* by Theodore Watts-Dunton in *The Coming of Love* (epic poem) and *Aylwin* (a novel), and largely negatively by Charles Dickens, particularly in *Barnaby Rudge.* The Gypsy Lore Society was founded in England in 1888 to further the study of Romani history and lore, but its membership then and now consists mainly of non-Gypsy scholars rather than actual Romanies; one of its early adherents was Sir Richard Burton. Other prominent members included Lady Sibyl Grant (1879-1955), who set aside some of her land for Gypsies to live on during Epsom Derby week, and the artist Augustus John (1878-1961), the Society's president for more than twenty years, who spent some time travelling in a *vardo* with his wife and mistress and their collective children. John spoke Romani well and was a friend of John Sampson, Librarian of Liverpool University, who wrote an important dictionary of the North Welsh Romani dialect, helped by an assistant librarian, Dora Yates (1879-1974). *The Journal of the Gypsy Lore Society* subsequently metamorphosed into the twice-yearly *Romani Studies* (published by Liverpool University Press) and the Society is now based in the United States. Dora Yates's historical archive is divided between the University of Liverpool and the McGrigor Phillips collection at the University of Leeds.

Leading scholars in Romani studies are professors Thomas Acton and Ian Hancock, the latter a Romani. In the UK the University of Hertfordshire Press publishes extensively in the field.

Primitive Methodism

Primitive Methodism originated in the early nineteenth century as a breakaway movement from the Wesleyan Methodist Church. Its founders were Hugh Bourne (1772-1852), a wheelwright from Bucknall, Staffordshire, and William Clowes (1780-1851), a potter from Burslem; neither were ever ordained, although at a later stage in the history of the movement the Primitive Methodists did formally train and ordain its ministers. As the name suggests, the 'Prims' sought a simpler form of worship – closer, in their view, to the origins of Methodism, with an emphasis on local control, including local non-ordained preachers, spontaneity in worship (earning them early on the offensive name of 'ranters') and fidelity to biblical sources. Worship initially took place in the open air (at camp meetings) as well as in adherents' homes, prior to the acquisition or building of chapels. Until the 1860s a number of preachers were women. Church members tended to be drawn from the poorest strata of society: agricultural labourers, millworkers and miners. The movement was closely linked to the growth of trade unionism, with a number of Prim preachers also being union leaders (Peter Lee, Joseph Arch, George Edwards amongst them). By the mid-nineteenth century, its adherents exceeded one hundred thousand but its influence extended much further through attendance at Sunday schools (for which membership of the connexion was not a requirement), often the only access to education for the children of the poor prior to the establishment of compulsory state education. In literature the Prims notably figure in Arnold Bennett's *Clayhanger* novels. As a boy Darius Clayhanger is rescued from the workhouse by the Prim Sunday school teacher Mr Shushions. This excerpt from *These Twain*, describing an incident at Edwin Clayhanger's print-works, encapsulates the sometimes unsophisticated nature of the movement far better than I can describe:

> *The programme was not satisfactorily set up. Apart from several mistakes in the spelling of proper names, the thing with its fancy types, curious centring, and superabundance of full-stops, resembled more the libretto of a Primitive Methodist Tea-meeting than a programme of classical music offered to refined dilettanti on a Sunday night. Though Edwin had endeavoured to modernise Big James, he had failed.*

Whilst never a wealthy movement, Primitive Methodism had one major patron: the self-made jam manufacturer, Sir William Hartley, for whom the Prims' training college in Manchester was named. Over time the differences between the Prims and mainstream Methodism became less marked, and in 1932 Primitive Methodism, along with other Methodist movements, reunited with the Wesleyans to form the Methodist Church as it is today.

The Museum of Primitive Methodist and library at Englesea Brook, Cheshire, is an invaluable source for the study of the movement (http://engleseabrook.org.uk).

Locations

Chingestone

Chingestone is the name given in the Domesday Book to the village now known as Kingston Blount, located on the B4009 on the Oxfordshire side of the Chiltern Hills, about six miles from Thame. The Chingestone of the novel is a partial but not faithful portrait of this village, which did in fact still have four pubs in the 1940s (the last one has closed and is at time of writing up for sale). The three places of worship in Kingston Blount are now private houses, being the Primitive Methodist chapel at the far end of the village, the Congregationalist (not Wesleyan) chapel and the Anglican chapel of ease. There is no Surman's Wood, although Surman is a local surname.

Canterbury

The Cricketers, the Millers, and the Black Griffin are all actual pubs in Canterbury. The sixteenth-century the Flying Horse, just outside the city walls, was sold in 2015 to a restaurateur; it does have bedrooms on the first floor, but I have taken some liberties with the internal layout of the building. Percy Cooper was the landlord in the 1920s.

The former Primitive Methodist chapel on the Borough is now part of the King's School, whilst Lenham Heath Primitive Methodist chapel is now a private home.

Denne's Mill burned down in 1930. The mill race and part of its machinery can still be seen in the St Radigund's district of Canterbury; there are plans to reconstruct the mill wheel.

St Mildred's Tannery opened in Canterbury in the 1790s and, despite complaints about the smell, did not close until 2002.

Canterbury Cattle Market was located more or less where the Whitefriars shopping centre is now.

SELECTED BIBLIOGRAPHY

British Romani history and literature:

Memoirs written by Gypsies:

There are others, most notably Damian Le Bas's *The Stopping Places* (2018); I have deliberately limited this list to those that most correspond to the period of the novel.

Ronald Smith, *Gipsy Smith: His Life and Work,* (London, 1901)

Dominic Reeve, *Smoke in the Lanes* (Edinburgh, 1958)

Silvester Gordon Boswell *The Book of Boswell* (Harmondsworth: *Autobiography of a Gypsy* 1970)

Manfri Frederick Wood, *In the Life of a Romany Gypsy* (London, 1973)

Alex Smith (ed. Mícheál Ó hAodha and Thomas Acton), *Memoir of a Travelling Showman* (2017)

Memoirs written by non-Gypsies:

George Hall, *The Gypsy's Parson His Experiences and Adventures* (London 1915). (Hall learned Romani and travelled with Romani families.)

Rupert Croft-Cooke, *The Moon in My Pocket: Life With the Romanies* (London, 1948)

Dora E. Yates, *My Gypsy Days: Recollections of a Romani Romnie* (London, 1952)

Denis Harvey, *The Gypsies: Waggon-time and After* (London, 1979)

Contemporary studies:

Angus Fraser, *The Gypsies* (Oxford, 1995)

Thomas Acton and Gary Mundy (ed.), *Romani Culture and Gypsy Identity* (Hatfield, 1997)

Thomas Acton (ed.), *Gypsy Politics and Traveller Identity* (Hatfield, 1997)

Simon Evans, *Stopping Places: A Gypsy History of South London and Kent* (Hatfield, 2004)

Colin Clark and Margaret Greenfields, *Here to Stay: The Gypsies and Travellers of Britain* (Hatfield, 2006)

Becky Taylor, *A Minority and the State: Travellers in Britain in the Twentieth Century* (Manchester, 2008)

Janet Keet-Black, *Gypsies of Britain* (Oxford, 2013)

Selected fiction:

George Borrow, *Lavengro*, (1851), *The Romany Rye* (1857) and *Romano Lavo-Lil: Word-Book of the Romany or English Gypsy Language*. The first two of these are novels; the third is an anthology of anecdotes, sayings and memoirs of Romani life in Britain and abroad, and includes a short Romani-English dictionary.

Francis Wylde Carew (Arthur E. G. Way), *No. 747. Being the Autobiography of a Gypsy* (Bristol and London, 1891). (Despite its title, a novel.)

Theodore Watts-Dunton, *Aylwin* (London, 1898)

Rupert Croft-Cooke, *A Few Gypsies* (London, 1950) *Harvest Moon* (London, 1953)

Primitive Methodism:

A. Victor Murray, (ed. Geoffrey Milburn), *A Northumbrian Methodist Childhood* (Morpeth, 1992)

Geoffrey Milburn, *Primitive Methodism* (Peterborough, 2002)

George Edwards, *From Crow-scaring to Westminster*: An Autobiography (London, 1922) (Edwards was a farm-labourer, union organiser and ultimately MP for South Norfolk, and a Primitive Methodist preacher)

J. Jackson Wray, *Nestleton Magna*, London, n.d. (novel)

Kate Tiller, 'The desert begins to blossom: Oxfordshire and Primitive Methodism, 1824–1860', *Oxoniensia* (Oxfordshire Architectural and Historical Society 2016)

Kenneth Lysons, *A Little Primitive*, Buxton, 2001

M.K. Ashby, *Joseph Ashby of Tysoe* (Cambridge, 1961) (The agricultural trade unionist was in fact a Wesleyan, but this biography gives a vivid account of the link between non-conformism and trade-unionism in the neighbouring county of Warwickshire.)

Rev. S.S. Henshaw, *The Romance of our Sunday Schools* (London, 1910)

Rev. Arthur Peake, *Plain Thoughts on Great Subjects* (London, n.d.)

Rev. David G. Sharp, 'Not Well Understood: Winchester Primitive Methodism 1837–1932 and its Congregational Supporters', lecture, 2007

'Warden Grey' (Rev. W. Graham), *Heatherfield: A Tale of Country Religious Life* (London, 1911)

Prison conditions in England in this period:

Gilbert Thomas, *Autobiography 1891-1941* (London, 1946) (The experiences of a conscientious objector.)

Stuart Wood (pseud.), *Shades of the Prison House: A Personal Memoir* (London, 1932)

Wilfred Macartney, *Walls Have Mouths* (London, 1936)

W.J. Forsythe, *Penal Discipline, Reformatory Projects and the English Prison Commission, 1895–1939* (Exeter, 1990)

ACKNOWLEDGEMENTS

Firstly, I would like to thank my agent Annette Green for her unstinting support and commitment to *The Gypsy Bride,* followed by Claire Johnson-Creek and the team at Bonnier Books UK for making my work as good as it could be, and championing its venture into the world, Laura Gerrard for copyediting and Natalie Braine for proofreading. I owe a great debt to Julie Cohen for her insightful comments on an earlier manuscript; without her input I would never have got this far. I have striven to be as historically accurate as possible, and if I have succeeded it's because of the many people who helped me. Firstly, I would like to thank Gary, Olby, Esther and Mary Brazil of the South-East Romany Museum at Twin Oaks, Marden, Kent for their warm welcome and their generosity in sharing time, anecdotes and expertise. Through them I also met Thomas Acton, Professor Emeritus of Romani Studies at the University of Greenwich, who fact-checked my manuscript and put me right on many things. On the Primitive Methodist side, I would like to thank my former academic supervisor at Durham University, Dick Watson, Professor Emeritus of English and currently editor of the Canterbury Dictionary of Hymnology. There is nothing he does not know about the history of Methodism, and he pointed me in the direction of many sources that helped me find the 'voice' of the Prim community in Chingestone. I owe a great deal to Dr. Jill Barber and the volunteers of the Primitive Methodist Museum at Englesea Brook, Alsager, Cheshire (https://engleseabrook.org.uk/), especially for their kindness in opening the museum for me during their closed season, and to David G. Sharp for sharing with me his research on West Country Primitive Methodism. Tina Machado's Historic Canterbury site (http://www.machadoink.com/) was invaluable, and I thank her for her quick response to my questions.

I have dedicated this book to my fellow author Anne Booth. Not only did she persuade me to study for an MA in Creative Writing, but it was she, the gentlest person I know, who finally gave me an ultimatum to stop making excuses and get scribbling (we were sitting in a pub in Kent, of course). Writing can be a lonely business sometimes, and the companionship of fellow writers, no matter the distance, cannot be underestimated, and so I would also like to acknowledge my Arvon friends. You know why, Lorraine Rogerson, Jane Wallace and Liz Kershaw.

I also want to remember my Primitive Methodist ancestors, whose footprints are still visible in rural Oxfordshire, and my distant cousin Ernest George Quartermaine, who lies in Bucquoy Cemetery, Ficheux, now under a little earth from his native village. He fell in the second battle of Arras on 2nd October 1918, aged eighteen, and is the original of Charlie Lambourne. His mother asked for this inscription on his gravestone: 'Jesus whispered Victory is won. Let us pass over to the other side.'

Lastly I thank my patient husband and best friend, Carmine Mezzacappa. Every time I asked 'should I do this?' he said 'yes!'.

Dear Readers

I hope you have enjoyed reading *The Gypsy Bride* as much as I enjoyed writing it. I'd love to tell you how the book came about.

I got my inspiration browsing in a charity bookshop (this often happens for my fiction, because I find so many avenues to explore there, and I relish a chance discovery). I was keen to write something rural, set between the two world wars, and knew it would be a love story (a common theme in just about all my writing is love and culture clash – this is probably something to do with coming from Northern Ireland).

In Oxfam I found a copy of W.H. Hudson's *A Shepherd's Life*, and was immediately intrigued by a chapter entitled 'The Dark Men of the Village'. I was expecting Morris Men or mummers, but what I found were Romani Gypsies, people then moving with the seasons and working on farms, be it digging up wurzels, getting in the harvest, or pulling the bines in the hopping season in Kent. They were part of the warp and weft of the agricultural year, seasonal workers for whom their employers didn't have to find accommodation because they, of course, came with their own caravans. From there I moved onto George Borrow's *Lavengro* and *Romany Rye* and was hooked, and I started to glimpse Sampson Loveridge through the trees.

The earlier literary images of Gypsies were not, by and large, written by Gypsies themselves, and so were sometimes highly coloured, romanticising, or derisory. I owe a huge debt then to the Brazil family of the South-East Romany Museum in Marden, Kent, who with great patience and kindness answered my questions and told me things not to be found in any book. They also advised me to 'ask Tom', meaning Professor Thomas Acton, Emeritus Professor of Romani Studies at the University of Greenwich, who kindly read my manuscript and put me right when I'd got the wrong end of the stick. If any inaccuracies remain they are not his fault, nor the Brazils'.

For Ellen Quainton, I looked to the history of the English part of my family, once part of a rooted rural community. My great-great grandfather was a Primitive Methodist preacher in a village in the Chilterns. I have a photograph of him looking stern and magnificently whiskered; he is the original of Ellen's grandfather. The 'Prims' united with other Methodist groups in 1932 to form the Methodist Church more or less as we would recognise it today, thus disappearing as a discrete entity, but the impact they and other strands of non-conformism had on working-class life should not be underestimated. Through their Sunday schools they provided education for children and adults – not all Prims, by any means – before legislation established free state education. Their involvement in rural trade unionism they saw as God's work, standing up for those at the bottom of the pecking order; they were similarly active in mining and other industrial communities. 'Prim' principles persisted long in my family; my mother signed the Temperance pledge as a child (she has since progressed to Campari and soda). There may well be a former Prim chapel somewhere near where you live, though it is likely now to be someone's home, a garage, a furniture store or even a pub, rather than a place of worship. My portrait of Ellen's vanished Prim community was only possible with the help of Dr. Jill Barber and her dedicated team of volunteers at Englesea Brook Museum of Primitive Methodism, housed in an early chapel and school-room near Alsager – a fascinating place.

I hope you enjoyed *The Gypsy Bride*. If you did, please do share your thoughts on the Memory Lane Facebook page MemoryLaneClub. I hope you will also want to read about Sam and Ellen's daughter. She is the heroine of my next novel, which is set mainly in 1950s Nottingham, and will be published next year.

Best wishes,

Katie Hutton

A Recipe for Spiced Crab Apples

This recipe for spiced crab apples was contributed by Mrs F. H. Wood, to Hornsea Trinity Methodist Church and Circuit's *Recipe and Quotation Book*, published in 1936 to support the annual bazaar.

Ingredients

1 pound of sugar
1 pint of vinegar
¼ ounce each of whole cloves and white pepper
A stick of cinnamon
2 pounds of Siberian crab apples

Method

- Boil the sugar and vinegar till they reach a syrup consistency.
- Add the whole cloves, white pepper and a stick of cinnamon to the syrup and mix.
- Add the apples to the syrup and mix until well coated.
- When the fruit is tender, remove from the syrup and set aside. Continue cooking the syrup until it has reduced to half the amount.

- Pour the syrup over the fruit and leave for three days.
- After three days, reheat the syrup and pack the fruit and spices into jars. Then pour over the boiling syrup, and cover.

This recipe book was published four years after the unification of the three main strands of Methodism, but very much follows the tradition of the Tea Meetings to which a Primitive Methodist like Ellen and her mother would have contributed. I particularly liked some of the encouraging quotes that preface the recipes: 'May a mouse never leave your cupboard with a tear in his eye' (from Mr G. W. Hardbattle of Aldbrough) and 'Don't kill time – work it to death' (from Mrs R. Gibson-Fisher of Woolwich).

Reproduced by kind permission of Driffield-Hornsea Methodist Circuit.